One of the most interesting explorations of the
many worlds theory that I've read in years ...
Original, intelligent, unputdownable'
Guardian

'Gripping ... this is the sort of tricksiness
Barry was put on Earth for'
The Times

'Dynamic, suspenseful action with a
light frosting of metaphysics'
Washington Post

'He navigates the multiverse and the concepts
of string theory and chaos theory with frightening
conviction. Let's hope he just made it all up'
Wall Street Journal

'Sci-fi wizard Barry sets a serial killer loose in the
multiverse with mind-bending results'
People

'A very enjoyable thriller with a very satisfying ending'
Mystery and Suspense Magazine

'There are the familiar dislocations and dilemmas
of a quest that flings its characters across separate but
related realities, but these are seasoned with the wit,
menace and pacy excitement of a nicely controlled,
neatly structured crime thriller'
ParSec Magazine

'Beware Max Barry. Once his story grabs hold, you
will forget to eat, sleep, and bathe until you're left with
the world's worst book hangover. An exhilarating
rocket shot of a thriller tempered with
Barry's trademark wit and warmth'
David Yoon, author of
Version Zero and *Frankly in Love*

'With unrelenting tension, Max Barry weaves a complex
tapestry where a sociopath's insatiable obsession knows
no bounds, not even time and space . . . I devoured
this novel in one sitting'
J.D. Barker, author of *A Caller's Game*

'A crime thriller that tripped and fell through a manhole
and into the multiverse. It's frenetic and funny and
gut-wrenching by turns, and I absolutely could not
put it down. You need to read this book'
Edward Ashton, author of *The End of Ordinary*

THE 22 MURDERS OF MADISON MAY

Max Barry

HODDER

First published in Great Britain in 2021 by Hodder & Stoughton
An Hachette UK company

This paperback edition published in 2022

1

A CIP catalogue record for this title is
available from the British Library.

B format ISBN 978 1 529 35213 9
eBook ISBN 978 1 529 35211 5

Printed and bound in Great Britain by Clays Ltd, Elcograf S.p.A.

Hodder & Stoughton policy is to use papers that are natural, renewable
and recyclable products and made from wood grown in sustainable
forests. The logging and manufacturing processes are expected to
conform to the environmental regulations of the country of origin.

Hodder & Stoughton Ltd
Carmelite House
50 Victoria Embankment
London EC4Y 0DZ

www.hodder.co.uk

For Finlay & Matilda

THE
22 MURDERS
OF MADISON
MAY

1

SHE PULLED TO THE CURB AND PEERED THROUGH HER CAR WINDOW AT the house she had to sell. The mailbox was lying across the lawn in pieces, as if someone had taken a baseball bat to it. "Oh, come on," Maddie said. The house was a dump. The mailbox had been one of the best things about it.

She retrieved her bag from the passenger seat, climbed out, and tugged down her dress. It was ninety degrees and humid. Her house's best feature was spread across the earth. But she had brought her sneakers, which meant she wouldn't have to do this in heels. She carried broken mailbox shards around to the side of the house and dumped them beside a pile of old wood and a deflated football. While she was picking clean the small lawn, she noticed two boys of about fourteen loitering on bikes outside the fence, so she straightened and waved to them.

"Bend over again," said one of the boys. The other laughed.

She went into the house. It was dark. The walls leaned close. There was a fusty, hard-to-mistake, neglected grandma smell. But it was hers to sell, so she drew the curtains, drained the sink, and opened the back door. She set candles in strategic locations: hallway, bedroom, and a weird L-shaped space that she'd decided to call a study. These were her special candles, which she'd found after an on-line search for *conceal stench*. She checked her watch. The candles were good, but for emergencies, she had another secret weapon: a spray can labeled JUST LIKE COOKIES. It was less convincing than the candles, closer to Just Like Burnt Dirt, but it worked faster. She moved from room to room, spraying in controlled bursts.

She was staring at a dark stain in the corner of the living room when a car eased into the cracked concrete driveway. "Shit," she said. She yanked off her sneakers, stuffed them into her bag, and squeezed her feet into stilettos. She swiped open her phone and keyed a play-list, SELL MUSIC, which was pianos and swelling strings, a little brass: classy, but also motivational. The car door thumped. She used her hand mirror to verify that nothing had gone horribly wrong with her face, then focused on reaching the front door without driving a heel through the floorboards.

The buyer was approaching the concrete front steps, removing his sunglasses, craning his neck to peer at something higher up. The drainpipe, she guessed. It wasn't actually attached to anything. She had meant to do something about that.

"Hi!" she said, and smiled, like: BZZZT. The saying went *Location, Location, Location*, but at Henshaw Realty, it was *Teeth, Tits, Hair*—at least according to Maddie's mentor, Susie, who'd been sell-ing houses for thirty years and presumably knew what she was talk-ing about. BZZZT: Head up, teeth out, shoulders back, little head tilt, hair falling to the side. She had long hair, red edging into auburn, which so far she had resisted blondifying. "I'm Maddie!" she said. "Thanks so much for coming."

The buyer shook her hand. He was about her age, early twenties, dimples, thin, but somewhat cute. Despite the heat, he was wearing a long-sleeved collared shirt over chinos. "I'm Clay," he said. "Wow, you're tall."

"It's the shoes."

He looked down, so she took the opportunity to turn one leg and do a little pose. When he met her eyes again, she went: BZZZT.

"You're really pretty," he said.

She laughed and turned to let him follow her into the hallway. Too much BZZZT. She would tone that down. "You're lucky," she called over her shoulder, as they entered the kitchen's chemical embrace of cookies-slash-burnt-dirt. "We've had a lot of calls about this house. You're the first to see it." Lies. Terrible lies.

"Is that right?" He had removed his sunglasses. Strong eyebrows. His hair was a little shaggy, not really her thing, but she liked the implication, that he had his own style. Went his own way. Was possibly uniquely into falling-down, unrenovated 1960s clapboard two-bedrooms in Jamaica, Queens.

She collected her phone, which was tinkling piano noises. "Do you mind if I take your photo?"

"What for?"

"It's a security thing."

He seemed confused.

"It's silly, but we're meeting people alone, so they like us to—"

"Oh, of course. I get it."

She raised the phone. He straightened and smiled, a little BZZZT of his own. He was kind of awkward. Beneath the dimples and the shaggy hair, she sensed a guy who wasn't comfortable with people.

She snapped. "Done," she said. "That goes to our office." Where they had his details from when he'd made the appointment. He was Clayton Hors, of Ulysses, Pennsylvania. Currently living with his parents, after dropping out of Carnegie Mellon, looking to start a new life with a move to the city, thanks to, Maddie was guessing, a push from the folks. She put down the phone. "Thanks."

"No problem. There are some bad people out there. You have to take precautions."

"I also know jujitsu." She did not. "So," she said, "I really love this window. You get so much light."

He nodded. "How long have you been selling houses?"

"About a year." He wasn't looking at the window. Although maybe that was a good thing: The backyard was thigh-high weeds and a quietly rotting shed.

"Is real estate your"—he searched for words—"long-term ambition?"

"Oh, I love houses." Technically the truth. Houses, she loved. Real estate, which, it turned out, was mostly about pressuring people into making decisions, not so much. She had been wondering lately whether she'd chosen the wrong career. For a long time, she'd dreamed about acting—never seriously committed to it, of course, because it was so impractical, like saying you wanted to be an astronaut, but if she was still thinking about it, did that mean something? That she should have been braver?

"You love this house?" he said, looking at the crooked cupboards, the blotchy curtains.

"Every house has something to love. You just have to look for it."

He smiled. A genuine smile. He had warmed up. "Well, good for you." He headed into the living room and she followed. "Although I'm a little surprised you're not an actress."

She stopped, startled.

He glanced back. "Sorry. I blurt out whatever I'm thinking. Is it okay if I look around by myself? I'll let you know if I have questions."

"Sure," she said, recovering. "Knock yourself out."

He moved off. She peered at a cupboard door that was hanging by one hinge, wondering if she could fix it. Susie, her mentor, would say: *Maddie, leave it. The house is shit. You can't make it not shit. Try to dress it up and all buyers will see is that you're lying to them.* It was true, Maddie supposed. But this kind of thing wasn't even about the buyers. It bothered her on a personal level to see something that needed fixing and not fix it.

The *Just Like Cookies* was wearing off, so she moved about the house to deploy a few more tactical sprays. On a pass through the kitchen, she checked her phone, because she had a boyfriend, Trent, who was supposedly going to let her know whether he would be home tonight or out with friends. Nothing.

Clay appeared in the doorway. "I'm just gonna grab something from my car."

"Sure," she said.

He'd pushed up his sleeves. On his right forearm was a discoloration, a patch of purple, red, and yellow all mixed together, like an injury that wasn't healing right.

He caught her looking. "I have a dog. Goes kind of crazy sometimes."

"Oh," she said. What was she doing? Staring like an idiot. "I'm sorry."

"She has a good heart. Just doesn't always know it. I'll be right back."

He disappeared. She felt mad at herself. She moved to the living room and watched him open the trunk of his car. A nice one, a new black Chevrolet SUV. Rental sticker, so she couldn't infer anything about his finances. She returned to the kitchen and her musical phone.

He clomped back inside the house. After a few minutes, she called: "Everything okay?"

There was no answer, so she put down her phone and set out to find him. He wasn't in the hallway, nor the laundry—"laundry," with air quotes—a tight cupboard of rusted steel and water stains. He wasn't in the room she was calling a second bedroom, even though the only way you were getting a bed in there was upright. The hallway ran down the middle of the house; possibly they were circling each other. But if so, he was being very quiet. She didn't think it was possible to move around this house without making a sound unless you were very intent on doing so.

When she entered the master bedroom, she found the curtains were closed. She had definitely opened those earlier. She reached to toggle the light switch, but of course there was no power; it had been disconnected months ago. In the gloom, she could make out a silver lump on the carpet: a case of some kind, possibly a toolbox. The lid was open, but it was facing the other way, so she couldn't see what was inside.

Her phone in the kitchen fell silent.

She turned. "Hello?"

The front door was ten feet to her right. It was open. Outside was a clear, bright day. Concrete path, low chain-link fence. The road was a cul-de-sac—rare in New York, a real jewel in this house's cardboard crown—so there was no passing traffic, but she could hear kids calling to one another, most likely the two who'd been out front when she arrived.

She had sent Clay's photo to her office. They had his details, which had been verified before she'd even come out here. Clay knew this. The security process was on her side.

She headed to the kitchen.

He wasn't there. Neither was her phone. That was less cool. "Hello?" she said again, more aggressively. "Can I help you?"

The outside noise fell away until she was standing in a closed-in bubble of quiet. The front door had closed, she realized.

The wind. You opened all the doors and the breeze can be strong, can blow right through, slam a door—

Only the back door wasn't open. None of the doors were open. And none of them had slammed. They had closed so softly she hadn't heard the click.

No breeze had blown her phone away, either.

She called: "Clay, my office has your information. They know who you are."

She was in an empty kitchen. The drawers were empty: no knives, nothing she could see to use as a weapon. Outside, though, were those kids. The house was clapboard; if she screamed, they might hear.

She bent down and unstrapped her stilettos. Whatever might happen next, she didn't want to face it on heels.

"Sorry." His voice floated toward her. "Sorry, Madison, I'm here."

She stayed where she was. "Do you have my phone?"

"I'm sorry, I needed it for a second."

"Why do you have my phone?"

Silence.

She opened her mouth to repeat the question. He appeared in the living room doorway. She tensed. She could be hitting the back door in about three seconds. Would it be locked? Would it stick? If so, he would catch her before she got out.

"I'm super-apologetic about this. I really didn't mean to freak you out." His palms were up to indicate his complete lack of threat. But he was moving toward her, one slow step at a time, which she did not like at all. She could see that discoloration on his forearm: the dog bites that weren't healing. A mix of old and new wounds, she realized suddenly. He'd been bitten over and over. By that dog he said he owned, who had a good heart but didn't always know it.

"Can you stop?" she said. "I am actually freaked out."

He stopped. "I'm really sorry to do it like this. I know how it looks. But I'm out of time."

"Can I have my phone back?"

He looked pained. "Unfortunately, no."

"Why not?"

"Madison, you have to trust me. I don't want to hurt you. I'm here for you." He began to edge toward her again.

"Stop. I want you to leave this house."

"I can't do that. I'm sorry. I need you to come to the bedroom."

The bedroom. Where the curtains were closed. Where a silver box sat in the gloom, facing the wrong way. She was not going to the bedroom.

He ran his hand through his hair. "This isn't going well. I'm sorry. I don't have time to explain."

She took a half-step to her right, just shifting her weight, and he leaned in the same direction. He was prepared to chase her, she saw. If she ran. If she tried to scream.

He said, "Please, please, just come to the bedroom."

She began to act. Not in the way she'd been thinking about before, for a stage, or a camera—the ordinary way, like when she met clients, or buyers, and had to be a slightly different version of herself for a while. For them, she was a sparkly, chatty Maddie, who was very interested in whatever you had to say and however long you wanted to take to say it. For Clay, she would be a person who did not need to be chased. She would be that person as completely as she could, until she saw the opportunity to be a person running for her life.

She nodded.

He exhaled. "Thank you. Thank you." He gestured, indicating for her to go past him. But that was a bridge too far, even for a person who did not need to be chased, and she hesitated. He nodded and backed away, making space. That was good. They were establishing trust. He was granting concessions, which she could abuse.

In the hallway, though, he stood with his back to the door. He gestured to the dark bedroom and she stared into his face but saw no other option. "Madison," he said, and pressed his hands together like a prayer. "I promise, I promise you can trust me."

She screams. Outside, the kids hear. Their heads turn in unison. Moments pass. Then they shrug and return to their bikes. It's a bad neighborhood; there are screams, sometimes.

No. Not this. She does not scream.

But she couldn't make herself enter that room. "Why?" she said, even though it was moot; he was close enough to seize her if he chose.

"I only want to talk. I swear to God."

She was terrified and possibly only seeing what she hoped for, but there was honesty in his face. She was a reasonable judge of character, from the acting: You learned what emotions looked like, which parts of the face moved when a person was envious, or sympathetic, or angry. Or lying.

She walked into the bedroom. Clay closed the door behind her. A thin shaft of light split the curtains and slashed across the carpet. The silver case sat in shadow, its mouth open to the far wall.

He moved to the curtain, opened it two fingers' worth, and peered out. Looking for . . . what? People, she guessed. Making sure no one was around. She reached behind her, seeking the door handle. She was only two closed doors to freedom. All she had to do was open this door, get out, fling it closed—this part was important!—so that it actually shut, and Clay would have to navigate the handle, and by then she could be pulling open the front door, and she would be outside, running, and, yes, it was a bad neighborhood, a terrible neighborhood, where there was every chance that no one would come to help, no matter how much noise she made, but it was her best option, she felt; it was far, far better than staying and finding out what was in the box.

Clay let the curtain fall closed. She tucked her hand into the small of her back before he could see. No one reaching for the door handle here. No, sir. No one who needed to be chased.

"I think we have a few minutes," Clay said. "I can tell you what's going on. But it won't be easy for you to hear. I need us to give each other a chance. All right?"

She nodded.

"Can you give me that chance?"

"Yes," she said, although she didn't like that: the push for affirmation.

"Like you said, your office knows who I am. They have my name, my photo." He held up his hands. "I've left fingerprints everywhere. Right?"

She nodded. Yes! These were excellent points. They could all agree that it would be crazy for Clay to do anything. There were security measures. Yes.

"So you can relax."

"Okay," she said. She was not relaxed. This situation had a long way to go before she would be anywhere near relaxed. But she was being agreeable.

He rubbed his hands together, a nervous gesture. He was still near the curtains. It was not completely impossible that she could get out the door before he reached her. "I'm just going to tell you. Madison, I'm not from this world."

Oh, God, she thought.

He came toward her. At first she thought he meant to take her hands, and that jolted her to her senses, because for a moment there she'd been snagged on the preposterousness of what he'd said: *I'm not from this world*—like, what did that mean, exactly, in what sense? But now she realized: the crazy sense.

The photo at the office didn't matter. The fingerprints didn't matter. He believed he was from another world.

"I've traveled here for you. Only for you, Madison." He hesitated. "How do you feel about that?"

She felt like vomiting from terror. But she said, "I'm . . . confused." Her tone was level, almost curious, and that was good; that was exactly what she wanted.

He glanced at the curtain again. When he next moved to the window, she was gone. She should have run the first time. "Of course you are. And scared, I bet. But you can trust me."

His face was hangdog, and here it was again, this weird insistence on her approval, even though he had all the power. It might be something she could use. For whatever reason, he cared what she thought, and if she were smart—if she didn't push too hard—she might be able to find a way to turn that against him. *I need us to give each other a chance,* he'd said. Maybe she could make him give her a chance.

"I . . . do feel like I can trust you," she said. "I don't know why."

His reaction was bigger than she'd expected: His loud eyebrows shot up and his mouth dropped open. "Really?"

"Yes," she said, rowing hard. "I felt that when we met. Maybe you remind me of someone I know?" No reaction. That was a swing and a miss. But he was waiting, his expression expectant, offering her another pitch. "Or . . . maybe we've met before."

Whack. A solid hit. His face lit up. "When do you think we've met?"

Oh, Christ. "I don't know. There's just . . . something."

"When?" he said again.

"College? High school?" But these were bad guesses, she saw. Not even close. She did something very brave and took a step toward him, i.e., away from the door. A small deposit toward the hope of a future return. "Or something deeper. More spiritual."

He exhaled shakily. "You're right. We have met before. But not in this world."

She nodded. *Yes, of course, that's probably it.*

"All this . . ." He gestured to . . . the room, the curtains? No, no: the world, of course. "It's a drop in the ocean. There are more worlds. More than you can count. They look the same but they're not, not if you pay attention. And you're in all of them. Everywhere I go, you're doing different things. Every time I leave, it's to find you again."

He gazed at her. She felt required to ask a question. He'd just told her there were a bunch of worlds; of course, of course, she would have questions, if she took that seriously, and was not devoting most of her brain toward figuring out the location of the door handle. She said: "Why?" He didn't answer, and she thought maybe that had been a bad question, but no, it wasn't that: He just wanted her to figure out the answer. "In these . . . other worlds . . . are we . . . together?"

He gave a rueful smile and shook his head. But that was the right answer, she thought. That was what he'd wanted her to say. "Sometimes I can't even get to see you. Sometimes I can get to you but it doesn't work out. There are people trying to keep us apart. People who move, like me." He glanced at the curtains again. "They're getting close."

She was interested in that: in people who wanted to keep them apart. She would like to meet them now, if that was at all practical. "Why do they want to keep us apart?"

"It's complicated. I'll explain on the way."

On the way. For a long moment she tried and failed to imagine what on earth that could mean. Then it hit her: His box was a portal. Inside would be a car battery or a dead opossum that he'd convinced himself was a transdimensional travel device, and he would hold her hands and ask her to close her eyes. Then: *Kazam!* They would be in another world. Which would look the same, according to him. So, very conveniently, there would be no evidence of whether they'd traveled. But all this was fine, Maddie realized, completely fine, because after that, he would want to leave the house, and then she could run.

"On the way to where?" she said, widening her eyes, like: *Interdimensional travel, how amazing.*

"I have a hotel room," he said.

Ah.

They said never let yourself be taken to a secondary location. That was where you got murdered. But she had to get out of this house. She would go with him, but not get in his car. "All right," she said.

He smiled. "I still can't believe you recognized me. That never happens."

She smiled back.

"I mean, never," he said.

She felt a touch of ice in her throat. Her smile felt welded to her face.

"You know, I love you, Madison. In every world. Even when you don't love me back."

"We should go," she said, "before those people arrive."

"Can I ask you something?"

She nodded mutely.

"Can I hug you?"

She said nothing.

"It's just, it's been so long. It kills me to get this close to you and not touch you." He spread his arms.

She revolted at the idea. She could shove him, she thought. He was standing in front of the silver box; she could move in for the hug, then push him over the box.

She moved toward him. She didn't know if she could really shove him. It was fine in theory, but dudes were always a little faster and stronger than you expected. It was easy to forget, but occasionally there was a situation, a game of mixed basketball, a guy getting out of hand at a party, which made you realize: *Oh, shit, they are quick.*

He spread his arms. His disfigured forearm caught the shaft of light and she saw it clearly: a mess of older scar tissue and newer bruising, a red scab that couldn't be more than a week old. None of it looked like it was made by a dog.

She stopped, unable to make herself approach any closer. He stepped forward and gently put his arms around her. She let it happen. He exhaled noisily. His cheek rested on her head. "This is nice," he said.

She could see over the lid of the case. She had been right earlier: It was a toolbox. It had levels. On each was a different kind of knife. It was a box of gleaming metal and pain. She saw a space, as if something belonged there but was missing.

She began to tremble. "Shh," Clay said. "Shh." But she couldn't stop. His hands moved to her shoulders and pushed her back until he was holding her at arm's length. She couldn't help throwing fear-stricken glances at the box, and a smile crept along his lips. "Oh, Madison. You don't need to worry about that. That's only for if it doesn't work out. This time is different. Because this time you know me, don't you?"

She nodded.

"You felt a connection, right? As soon as we met?"

"Yes."

"Or," he said, "you were messing with me. Stringing me along." His fingers tightened on her shoulders. "Is that what you were doing?"

"No."

He gave a short, dismissive exhalation. "You know what I find crazy? There are so many of you. You're as common as dirt. I can find another tomorrow. But you always think you're so special. You're a real estate agent, for God's sake. But I gave you a chance, like I always do. I was honest with you and you lied to me."

She seized on this. "You said you didn't want to hurt me. You promised."

"I *don't* want to hurt you. But this . . ." His eyes ran down her body. "This isn't you. I can't stand to see you like this. I honestly can't."

She couldn't stop thinking about the space in the box. There was a missing tool and he had it somewhere.

She fled. Tried to. He had her before she'd so much as twitched, and she opened her mouth to scream and he jammed his forearm into it. Then his bulk followed, forcing her to the floor, knocking the breath out of her. She couldn't breathe, choked by his forearm, by the horrible puckered wound. When she tried to bite him, her teeth perfectly filled the indentations of his scar tissue.

He was reaching behind for whatever he had in his back pocket. "I hate that you make me do this," he said, and even as she struggled, she could see that he did indeed look regretful, like a man forced to put down a pet dog, one he'd loved that had turned rabid. The knife loomed, fat and wide and evil. "I really hate it."

2

THERE WAS A CLOCK. EACH SECOND, IT JERKED FORWARD WITH A decisive, mechanical *thwack*. In Felicity's first month in the newsroom, she'd asked if maybe that clock could be moved, or replaced with something digital, or anything, really, that didn't emit a sound like nails being driven into a board sixty times a minute above her head. The answer was no, because the clock was an institution. It was an old-timey wooden box suspended from the ceiling and had been here longer than she had. In these challenging times (for newspapers), it was a comforting connection to the past, when they had been respected, and the *Daily News*'s editions always landed with an impact. *Thwack. Thwack. Thwack.* Like that.

On the phone, Felicity Staples was listening to a district attorney tell her she was making a mistake. He was hard to hear, because of the clock. "What you're insinuating simply isn't correct," said the D.A. He was the county D.A.; his name was Tom Daniels. He and Felicity had spoken several times before, and each time, his opinion of her seemed to drop a little more.

"I'm not insinuating anything," she said. "I'm only asking questions."

"Please." She'd seen him do this on TV, when pressed on something he didn't want to answer: *Please*, then a subtle change of subject. A pinch of the brow, expressing both amusement and pain at the question. Daniels was mid-forties, somewhat dubiously tanned, with a magnificently expressive face. "How long have you spent on this story? I have trouble believing that Brandon considers this a sensible use of your time."

Brandon Aberman was the paper's managing editor. She ignored the jibe, because, one, it was a diversion, and, two, yes, Brandon would definitely prefer her to work on something else, preferably involving bedbugs.

"A young man from a well-connected family walks away with no time served despite a plethora of evidence—"

"Plethora," said Daniels. "I'm so glad you've found an outlet for the English degree. If you were more familiar with the reality of prosecution, you'd understand we have to make the best deal we can, given the circumstances."

"Circumstances like the family mixes socially with the mayor?"

"Felicity Staples," he said, like a disappointed parent. *Felicity Staples, come here. Did you make this mess?* "I'm quite sure there's a better outlet for your talents than fishing for gotcha quotes from a D.A."

The newsroom was a huge open space with dark desks jumbled about beneath silent, hyperactive TV screens. Felicity's desk was near the front, close to the elevators, beneath the clock. Blind-shuttered glass offices lay to her left and right, while ahead, beyond a barren patch of deskscape that had lain bare for six months, were two glorious windows, offering skyscraper-framed glimpses of sky. In between was a message board, where stood Melinda Gaines, a political reporter and columnist, with a coffee cup. Melinda raised the cup and took a careful sip. On the message board, Felicity knew, was an internal job posting for "social media manager." She knew that because she'd studied it herself a few times already. Each time, she'd decided the position was irrelevant to everything she'd ever studied for, worked toward, and believed in, as well as offering less money. But it was also a job that would definitely exist in twelve months, which couldn't be said for her own. Watching Melinda Gaines contemplate it over coffee was terrifying, because Melinda Gaines was forty-four and had written a towering series of articles exposing three corrupt city judges. If Gaines was considering "social media manager," the writing really was on the wall for the future of journalism. Literally posted there.

"I'm comfortable with how I'm employing my talents, thank you, Tom," Felicity said, because she didn't want to verbally spar with Tom Daniels. She wanted to make him feel comfortable and eviscerate him in print. She was thirty-three. She could do plenty of things with her life. "Is it true that you met with the Hammonds personally the night before you dropped the charges?"

"I'd have to check my diary."

Her view of Melinda Gaines contemplating the future of journalism was broken by the gangling form of Todd the intern, flapping a piece of yellow notepaper. He wore round glasses and an anxious expression. "I've got a murder."

Felicity shooed him. She did not do murders. She did city politics, lifestyle, occasionally stories on people who died eating something they shouldn't have, but not murders. "You've met them, though, at some point? Socially?"

"I can find out and send you that information, if you like."

He would not. He'd taken her call, to rob her of the line *District Attorney Tom Daniels did not respond to requests for comment by the time this article was published*; now he would string her along until the next revolution of the news cycle, when nobody remembered the curiously lenient plea deal of James Hammond, a fine-looking college boy whose promising future was briefly threatened by an assault upon a girl who laughed at him at a party.

"Can you take a murder?" said Todd, moving into her eyeline.

She swiveled. "Is it standard procedure for a district attorney to involve himself in cases when he has a social relationship with the accused's family?" *Daniels admitted it was not standard procedure for a district attorney to—*

"It's standard procedure for the D.A. to prosecute all cases to the best of his ability. Is there anything else?"

"How would you describe your relationship with the Hammonds?"

District Attorney Tom Daniels admitted he had a "long-standing" relationship with the Hammond family—

Alternately:

District Attorney Tom Daniels claimed a "limited" relationship with the Hammonds, but has dined at their Hampton Bays mansion on at least two occasions—

"Someone needs to take this," said Todd, sounding anxious. "Levi's out."

She glared at him. Todd put on a wounded look and walked away.

"I've run into the Hammonds on several occasions," said Daniels. "They're active in society; if you get out enough, you're bound to meet them."

She probably should have known better than to try to verbally entrap an attorney. She plucked a yellow pen with a Goofy head from her basket and rolled it between her finger and thumb. Three years ago, she'd run from work to meet a guy for a blind date, scribbling notes for an article on the subway, and as she entered the restaurant, she checked herself carefully in a mirror, making sure her dirty-blond hair and face were in the right places, then, without thinking, tucked that Goofy pen behind her ear. It was whole minutes later, after they'd exchanged polite kisses and introductions, just as she was starting to think, *This one seems all right,* did the realization steal over her: *DID I PUT THAT FUCKING PEN IN MY EAR???* She reached up and felt it. She was mortified because it looked like she was putting on a kooky affectation, and she could not apologize enough, but the guy didn't seem to mind one way or the other, and from there the night actually went well. They were now living together, and she kept the Goofy pen as a reminder that things could work out no matter how much she tried to sabotage them.

She said, "What did you think of the victim impact statement?"

A moment of silence for her weird question. It was so easily deflected—*What I think isn't relevant*—that he didn't try. "I thought it was profoundly sad."

"I thought it was horrifying," Felicity said. "She said she doesn't laugh anymore. She laughed at a boy at a party, and he hit her so hard that her retina detached, and now she doesn't laugh. I can't stop thinking about that."

Daniels was silent.

"I guess that's not so shocking to you," she said. "You deal with worse all the time."

"The victim's injuries were very serious and saddening," Daniels said, and they were back to the game.

"Thank you for your time, Tom," she said. "Please do send me those dates."

As soon as she lowered the phone, Todd the intern turned in her direction, his face brightening.

"No," she said. She stood. It was after one; she needed to eat something.

The meeting room door opened, revealing the neat, tucked-in figure of Brandon Aberman, her boss, in a duck-egg-blue sweater over a collared shirt, tan slacks, and brown loafers. His hair was a swept-over coif that Felicity always felt could be popped right off and placed on a desk, like that of a LEGO man. He beckoned to her. Todd drifted behind her, covering her exit.

"Hi, Felicity," Brandon said. "How are you?"

Every conversation she and Brandon had ever had began this way, no matter how recently they'd spoken. She suspected a management book somewhere, a chapter titled "Building Trusting Partnerships with Subordinates."

"Great."

"How's the recycling piece coming along?"

"It's coming." That was what she was supposed to be doing instead of harassing District Attorney Tom Daniels. Someone at a recycling center in Hoboken had filmed a truck dumping citizens' carefully washed plastics and glass into the landfill, and it had become a thing on social media; therefore, the paper needed something on its website as quickly as possible. Felicity had phoned a few people and discovered that the recycling center's position was more reasonable than it had first appeared, for reasons that were complicated, which prevented her from writing the kind of article Brandon wanted, i.e., "More Secret Trucks Revealed; Recycling Center Has Links to Underworld Crime." "I'll have it for you by five."

He glanced at his watch, which was full of icons. "Do you have enough for a VC spot? They want to post something in the next half hour."

VC was Visual Content, or possibly Video Content; she couldn't remember. Either way, it was a bunch of smart twenty-six-year-olds in bright sweaters and delicate blouses compressing news into thirty seconds of hot-button phrases. Felicity occasionally did VC spots—not as many as five years ago, when it was going to save the news business, and no one had realized the social media numbers were lies—and it was always slightly soul-crushing.

"Oh, ah . . . I don't know if I'm quite there yet."

"If you've spoken to the recycling center, that's enough. I'd rather have something now than later."

"They say there's no way to recycle it cost-effectively," she said.

"Since China closed up, there's literally nowhere for it to go that doesn't cost more money than sending it to the landfill."

Brandon pursed his lips. "So it's a systemic issue."

She nodded.

"Why don't they tell people? Why waste our time sorting plastics if it winds up in the same place?"

"They said it took years to train households to recycle properly and they don't want us to get out of the habit. A new buyer might enter the market in the future."

"That sounds deceitful," said Brandon. "I will have you do a VC, if you don't mind."

"Ahh," she said. "The thing is, also, I was about to cover a murder." She turned and clicked her fingers at Todd. He jerked toward them. "There's a big one and Levi's out."

Todd cleared his throat. He was only three weeks old, nervous around the rest of them. "I took a call from Detective Jim McHenry of the Crime Scene Unit, who said Levi would want to know about this right away. They have a single white female victim, fatally stabbed while showing a house on 177th Street in Jamaica."

Brandon touched his chin thoughtfully. There were a lot of murders; the paper didn't cover most of them. "Suspect?"

Todd shook his head. "He didn't say."

"Always ask," said Brandon. "What else?"

Todd looked at his note. "The victim's name is Madison May."

Brandon dug his phone out of his pants and began to manipulate it. "M-A-Y? And she's a real estate agent?"

"Was," said Todd, gaining confidence. "Worked for Henshaw Realty out of Laurelton."

Brandon turned his screen toward Felicity, revealing a website. Beneath a sky-blue banner were the words MADISON MAY, SALES ASSOCIATE, and a picture of a woman with auburn hair spilling over a dark blazer.

"Pretty," Felicity said.

Brandon was silent. She could see him imagining how this picture would look above a headline that included the word *slain*. It would look fantastic.

"What's Levi doing?" asked Brandon.

"I don't know," Todd said. "He's not answering."

He was doing Annalise from Ad Sales, Felicity suspected. Levi's desk was connected to Felicity's, and most days, as the clock *thwacked* its way toward twelve-thirty, Annalise from Ad Sales would slide into the newsroom, ease her ass onto the space between them, cross her legs, push back her shoulders, and ask if she could get Levi's opinion on something. Then, every few minutes, Annalise would tip back her head and give voice to high, girlish peals of laughter that were unlike anything Felicity had heard from her during the office Christmas party, in the company of her husband.

Brandon tapped his chin. Felicity waited.

"All right," Brandon said. "Check it out."

"Okay," she said, buoyed. With any luck, by the time she got back, they'd have found someone else for the VC spot. "Photographer?"

Brandon shook his head. His hair gleamed. "We can get something from the police."

Even better. She could enjoy her own thoughts instead of sharing a ride with a camera jockey. She could pick up some lunch. And she could figure out what she was going to do about District Attorney Tom Daniels, who expressed sincere sympathy for poor assaulted girls without ever using their name. "You got it."

THE WIND SWITCHED around, and by the time she reached 177th Street, the sky was beginning to dispense fat drops to puncture the city heat. The police had taped off a perimeter, and at its center was one of the saddest houses Felicity had ever seen. Uniformed cops spilled out of the driveway and onto the street. Through dirty windows, she glimpsed people moving about, uniforms and suits and people in loose white plastic. Every few seconds, one of the windows lit up with flashes.

"Such a terrible thing," said a woman holding the neck of her top closed against the wind. Beside her stood a broad-shouldered, bearded man in a trucker's cap, staring at the house with no visible emotion.

"Did you know her?"

"Oh, no. They say it's the real estate agent. I never met her." She lowered her voice. "They're thieves."

"Pardon?"

"Realtors," said the woman. "They rob you blind."

"Oh," Felicity said. "I see."

A uniformed cop strayed near the yellow tape and Felicity waved to catch his attention. "Is Detective McHenry here?"

"Who are you?"

"Felicity Staples." She reached for her press pass. "I'm with the *Daily News*."

"No media," said the cop, turning away.

"I need Detective McHenry. Can I speak to him, please?"

The cop ignored her. She shivered. Rain trickled down the back of her neck. If she hadn't blown off the VC spot, she would be warm and dry, smiling for the camera, warning people about the dangers of deceitful recycling operators. She hadn't done real crime reporting for a while. She'd forgotten it could be so wet.

A short man in an olive coat approached the tape, water dripping from the brim of a dark hat. "Who are you?"

"Felicity Staples." She found her pass again.

"Where's Levi?"

"Indisposed."

"I didn't call you. I called Levi." He glanced over his shoulder.

She shifted from one foot to the other. Her shoes squelched. She'd assumed the tip wasn't especially secretive, since it had been left with Todd, but maybe that wasn't the case: Maybe it was too good to wait. "Levi sent me," she lied.

McHenry eyeballed her.

She pulled out her phone. "You want me to call him?"

He gave a short shake of his head, spraying water. "Okay, stay here. I'll see what I can do."

Felicity glanced around. The woman had left to seek shelter from the increasing rain, but her husband remained, watching the house. Rain ran down his cap and beard. He looked like a woodsman. Like he'd just emerged from the wilderness after a month of hunting boars. With a handcrafted spear. Half naked. She looked away. She had an active imagination.

The window that had been flashing became a solid rectangle of light. A man edged by it with a shoulder-mounted video camera aimed downward, at the carpet, or whatever lay upon it. "What a shit-hole," she said, meaning the house, and the street, and the weather, and the situation. The woodsman didn't respond.

The CSU detective, McHenry, gestured to her from where the police tape was tied to the chain-link fence, and Felicity hurried to meet him. "It's a messy one. Vic was stabbed half a dozen times. Throat cut."

She fumbled for her notebook and wrote: THROAT, 6+ STAB. "Can I get in there?"

He shook his head. "No, no."

"Why not?"

"Because it's not worth my job. The deputy inspector's in there with his detectives. This is all background, okay? You don't use my name. That's how me and Levi do it."

In the top-right corner of the page, she wrote: BG. "Why did you call Levi?"

"I knew he'd be interested."

"Because of the vic?" She'd never used the word *vic* to a cop before. She felt professional. "Because she's photogenic?"

McHenry looked at her like she was crazy. "What?"

"The victim was pretty."

McHenry gestured impatiently. "I got no friggin' idea what she looked like. It's somethin' else."

A light flared on the street. She turned to see a TV crew setting up: a white van, a guy with a camera, a thin woman in a green blazer beneath a black umbrella. A moment later, a man in a gray suit appeared at the front door of the house: the deputy inspector, Felicity assumed. He was tall, in his fifties, with deep lines in his face. He put his hands on his hips to survey the TV crew. Behind him emerged a young woman in a black skirt, who shook out an umbrella and opened it. They descended the steps, the woman awkwardly holding the umbrella for him.

"You want a look inside?" said McHenry, once they'd passed. "Now's your chance."

She hesitated, but why else was she here? She ducked beneath the tape.

"That's Deputy Inspector Moth," McHenry said over his shoulder, walking quickly toward the house. "Drawn to bright lights." He climbed the concrete steps. "You get thirty seconds. In and out. No pictures. You got it?"

She nodded. McHenry spoke to a uniformed cop, handed Felicity thin blue gloves and shoe covers, and waited while she tugged them on. Inside was a close hallway and the smell of damp. McHenry knocked on the door to his left, which was opened by a man dressed in white plastic. Behind him stood a light tower, painful to look at.

"Can I open this all the way?" McHenry said. The man in plastic said to wait; the door closed.

"So what's the 'something else'?" Felicity asked. She was dripping on the carpet.

He inclined his head toward the door. "You can see for yourself in a minute."

Obviously. But she wanted to know what she was in for. Was

there a body? She wasn't totally ready to see a dead real estate agent, a woman who'd been stabbed *half a dozen times, maybe more*, let alone the *something else*, the extra *frisson* that made it especially interesting to a newspaper.

The door swung back. Felicity squinted against the light. It was a bedroom, the carpet dark and heavy. A smell reached out to her, rich and wet. She saw yellow-and-black markers. No body, though. Definitely no body.

"Stay where you are," said the plastic man. "Don't come in."

A stain lay near the door, a big one. Then others, smaller, beside plastic markers. It was repulsive and terrible, but she had been braced for worse and it was almost a relief. She didn't see any *something else*.

"Look up," said McHenry.

The drywall had been carved open with thick slashes. There were five angled prongs crossing a circle. Some kind of insignia, she guessed. But none she recognized.

Below that was a word in sharp, furious lines:

STOP

McHenry was so close behind her, she could feel him breathing. She said, "What is that?"

"Beats me."

The white plastic man raised a camera. The flash discharged, momentarily inverting the colors of the room.

She said, "Can I get that? These pictures?"

"I don't know about that." McHenry stepped back. "You gotta go."

"Wait," she said, but McHenry began to bundle her out of the house. The plastic man closed the door, and she lost her view of the wall and its message behind it.

SHE DIRECTED THE UBER TO HER BROOKLYN APARTMENT, BECAUSE SHE
was soaked. She meant to return to the office—it was only four—but
once she was in the shower, with hot water pounding her back, she
couldn't seem to get out. There was a chill at the core of her, as if
she'd brought it home from that house.

When she finally entered the living room in a towel, her brave
cat, Percival, curled around her ankles, while her anxious cat, Joey,
watched from beneath the dining table. She collected her phone and
tapped out: *Working from home for rest of day if that's ok.*

A few moments later, Brandon's reply: *Certainly.*

For all his LEGO hair and careful conversations, Brandon did
seem to give a shit about the workers, for which she was grateful. He
probably even guessed why she wanted to stay home. She fell into
sweatpants and a loose top, sat at the dining table, and cracked open
her laptop. Levi was back on deck, his physical appetites satisfied
(she assumed); he'd already spoken to the police. She brought up the
document he was working on, which was a dozen paragraphs with
new words spilling across the bottom even as she watched.

*The victim of a brutal stabbing in Jamaica this afternoon was "tk tk
tk", Tk say.*

Tk was what you wrote when you knew something belonged but didn't know what. Beside it hovered a yellow bubble: *Quote family / colleague / etc.*

She picked up her phone. Levi answered immediately, but the words continued. She could hear him typing. She said: "Do you want me to call her family?"

"Don't bother. They're not taking calls. Can you try her office, though? That'd be helpful."

a ferocious, unprovoked attack

"The real estate people?"

"Number's in the notes. I need to establish character. 'She was a bright, beautiful girl with everything to live for.' You know."

"Okay."

"But not that. That, with details. She was planning to go kayaking next month. She collected stamps. She was engaged to be married. Yes?"

"I have written stories before," she said.

promised to expend every available resource

"Not crime stories," Levi said. "It's a different beat from what you're used to."

"How so?"

"For one thing, you can say what you mean. You don't have to run everything by Legal first."

"I say what I mean," she said, mildly offended.

"Here's a tip. Get the receptionist talking. She put me straight through to the head guy and he's saying nothing. Probably worried about his legal exposure. As he should be, sending a twenty-two-year-old out to empty houses by herself."

"What about the message on the wall?" she asked. She couldn't see it mentioned in the article.

"We're holding that back. NYPD is actually a little pissed we know about it."

"We're not publishing it?"

"Not yet. When it's time."

She supposed he knew what he was doing. There was a dance: the desire to publish on the one hand, the need to nurture and protect sources on the other. "What does it mean, do you think?"

"'Stop'? Beats me."

"I can't even figure out who it's aimed at. Who does he want to stop? The cops?"

"It may not even be related. Could have been there for days."

It had looked fresh to her. Like a new wound. "Mmm," she said.

Levi snickered. "Don't use your imagination. That only gets you into trouble. We find out when we find out."

would not disclose whether they had identified a suspect, but it is believed a person key to the inquiry will be brought into custody shortly

She asked, "The police know who did it?"

"Some college dropout from Ulysses, Pennsylvania. Goes by the name of Clayton Hors."

"How did they identify him?"

"Don't know. But they're confident he's their guy."

Felicity chewed her lip.

"Call me when you have a quote," Levi said. "Unless there's something else?"

"No," she said. "Yes. How do you talk and type at the same time?"

"Practice," Levi said, and hung up.

SHE SET HER elbows on the table, stuck her phone to her ear, and waited while it rang.

"Henshaw Realty, this is Alexandra, how may I help you this afternoon?"

"Hello, Alexandra. My name is Felicity Staples. I'm a reporter for the New York *Daily News*. I'm so sorry about Madison."

A brief silence. "Thank you."

"Do you have a minute? I'm hoping you can tell me something about the kind of person she was."

"I'll put you through to Simon. One moment, please."

"Please don't. I don't want to talk to Simon."

"I'm not allowed to speak to the media."

She closed her eyes. "Alexandra, I know I'm not the first reporter to call. But Simon is giving us no comment, and what that means, Alexandra, is when this story goes up, Madison won't have a face. She'll be a name and an age, and that's not enough for people to care. I want them to care, Alexandra. I want them to know who she was, so they can understand." The line was silent. "I was at the house this afternoon. It was the worst thing I've ever seen."

The receptionist exhaled. "Only clients called her Madison. She's Maddie."

Felicity typed.

"She was . . . She was going to be somebody one day. She was young and had a lot to learn, but she was learning it. She was on her way to something better."

"Thank you."

"She wanted to act," the receptionist said suddenly. "She talked about taking acting classes once."

That was good detail. "Did she—"

"Have the police arrested him?"

Felicity hesitated. "They haven't made any statement about a suspect."

"*Clayton Hors,*" the receptionist said, with venom. "We have his picture."

She hadn't expected the receptionist to know that. "Did someone—"

"Our system has their details. When they arrive on-site, the agent verifies them with the app."

"He left you his ID?"

"His driver's license. And when she met him on-site, Maddie took his picture. He let her take his picture and then he killed her."

Jesus Christ, she thought. She was momentarily unsure how to record that. She typed: *MM pic of CH at house → app → office.*

Voices rose in the background. "I have to go. I hope you have what you need."

"Yes," Felicity said. "Thank you." The receptionist hung up without replying.

SHE DUTIFULLY PHONED Levi and filled him in. Then she set down her phone and got back to her real work, the kind that didn't involve murdered real estate agents. No diary information yet from District Attorney Tom Daniels, the protector of well-heeled rich boys, so she typed out an email, just to let him know that she intended on making herself annoying. Her recycling story hadn't been reassigned and hadn't gone anywhere, she discovered, so she picked it back up. She worked for ninety minutes, and every five had to resist the temptation to check whether Levi had filed.

He let her take his picture and then he killed her.

That was really awful. All of a sudden, Felicity decided not to check the *News.* She was off the clock; her boyfriend would soon be home; she would do something wholesome. She went to the kitchen and searched the cupboards for something cookable.

Gavin arrived at seven, as she was scraping green paste out of a pot. His face contorted in alarm. It had not been a happy cooking experience. "What's wrong?"

"This is disgusting," she said.

"What is?"

"This," she said, dumping the pot into the sink. "I wanted to cook, but the sauce is *foul.*" It stuck to the side of the pot. She had burned it. It was half leftovers to begin with. She hadn't even made it from scratch.

He came and put his arms around her. "What's the matter?"

She rested her head on him. He was tall and huggable. He was a lawyer; not the exciting kind, a lawyer for patents. A dependable lawyer. He worked for Heron Law Group, a medium-sized firm specializing in corporate telecommunications disputes. He had sandy hair and a nice smell. She enjoyed that for a few moments.

"Nothing," she said. "Just a rough day."

"Want to talk about it?"

"No," she said, deciding. She didn't want to talk about murder anymore.

"Are you sure?"

She looked at her sad pot. On the stove, pasta was bubbling, useless without sauce. "We should order takeout."

"Well, wait," Gavin said. "Let me try that." There was some sauce left in the pot, and he spooned a sample into his mouth. She watched him roll it around and swallow. "Fuck," he said. "This *is* disgusting."

"I know."

"Did you put something in that?"

"Salt. Garlic. Some random spices."

"Why did you do that?"

"I don't know," she said. "I wanted to cook."

"Let's get Thai," he said, and she nodded.

THEY ATE AT the table: no Netflix, no phones. Gavin told her a story about work, some patent-related process of discovery, which involved filings, rulings, and a transmission protocol that was maybe one thing or maybe something else. He had an incredible ability to be absorbed by the mundane, Felicity had learned, during the three years they had been together since the Goofy-pen incident. He was easily content. Felicity had struggled with this for a while, because it was hard to believe him when he said that he didn't care what they watched, or where they went. She used to peer at him and say things like, *So I could put on* Bridesmaids *and you'd be totally fine with that,* and he would nod, and she would glance at him throughout the movie, seeking any hint of deceit, but it was true: He could be happy almost anywhere, with anything, no matter what was happening. He was four years older than her, approaching thirty-seven, so maybe this was the kind of equanimity that came with age, and when Felicity was thirty-seven, she, too, would possess a quiet, mature big-picture perspective, a contentment with the world around her and with her place within it. As opposed to now, when it seemed like almost everything was either terrible or in the process of being made that way by entrenched assholes, while nobody gave a shit.

Toward the end of the meal, her phone dinged. She glanced at it. An email notification, sender *Levi Waskiewicz,* subject *crime scene pics.*

"What is it?" Gavin said.

What would Levi want her to do with crime scene pics? Look them over? See if they triggered anything?

She shook her head. She would not look at those tonight, she decided. "Nothing."

"Good." He set down his fork. "Want to go to bed?"

She raised her eyebrows. There were disemboweled tubs everywhere. It was barely eight-thirty. "Yes."

"Good," he said again. He pushed back his chair and came to help her out of hers, like a gentleman. They kissed. Until that moment, she hadn't realized how much she needed it, and she kissed him back hungrily. He began to unbutton her blouse. She bit his lip, just hard enough to make it interesting. "*Nmf,*" he said, a sound she had always liked. She inhaled him and there was more after that.

AFTERWARD, SHE BRUSHED her teeth. The whole time, her phone sat on the bedside table, dark and inert. She was very aware of it. But she didn't look at it. She returned to bed and read a novel, a paper one, while Gavin lay beside her, scrolling work on a tablet. Then she turned off her lamp and rolled over. At some point, Gavin kissed her shoulder, and the room went dark.

She lay awake for a long time. *I saw the crime scene firsthand,* she thought. *Whatever Levi sent, it can't be worse.*

But it could, of course. Would Levi send her corpse pictures?

He might. He was a crime reporter. They had ghoulish senses of humor, like doctors.

Just get a sense of what's there. You don't have to look right at it. Get a peek and stop wondering.

She extracted herself from bed. Gavin was a deep sleeper; he didn't move. She closed the bedroom door and padded into the living room. Percival was on the sofa, a vague white ball against dark fabric. The table was striped with slatted streetlight from the vertical blinds.

She went to the sink and poured herself a glass of water, to give herself time to make sure she really wanted to do this. Then she sat at the table and opened her phone. Levi's email was second down, beneath a gym promotion. She held her phone at arm's length and squinted so it was out of focus.

The first pic was an exterior of the house; she could tell that. She scrolled. Another exterior shot, this time with more of the street. Next, a room. *The* room. Her sense was that it was geometrical: floor and walls; no desperate lump; no body. The next was similar. She worked her way through twelve photos this way, and none of them were of Maddie.

She exhaled. She scrolled to the top and began to review the pictures properly. The only text was a brusque *fyi,* so presumably Levi merely wanted to know if anything jumped out at her, a detail they might include in a follow-up. Because there were sure to be follow-ups. If the clicks came through like she expected, there would be many.

She spotted the detective, McHenry, in the second exterior shot, standing with his mouth open and his eyebrows raised, like he'd thought of something good to say to the other cops and was waiting for the chance to get it out. In the background, she spied herself, blurred but recognizable, behind the police tape. Waiting for McHenry. Beside her was the woman she'd spoken to, as well as the man Felicity had presumed was her husband, the woodsman in the cap.

She peered at the screen. She spread her fingers, making the man's face balloon on her screen.

He was younger than she'd thought at the time. Late thirties. Dark eyes, partially hidden beneath his cap, which was pulled down hard. Above the brim was a logo, a fuzzy circle that struck her as vaguely familiar—

No, she thought.

She scrolled to the despoiled wall. The word, STOP, and the strange insignia.

The woodsman's cap was horribly out of focus. She couldn't be sure. But they were similar. They were very, very similar.

She dialed Levi. He answered on the fifth ring, right before she was sure she was headed to voicemail. "Hello?" His voice was thick with sleep.

"Did I wake you?"

"It's after midnight."

"Sorry. I just saw something in the pictures you sent me. The crime scene photos." She explained about the man and his cap.

"Hold on," Levi said. "I'm getting my laptop."

She waited.

"Second pic? House, lawn, cops?"

"Yes. We're behind the tape. Right side."

There was a long silence.

"The bearded guy," she said. "Zoom in on his cap."

"I'm not even sure he has a beard. He's fifty feet out of focus."

"He was right beside me."

"You remember what his cap looked like?"

"No. I wasn't paying attention to the guy in the cap."

He exhaled. "It's late. You're seeing things that aren't there."

"Are there other photos? Maybe there's a better shot."

"I'll check tomorrow."

"Can you check now?"

"Let's say you're right," Levi said. "It's the same logo. It doesn't have to mean anything. It could be a baseball team our guy hates. It could be a burger chain. Life is full of coincidences."

She held the phone, unwilling to say: *I guess.*

There was a rustle of bedding. Levi was divorced. She presumed he slept alone, dreaming of Annalise from Ad Sales. "Felicity, I get that you're eager to see justice done. I was the same, before this job kicked all the humanity out of me. But the police will get there. They already know who did it."

"Have they made an arrest?"

"I don't know, because it's one in the morning. We'll pick this up tomorrow. Today."

She couldn't argue any longer. "All right."

"I led with the quote you got from her office, did you see? It was good. But you don't need to come at this at a hundred miles per hour."

"Okay. Thanks. Sorry for waking you."

"Forget it." He snickered. "You're getting a taste for it. For crime."

It was more that she was really disgusted by this particular case. "Maybe."

"Careful. It's hard to get out of it, once you're in. Good night, Felicity."

She stayed at the table for a minute. The *Daily News* app icon was on-screen and she eyed it. Then she tapped. And there it was: the photo of Maddie May, the one she'd seen on the Henshaw Realty website.

WOMAN, 22, SLAIN IN "AMBUSH" WHILE
SHOWING HOUSE

She opened the story. Inside were words she'd collected from the receptionist. The article was last updated six hours earlier, which meant no one on the night crew had heard anything worth adding. No news of any arrest.

Something brushed against her ankle. Percival, her brave cat, had grown tired of waiting for her to join him on the sofa. She lifted him onto her lap and stroked him, feeling him rumble. Outside, a car slewed through the rain-soaked street. She carried Percival back to the sofa and returned to her own bed. This time she slept.

SHE WOKE TOO early and went for a run in Prospect Park. Her eyeballs felt gritty. She drank coffee before she left for the newsroom, then poured another in the break room when she arrived. She had a budget meeting at eight-thirty and spent it staring through the glass wall at Levi, wondering if he'd told the police about the man in the cap.

"Felicity," said Brandon, and she blinked. "Late night?"

She frowned and tried to focus on the topic at hand, which was whether the Queens comptroller was actually going to run for mayor or just making a lot of noise about it like usual.

"Have a coffee," Brandon said.

She didn't need a third, but made it anyway. When the meeting broke up, she wended through the desks to Levi, who was on the phone, his feet up, his laptop open. "I have a call in to DeLuca about your cap theory," he said, hanging up and swinging his shoes to the carpet. "Should hear back this morning."

"Can you let me know when you do?"

"Sure."

"Still no arrest?"

"Nope."

"Why not?"

Levi shrugged slightly. "Their suspect has gone to ground. Shouldn't take long with someone like him, though. They'll nab him later today, most likely."

"Okay," she said.

"Okay?"

"Okay," she said. She returned to her desk, from where she could see him typing, staring at the window, and making calls. Twice he got up and moved around the office: once to talk to Melinda Gaines; once to stand in the corner with his phone for no apparent reason.

She had to go to the bathroom, because of the coffee. Each time, she worried she'd return to Levi's empty desk, his jacket missing from the hook. Finally, as the terrible clock hammered out twelve-thirty, Annalise from Ad Sales bounced into the newsroom, which meant Levi was about to disappear. Felicity rolled her chair across before Annalise could get there.

They smiled wanly at each other. There was a blob of mascara on Annalise's eyelashes, but Felicity didn't say anything. "So true," Levi said to his phone. "You get no argument from me there."

"Felicity, isn't it?" Annalise said.

"Yes," she said. "Annalise."

Levi was looking at her significantly. This was the call, she realized: He had Deputy Inspector DeLuca on the other end. "One more thing. One of the girls in our office was looking through the photos and thought she saw your murder-wall logo on a cap worn by one of your looky-loos." A pause. "Ahh . . . it's thirty-eight. The wide shot. Yeah. Right at the back." More silence. Levi laughed. "Hey, I passed it along. I'm being a good citizen." DeLuca said something else and Levi laughed again. "I'll hold you to that," Levi said, and hung up.

Felicity stared at him.

"Levi, can I borrow you for a minute?" Annalise said.

But Levi was looking at Felicity. "What?"

She was so furious she could hardly speak. There were so many things wrong with what had just happened. "What was that?"

"I passed along your tip."

"You didn't say I was *there*. That I saw the cap myself. Not just in the photo."

"You weren't supposed to be there. I don't want DeLuca knowing his office is leaking. And you didn't see it. You only think you did."

"You said it like it was a *joke*."

"Felicity, that's how these guys are. I tell them how to do their jobs, they get their backs up. This way, they can pick it up like it's their own idea."

This didn't make her feel any better. She turned and walked away in disgust. Then she came back. "I'm not a *girl in your office*. I'm a reporter."

"I know that. I was playing to the cheap seats."

"All of that was bullshit," she said, and walked away for real. She had attracted attention from Todd the intern and Melinda Gaines the future social media manager and all the other hacks scratching away at their keyboards like it ever made a difference. Levi's chair creaked, which probably meant he was preparing to leave for his lunchtime rogering. Annalise murmured *feisty*, or something like that, maybe it wasn't that at all, but the tone was condescending and set Felicity's blood to bursting in her brain. She felt like going back and shouting that someone had died, a woman had gone to show a house and been stabbed to death, but people died all the time and no one really cared. So she made herself keep walking all the way out the door.

THERE WAS A deli two blocks away run by a Turkish family who served amazing pide bread and occasionally screamed at one another across the counter. Today was Tuesday, which meant the tables were dominated by arts college students, filling the air with insistent, laugh-punctuated chatter, making Felicity feel a hundred years old. She had been like them, not too long ago. Young and dumb and thrusting herself into the world in bright, optimistic forays. Now she was stuck under a clock in an industry that was starving to death, writing stories about people who did bad things yet rarely suffered consequences. Sometimes she wondered if she'd taken a wrong turn somewhere, because this wasn't the life she'd imagined for herself, but then again, maybe not, because it wasn't so terrible, what she had here, with her semi-respected job and her ability to lunch alone at a Manhattan deli in the middle of the day.

She wanted to act, the receptionist had said. *She talked about acting classes once.*

If Felicity were stabbed to death, this was the kind of thing people would say. *She wanted to get out of journalism. She once talked about becoming a social media manager.*

She set up her laptop and took a big, crunchy bite of her pide. She opened a browser and typed *reverse image search*. She didn't know a whole lot about what that was. But she knew it existed and had identified things for other reporters. She dug the crime scene photo out of her messages, what Levi had called *your murder-wall logo*. As it was uploading, Todd the intern walked by her table, offering an awkward wave. She felt mildly guilty—she wasn't supposed to be working on this—but he couldn't see her screen. Her search results arrived and were garbage; nothing close to the same design. She picked her way around the page.

"Todd," she said. "Do you have a minute?" She swiveled her laptop. "What am I doing wrong here?"

"What are you trying to do?"

She pointed to the murder logo. "Figure out what that is."

He peered. "Uh, you can't really do that. A reverse image search is for finding copies of an image. Not the things in the image."

"Oh," she said.

"And what you're really looking for isn't even that. This is a design someone carved into a wall, right? So what you really want to find is the original. Whatever this person was trying to copy." His fingers hovered above her keyboard. "Can I?"

"Sure."

He began to type. She was looking at a Web page called Logo Monkey, where a cute cartoon monkey told her: *Avoid monkey business! Make sure your logo is original!*

"So," Todd said. He was excited, she noticed. He was even more geeky than she had imagined. "Here we can upload a sketch to compare to basically every registered logo. But don't use the photo. Make a clean drawing yourself."

She found a napkin and carefully drew the logo, the circle and five slashes, trying imagine what it was supposed to look like when it wasn't being carved into drywall by a maniac with a knife.

"Good," Todd said. "That's great."

They used her phone to capture the drawing and shared it to the laptop. A blue progress bar crawled. The monkey hopped from side to side.

"This place is great," Todd said, meaning the deli. "I only just discovered it."

The screen spilled designs. A flaming baseball belonging to BALTIMORE REBELS. A smiling sun from PROVIDENTIAL HEALTH. A parade of conceptual circles, none of which were her drawing. Then she saw it.

THE SOFT HORIZON JUICE COMPANY

"Does that seem right?" Todd said.

It looked right. It was the exact design. But it couldn't be connected, surely.

Stop, Soft Horizon Juice Company. Or I will kill again.

"I have to get back," Todd said. "Let me know if you need help with anything else."

She nodded, distracted. "Thanks, Todd."

After he left, she plugged *Soft Horizon Juice* into a couple of public-records databases, the *News*'s media archive, and the two major corporate registries. The Soft Horizon Juice Company had been founded in 2007, she learned, with the goal of bringing to the world the unparalleled freshness of Californian oranges. It had a website, which listed a number of offices worldwide, including one in Hell's Kitchen. She scrolled through a gallery of products, none of which she could ever remember seeing in a store.

She checked the time. She needed to get back to real work.

Just in case, she typed: *Soft Horizon Juice Madison May.*

Nothing.

She highlighted *Madison May* and tapped delete. Instead: *Clayton Hors.*

Again, no connection. But the fourth result was the Facebook page of Clayton Hors. She found herself looking at a young man in his early twenties, tall, thin, Caucasian, shaggy brown hair. He was on a beach, wearing a green top, grinning at her from beneath a pair of sunglasses.

She didn't want to look at him. Abruptly, she closed the laptop. But when she next opened the laptop, she realized, he would be there, grinning at her. She opened the lid and moused up to the browser tab and Xed him.

SHE LEFT THE office early to catch a look at the registered office of the Soft Horizon Juice Company on West 50th Street, even though it was probably nothing. It was a grand, Gothic tower with a wooden revolving door and a quietly residential feel. The website hadn't listed an apartment or floor number, so that was the end of this particular line of inquiry, unless she wanted to hang around and harass people who came in and out. She loitered, considering. Across the street was a narrow laundromat.

What the hell, she thought. She went inside and played with her phone, occasionally glancing up when she saw the tower's door revolve. No one who looked very corporate, she noted. Not unless Soft Horizon Juice was staffed by middle-aged, well-heeled Manhattanites. She stayed for another hour or two, working her phone, until she glanced up and saw the woodsman.

He was coming out of the tower in jeans, a red checked shirt, and a cap. He looked bigger than she remembered, like a walking tree, sauntering eastward. She hurried out of the laundromat and began to follow him from the opposite side of the street.

Levi picked up on the third ring. "Let me go first," he said. "I'm genuinely sorry for how I came off before."

"Sure, sure," said Felicity.

"So I did some digging for you. And guess what? I found your guy."

"What?" The light changed. The woodsman began to cross the street toward her. Caught, she turned and studied the storefront of a pizza place.

"The guy with the cap. His name is Hugo Garrelly."

Hugo, she thought, watching him in the reflection. He came and stood behind her, waiting to cross Ninth Avenue.

"I assume your silence is shock that I managed to ID a guy from his hat," Levi said. "Turns out the CSU had a bunch more pictures, including one where your guy is in focus. You were right: It *does* look like the same logo. And the cap has some writing, too. It says, Soft Horizon Juice."

The light changed. She stepped onto the road, following Hugo. "Okay."

"Which sounds like nothing. Because whatever the murder-wall logo is supposed to be, it's probably not an ad for a juice company. You know?"

"Right."

"But then a funny thing happened. I got on the phone to one of my guys in Queens South and guess what? He recognized him. Because Hugo Garrelly is BOLO."

Ahead of her, Hugo turned abruptly into the subway entrance at West 50th and Eighth. She followed him down into thick, humid air. "He's what?"

"'Be on lookout.' Like an APB. There will be some sore asses in the 113th Precinct, Felicity, because half the city's on alert for this guy, and he's in their crime scene photos."

Hugo swiped through the turnstiles. Felicity followed.

"I mean, to be fair, the BOLO was only issued this time yesterday, so maybe by then they hadn't distributed it to everyone in the field. But it's a hell of a thing."

A train rattled. People streamed from an A train, forcing her to the side. "What is he—"

"Why is he BOLO? That's the delicious part. They wouldn't even tell me at first. I had to make another call. Hugo Garrelly is—" A train honked.

She plugged her ear. "Say again?" So far, her phone reception had held up, but that wasn't guaranteed: It could drop out at any moment, leaving her with a dead line.

Levi's voice returned. "Hugo Garrelly is serving a life sentence in Sing Sing for murdering his wife. Only he's not. Because he's BOLO."

She was walking six feet behind him. She chose her words carefully, because she wasn't sure how much he could hear. "I know where he is."

"Who? Garrelly?"

"Yes, we're together now."

Levi's voice filled with concern. "You're with *Garrelly?* Felicity, he's Do Not Approach. You need to get away from him."

He hadn't turned the whole time she'd been following him; she felt sure she hadn't been noticed. And the day before, when they'd stood side by side behind a strip of police tape, he'd barely glanced in her direction. So he might not recognize her even if he stared right at her. "I'm in the subway at West 50th and Eighth," she said blandly, as if she were organizing logistics. "I'll be on the southbound platform soon."

She heard Levi clicking his fingers. To someone she couldn't see: "Call nine-one-one and tell them their escaped felon Hugo Garrelly is on the southbound platform at West 50th and Eighth." He returned to her. "Felicity, you don't want to be anywhere near this guy. He's dangerous."

"I'm fine." She was keeping her distance. There were people everywhere. She had been very lucky to find him and didn't want to let him go. On the platform, people were spilling from a train. Hugo waited patiently to let them pass. Then he stepped on board. Felicity followed.

She kept close, so that when he took up a position near the far doors, she could set herself behind him. The doors chimed: *bing-bong*.

"What are you doing?" Levi said in her ear. "Because it sounds like you're getting on a fucking train."

"Yes, honey," she said. "I should be home in about twenty minutes."

"Is he with you? On the train?"

"That's right."

"Jesus Christ," Levi said.

The train moved off. She stared at the back of Hugo's head. Thick hair poked from beneath his cap. The lights flickered. A guy in a Mets cap sprawled across one of the seats slapped his thigh, watching his phone, and said, "Oh, *damn*."

In her ear, the line fell silent. She hummed nervously to herself, like an idiot, like someone pretending to be on the phone.

Hugo's wristwatch beeped: a tinny, electronic sound. He was holding the pole and so she could see it: a chunky silver thing with a blue face, the kind of device she'd thought they stopped manufacturing in the 1990s.

Levi materialized in her ear, speaking to someone unknown: "She's going southbound."

"Hello," she said.

"Felicity, they want to know if he's armed. Is he carrying anything you can see?"

"No, I don't think so."

"Tell them yes," Levi said to somebody. "He's got a gun."

"Ah," she said, "that's actually incorrect."

"You're on a train with a guy who cut his wife into pieces. I'm getting the police to you as fast as I can."

"Mmm," she said.

"Next stop, if he gets off, you stay on. If he doesn't, you get off. Is that clear?"

She would hate to lose Hugo now. But it was a good point. She had been eyeing Hugo throughout this conversation and he had remained very still. In a train full of people shifting about and scrolling on phones, he was a statue. Maybe that was what happened to you in prison. Maybe you got Zen, from all that time sitting alone in your cell, gazing at the wall, after murdering your wife.

The train lurched. The wheels began to squeal. They were coming into 42nd Street.

Hugo wasn't gazing at nothing, though. He was actually watching the door to the adjoining train car. Or looking through it to the passengers beyond? From behind, it was hard to tell. Felicity shifted, thinking to use a reflection, and when she did, in the black glass of the doors, she saw his eyes on her.

"Felicity," Levi squawked. "You still there?"

The train stopped. There was a surge of movement in the adjoining train car. Abruptly, Hugo shouldered his way between the doors. There were shouts. People heaved out of his way. Hugo forged through them toward the stairs, and there was something else, Felicity realized: a second disturbance, a man in a long gray shirt also running for the exit, who had come from the next train car.

"He's running!" she yelped into her phone.

She went after him. But she lost the line of sight and at the top of the stairs there were several ways he could have gone: to the other platform, to the street, or into the tunnel to the 1, 2, and 3 trains. She chose the latter at random, but within twenty seconds could see that it was too calm, not at all the kind of scene that would be left in the wake of men barging down a cramped space, so she headed back to the gates. She arrived in time to see a flash of red checked shirt crossing back toward the northbound platform.

She pressed the phone to her ear, but Levi was no longer there. When she reached the platform, she found Hugo standing motionless, staring across the tracks. He glanced back at her.

"I'm on the phone with the police," she lied. "Stay where you are."

He ignored her. She followed his gaze across the tracks and saw the man in the long gray shirt looking back at them. He was young, early twenties, longish brown hair. She recognized him: Earlier today, she'd been looking at his Facebook profile picture. It was Clayton Hors.

The police were on their way; she could point them to Clay, have him and Hugo arrested—

Hugo took a step toward the edge of the platform, as if he were about to leap down to the tracks. Clay didn't move. Hugo hesitated. He glanced at his watch, then at Felicity. The air began to stir with the advance of a train. "I need your help." His voice was low but firm, like he was speaking to a child, or a skittish animal. Not as rough as she'd expected from the woodsman exterior. "I need you to hold something for me."

She backed up a step. She wasn't going to do that.

"There's a cavity beneath the platform. You'll be safe. Just don't drop it."

He held something out to her: a dull egg the color of old metal. And she wasn't going to take it, of course, but her hands instinctively came up to repel him, and she was momentarily distracted, thinking, *What is that, some kind of weapon?* and he seized her wrist.

"Hold it," Hugo said. He pressed the egg into her palm. Then he shoved her off the platform.

SHE SPRAWLED ON THE TRACKS, BANGING HER CHIN AND ELBOW AND knee. Her bag hit the ground and vomited forth her belongings. She raised her head quickly, because there was a train approaching, she recalled, a *train*, its lights blooming, and as she did, the air split with a bone-rattling blast from its horn. Its wheels began to scream. Felicity had covered her share of subway-misadventure stories, and often snared a quote like *It came out of nowhere*, which was great because it spoke to the mentality of people who found themselves on subway tracks—people who were, for the most part, there for ridiculous reasons, such as trying to recover a dropped phone, or take a shortcut to the opposite platform, or, in one memorable case, record a hilarious TikTok. So, as a newspaper reader, you heard this person saying, *It came out of nowhere*, and shook your head, and knew that such a thing would never happen to you. But fuck her if this train wasn't coming out of nowhere.

She saw the cavity, a thin space with a curved wall only a few feet away, and scrambled toward it on her hands and knees. Wind whipped at her. She jammed herself into the space. Her bag and contents lay scattered on the tracks. Her phone seemed miraculously undamaged. Among the stones was the strange metal egg Hugo had given her, glowing in the lights of the train.

I thought I had time. Another popular line among people who did not, as it turned out, have enough time. But the egg was right there and she lunged out and snatched it up.

She threw herself backward. The train's undercarriage thundered by, its wheels gigantic, shrieking pizza cutters, throwing sparks and grit and steel dust. She felt a terrific sensation, a squeezing, like the air was crushing her. The pizza cutters revolved and slowed and stopped.

Her mouth was full of dirt. All she could see was half a wheel and its housing, thick with oil and filth. Ten seconds passed. Then, somewhere above: *bing-bong.*

To her astonishment, she could hear people moving about, getting on and off the train. Felicity was familiar with normal procedure in this kind of situation: It was for the driver to leave the doors closed while radioing control to bring cops and medics, who would yell for nobody down there to move until they were able to cut the power to the third rail, and, as a by-product, fuck up the New York transit system for three hours. She tried to yell, but the sound was swallowed by concrete and train. She tried again, because this was really incredible: first, to be pushed, and second, to be ignored. The first was shocking; the second infuriating. "Don't start the train!" she shouted.

It began to move. The pizza-cutter wheels protested like spoiled children. They picked up speed and swung dust-filled air around her and she pressed her lips together and closed her eyes. When the final train car passed by, the wind turned around and tried to suction her right out of the cavity. She stayed curled tight until she was sure she was safe.

She emerged slowly, not prepared to discount the possibility that another train was lurking somewhere nearby, waiting until she lowered her guard. Her arms and legs trembled. On the platform, people gaped at her. *Didn't they see me be pushed?* she wondered. Surely those people hadn't simply jumped on the train and left.

A man with gigantic arms popping from a black tank top moved toward her. "Are you okay?"

"No," she said. *I'm on the train tracks, you see.*

He bent at the platform edge and extended his hand. "Can you reach?"

She remembered her things: her phone and bag. But they were gone, blown away by the train. She stared at the empty tracks in dismay. She still had the egg, though. She had preserved that.

"I got you," said the man with the arms. "Right here."

"I can't find my things."

"Let's just get you off the tracks, darling."

More people had gathered at the edge of the platform. It was becoming a community. A woman said, "Are there steps?"

There was indeed a ladder. "Yes," she said. The handholds disappeared at the top, which made the last part difficult, but the man helped her. Then she was on the platform, with no phone or bag, and no sign of Hugo Garrelly or Clayton Hors, and an egg. "I lost my phone."

"Well, that's not too bad," said the woman. "You're okay, that's the thing."

"Hey," said the man with the arms to two approaching men in bright orange MTA vests. "Over here. She fell on the tracks."

"I was pushed," Felicity said.

The first MTA man to reach her was turbaned and had a thick black beard. He unzipped a red bag and began to pull things out. "Ma'am, my name is Ravneet. I'm going to help you. Are you hurt?"

"I need to use a phone."

"Are you hurt?"

She shook her head. There had been pizza cutters near her head, but they hadn't touched her.

"I want you to sit down a moment." He began to illuminate parts of her with a penlight. "May I touch your face?"

She nodded. He probed her forehead. Her legs were bloody and scraped around the knees. She looked at her hands and they were cut and dirty, too.

Light shone into her eyes. "You fell on the tracks?"

"Someone pushed me."

"Who?"

"He's gone now."

He lowered the penlight. "Ma'am, you don't appear to have any serious injuries, so I'm not going to call an ambulance. But if you think you need an ambulance, you can dial nine-one-one yourself."

She was thinking more clearly now. "The NYPD is on the way. The man who pushed me is wanted by the police. I'm a reporter for the *Daily News*." None of this left any visible impression on Ravneet. "I don't have my phone. Can I use your phone?"

"Ma'am, you cannot use my phone, but I want to make sure you're okay. Will you come and sit with me until the NYPD arrive?"

"Sure," she said.

She was taken to a small, dingy office with a single fluorescent overhead light and the lingering scent of man-sweat. Ravneet began to flick through grainy video footage of platforms while peppering her with polite questions that were, Felicity figured out, mostly about establishing her cognitive state. Eventually there was a knock and Ravneet opened the door to two uniformed cops, a man and a woman. "Hi, there," said the man. "How you doing?"

She explained what had happened, emphasizing the parts where she'd been pushed onto the tracks by a wanted fugitive. The cops remained impassive, their eyes occasionally flicking to Ravneet.

"Where do you live, Felicity?" the woman asked. "Can we drive you home?"

"What about Hugo Garrelly?"

"That I don't know. We're just here for you."

This was pretty unsatisfying. But her options were limited without a phone, so she allowed the cops to escort her from the station. In the back of a cruiser, as the city passed by, she turned the egg over in her hands. She wasn't sure what it was: metal or mineral. It might have been machined in the past, but if so, it was a long time ago, and any corners had worn away. The ends were pockmarked, exposing a gray, layered core, which appeared kind of brittle, as if she might be able to do serious damage with a screwdriver and some motivation. It was too cold to hold for long. She set it in her lap. "Do you want this thing?"

The female cop turned in her seat. "What thing?"

"The thing Hugo Garrelly gave me. The egg."

"What is it?"

"I don't know. Maybe nothing. He might have just wanted to distract me." The cop was silent. "Do you want it?"

"You keep it for now. We'll let you know."

"O-kay," Felicity said. She was not super-impressed with this, either. "And you can't tell me whether you arrested him yet?"

The cop just looked at her. The man said, "St. Paul's Place. This is you?"

She thought they might let her out at the curb, but this wasn't an Uber, and they accompanied her all the way up the steps to her building. It was late and she had no keys, so she buzzed for Gavin. "I'm here with two NYPD officers," she said, which felt like a coded message, *Hide the weed*, but really wasn't. The cops followed her to the apartment and loitered nearby while she explained to a startled Gavin what had happened.

"You're all right, though?"

"I'm fine." She thanked the cops and, finally, they nodded, releasing her. She went inside and found Percival on the sofa. She sat and tickled his ears. "What a day," she said.

Gavin took a minute, hanging out in the hallway to talk to the cops. "They said you seemed disoriented," he said, closing the door.

"I'm fine. Just tired." She'd put the egg on the table, and Gavin stopped and bent to peer at it. "Do you know what that is?"

He shook his head.

"Can you bag it up? It might be important."

He fetched a clear Tupperware container and sealed it inside. "How's that?"

"And I need your phone. I have to call Levi."

"Felicity," he said. "You need to relax. I'll call Levi. You stay there." He took the egg tub to the kitchen. "What's the number?"

She didn't know. Everything was on her phone. "Call the general number. 210-2100."

"We need to report your cards missing, too." He leaned his butt against the counter. "210-2100? Wrong number."

She felt confused. She knew the general number.

"I'll just look it up," he said, and poked at his phone. She waited on the sofa. It was the kind of moment when she might have pulled out her phone and done something. But she had to just sit there, in a kind of forced mindfulness. She stroked Percival, who purred. She looked for Joey, because this felt like a two-cat scenario, but he was nowhere. "Hello, this is Gavin Erlich. I'm the partner of one of your reporters, Felicity Staples." He walked to the bedroom, came out with a white blanket, which had been Felicity's since she was a teen-ager, and spread it across her legs, like a good boyfriend. "Yes. Thank you." He hung up. "Levi will call me back."

She nodded. She wanted to find out what had happened with Hugo Garrelly and Clayton Hors. But it was feeling decreasingly urgent. She kept thinking about falling. About trains with pizza-cutter wheels.

"Let me take care of you now," Gavin said, and she nodded.

LEVI DID NOT call back before Felicity went to bed, where she fell asleep instantly. When she woke, it was in a panic of murder and cats, feeling as if it had been only moments, but the bedroom was awash in morning light. Gavin was at the breakfast table, pecking at his laptop. "You slept well."

"Yes," she said, although she didn't feel it. Her heart was pounding. "Did you feed the cats last night?"

He nodded. "Why?"

She wasn't sure. She had woken with generalized anxiety about cats. "Did Levi call?" Gavin shook his head. "Can I check the news on your phone?"

He slid a tablet toward her. "Use this until you get your phone back."

She sat. Then she looked at him. "Why aren't you at work?"

"I'm looking after you," he said.

She smiled. She didn't feel super-grateful, though. She felt off-balance. There was something wrong and she couldn't figure out what. "You don't have to hang around. I'm fine."

"It's no problem."

"I mean it," she said.

"Are you sure? Because it would be easier. I can be home early."

She nodded. There was a little more negotiation, then he kissed her on the head and the apartment door closed and it was just her at the table, feeling weirdly relieved that he was gone.

Stress, she thought. *Post-trauma what-have-you. It's normal to experience strange emotions after a near-death experience.*

She scrolled the *Daily News* app, looking for the Madison May story. That was odd: Maddie wouldn't have left the front page unless the click-throughs had been truly awful. She navigated to CONTACT US and launched an audio call on the tablet. This was what she would be doing for a while, she guessed: making calls with a giant slab of glass. While it rang, she twisted in her chair, looking for Joey, her clandestine cat. She stood and wandered the apartment, holding the tablet like an offering.

"New York *Daily News*, this is Annette, how may I help you?"

Annette had appeared in the *News* more than anyone on the planet. When they needed a generic picture in a hurry and weren't too particular about it, they would say, *See if Annette has a minute.* She asked for Levi and entered the kitchen while waiting on hold. Percival was in the corner, eating from his bowl. But Joey's bowl was missing.

She was peering under the bed when Annette returned. "Hello, Felicity?"

"Yes."

"I have Levi for you. Please hold."

"Thank you." She had exhausted Joey's usual hiding places and was beginning to feel touches of genuine alarm, not just foggy vestiges of cat/train/murder panic, but specific concern that Joey had gotten out. He'd done it a few times before they'd wised up to his talent for dashing between their legs when they opened the front door.

"Felicity," Levi said in her ear. "What happened to you? I heard you had an accident on the subway."

"Not an accident. Hugo Garrelly pushed me." She opened the apartment door and peered out in both directions. No cat. "And he gave me something. I've still got it. Some kind of metal egg."

"This guy gave you something and pushed you onto the tracks?"

"Yes."

"What a psycho. Have you spoken to the police?"

"They didn't seem very interested. Maybe you can have more luck." She turned the corner. Once, she had found Joey cowering near the stairwell door. But not today.

"Do they know who it was?"

"Hmm?" she said, distracted.

"The guy who pushed you."

"It was Garrelly. I followed him off the train. And I saw Clayton Hors there, too. I think Hugo and Clay know each other."

"Wait a minute. Who pushed you?"

"Hugo." She called: "Joey."

"Hugo Joey?"

"No," she said. "Sorry, I've lost my cat."

"Look, you sound a little fried. Get some rest. We can handle things here."

"I'll be in later. I need to organize a new phone. I lost everything on the tracks."

"Well, if you think so. See you then."

"Wait." Could she have missed Joey in her sweep of the apartment? Could he have been kidnapped? Catnapped? People did do that. After six and a half years with the *News*, she knew they did anything. "What happened with Hugo?"

"Who?"

"Hugo Garrelly. The guy in the subway."

"The guy who pushed you?"

"Yes."

"I have no idea. What do you mean?"

There was an awkward pause. "What?" she said.

"You're asking about this man who pushed you onto the train tracks?"

"Hugo Garrelly. The man from the crime scene. The dude in the Soft Horizon hat with the murder logo."

"Felicity," Levi said, "I'm sorry, but I don't know what you're talking about."

She tried to figure this out. "Which part?"

"All of it. Why don't you stay home and rest up? It sounds like you've had a hell of a time."

She stepped into her apartment and closed the door. Percival sat beside his empty food bowl, looking at her. He meowed.

"Where's my fucking cat," she said.

"Is your boyfriend with you, Felicity? What's his name? Gavin?"

She went into the kitchen and began to pull open cupboards. She put the tablet on the counter and crouched to peer around pots and bowls. "He's at work."

"Maybe you shouldn't be alone right now."

She stood and peered down at the tablet. "Two days ago, Madison May was murdered. It was on the front page. Yes?"

"Okay."

"Not 'okay.' Yes or no?"

"I don't remember seeing the article, but it's possible."

"Levi, you *wrote* the article," she said. "We worked on it together."

There was a long pause. "Felicity, I really think someone should be with you. Can you give me your boyfriend's number?"

"Do you remember working with me on the Maddie May case or not?"

"You don't do crime, Felicity," Levi said. "You do politics."

She felt a burst of irritation. She was trying to find Joey, who could be lost or stolen, and Levi was making no sense. She tugged the sofa away from the wall. Cat hair. A masticated feather that had once been part of a cat toy. "I *know* I don't do crime. But you were out, so I went to the scene. 177th Street, Jamaica. A real estate agent was killed. Her name was Madison May." Silence from the phone. "Hello?"

"I hear you, Felicity, but I don't know anything about that. I need to ask you something. Did you hit your head?"

"What?"

"When you fell on the tracks, did you hit your head?"

"No," she said, although she wasn't completely sure. She had hit her knees and elbows. She might have.

"You sound disoriented. I think you should get yourself to an ER. I've found Gavin's number. He left a message earlier. I'm going to tell him to come get you."

"Levi, go to my desk. There are handwritten notes there."

"I really think—"

"Please, just do it." She stared around the apartment. She was going to find the little fluffball here somewhere. It would be a hilarious story for Gavin. *You won't believe where Joey was.*

"I'm looking at your desk. I see no notes about a dead Realtor."

"What's your number?"

"What?"

"I lost my phone," she said. "Let me call you back with video."

There was some messing around. Her tablet flickered. She was seeing Levi from an unflattering angle. The picture swiveled. There was her desk. She bent over the tablet, trying to discern detail. She couldn't see her notes. Levi's face loomed again. "See? It's a clean desk. Go sit down. I'm serious."

He was holding his phone so low that she could see up his nostrils. Behind him was the ceiling. She stared.

"Where's the clock?"

"Which clock is that, Felicity?"

"The *clock*," she said, and her voice sounded strangled and panicked. "The loudest fucking clock in the world, which has hung from the ceiling since 1803."

He didn't even turn to look. Just gazed at her, his eyes full of concern.

She was holding some items from the sink. Without warning, a glass slipped from her grip and bounced off the floor near Percival. He streaked from the room and disappeared behind the sofa.

Joey's food bowl was not in the sink, she could see now. Like Joey, it was nowhere. It did not exist.

"Felicity," Levi squawked from the tablet. "Felicity."

"Something's wrong with me," she said.

MADDIE'S AUDITION RAN LATE. IT WAS A COMMERCIAL FOR A HAIR-
loss spray, shot documentary-style. Her role was "Girlfriend." Her
purpose was to express amazement at the physical transformation of
her costar, "James." She had four lines, which she had practiced a
variety of ways over the preceding week until landing upon a take
that felt solid and interesting and (dare she say) true, but which had
turned out to be, as the saying went, not what they were looking for.

"Maddie, is it?" said the director, who was English, and, inciden-
tally, bald as a cantaloupe. "Can you give me some more childlike
wonder?"

"More what, sorry?"

He clasped his hands, as if in prayer. "You're giving me 'I have a
newfound respect for my boyfriend since he got hair.' But what I
want to see is: 'I am *tits-out drooling* since he got hair.'"

James coughed into his hand. He did have great hair. Maddie
doubted it was from a spray. She said: "Sure, okay, I see."

"Also, when you speak, you keep turning to camera." Was this
bad? From his expression, it was bad. "James has become a god to
you. You can barely believe your luck to be in his presence. So where
will your eyes be?"

"On James."

"Exactly."

"I don't want to look away," she said, "in case that's the moment I lose him."

"Brilliant," said the director. "Let's go again."

They ran the scene three more times. She invented a thing where just before one of James's (fourteen) lines, she opened her mouth like she had a thought, then just let her lips dangle, as if his words had blown it away. She breathed only when he glanced at her. When he looked away, she untethered a sliver of panic and let it slide across her face.

"Amazing, thank you," said the director. "We'll be in touch."

But they always said, *Amazing, we'll be in touch.* She was yet to be cast in something that paid.

Her train was pulling in as she approached Marcy Avenue station. She took the steps at a run, her bag bouncing, dodging a group of dudes coming down and taking all the space. She tapped her pass and sprinted to the platform, but the doors closed in front of her. A girl behind the glass looked at her with interest. "Gah," Maddie said, as the train pulled away.

While the platform emptied, she took out her phone and plugged in her earphones. She messaged Trent: *On my way!* ♥ *Missed a train how did it go?*

A man paused near the exit. He was the last to leave. She glanced across the tracks, as if attracted by the billboards, to get a sense of him without making eye contact. He seemed fairly tall and thin. Longish hair. Possibly watching her. She adjusted her bag. She was made-up for the audition, wearing bright shoes and a snug sweater and a sprinkle of accessories that signaled she was super-friendly and accessible, which she didn't want to do anymore. She put her phone to her ear like she was making a call and walked away. Then she stopped and looked at the screen, like *What's with this thing, no reception?* In her peripheral vision, she saw the man by the exit, facing her.

A couple entered the platform, a middle-aged man and woman, talking loudly about soup.

She risked a direct glance at the man. A guy in a filthy khaki jacket, his cheeks hollowed out, his fingernails dark, and he wasn't staring at her; he was gazing into space. So she had totally profiled him. Not very inclusive of her. Not very liberal. She returned to her phone. The platform filled over the next ten minutes, and when the train arrived, she was one of a half-dozen boarding the end train car. She circumnavigated an exploded hamburger and took a window seat.

They're going to let me know, she messaged Trent.

He would be on the sofa in their shitty one-bedroom apartment, playing video games. The air-conditioning would be off, because he didn't feel the heat. The sink would be full of dishes. They had been dating for twenty-two months, and occasionally she felt like they'd stopped trying. Well. That was generous. She felt like *he* had stopped trying. Somehow over time he had become more important and she less, until she was orbiting him like something trivial and supplementary.

She said: ?

He would be on the sofa in their shitty one-bedroom apartment,

The train stopped at Myrtle Avenue. A handful of people disembarked. Just before the doors closed, the homeless man stumbled into the car.

She looked at her phone. The man gripped a pole. The train set off. He swayed. When she looked up, he was staring at her.

He must have boarded with her at Marcy Avenue. Working the train cars, she assumed, begging for change. She lowered her head, letting her hair fall forward, focusing on her phone.

Want me to order?

Pepperoni ok?

She could imagine Trent's eyes sliding to his phone. A quick tap and then his attention back to the exploding bodies on the TV. He was a good guy. He was tall. He worked out. He earned money, actual money, the kind that could pay the rent, which she, pulling five or six shifts a week at a coffee shop between classes at NYU, absolutely did not. She could forgive his perfunctory emojis, couldn't she? At least until she was pulling her own weight, financially speaking.

Ain't no one got time for a fixer-upper, a friend from NYU, Zar, had said once, not specifically about Trent, but boyfriends in general. Maddie had thought about that often since. She was a fixer, though. When she started a thing, she hated to leave it.

The homeless man collapsed into a seat. Not beside Maddie, thankfully. But facing her. Eight or ten people remained: There was a guy in front of her, facing away, with strong-looking shoulders, his head bent, scrolling his phone. A father and a young girl by the doors. Two older women to her right, talking over the top of each other. But at Central, the father and daughter stepped out, and then at Myrtle-Wyckoff, the two older women rose and moved to the doors. "I love your hair," one of the women said to Maddie.

"Oh, thank you," she said.

"Mine was just the same shade of red, when I was younger," the woman said.

"Oh, it was not," said the other woman, and swatted her with her hand.

The train moved off. It was quiet and Maddie felt self-conscious because of the hair comment. The only other remaining guy commenced a phone call, telling someone he was ten minutes away but she could eat without him. When Maddie glanced at the homeless man, he was staring straight at her.

The train shook. Two more stops, a short walk to her apartment along a route she knew well, key in the lock, and she was home.

Maybe she should have taken a taxi. The train was usually fine, but occasionally not, especially not this late, after seven. Once, also late, she'd been stuck beside a man who slid a hand into his pants pocket and began slowly but determinedly to masturbate. She only realized when his breathing quickened and then it was over before she could move. At the next stop, he'd left without looking at her, like she hadn't even mattered much, like she was a prop.

She was fine. To give herself something to do, she messaged Trent.

Almost there.

The train slowed. The guy in front of her told his phone, "Okay. Love you. See you soon," and stood. Maddie felt a flash of panic: She was about to be left with the staring homeless man. The train stopped. The doors opened. The guy with the phone stepped out. The homeless man leaned forward as if he was about to get off, too—no, she realized, more like he was switching seats, shifting closer to her, maybe, or right beside her, just the two of them, alone in the train car.

She hoisted her bag and walked off the train. In the cool air and bright sodium lights, she felt immediately better. She followed a trickle of people onto the street.

Walking from Seneca. Got off at the wrong station. 😬

Want me to pick you up?

She was slightly annoyed that he believed her. She wasn't the kind of person who got off at the wrong station by accident. That was something she would never do. She resolved not to accept his offer. She was out, she was walking; she could do things by herself.

No thanks. Home soon. 😊

She reached the crossing. The guy from the train who'd told his girlfriend that she should eat without him was waiting there. His hair was long enough to blow in his face. Maddie glanced behind her in time to see the homeless man shamble out of the station toward her.

The light turned green. She crossed in a kind of panic. When she reached the curb, she was caught on trying to figure out which route involved the least shadow and isolation, and the guy from the train noticed and said, "Are you okay?" He followed her gaze to the homeless guy, who was now running, he was literally *running*, to make the crossing, and added: "I'm going this way, if you want to walk with me."

He was pointing in the correct direction. "Yes," Maddie said, "Thanks." He nodded and they fell into step.

"Warm night," he said.

She glanced back. The homeless man was at the corner, looking agitated. "Yes," she said, remembering to respond. She looked at the guy and laughed. "Sorry."

"No problem." He smiled, revealing dimples. He had nice eyebrows. He walked without crowding her, leaving her room. "I'm headed to Woodward and Cornelia, but I can walk you somewhere else, if you want."

"Woodward is great, thank you."

He nodded. "I'm Clay," he said.

"Maddie." Then, for conversation: "Are you meeting your girlfriend?" He looked surprised. "I was sitting behind you on the train."

"Oh. Yeah, I'm headed home."

"I didn't mean to eavesdrop."

"That's cool." He smiled again. He was kind of endearing, in a goofy way. She had a crazy thought: She had been traveling home from a failed audition, thinking about her dying relationship, and got off one station early, and met the love of her life.

"Have you been together long?" she said, asking bold questions.

"Not really."

Interesting. "What's her name?"

"You're going to laugh."

She smiled. "Why?"

"It's Madison."

She did laugh. "There are a lot of us around."

"There sure are," he said, and laughed, too. "You're right about that."

She glanced back. The homeless guy was nowhere to be seen. She had overblown the whole thing. But it was all good. It had happened for a reason.

He said, "How's your day been?"

A polite question: not super-personal, like hers had been. "I spent most of it waiting around at an audition."

"Like for a movie?"

"A TV commercial."

"Oh," he said. "That's still pretty cool."

"I don't think I got it."

"That's still impressive," Clay said. "It takes guts to put yourself out there even though you might get rejected."

"It goes with the territory."

He shook his head. "I couldn't do that. I hate getting rejected. I can't stand it."

"You get used to it."

He was lost in thought for a moment. "Maybe," he said. "What's the commercial for?"

"I don't want to tell you. It's stupid."

"I promise I won't laugh."

"Hair loss."

"You're advertising hair loss?"

"A spray," Maddie said, "which cures hair loss. Or covers it up. I don't know. I'm the adoring girlfriend. Only I'm not, because I didn't get the part."

"It's probably for the best," he said. "It wasn't meant to be."

"You're probably right." She could see her street now. The next block was mostly brownstone walk-ups, and she began to think how to play it so that Clay wouldn't disappear from her life forever. She was performing at Narrows in a few weeks; could she offer him tickets? He might not be her fated love, but he seemed friendly and thoughtful, which wasn't easy to find.

"You'll get a better job. One you deserve. I'm sure of it." He said this with so much conviction, she kind of believed it herself. Clay pointed to a car, a blue Accord parked beneath a streetlight. "Hey, this is my car. I need to grab something, if that's okay."

"Sure," she said, although she didn't quite understand that: why he was catching trains, then walking, then collecting things from his car.

"It's for my girlfriend." He popped the trunk. "She might not even need it. But, you know." He rolled his eyes. She smiled, even though she didn't know, actually. He withdrew a silver case. It was large, like something she might expect a tradesperson to carry. A toolbox. Which didn't really fit with the idea she'd built of this guy in her head.

"Anyway," she said, taking a step away from him. She didn't like the case. "My street is right there. Thanks so much for the walk." Forget the tickets. Forget this guy.

"No problem. You don't want me to come with you all the way?"

"No, I won't hold you up."

He was silent. Her phone dinged. She glanced at the screen.

Hi Maddie, this is Damien from FTR Campaigns. Can you return tomorrow at 6am sharp for production? Pay is standard scale, $800/ day plus o/t if required etc.

She gave a squeak of joy. "Oh my God, I got it!"

Clay reached the sidewalk. "The part?"

"Yes!" She began to walk, her fingers working the phone. She had so many people to message.

Got it got it got it!!!!!

"The hair-loss girlfriend?" Clay sounded disapproving, for some reason. "Didn't you say it was stupid?"

"It's *so* stupid."

"But you're going to do it?"

"Yes," she said. "Yes, yes, yes." She found Zar, with whom Maddie had invested in a bottle of sixty-dollar champagne, to be opened in the event that one of them booked a commercial job. *Got that bottle ready???*

Trent: *Are you serious?*

Zar: *No way!!!!!! Who / what / howwwww?????*

"Why?" Clay said.

She didn't answer. Her phone was blowing up. She was walking fast, excited to get home. Clay kept pace with her, carrying the case. "Um, because that's how you get started. You have to do the dumb ones."

"I don't think you should," Clay said. "You shouldn't do the dumb ones."

She laughed. "Well . . ." She trailed off, because messages were still coming in, demanding answers.

Hair-loss girlfriend, which one was that??

OMG that's so so so amazing I am literally THROWING UP with jealousy

"I think you're better than that," Clay said.

She glanced at him. "That's kind." The comment was unsettling, though. She tried to turn it into a joke. "But you haven't seen me act."

"Actually, I have."

"When was that?" She tried to keep her voice light. She didn't recognize Clay. She had no recollection of ever seeing him before. He had seemed kind and decent, but these last two minutes, there were red flags everywhere.

"In a movie."

"I haven't done a movie. You must have me confused with someone else."

He shrugged, smiling.

She wanted to get away from him now. The corner was fifty feet away. But there was no one around, she realized. She was on a residential street and it was just her and him. "Where are you meeting your girlfriend?"

"Actually," he said, drawing the word out, so that it felt vaguely condescending. *Aaaact-u-ally.* "I've already met her."

She tried to make sense of this. "I don't understand."

"Hold this," he said, and handed her the case.

She squawked a protest. She was holding her phone and almost dropped it, then almost dropped the case. She was off-balance and he grappled with the case, trying to help her, but her feet kept going backward, and she was backing into a driveway, she realized; no, no, she was *being backed* into a narrow driveway. He was pushing her. She couldn't stop retreating without dropping the case on her feet. She let it go anyway. He pushed his body against hers, jamming her against the brick wall. She inhaled, and he thrust his forearm into her mouth.

"A TV hair-loss commercial?" Clay said. He sounded angry but she didn't know why. "Really?"

She choked. His body was smothering her, too close for a kick or knee to the groin. When she scratched at his face, he grabbed her wrist like he'd known what she would do. She couldn't breathe with his forearm in her mouth and she bit down as hard as she could, but he barely grimaced. His flesh was hard and cracked, like scar tissue.

On the street, a figure appeared, hitched toward them, and stopped.

"Later," Clay said, sounding angry.

"I followed you," said the figure.

"Wait around the corner."

It was the homeless man. Maddie gave a muffled whine.

The homeless man said uncertainly, "Is she okay?"

"She's fine," said Clay. "Go around the corner, if you want your money."

She could barely breathe, but she called to the homeless man with her eyes. *Please,* she said. *Please help me.*

He turned away. She put everything she had into screaming into Clay's forearm. It was a poor, strangled sound, but enough; the homeless man's shoulders hitched. He turned and came toward them, walking stiffly, as if his legs were stilts. "Leave her alone," he told Clay, his voice shaking.

"For fuck's sake," Clay muttered, his breath hot on her face.

He stepped back. As soon as the pressure of his body lifted, she tried to move. His hand came up and shoved her head hard into the brickwork.

She was on the ground. She felt very sick. Her eyes weren't working properly. There were people fighting. She began to crawl, but her arms and legs weren't working properly, either.

One of the people fell to the ground. The other stood over him. Maddie continued to crawl. She reached a silver case, which she recognized. The case was open, like a flower, with unfolding trays. The top tray was empty. The tray beneath it held a gleaming knife. Beside it lay a lock of hair tied with green ribbon: auburn hair, glinting gold and brown, like her own. And there was a brooch, an ivory sparrow, which she was absolutely, one hundred percent sure was at home in her drawer.

The person on the ground stopped moving. The other man came toward her. There was something in his hand, which looked like it belonged in the case.

"No," she said. Her voice was thick and slurred.

"Yes," he said, and bent over her.

THE WAITING ROOM OF NEWYORK-PRESBYTERIAN BROOKLYN WAS FULL
of heat and bleeding children. At one point, a tiny Slavic woman rose
unsteadily from her seat and began to totter toward the restroom.
Felicity opened her mouth to say to Gavin, *I think she needs help,* and
the woman fell to the ground. By the time they had made sure she
was okay—no staff in sight, so Felicity took her to the restroom and
stood outside the stall until she was done—their seats were occupied
by two teenagers, one of whom was pregnant and huffing like a
steam train.

Eventually Felicity and Gavin were admitted to a small room
with three stools, an untidy desk, and a poster advertising skin treat-
ments. They sat quietly, holding hands. On Gavin's lap rested the
metal egg in the plastic tub, which they had brought just in case.
Those were Gavin's words: *just in case.* The rest of that sentence, she
assumed, was: *it's made of chemicals that cause you to hallucinate cats.*

A short woman in blue scrubs entered. There was a spray of dark
freckles across her nose. According to her nametag, she was Charu
Kapadia. "Felicity Staples?"

"Yes."

She sat on the remaining stool and prodded a keyboard. "What brings you here today, Felicity?"

"I'm having trouble remembering things."

"She fell off the platform in the subway," Gavin offered.

"When did you fall?"

"Yesterday afternoon."

"And you hit your head?"

"I might have."

"Do you have any pain?"

"No."

"No pain anywhere?"

"No."

Charu tapped at the keyboard. Felicity could see the screen: *nil pain.* "Any nausea, vomiting?"

"No."

"No dizziness or fainting?"

"No."

"Any difficulty walking or moving about?"

"No."

"Can you open your mouth and poke out your tongue?"

She did that.

"You can close your mouth." Charu used a penlight to study Felicity's eyes, just as the MTA man had done. "When you say you've had trouble with your memory, can you give me an example?"

"We have two cats, Joey and Percival. Joey has always been shy. He hides. But today . . ."

"We have one cat," Gavin offered. "Percival. We've never had two cats."

Charu looked between them. "There's no second cat?"

"No," Gavin said.

Charu was silent. "I asked you this morning," Felicity said. "I said, 'Did you feed the cats last night?' And you said yes."

"I thought you said 'cat.' Singular."

Charu typed: *altered mental sta*. Then she glanced at Felicity and tilted the screen away. "Did your memory of the second cat begin yesterday?" She blinked twice. "I'm sorry. I mean, when did she first mention a second cat?"

"This morning."

"Until today, she never said anything about a second cat?"

"No."

Charu typed. "Are there any other inconsistent memories?"

"Yes," Felicity said. "I remember a clock at work that isn't there anymore. And working on a story that no one knows anything about. I went to a crime scene where a woman was murdered." In the waiting room, she had looked up the Henshaw Realty website on Gavin's phone. She had scrolled down the staff page and up again. There was no Madison May. "But it's like it never happened."

"She came home with this," Gavin said, offering the plastic tub. "After she fell, she was carrying it."

Charu made no move to take it. "What is it?"

"I don't know," Felicity said. "Someone gave it to me. Then he pushed me off the subway platform. That's when I fell."

Charu was silent.

"Could it be toxic?" Gavin said.

"We may want to look at it later. For now, I'd like to check your head for bruising." She opened a drawer and extracted a pair of blue plastic gloves, identical to the ones Felicity had been given by Detective McHenry at the house in which Maddie May had been murdered. In Felicity's memory, at least. Not in real life, it seemed. Charu's fingers probed Felicity's skull and pressed behind her ears. "Any pain when I do that?"

"No."

Charu peeled off her gloves and dropped them into a canister. "I'd like to run some more tests."

————

THE CT MACHINE was a giant plastic doughnut. It sucked Felicity in and out. Then there was a room with a bed and a TV on the wall. It was small and bare but private, which was more than she'd expected: This was thanks to Gavin's insurance, which was infinitely better than her own. Felicity had been dismissive at times about Gavin's attention to mundane things, such as insurance. But now look at this.

He parked his butt beside her bed, fiddling with the TV remote. She was sitting atop the sheets with the tablet. Gavin glanced at her. "Should you be doing that?"

"I'm just Googling." She showed him the screen. "There *is* a Hugo Garrelly. He did murder his wife, and he is in Sing Sing."

"Okay."

"But I remember him at the crime scene." She looked at Gavin. "How do I know he exists?"

He shrugged. "You work in a newsroom. You pick things up."

"Mmm," she said, unconvinced.

"I'm going to ask someone if you should be doing that," Gavin said.

She watched him leave. He'd been the picture of concern all day. She couldn't have asked for more. But she was not comforted. She was suspicious. As a reporter, she was used to being lied to, and that was how this felt, like someone trying to rewrite history. Trying to gaslight her. She couldn't think why Gavin would want to convince her that she'd never owned a second cat. Or why it would involve the newsroom and the removal of the world's loudest clock. But she felt hella gaslighted.

Gavin returned. "I couldn't find anyone," he said. "But I don't think you should be doing that."

At eight o'clock, she was visited by a specialist, a short, balding man who wore scrubs rolled up over enormously hairy forearms. She repeated her story and he ran her through the same questions the ER doctor had, plus one about whether she'd been handling snakes. Her CT and blood work had come back clean.

"That's good?" she said.

"It's terrific," said the specialist. "No obvious bleeding or swelling. So next step is likely to be an MRI, either tomorrow or the day after. All right?" He showed white teeth.

When Gavin had left, she watched a TV reality series about terrible people doing terrible things. When it was over, she picked up the tablet and navigated to the *News*. She'd checked a hundred times already, but now there was something new:

STUDENT, 22, FATALLY STABBED OUTSIDE HOME

Ordinarily, "Student murdered outside home" was not an article. There had to be more juice than that: a moral failure, a grieving parent threatening to sue somebody, a startling coincidence. In this case, the juice was the photo, because the victim was young and white, with an open, affable smile. It was a *so much to live for* photo. The kind of shot that could, juxtaposed with that headline, strike terror into the hearts of parents, and bring forth thousands of clicks.

It was Maddie.

Her chest tightened painfully. She felt her own brain struggle to make sense of it, as if it were one of those illusions that would change from one thing to another as you looked at it: bird, woman, bird, woman. *What am I looking at?* Student, real estate agent. Inside, outside. Yesterday, today. She felt afraid to move, as if she might disturb the tablet and the image and headline would disappear. Finally she raised a finger and tapped.

Police are seeking a man in connection with the stabbing death of Madison May, 22, a performing arts student at NYU.

Felicity swung her legs out of bed and entered the hallway. There was no one in sight, so she walked barefoot to the desk, which was staffed by a thin woman in a red bandanna, studying her phone. Felicity put her hands on the counter. "Can I see a doctor, please?"

The woman raised her eyebrows. "Excuse me?"

"Is the specialist still here?"

"You need to go back to your bed," said the woman.

"No," she said, "I need to see the specialist," and this evolved into a scene where the woman in the bandanna made some threats and then a call in which she called Felicity "uncooperative." A few minutes after that, the short, hairy-armed specialist came by, and Felicity showed him the tablet.

His eyes flicked across the screen. "What am I seeing?"

"I called security," said the bandanna woman.

"I told you I remembered this murder. This is her. It's happened."

The specialist scratched his cheek. "This is the real estate woman?"

"Yes," Felicity said, although, according to the article, no: Maddie was a student. "The details are different. But it's her. It's the same person, murdered in a different place." This came out before Felicity realized quite how it sounded.

"This is fine," the specialist said, his voice soft. "You've got bits and pieces in your head and they're all scrambled around. If a few are starting to come together, that's a great sign. Take yourself back to your room and I'll check on you tomorrow."

She stared at the tablet.

"I have a patient who needs me," said the specialist. "We'll reconnect tomorrow, okay?"

The woman in the bandanna was staring, Felicity realized. Staring aggressively. Felicity padded back to her room and climbed into the bed. She could hear the burbling of a television from somewhere.

On her bedside table sat the plastic tub with the metal egg inside. No one from the hospital had been interested enough to take it away yet. She eyed it.

Outside her room, someone coughed. There was a peal of laughter. She raised her tablet and began to research Maddie May.

IN THE MORNING, a short nurse with dubiously long lashes took her blood pressure. The man in the next room was a complainer, the nurse said. He had complained about her perfume. "Do I smell funky to you?" the nurse asked, and Felicity shook her head. "Exactly," the nurse said.

Her blood pressure was fine. Everything was fine, except for how Felicity's memory disagreed with everyone else's. At nine o'clock, her tablet trilled, and it was Gavin. "You won't frickin' believe this," he said. "We've been burgled."

Ah, yes, she thought. *Of course we have.*

"I went out for breakfast. I was gone all of forty minutes. When I came back, the place was trashed. I mean, it's destroyed. Everything's on the floor. They cut open the *sofa*."

She glanced at the plastic tub on her bedside table.

I need you to hold something for me, Hugo had said. She'd been focused on the *something* part, trying to figure what the thing was. But there was another implication. *Hold.* Not *take.* Like it was temporary. Like he'd want it back.

"I've called the police, but who knows how long they'll be. How are you? Do you feel any better?"

"I think so," she said, which was the truth: She did feel better. She felt increasingly confident that she wasn't crazy.

"If you're doing okay, I'm going to hang around and deal with this mess."

"Sure."

"I'll let you know when I know anything. Love you."

"Love you," she said, and put down the tablet. She climbed out of bed and eyed the tub with the metal egg inside. Then she began to look for somewhere to hide it.

SHE SPENT THE afternoon lying with her back to the door, the sheet pulled up to her chin, as if she were sleeping. She wasn't. She was waiting, with one arm beneath a strategically placed pillow, her hand resting on the call button. Someone brought her lunch. The room filled with the smell of cooked vegetables. Voices echoed in the hallway. Someone dropped a stack of something—folders?— and someone else said, "Those had better not be for Dr. Bolton." Felicity began to feel drowsy. She caught herself drifting off, then did fall asleep. When she woke, someone was moving about the room.

She lay still. The person was moving quietly, but that could be for a couple of reasons. She heard drawers open and close. The lifting of the chair cushions. A rustling that could have signaled the emptying of her plastic flowers from the beside vase. Then, unmistakably, someone on hands and knees, inspecting the underside of her bed. And was there not a distinctly male smell filtering through her neglected lunch? Yes, she thought. There was.

The sheet was ripped from her body. She gasped. He glowered down at her: Hugo Garrelly, the man she'd stood next to at the murder house and later pursued onto a train, no cap, a blue shirt this time, but the same beard, the same intense eyes. "Where is it?"

She pressed the call button. What she hoped was the call button. Press, press.

"I need it back," he said. "Where did you put it?"

"You're supposed to be in Sing Sing," she said.

He seized the bottom of her mattress and lifted. She tilted toward the wall. Then he dropped her. "You're sitting on it. Get off the bed."

"I'm not," she said, but he advanced and she scuttled out of the bed. He patted around the sheets. Then he looked at her. She understood: There was nothing else in the room. "I don't have it." She held out her arms, spreading her pajamas to prove it. He gripped her and patted and squeezed, his touch passing over her arms, stomach, and thighs.

"Where is it?"

"How did Madison May die twice?"

He squinted at her.

"I'm in a hospital because people think I'm crazy. But I'm not, am I? And you know why."

His watch beeped. He glanced at it. She recalled that it had done that before, in the subway. He had a bunch of alarms, for some reason.

"Tell me," she said.

He walked out.

This she hadn't expected. She went after him. "Where are you going?"

"There are other ways to do this."

She caught him at the elevators. "Why does no one else remember? What does the metal egg do?"

The elevator doors opened. Hugo stepped inside. She made to follow and he pushed her back by her shoulder. "No."

"Yes," she said, and tried again. The doors began to close and she managed to get a leg between them and they opened again. Hugo gave a grunt like he was about to send her skating across the floor on her butt. Then a mother with a young boy appeared and Hugo hesitated and then stepped back to let them enter. Felicity slipped inside with them. The doors closed.

"I'm hungry," said the boy.

"Where's my cat?" Felicity asked Hugo, who ignored her. "Where's my goddamn cat?"

The boy gazed at them. "Is your cat lost?"

"Shh," said the woman.

"He took it," Felicity said.

Hugo said, "I didn't take anyone's cat."

"Yesterday, I had two cats. Now I don't. Where's Joey?"

Hugo didn't answer. The boy said, "Do you know where Joey is?"

"No," Hugo said. The elevator doors opened and Hugo strode between them toward the lobby.

"I will scream like a child," Felicity said, hurrying to keep pace. "You're a felon. I'll have security tackle you before you reach the sidewalk." He didn't answer. "Why won't you tell me? What's so wrong with you that you can't just say what's happening?"

He stopped so suddenly that they almost collided. "I'm sorry you lost your cat. But you need to back up. This is nothing to do with you." He began to walk away.

For a moment she just watched him, astounded. "It's nothing to do with me?" She raised her voice. "Everyone thinks I'm insane!" She went after him and grabbed his arm. "Where's my cat?"

He pulled free without slowing. She grabbed at his shoulder, stretching his shirt. Hugo's hand closed on her wrist like a clamp. She cried out. "Calm down," Hugo said, and, at last, she saw a security guard ambling toward them.

"Everything all right with you folks?"

"Talk to me," she said to Hugo. "Give me answers. That's all I want."

Hugo looked from her to the guard. "Fine."

"We're okay. Thank you." The security guard shrugged and moved away.

"Three minutes," Hugo said. "Then we're done."

"Yes," Felicity said. "Deal."

He glanced around. A pair of elderly women shuffled by. "You're not crazy. Your memory doesn't match anyone else's because you moved. In the subway, you left one place and came here. It looks the same, but it's not."

She blinked, because he seemed to have finished. "That's it? That's your explanation?"

"What else do you want to know?"

She stared.

"Your cat is fine, by the way. He's back where you left him."

"Joey's fine?"

"He's right where he was. Everything back there is the same. Except you're gone."

"Are you talking about . . ." She didn't know what he was talking about. "Time travel?"

He shook his head impatiently. "There's no time travel. You're in a physically different place. It shares an ancestor with where you're from, but at some point it split. Since then, it evolved independently."

"You're saying there are two worlds? The real one and a . . . a secret—"

"Many worlds. Detaching and refolding all the time. Nothing makes one any more real than the other."

"Parallel dimensions?" she said, groping for a concept. "Is that what you're saying?"

"Sure. There you go."

"This is a parallel world. That's what you're telling me."

"Right. And here, you never got a second cat. You went to the pet store, you—"

"Shelter."

"You went a day late, or you missed a train, and someone took him before you got there. So he's fine. He's just not your cat."

She stared. This was a horrible story. "And Madison May?"

"What about her?"

"She decided to study acting here instead of going into real estate?"

"Right."

"But she died both times. I mean, in both places."

He nodded shortly. "And she'll die again, unless I get out of here."

"What does that mean?" He was throwing glances at the door like he was about to leave.

"*This* is what you want to know? The history of Madison May?"

It would be a start. "Yes."

He blew air. "Fine. Someplace else, not anywhere you know, Maddie was an up-and-coming actress. Ten months ago, her first movie comes out, *By the River Blue*. Maddie is on-screen for all of ten minutes. Wears little shorts and gets a glass of water thrown over her. Can't say I found her performance anything to write home about, but there's a kid named Clayton Hors who disagrees. He sees this movie and falls in love. Ordinarily, he'd have gone home and jacked off and that'd be the end of it, but Clay is special. He knows how to move. Move like I do. He hasn't got it all figured out yet, but he knows it means he can try things, and if they don't work out, move somewhere and it's like it never happened. So that's what he does. And the thing he tries is meeting Madison May. He gets himself arrested trying to break into her house; never even speaks to her. But here comes the real disappointment, because Clay is a moron who doesn't know anything about moorings, so when he moves, he winds up someplace Maddie isn't an actress. She's a TV weather girl, or a waitress, or a student. Everywhere he goes from then on, she's like that, and not a movie star. Clay finds this frustrating. In fact, he's so frustrated, he kills her. Why, exactly, you'd have to ask Clay. It makes no goddamn sense to me. But that's why I'm here. To stop him from what he keeps doing, which is finding Maddie and killing her."

A man at the desk coughed meatily.

Felicity said, "How many times? You said this started ten months ago. How many times has he killed her?"

"About twenty."

"*Twenty?*"

"Give or take." He glanced at his watch. "I have to go."

"Wait. How do I get back?"

"That was your three minutes plus some. We're done."

"How do I get back? It's the egg, right? I have to use the egg."

He gestured vaguely. "You can make a life here. It's not so different."

"I'm short a cat," she said. "I don't want similar. I want to go home."

"You can't."

"Why not?"

"It's one-way. You can't go back. I'm sorry." For a moment, there was a hint of sympathy in his expression. Then he turned away.

"What?" she said again, loudly. "Excuse me?" She went after him. "What do you mean, I can't go back?"

"If people could go back, Clay would have returned to his dream Maddie a long time ago. You can't go backward. It's impossible."

She stopped. He had left this part until the end. He hadn't wanted to tell her at all. "You son of a bitch." He ignored her. The doors slid apart, opening onto the street. "Wife-murderer!" she shouted.

He turned and crossed the space between them quickly, fury on his face. He raised a hand and for a moment she thought he meant to hit her. But he only stuck a finger in front of her face. "I did not kill my wife."

She didn't move. Anger drained from his face. He glanced around. People were watching. He turned and walked out.

———

SHE RETURNED TO her room and began to pack things into her overnight bag. As she was zipping, the tablet trilled, and the screen lit up with Gavin running toward the camera, his mouth open, his hair flying. They had been horsing around in Central Park the previous August—no, September, it was the Labor Day weekend. It had been too warm to stay inside. She remembered this.

It's not so different.

She swiped. "Whew," Gavin said. "I thought you weren't going to answer. Police are gone, but the place is still a wreck. We need a new sofa. Unbelievable. How are you? Any news? Test results?"

On their first date, had she stuck a Goofy pen behind her ear?

"Babe?" he said.

"No test results."

"How are you feeling? You sound strange."

"I'm just tired."

"They want me at work, but I can come by the hospital first."

"No, don't. I'm fine."

"All right. I'll check in with you soon. Take care of yourself. I love you."

"Okay," she said, and tapped to end the call.

She stuffed the tablet into her bag. Then she went to the door and closed it. She wrestled a chair onto the hospital bed and climbed onto it. She felt like she was three seconds away from a broken wrist, but she hadn't fallen the last time she'd done this, and she didn't fall this time. She eased the ceiling tile aside and groped until her fingers found the tub.

At the floor desk, the bandanna woman was talking to a younger woman with heavy eye makeup and severe bangs. Felicity waited, but there was no incipient end to the conversation. "I'm going home," she said.

The bandanna woman looked at her. "Did a doctor tell you that?"

Felicity shook her head. "It's fine. I figured it out."

"You figured it out?" the woman said, her voice thick with sarcasm.

"Yes." Felicity walked away. She thought the woman might come after her or call for security, but neither of those things happened. She reached the elevator and pressed the button and waited. She had no idea what she was going to do.

7

EVERYTHING ABOUT HER APARTMENT BUILDING WAS THE SAME: DULL hallway carpet, big ball light globes, even the scuff mark on the bottom of the door from when the movers had banged it carrying their dining table. She inserted her key and it didn't turn; she had to force it. That was new, but when the door swung open, it offered a prosaic explanation: The apartment had been burgled. Hugo, she assumed, searching for the metal egg. Broken drawers and burst cushions were stacked on the sofa. A potted plant sat in the kitchen sink, rescued by Gavin, she assumed. The bedroom was a blizzard of clothing. Every door was open.

She began to tidy. The third thing she picked up was a salmon-pink summer dress she had never seen in her life. She looked at it awhile and hung it in the closet.

By the time Gavin arrived home, she'd put away everything that wasn't broken and carted the remainder down to the basement. She had thrown a bedsheet over the mess of a sofa, which lent it a college dorm feel. She had restored knickknacks to the TV shelf. Every now and then she came across something new, like a mechanical clock with a carousel of little bears on bicycles, something that might have been sentimental and beloved, but wasn't. Not by her.

Who was here before? she wondered. There must have been someone. A woman named Felicity Staples, who'd bought a salmon dress and a bear clock. Who had a job at the *Daily News* and shared a bed with Gavin. Where was that Felicity now?

She could figure two possibilities. In one, they had swapped, which meant the other Felicity was currently coming to terms with a world in which she owned an extra cat. In the other, the woman had been replaced, and Felicity's arrival was like Dorothy entering the Land of Oz in a spinning tornado house, landing on the Wicked Witch of the East and squashing her flat.

GAVIN ARRIVED HOME and began to organize pots. She watched, interested. He had never been a cooking guy before. He filled a pot with water with one hand, flicking on the heat with the other, like he'd done it a million times, then pulled a stick of something she didn't even recognize from the fridge and began to chop. Spring onion. That was what it was. "Before I forget," he said, "that position with Twine Medical is available. I ran into the guy." He looked up. "Do you remember?"

She shook her head.

"They're after a technical writer. You said you were interested."

Huh, she thought. Even here, she was losing her job.

"The position will be open next week," Gavin said. "No rush."

She watched his hands. No wedding ring. She had kind of gotten it into her head that their marriage was inevitable. But this Felicity and Gavin weren't engaged, either.

The meal was an Instagram-grade concoction of noodles and eggplant. The Gavin she knew could never have cooked this in a million years. "Hey, I bought you a new phone," he said. "You just have to sign in. It restores from the cloud, so it's like you never lost it."

"That's neat." She was reacting badly: to the meal, to Gavin, to all of it. She was being like her college friend Alice, who had spent a summer traveling across Europe, and afterward, they couldn't go anywhere without Alice pointing out everything that was different. "In Paris, they have bicycles you can just take for free," Alice would say, and, "In Amsterdam, they leave their babies outside in strollers even when it's snowing, it's actually much healthier." At a bus station: "Pharmaceutical ads like this are illegal in Europe." In a McDonald's, Alice gazed at the menu and said, "You really do get a new perspective on your own country when you go abroad," and it was really unbearable.

Where I come from, Gavin doesn't really cook.

Where I was before, I actually had two cats.

When you move, you really learn a lot about where you came from.

He slid a white box toward her. Her old phone really was lost forever, she guessed. It literally no longer existed.

While she was tapping, Gavin dug out his own phone. He began to read, forking noodles into his mouth. She found herself watching him. She was sure his hair was longer.

"Huh," he said, not looking up.

"What?" she said.

Seconds passed. She watched his eyes move back and forth across the screen. "Huh."

"I hate it when you do that," she said.

He looked at her. "What?"

"When you're reading and say, 'Huh,' and I say, 'What,' and you ignore me. Then you say, 'Huh' again."

Gavin blinked.

"You do that all the fucking time," she said, and got up and walked into the kitchen, her arms swinging, she was so mad.

"Can you come back here?"

She went to the cupboard and took out a bottle of wine. She poured a glass and drank it all. She was considering a refill when he walked in.

Behind his glasses, his eyes were calm, composed, and too green. "Can we talk?"

"What do you want me to do? Sit there saying 'What?' over and over?"

"I didn't realize I was doing that."

"You were." He was being reasonable. She was the crazy one. "I'm going out." She grabbed her bag and walked to the front door.

"Felicity," he said. "Wait."

She slammed the door on her way out.

AFTER A WHILE it became clear that she was heading for the subway. Because of course she was: That was where it had all started. She had her bag and the plastic tub and the egg. She had a phone. It was after eight when she arrived, and the northbound platform at 42nd and Eighth was populated with teenagers. She loitered. A train came through; the teenagers piled on board; the train pulled out. She walked to the platform edge and looked down. She sat, dangled her legs, and jumped down.

She landed awkwardly. No one shouted; no one came rushing to the platform edge. She dug out her new phone and activated its light. The cavity beneath the platform was larger than she remembered. Maybe it felt smaller when you were trapped inside it with a train rolling by. She crawled inside, trying to avoid catching her clothes on the pipes.

She didn't know what she was looking for. A door? A latch that, when pushed, revealed a tunnel of swirling light? There was nothing like that. She unzipped her bag and opened the tub. She had no idea what it was or why Hugo had given it to her. But it was connected somehow. She hesitated, remembering Gavin's theory of toxic chemicals, then grasped it. It was ice-cold, but did not change anything.

She looked around. What had she done the first time? Cowered here with her eyes shut. She tried that: shifting into the same position. She opened her eyes. She knocked the egg gently against the wall. She said, "Open sesame."

Maybe she'd moved worlds and not realized. Could it be that subtle? She didn't think so. There had been a sensation of pressure, which at the time she'd thought was from the train.

A wind stirred. She was expecting it and stayed where she was. The light grew. The wheels began to scream. She plugged her ears with her fingers. The egg was a deep chill in her palm. She closed her eyes against the bite of flying dirt, and when she opened them she saw one of her old friends, a steel pizza cutter. Above, the rumble of doors. Voices, too, raised in alarm. "She's down there," a woman said. "She went down there."

"Hold the train," called a man. There was more shouting. For the next forty-five minutes, the train sat still while a procession of people spoke to Felicity to verify that she was safe. Then, with plenty of warning, the train began to roll forward, very slowly. The tracks were full of brightly jacketed workers. They helped Felicity out of the cavity and onto the platform.

"Thank you," she said. They were being very nice, considering what an asshole move she had pulled. She had, she was pretty sure, inconvenienced about a million people.

She recognized an MTA man with a turban: Ravneet, who had attended to her the last time. "Are you hurt?"

She shook her head.

"I must tell the police that you have done this before. You will be in trouble."

"Okay," she said. A question occurred to her. "Am I the only one? Has anyone else been down there lately?"

"I assure you, it is only you."

She nodded. Two officers were already approaching. She tried to think of what she would say.

SO IT PROBABLY wasn't the cavity. There might be nothing special at all about that place. Because Hugo hadn't used it, if she believed Ravneet. On the Q, heading home after an hour spent refusing mental health services from the police, she turned ideas over in her brain. Her phone kept pinging. It was restoring from the cloud, and during her iBlackout she had missed a lot of calls and messages. Her family seemed to have the idea that she was barely clinging to life. Felicity tapped out a few replies, just enough to reassure everyone that she was still kicking, then put her phone away. She didn't want to speak to anyone. She didn't want to hear her mother's voice slightly altered, or her father's stock of well-worn expressions, but with changes.

A loss isn't a loss until you sell. That was one of his. It meant you shouldn't give up just because things were going badly. But another way to interpret it was: You could avoid dealing with a situation by ignoring it.

When she unlocked the apartment door, Gavin was in a chair, reading a book by the tall lamp. He set it down and looked at her, his glasses reflecting. "Are you all right?"

"Yes." She owed him an apology, of course. It was nearly midnight.

"Are you going to bed?"

"Yes," she said. They did that. She rolled over, putting her back to him, and he turned off the light without a word.

IN THE MORNING, when Gavin went to work, she absorbed herself in cleaning the apartment. She left her phone on mute to concentrate on where things were supposed to go. She opened the fridge and stared at its contents, trying to imagine how one might combine the menagerie of ingredients within. Then she went to her local deli, which was familiar.

Her inbox was filled with work: follow-ups to stories she didn't know, replies to emails she'd never sent. She would have to figure all that out, she supposed. If she was stuck here, she would need to integrate. But instead of dealing with that, she dug through her contacts for the name of a professor at Columbia, a man she'd interviewed previously about budget cuts to science who had given great quotes. He agreed to meet her on campus.

She wasn't sure whether to take the egg—it seemed risky to bring it along and risky to leave it—and wound up stashing it inside her mailbox in the lobby. On the train, she sat opposite an ad for something called Medivox, a spray that promised to cure colds. What was that, she wondered: a miracle product that didn't exist in her own world? Or just run-of-the-mill bullshit, like herbal teas?

Professor Ken Creighton's office was a narrow slice of the Northwest Corner Building, between the elevators and a supply closet. One wall was shelves, stuffed with books and papers. On the desk sat a travel mug that said: SWEETENED WITH THE TEARS OF MY POSTDOC STUDENTS. Creighton didn't look the type to evoke tears from anybody, though: He was a small, tidy man with silver hair and a warm smile. He shook her hand with both of his and took a seat not behind his desk but directly across the cramped space from her. "So you're interested in the Multiverse," he said, as if this was amusing.

"It's a kind of 'imagine what's possible' piece," Felicity said, even though the *Daily News* would never run an article like that, not in any universe.

"Amazing," said Creighton. He was fiftyish, or maybe older, but in a way that suited him. If Felicity had been taking physics classes, she would not have been devastated to get Professor Creighton. "They say everything comes back into fashion, if you wait long enough."

"The Multiverse isn't fashionable?"

"It was exciting for a while. As ridiculous as it sounds, once you accept that the universe runs on quantum mechanics, it follows logically that our world is only one of many. You need a good reason to believe otherwise. However, it's untestable. Which means it's not a hypothesis so much as an open box you can rummage around in for whatever kind of theory you like. It won't completely go away, though, so we kick it between the Math and Physics Departments every few years."

"It's not disproven, then." She took out her notepad. "It might be real."

"I cannot disprove the existence of invisible pink unicorns," said Creighton. "Those, too, may be real."

"I see," she said. "If it's real, how does it work?"

"Depends which theory you believe."

"Could I describe a scenario and you tell me if there's one that fits?"

He looked delighted. "That is, in fact, how most people do Multiverse thinking. Go ahead, and I'll do my best."

"In the scenario I was thinking about, people can . . ." She hesitated. "Move. They travel from one world to another."

His eyebrows jumped. "Well, then. Travel eliminates ninety-nine percent of all possibilities."

"But not all of them?"

"Oh, no. There are always more possibilities with a Multiverse."

"Well, there are at least two travelers. Three," she said, including herself. "They use something to make themselves move. Some special metal object, which they hold. And there might be some more steps. Things they have to do. But then they move." He didn't respond. "What do you think?"

He leaned forward, as if taking her into a confidence. "I think it's extremely ridiculous, even for Multiverse theories."

"There's no theory for that?"

"Of course there is." He reached over, plucked a pen from the desk, and began to waggle it for no apparent purpose. "Let's see. A transfer—of information, at least—so we're dealing with bubble collisions, where multiple universes press against one another. The process is repeatable, yes? A traveler can keep moving, meeting their alternate selves, say, and taking them out for coffee?"

"They can keep moving, but they can't meet themselves."

His eyebrows shot up. "No doppelgängers? That's a shame. That's the fun part." He tapped his chin. "Curious. Was there a doppelgänger previously, in this scenario?"

"How do you mean?"

"Does the traveler enter a universe in which he never previously existed? Or does the transfer itself destroy the double?"

"I'm not . . ." She was caught on the word *destroy*. "What do you mean by . . ."

"Replacement," Creighton said. "There is evidence that the traveler existed prior to his arrival."

"Yes," Felicity said.

"Then we have information conservation. How delightfully retro. This was actually the foundation of early Multiverse theory. There was even a project, back in the day. A hush-hush study, sponsored by the military."

"What happened?"

"Oh, nothing very exciting. They only managed to make a bunch of math professors disappear." He laughed at her expression. "Figuratively. They were hidden away on a secret base somewhere for years."

"Oh," she said.

"The Soft Horizon Project. It still upsets me to think about the waste of talent. If we had any sense, we'd let our best and brightest work on whatever they pleased. Not lock them away every time the Pentagon has a flight of fancy."

She was frozen with her pen above her notepad. "*Soft Horizon?* That was the name?"

Creighton nodded. "It was all declassified in the early 2000s. A few of us went through their work to see if there was anything worth salvaging."

"And?"

"As I said, nothing. The basic premise was flawed."

"How do you know? Could they have released material to mislead you?"

He was smiling. "You have a journalist's nose for a conspiracy. But these are our colleagues. When they returned to campus, it was discussed. If they'd done anything worth a dime, we would have heard all about it, believe me."

"Hmm," Felicity said.

Creighton's lips twitched. "Although . . ."

"What?"

He leaned forward. Unable to resist, so did Felicity. "We had a joke. I can't remember how it began. But each time we saw Nikolas— one of the Soft Horizon researchers—we'd greet him by saying 'Apple.' And we'd make him reply 'Banana.' The joke was that if he didn't, we'd know we had a problem."

"Why would you have a problem?"

"Because it wouldn't be Nikolas. It would be a version of him who traveled here from a universe in which Soft Horizon had succeeded." He laughed. "A smart Nikolas, you see. One who had found a solution to problems that confounded our own, stupid Nikolas." Unexpectedly, he reached across and patted her knee. "You look shocked. These are just games played by bored professors."

"Yes," she said. "Of course."

"Nikolas de Boer and I worked together for another four years," Creighton said. "I assure you, he never stopped saying 'Banana.'"

But that was years ago, she thought. In the meantime, Smart Nikolas had been hopping between worlds. Making his way toward this one, one step at a time. Smart Nikolas and whoever he traveled with. "Your code. Apple and banana. That could work both ways. Travelers could use a code to identify each other. A code or a logo."

"Not a bad thought. If you were a Multiverse traveler, you wouldn't want to confuse one of your companions with a naïve version." He smiled, but this time it was different. "I have a class in a moment, but I'm free to meet later, if you're interested. There's a bar on 23rd I find tolerably student-free."

Was he flirting with her? He was twenty years her senior and wore a wedding ring, but maybe that didn't matter. Maybe once you were in the bar on 23rd, it belonged to another universe. "Can I ask one more? Does the theory describe anything called 'moorings'?"

"Not that I'm aware. What's the context?"

She tried to recall Hugo's words. *Clay is a moron who doesn't know anything about moorings so when he moves, he winds up someplace Maddie isn't an actress.* "When you have a mooring, you get to choose things about the world you travel to. You can make it a certain way."

He frowned. "There's no way for . . ." Then his face cleared. "Ah. All right, yes. Under information conservation, that does make sense. You see, one of the problems with the idea of travel, if there really is an infinite array of universes, is that most of them would kill you. Our world is a one-in-a-billion-trillion shot. In many other universes—the vast majority of other universes—the Earth wouldn't have evolved its current climate. It may not even exist. Which means you would not want to spin a roulette wheel and travel to a random alternate universe. With information conservation, however, it is impossible for a traveler to inject something new into the destination universe. He may only replace what is already there. And this means he *must* arrive in a universe like his own, which contains a copy of himself to replace. All other possibilities are unreachable—filtered out, effectively. Does this make sense?"

"I think so."

"Then consider what he might choose to bring." Creighton seized a book from the desk, a red hardcover. "This novel, say. If I carry it to the next universe, it must, according to the law of information conservation, already exist there. Which, by extension, means its author must exist. Its publisher. The world must have books. With this one object, I've determined many things about the world."

"So the book is a mooring."

"I'm not familiar with that term, but it sounds appropriate. Where did you pick it up?"

"I'm not sure," she said. "I've been interviewing different people. If I have a mooring, what do I do with it? How do I actually travel?"

"There's a well-known oscillating function that describes the timing of bubble collisions—moments where multiple universes come into contact with each other in curved spacetime. This was Soft Horizon's premise: that in those moments of overlap, transfer could be possible. Given the right technology, of course. And assuming one was free from the observer effect. But I can't tell you what that technology would be, or how it would operate, because it didn't work."

Timing matters, she thought. She remembered Hugo's old-fashioned watch, how it had beeped on the subway. "I could know when it was time to travel. From this oscillating . . ."

"Function," Creighton said. "Yes, if you can handle the math. The time between collisions varies in a predictable way, from about fourteen to fifty-seven hours."

"Can a traveler go home? Back where she came from?"

His smile became puzzled. "You must be a good journalist. You know so much about a project you've never heard of."

"That was part of Soft Horizon? The idea that you can't go back?"

"Of course. You must travel to a universe that possesses a version of yourself. But this is no longer true of the universe you came from."

She blinked, startled. "Why not?"

"Because you disappeared." He gestured, like a magician performing a trick. "Out of sight, to avoid the observer effect. You left a letter, I hope, to inform your friends and family that they'll never see you again." He gazed at her. "I'm quite serious about the bar. I'd enjoy answering more of your questions there."

She stood. "You've been very helpful, thank you."

He rose. "I'm late for my class now. It's the least you could do."

"Thank you again." She shook his hand, not even really thinking about the come-on. There was a pit of nausea in her stomach and she wanted to get out of the building.

"When will the article run?" Creighton asked. "I'd like a copy of it."

"I'll let you know," she said.

SHE SAT ON the steps of the Low Library, trying to research on her phone while students moved around her, laughing and talking about TV shows she'd never heard of—because she was older than them or because the shows didn't exist; one of those, she couldn't be sure which. Creighton had said that Soft Horizon was declassified, but Felicity couldn't find any references to it. She tried *oscillating bubble collision function*, which only brought her to an academic paper drenched in symbols she would never understand. At the bottom, though, was a simple table, the output of the function, as a long, repeating pattern. *Like a bus schedule*, she thought. But with no dates or times: only the length of time between buses. So unless she already knew where she was in the pattern, it wouldn't help her.

The sun was warm. She was tempted to stay for the afternoon. Sit here and think until she'd figured it all out.

If you could move between worlds, what would you do?

Murder real estate agents, apparently. Although only Clayton Hors was doing that. Hugo was trying to stop him. Why was that? Out of the goodness of his heart? She wasn't sure she was ready to buy the idea of a traveling group of do-gooders. Specifically, do-gooders who acted like Hugo.

Riding the Q home, she forged into her email. There was a message from the office of District Attorney Tom Daniels; the last time they'd spoken, in a previous world, he'd promised to get back to Felicity about the case of an eighteen-year-old boy who assaulted a girl during a party. Maybe in this one he was genuinely interested in prosecuting the scions of wealthy society families. She scanned the email. The way Felicity remembered this case, the girl had laughed at the boy, and in response he'd punched her hard enough that her retina had detached. Here, that didn't seem to have happened, but for some reason, there was still a case. She dug into the conversation history and found that there had been an argument; that part was the same. And the D.A. had decided not to prosecute. But this time no one had seen James Hammond hit her. Instead, she had supposedly slipped and hit her head on the edge of the pool. By the time the ambulance arrived, she had died.

She exited Church Avenue station, furious. This was bullshit, obviously. It was the same event with a different spin and a worse ending. And once again, no one was going to care enough to make anyone pay for it. As she crossed Crooke Avenue, though, she realized she'd been inside her head for a while, and someone was following her. The knowledge popped into her brain fully formed, like an unread message notification that had been awaiting her notice. She kept her head down, fishing her keys out of her bag and sliding one between her ring and middle fingers, the way they said you should, to make a weapon. Behind her, she heard footsteps, brisk, like her own.

It's Clayton, she thought. He'd found out who she was, somehow, and come after her. She threw a glance over her shoulder. There was someone back there, and as she turned he lunged toward her and she yelped and began to run. She made five steps, enough to think that she was getting away, then he caught her bag and swung her against the brick wall of an apartment building. "Where is it?"

"Get off me," she said. Fingers jabbed into her armpits and crotch.

She had done self-defense, a million years ago, and learned the three key target areas to strike: *eyes, groin, instep*. She tried them and they didn't work, because he was too strong.

He flipped her around like a sack. The back of her head knocked the brickwork. His face was pale and puffy, his forehead enormous, blond hair plastered across it. His nose was thick, like an old boxer's, and lined with red veins. He was not Clayton Hors. He was no one she'd seen before. "Where is it?"

"What . . . *ack*," she said, which was supposed to be *What are you talking about?* Her throat had closed.

"Do you realize what's happening?" And before she could answer: "I *will* hurt you." He drew back a fist. "Where did you hide it?"

"I don't have it."

His fist moved. She flinched. But he didn't hit her. Instead, he seized the front of her shirt and pulled her to him. She felt her buttons go. "You have one day. Then I will begin fucking up your life in ways you can't imagine." His eyes burned into hers. Then he let her go and walked away.

She breathed. Her legs were shaky, so she sat. After a minute, a woman came along with a dog and asked if she was okay, and Felicity said yes, she was just tired. She cried for a few moments. Then she laughed, remembering the man's threat to begin fucking up her life.

Begin, she thought.

SHE COLLECTED THE egg in its plastic tub from her mailbox and carried it up to her apartment. Then she sat at the table and stared at it. She didn't want to give up the egg. It was practically the only thing she had: the only thing that had come with her aside from the clothes she'd been wearing. But she couldn't hide it for much longer. Eventually, they would find it.

She opened the tub, took out the egg, and tucked it beneath her pillow until she could think of somewhere better. As she emerged from the bedroom, there was the sound of a key in the lock. Gavin entered. She was surprised at her own excitement. "Hey!" he said. He had brought home snapper. Snapper! He kissed her and began to prepare it and sizzle it in a pan. She should give this Gavin a chance, she decided. He cooked and cared about her. He was a good guy. Her guy. With alterations.

They ate at the counter, side by side, with only the low kitchen lights on, so it felt like candles. "You have a little scar," she said, during her second glass of wine. "On your cheek."

He touched it. "This?"

"What's it from?"

"Chicken pox. As a kid."

She kind of liked it. It added character. A little imperfection to make things interesting. Then, without thinking, she said: "What would you do if I disappeared?"

He raised his eyebrows. "How? Like kidnapped?"

"Just disappeared. Vanished without a trace."

"I'm not sure."

She was trying not to think about Gavin, her old Gavin. She was giving new Gavin a chance. But now she couldn't leave it alone. "Think about it."

"Do I have to?" He refilled his glass. "It's a horrible hypothetical." She stared at him.

"What would you do if *I* disappeared?" Gavin said.

"That's not going to happen."

"Well, there you go," he said.

"God, you can be infuriating," she said.

"How am I being infuriating?"

"It's a serious question. I disappear tomorrow. What do you do? Do you miss me? Do you find someone else? I want to know."

He sipped his wine. "I'd go looking for you."

"Where?"

"Your office. Your parents' place."

"Would you call them or drive there?"

"Both," he said, warming up. "Phone first, then drive there."

"Why?"

"They could be hiding you."

She smiled. "They're not."

"Then I take out an ad. A full page in the *Daily News*. I could get a discount, I assume."

"You're not staff."

"They'd probably do it for free. Given the circumstances, they'd put you on the front page."

She hadn't thought of that. He was right.

"I would be interviewed a *lot*, assuming you're missing for a good length of time, in appropriately suspicious circumstances. I'd have to give them a photo. They always have exactly one photo of a missing person and use it over and over." He snapped his fingers. "The one of you on the pier."

She was appalled. "My hair is terrible."

"It's my favorite picture of you. You're so happy."

"Stop," she said. "I don't want to do this anymore."

He blinked. "But it's your game."

She began to cry.

"Felicity," he said, bewildered.

"I'm tired," she said. She hunched so that her hair fell over her plate.

She heard Gavin's chair scrape back. He touched her shoulder. When she didn't respond, he lifted her out of her chair, scooping her up as if she were a new bride, and carried her to the bedroom.

"I don't want to disappear," she said.

"Then don't." Gavin kissed her face, gently, in several places. She kissed him back, and it was good, like it was really him, like she couldn't tell the difference at all.

IN THE NIGHT, she rose to use the toilet and padded across the living room floor. She was trying to be quiet but caught her hip on the corner of the table. "Ow," she said. "Shit, ow." She moved to her right but somehow there was more table there. She groped toward the light switch and threw illumination into the room. The table was facing the wrong way, filling up space it hadn't before. She stared at it, realizing what it meant. The table hadn't moved. She had. She was somewhere new.

IT WAS A HOT JUNE AND A HOTTER JULY. ON THE FINAL THURSDAY,
Maddie's air-conditioning unit, a SeaBreeze 2000 that dated from
sometime when that moniker sounded futuristic, emitted a tired
wheeze and quietly died. Maddie, sitting on the sofa in white shorts
and a bra, her sociology books spread out around her, looked up. The
unit's green light was dark. Its fins were still. "Oh, come on," she said.

She got up, peered at it, and gave the remote a few optimistic
jabs. But the SeaBreeze 2000 did not respond. It had never been
very effective, hence the shorts and bra, but she was going to miss it,
she could tell. She went to the window and hauled it open. What
came inside was traffic noise, a rich mix of gas and food smells, and
heat like a solid object. She let the window fall shut.

This could have been avoided. The unit had been making odd
noises for a while, grating noises, and she'd ignored them because the
super was a pain and would, Maddie knew, stand in front of it for a
minute before shrugging and saying, *Sounds okay to me*, making her
feel like an entitled white girl complaining about an air-conditioning
unit that worked fine. A month ago, she would have phoned him
anyway, because Trent would have been beside her, to lend a shrug

and a smirk that would banish what the super thought into mean-inglessness. But Trent, like her air conditioner, was no more. She had come home from a shift at the coffee shop and set her bag on the table, and Trent, playing video games on the sofa, hadn't looked up. At this moment, Maddie hadn't been thinking of anything of substance—certainly not whether she still wanted to be in a relation-ship with Trent Haversham after twenty-two decreasingly fulfilling months—but a moment passed and then another and he still hadn't glanced in her direction, and she said, "I think we should break up." Out of nowhere, like a hiccup.

He turned. "What?"

She didn't answer right away, she was so surprised. It was the kind of thing she might say in improv, where you had to speak with-out thinking. Because that was the point: to find truth through feeling, not thought.

"What?" Trent said again, louder. He was still holding the con-troller. A beer can balanced beside him on the arm of the sofa. That was a thing, actually. Maddie always asked him to use the coffee table, which was twelve inches away and a whole lot less likely to result in the loss of their security deposit, and Trent always gave a patronizing look, like: *Me? Spill a beer?*

To be fair, he had not yet spilled a beer.

"I think we should break up." The second time wasn't as good. Less spontaneous, less authentic, and she always felt you had to do something different with a repeated line, really change it up, or it would undermine the first one. But this wasn't a scene. She wasn't playing to anyone. It was just her and Trent. It was going to be stupid and messy and some of the lines would be bad.

"What the fuck are you talking about?" He didn't look confused, though. He did know what the fuck she was talking about. "*Why?*"

A dangerous question. There was no right answer here. But si-lence was bad, too, apparently, because Trent pushed himself from the sofa like a spasm. His elbow brushed the beer can. She watched it fall, turning end over end, landing on the carpet, and discharging its contents: *chug-chug-chug.*

"Ah, fuck," Trent said, then again, louder: "*Fuck!*" He grabbed the can and slammed it onto the coffee table. Then he sagged back into the sofa. She felt grateful for this incident, which had explained things better than she ever could.

"I'll get a sponge," she said.

NOW, IN THE rising heat, sans Trent, she wondered how hot the apartment might get. Ninety? A hundred? On the topic of sponges: These old buildings soaked up heat like thirsty drunks in the day and leaked it at night. She had exactly one portable fan, which was the size of her hand.

Call the super. Who cares how he looks at you?

But no. She wasn't going to do that. It was late. She was, at heart, a coward. Also, it was maybe genuinely not a great idea to invite a man she barely knew into her apartment. She would call him in the morning.

Her phone rang. She jumped a little. *The super,* she thought. Somehow he'd heard her unit had broken down. *Hot night,* he would say. *Too hot for a girl like you to be sitting around in your bra and little pants.*

She shook her head and picked up the phone. It was a number she didn't recognize, ergo a robocall, or someone wanting to sell something, which she generally let go to voicemail, but she wanted to prove to herself that she wasn't *that* timid. "Hello?"

"Is this Madison May?" A male voice. No one she recognized.

"Who's calling?" A little trick she'd learned from her friend Jahzara. Admit nothing. Turn the question around. Did it make any difference? Probably not. But she had liked how Zar sounded when she did it.

"I'm with Emergency Services at New York–Presbyterian Brooklyn. I have some important information regarding your father's health."

She was silent. Her father had passed away five years before. She had been in class and suddenly glanced through the glass to see her mother standing in the hallway. Somehow, she had known immediately, the knowledge sinking into her like a knife. *It was peaceful*, her mother said. *It was just his time.*

It was an embolism, technically. Maddie had read the autopsy.

"Hello?" said the man on the phone.

"I'm here."

"I can send a car to bring you to the hospital. Where are you?"

"What is this about?"

"Your father," said the man, but a thin note of doubt had entered his voice, a timbre that said: *Ah, shit, her father's dead, isn't he?* "I can't discuss it over the phone, but it's important."

"You want to talk to me about my father's *health?*"

"The hospital may have made an error in his treatment," the man said. A pretty smooth transition, she supposed, to a scenario that worked with a dead father, but still bullshit, because her father sure as hell hadn't been taken to any hospital in Brooklyn. "You could be entitled to compensation."

She felt a rush of anger. He sounded sincere, and they always did, of course—the scammers, the con men—but to try to get to her with a story about her *father?* "Go fuck yourself."

A short, surprised silence. When the man spoke, his voice sounded different, his tone became urgent. "Maddie, we have to meet. You're in danger. I want you to—"

She killed the call. Dropped the phone to the sofa.

Scam call, she thought. *Clearly.*

Had she heard those last words correctly? She was in *danger?* He wanted to *meet?*

She felt abruptly cold, as if the apartment weren't ninety degrees.

She brought up her recent calls and blocked the number. Then she dropped the phone again, not wanting to touch it, in case the guy could travel down the line and ooze out into her apartment.

What *was* that?

She wasn't good with random events. It was the actor inside her (she liked to think): There had to be motivation. *Maddie,* Trent said impatiently, when she fretted about why she didn't get this role or that; why she was assigned a mentor with a stage background rather than screen; or even how Trent had come to a particular decision, such as disliking her friend Zar, who was—objectively—impossible to dislike. *Sometimes there's no reason. It just is.*

There was always a reason, though. If she didn't know it, she hadn't studied the scene long enough.

What kind of scammer wanted to meet in person? That part was strange. Those people generally didn't want you to know who they were. They stayed at the other end of a phone, safely anonymous, so that when the scam was exposed—when the son noticed his mother emptying out her life savings, or packing her bags to meet her online lover (*Have you ever actually met this person?*), they could blow away like smoke.

Bad people who want to meet you, Maddie thought. *Thieves. Rapists. Murderers.*

Thieves? He hadn't known where she lived. Not thieves.

Rapists. Murderers.

Her friend Zar lived in Cambria Heights, a thirty-minute, two-train transit, in a share house with three other girls. Maddie had been over twice and felt super-white the whole time, but also incredibly welcomed. She picked up her phone.

"Hey, Mads. What's up?"

"Hey," she said, the word coming out weird, like she'd been sitting on it.

"What's the matter?"

She tried to laugh. "Um, this is silly, but my air went out and I'm baking. Is there any chance I could sleep at your place?"

"Sure you can. Get your butt on over here."

She bit her lip. "Thank you."

"Anytime," said Zar, and then, because they took classes together and Zar knew what a bum performance from Maddie sounded like: "You sure you're okay?"

"I got a weird call," she confessed.

"What happened? You want me to come get you?"

"No," she said, and felt stronger hearing it. She was rattled—she was very rattled by the strange man who wanted to know where she was and whether they could meet—but she was capable of skating her butt across town. Not on the train, though. She would take an Uber. Maybe even an honest-to-God cab.

"I'll make you up the sofa. These bitches here need an early night anyway." There was a background squeal of protest.

"Thank you," Maddie said, clutching the phone.

"No problem. Just get here. Be safe."

"I will," she said.

SHE STEPPED OUT of the cab in Cambria Heights, leaving a tip she couldn't afford. She swung her bag onto her back and approached the house, which was a detached two-story red brick and white clapboard, the roof two big happy angles with bold white gables up front and goofy overhangs at the side. A friendly house. You could see that, despite the broken front steps and the faded paint. Maddie had always enjoyed houses, had even occasionally wondered, in her weaker moments, whether she should pack away the acting thing—which, let's face it, had a shockingly low probability of going anywhere—and get a real job, one that allowed her to take a cab ride without mentally crossing out future expenditures. Interior decoration, maybe. Or real estate. She would be good at selling houses, she thought. It would be a practical application of her acting classes.

She strode up the steps and rang the bell. The front door popped open, framing Jahzara in light. Zar was tall and slim, with shoulders like perfect gleaming rocks. Zar was also, Maddie had discovered, a better actor than she was. So whenever Maddie started to get down about her prospects of ever breaking in—when she had thoughts like *It's too hard* or *Maybe I should go into real estate*—she tried to remind herself of Zar, who had talent, beauty, and determination, and never once made a thing out of how when they went to casting calls together, all the producers would be white, and the director, and the casting director, and some would ask if Zar had considered reading for this other part, the friend.

Part of the game, Zar said, when Maddie brought it up. *Makes me work harder.*

Zar ushered her inside, which was not actually a whole lot cooler. But, then, Maddie wasn't really here for the air. She let Zar steer her into the living room, where three girls huddled in front of a laptop, pointing and talking over one another.

"This is Maddie from class. You remember Maddie?" There were *Hi, Maddies.* "Marieke, Jasmine, Nia," Zar said, pointing, for which Maddie was grateful, because she'd been scratching around in her brain for those names. "Drink?"

"Sure." Zar marched into the kitchen and came out with a bottle of red wine. A thought occurred to Maddie, popping into her brain from nowhere: They should buy a bottle of something expensive, and open it when one of them finally landed their first real part. "Trent?"

Maddie blinked. "What?"

"Was the phone call from him?"

She shook her head. "No one I know."

Zar decapitated the bottle and set two plastic cups on the counter. "You sure? One of his friends?"

"I don't think so." She had lived with him for almost two years; this didn't feel like a Trent thing.

Zar pushed the cup across to her, planted her elbows on the counter, and raised her own cup. Maddie dutifully knocked hers against it. "I dumped a dude once. Sweetest guy in the world. But when I gave him his marching orders, he's leaving crusty socks on my front doorstep."

"Crusty as in . . ."

"I assume so," Zar said. "I didn't inspect them up close."

She squinted. "But why?"

Zar spread her arms dramatically. "They blame you for making them feel something. And instead of dealing like a normal human being, they want to make you feel something back. Scared, angry, doesn't matter. It's a power thing. They all do it. Even the nice ones. *Especially* the nice ones. Wouldn't surprise me if Trent is dishing you some freaky night calls."

On the sofa, the laptop gave a burst of sound. The girls cackled.

"Come away with me this weekend," Zar said. "Me and Jorge are driving to his parents' lake house in Carmel. Forty-eight hours of pure escape. Come with us."

"Oh, I don't want to get in the way of you and Jorge."

"There's nothing to get in the way of. I need an excuse to slow him down. Don't answer yet," Zar said, because Maddie was shaking her head. "This isn't a third-wheel kind of situation. I'm asking another friend as well."

She had to admit: After weeks of broiling in a one-bedroom apartment with the ghost of her ex-boyfriend, it sounded like heaven. "A lake house?"

"Honest-to-God lake house," Zar said. "Jorge's parents have that restaurant money. It's tucked away in a forest like some fairy-tale house. You'd think you were the only people in the world. Can you imagine that? Not being surrounded by people every damn second?"

"We can hear you," called one of the laptop girls.

"Not you, Marieke, I love you," said Zar. "It's Jasmine who's driving me bananas."

Jasmine raised a middle finger without turning around.

"I can't buy any good conditioner with that girl around," Zar said. "I swear she drinks it, she uses so much."

"A lake house," Maddie said, testing the words.

"Everything is organized. All you need to do is say yes."

She smiled. "You're a good friend."

"Aw," Zar said. "Got a swimsuit?"

She nodded. She had bought it months ago and not yet found an opportunity to wear it.

"Good." Zar grinned. She raised her plastic wine cup and held it there until Maddie tapped it with her own. "Cheers."

IN THE MORNING, Maddie returned to her apartment, aiming to put a solid dent in a sociology paper that was due the following Wednesday. But when she was alone, the place felt small and foreboding in a way it hadn't before. Maddie was rehearsing a production of *A Streetcar Named Desire*, playing out of the 13th Street Repertory Theatre, and she was reminded of the words of the director, a tiny geriatric named Oren Hutchins, who was not yet satisfied with Maddie's portrayal of the lead. *Blanche isn't scared by what she's seeing*, Oren had told her. *She's not reacting. It comes from inside. She carries the fear within her.*

Maddie might have been carrying a little fear within.

If she believed Oren Hutchins, a weekend away at the lake would do her no good: She would bring the fear with her. Still. *Screw you, Oren*, she thought. *And screw you, sociology*. Five minutes later, she was riding the elevator to the ground floor, her bag across her shoulder. The doors opened. There was no strange man waiting for her. No furtive figure loitering on the sidewalk. She headed for the train station and felt lighter with every step.

SHE SPENT THREE hours in the city, moving between bookstores and coffee shops. When she passed the Roxy, her favorite theater, she stopped to see what was playing and noticed a family drama, *By the River Blue*. One of the characters was played by an actor Maddie had met while auditioning for an off-off-Broadway play. The girl, Aria Astwell, had beaten out Maddie for the part, and the play had gone on to have a wildly successful run, at least relative to anything Maddie had been in, and catapulted Aria into roles like this. Maddie had followed Aria's career ever since, because it was half inspiring and half infuriating how this girl had been in the same place as Maddie but then crossed over a magical threshold into the enchanted fairytale kingdom.

She was about to move on when she noticed a reflection in the glass: a man behind her. Maddie couldn't make out detail, but he seemed to be studying her. She resisted the urge to turn, and waited, pretending to study the cast list at the bottom of *By the River Blue*. Still the man didn't move, so finally she hoisted her bag and began to walk, watching out for him in store reflections.

Half a block later, she caught a good view of the guy trailing her, big, like scary big, late thirties, bearded, rugged, arms popping out of a collared plaid shirt. When they reached the corner, she risked a direct look. He was gazing amiably across the street, like he didn't even know she was there. *It's no one*, she thought. *Only Blanche, carrying her fear.*

The light changed. She began to cross. On the far corner was the subway entrance and she angled toward it. Just before the first step, she stopped and turned. The bearded man passed without so much as a glance. She watched him trot all the way down the steps and disappear toward the barriers. She stayed another thirty seconds, to be sure. He didn't come back.

"Pardon me," said an elderly woman, squeezing by.

She apologized. She was blocking traffic. Most likely, she was imagining problems. It was a city of eight million people; some of them would stop and look at you.

Stop being a Blanche.

She walked two blocks to the next subway. By the time she reached the platform, she'd almost forgotten about him.

SHE ARRIVED AT Zar's a little before three. Parked by the curb was a gleaming red Jeep, the kind of car that struck her as excitable and careless. The rear hatch was up. A muscular boy in a tank top was loading a case of beer. Someone was in the backseat. Before Maddie could decide whether to introduce herself, Zar emerged from the house with a bright orange carry bag and waved.

"This is Jorge," Zar said, like she was introducing a disobedient dog. "And this is the nicest girl I've ever met in my life, so you be nice to her."

"I'm Maddie," she said, and stuck out her hand, smiling.

Jorge gripped it, grinning. He wore a black Mets cap, a light silver chain, and baggy shorts with sneakers that struck her as the designer kind. He had good teeth and smelled faintly of wood. Or aftershave, she guessed. Wood-scented aftershave. "Hey."

"That's Liam in the car," Zar said, turning away before Maddie could react. When she glanced back, her expression was like: *Oh, didn't I mention that my other friend is a dude? Sorry, I totally didn't realize that you never would have agreed to this trip.*

Zar climbed into the car. Jorge said, "Take your bag?"

Maddie imagined Jorge and Zar canoodling in the cabin while she and—what was his name? Liam—sat an awkward two feet apart, trying to decide where to look. The same scene repeated on the lake, in the woods. How many bedrooms did this cabin have? Nightmare. It was a nightmare.

The Jeep's window slid down. Zar leaned out. "It's all good, Maddie. Trust me."

Maddie looked at her. Zar hadn't let her down before. She handed Jorge her bag.

"Cool," he said.

She pulled open the rear door and slid inside. She could feel the presence of Liam but waited until she'd belted in and arranged herself before looking in his direction. He wore glasses. He had light, almost fluffy hair. His eyes darted, like those of a cornered animal, which was actually good, since it made Maddie think that Liam, like her, was learning about this situation right now.

The rear hatch thumped down. Jorge climbed into the driver's seat and pulled shut the door with a bang, like chopping wood. The engine kicked into life. She gripped the armrest against the sudden acceleration, and in the side window, a parked car slid by, a blue sedan, a man inside with his forearms folded over the steering wheel, bearded, wearing a collared shirt. Fear rose in her throat all at once, like it had been there all along.

She jolted in surprise. "Is—" She twisted in her seat. The blue car was shrinking in the rear window.

"You okay?" Zar said, looking back.

"I thought . . ." She wasn't sure what she'd seen. And she didn't know if she wanted to voice this in front of Jorge and Liam. "I felt like I was being followed earlier."

Zar's lips made an O of surprise. "By Trent?"

She shook her head. "Older guy. Beard. Big. I thought I saw him in a parked car back there."

Zar turned to Jorge. "She's gotten out of a bad relationship."

Not that bad, she wanted to say.

Jorge's eyes flicked to the rear mirror. "He's stalking you?"

"It's not him. It's probably nothing."

"What kind of car?"

She tried to think. "A sedan. A wide one. Light blue."

Zar told Jorge, "You keep your eye on who's behind. See if anyone's following."

"No one's following us to Carmel," Jorge said. "I can guarantee that."

"How can you guarantee that?"

"I drive too fast," Jorge said. The Jeep jumped as if it had been kicked. Zar let out a squeal. Maddie clutched at the seat. She didn't approve of this, the reckless driving, but it did make her feel better. He slung the car between lanes, throwing glances over his shoulder like he was a wide receiver preparing for a pass, and that was good, too, as if his confidence was contagious.

"You idiot," Zar said. "You're going to get us killed." But she was laughing. Jorge grinned. Within twenty minutes they were on the Bronx–Whitestone Bridge, pointed north. As far as Maddie could tell, the blue car had been left far behind. And so had Blanche, she decided: Blanche, who carried her fear. All that was behind her. It would wait until she came home.

SOMEWHERE AROUND BAYCHESTER, Zar opened a cooler that must have been nestled by her feet. She passed Maddie a silver can that said O-GASM in big type, and, smaller: VODKA + ORANGE.

"What's this?" Maddie said.

"I don't know," Zar said. "Try some and tell me." She popped an identical can and took a swig.

"Liam, you want a beer?" Jorge asked.

"Uh," said Liam. "I mean . . ."

"Give him a beer," Jorge told Zar, who passed a dark bottle that was beaded with moisture. Liam accepted it and held his bottle toward Maddie. She knocked it with her can. Then she popped the top and drank. It was cold, but less aggressive than she'd expected, sweeter, almost not like alcohol at all.

"Good, yes?" Zar inquired.

"Yes," she said, although *ridiculous* was what it was. She felt as if she'd traveled back in time to circa 2018, when she was a teenager and could climb into a car with a friend and two boys she didn't know and drink and scream and have the best time. Although had she ever actually done that? Not really.

"Maddie, you smoke?" Jorge said. She realized he meant: *weed.* In the rearview mirror, his eyes were deep brown. He was an okay guy, she thought. At first glance, he came off a little brash, but he was genuinely asking, not pushing. "Maybe," she said.

"All right. Now we've got a party. Liam, you down?"

"I'll pass, thanks," Liam said. "But you guys enjoy."

"Liam is responsible," Zar said, turning in her seat. "Always thinking of his future. What are you studying again? Kids' bikes?"

"Macroeconomic trade cycles."

"That's what I said." Zar giggled.

Maddie said, "How do you two know each other?"

"He's my cousin," Zar said, and then, to Maddie's expression: "We went to high school."

"Oh." She drank. "What are macroeconomic trade cycles?"

"Well," Liam said, "you know how countries trade with each other?" There followed an explanation involving words Maddie had not encountered in her studies of the performing and social arts. "Anyway," he said suddenly, as if realizing how long he'd been talking. "That's the gist." He gave a quick, embarrassed smile.

"And you actually find this interesting?" Zar said. She looked at Maddie. "This is what the smart people sound like."

She was sure Liam was smart. And nice. And Zar did know people, so maybe he was even suited for her. Under different circumstances, something might happen. But not this weekend.

She took another drink. The sun through the window was hot, the air on blast was frigid, and she was developing a pleasant buzz in her head and a tingle on her skin. Jorge put on music, something electronic, which Zar changed, and they began to argue in a friendly, teasing way. Liam asked how long she'd known Zar, which led to a series of anecdotes. Cans were passed, which Maddie accepted, and seemed to drink themselves. When the Jeep turned onto a narrow tree-lined road, she felt mildly astonished, because it was like they'd only just left the city.

Stitched along both sides of the narrow road were driveways and mailboxes, but the houses themselves were all tucked away behind tall conifers. At a sign that read PRIVATE PROPERTY STRICTLY NO ENTRY, Jorge turned onto a packed-earth driveway. They bumped along for thirty or forty yards, the trees pressing close, chopping the afternoon sunlight into thin slices. Then they rounded a bend and there it was, the lake house, a neat white clapboard house with a wide porch and shuttered windows. On the front door hung a wooden relief of a smiling sun.

Jorge killed the engine, fell from the car, and whooped. *Like a movie*, Maddie thought, and that was a better description of the sensation she'd felt earlier, when she'd thought they'd turned into teenagers. They weren't real teenagers, not themselves six years ago; they were idealized versions, carefully distinct characters who hit the road with booze and weed and unbridled excitement for a too-good-to-be-true getaway to the lake. And then? Was it a road-trip movie? Did they have a coming-of-age experience? She wasn't sure.

"Swimsuits," said Zar, lurching from the car.

Maddie looked at Liam, who shrugged. She extracted herself from the vehicle, which took longer than she expected because her legs had quietly filled with O-gasm, apparently. Jorge had the hatch open and was already carrying gear up the front steps. He dumped it by the door, lifted the smiling sun to retrieve a key, and went inside.

"There is a pier," Zar said, articulating carefully, as if they were doing Shakespeare. "We shall leap from it."

"Is that a good idea?" She meant: *When we're this drunk.*

"Mmm-hmm," Zar said noncommittally. Liam passed, carrying bags. He was significantly more sober than them, Maddie sensed. He had paced himself. Zar was right: Liam was thinking of the future. "Imagine," Zar said. "Cool. Water." She made a horizontal gesture, indicating a flat ocean, or a horizon, or something.

Maddie followed Zar into the house. It was clean and minimalist, with broad white shelves and countertops graced by a few singular pieces: a twist of birchwood, a copper fish, a conch shell. Like an Airbnb. Not a lived-in place, with hair on the benches and bread crumbs on the floor. A model house.

A set, she thought.

Jorge emerged from a darkened doorway. His tank top had disappeared. His shorts had become a tiny, bright red pair of swim briefs. His torso was full of amazing bumps. He walked to the kitchen, retrieved a bottle of beer from the fridge, and banged the top open on the countertop. The lid dropped to the floor and rolled somewhere. He tipped the bottle back and began to drink in slow, authoritative gulps.

Zar bounced into a bedroom. Maddie was looking for that bottle top (*Keep the set clean, people!*), but Jorge was drinking steadily, looking at her. She began to feel awkward. She collected her bag and explored the hallway until she found a free bedroom. Inside, alongside bunk beds, was a box of beach toys. *Who are they for?* she wondered. Jorge, when he was younger?

Or no one, she thought. *They're just props.*

She fit herself into the bikini, which felt a little smaller than it had when she'd tried it on in her apartment, like her ass might be hanging out of her pants. The frill across her breasts, merely cute at home, felt as blatant as a half-raised stage curtain, commanding attention toward the main show. There was a small en suite with a tall mirror, and she used it to inspect herself, trying to put herself into the mind of Liam. Because that was the issue. The suit was fine for a swim with Zar. She wasn't sure it was okay for a swim with a guy Zar wanted to set her up with, with whom Maddie didn't want to be set up.

She exhaled. This was the swimsuit she'd brought. She opened the door.

Liam was passing. "Oh," they said at the same time. Liam's hands twitched up to his chest, then dropped. He was naked except for green shorts. Even in the dark hallway, his skin was so white it was almost luminescent. But he had nothing to be embarrassed about; he wasn't muscular, like Jorge, but he was lean, which was fine. That was totally fine.

He gestured for her to go first. She accepted before realizing this put Liam behind her as she paraded her ass to the front of the house. Averting his eyes, maybe. He seemed like the kind of guy who might do that. On the porch, Jorge and Zar were squeezed together into a hammock-chair contraption beside a bunch of towels, drinking and giggling. Zar was in a yellow one-piece, which sported a series of artful cuts that made her appear eight feet long. She saw Maddie and clambered out of the chair, momentarily threatening to tip Jorge onto the floor. "You're beautiful!"

"You look amazing," Maddie said.

"Everyone looks amazing," Jorge said. "Let's do this."

The path to the lake was steep and winding, the earth cool beneath her feet. After a minute, Zar raised her hand, and Maddie, trailing behind, stopped. "Listen," Zar said.

Wind in the leaves. Buzzing insects.

"No *people*," Zar said.

The boys continued on, but Maddie and Zar stayed, listening. When was the last time her ears hadn't been filled with noise? A year? "It's like another world."

Zar smiled and took her hand. They hurried after Jorge and Liam, and Maddie felt delighted, because although Zar was a close friend, they hadn't been, you know, *holding hands* friends. She was glad she'd come. It was already better than she could have imagined. They were headed to the lake and Jorge seemed nice, and, by the way, wasn't their group pleasantly racially diverse? Like, almost ideally so. Like an ad for a college.

Or a movie, she thought. *The white girl has a Black friend. And there's a Hispanic guy, but mainstream audiences aren't totally comfortable with interracial relationships, so the romantic interest is white, too.*

What kind of movie was she thinking of? Not an indie coming-of-age pic. Something more obvious.

Ahead, Jorge whooped and began to run. The trees were thinning, the earth turning gritty beneath Maddie's feet, and she emerged into sunshine and bright sand. On either side, the water curved to promontories of dark rocks. Here, at last, were people, but only a few: a middle-aged couple walking barefoot on the sand; a family with a dog; teenagers exploring the rocks. Jorge sprinted toward a sun-bleached pier that was spackled with ancient birdshit, leaped off the end, and disappeared. Water fountained.

Zar let go of Maddie's hand and ran, passing Liam, who was still on the sand. At the end of the pier, she jumped, her hair trailing in a long black streak.

Maddie and Liam followed at a walk. A board creaked beneath her foot. At the end of the pier, they found Jorge and Zar treading water.

"It's so amazing," Zar said.

Liam glanced at her, then launched into a fairly impressive cannonball. He came up and shook his head, flinging droplets.

Out of nowhere, the answer to the question that had been bugging Maddie popped into her head.

Oh, she thought. *It's a horror movie.*

She'd been misled by the opening. Four happy young people; her brain had been searching for something upbeat. But the characters were always happy and overconfident as they headed off to their cabin in the woods, or their house on the lake. Only later did the tone change, when night fell.

"Maddie!" Zar shrieked. "Jump, you coward!"

Actually, it began even earlier than that, didn't it? Before the road trip, there was a prologue to establish a sense of danger. Usually something creepy involving the lead. A close encounter, to establish the idea that she was marked.

"*Maddie!*"

Below her, the water sparkled like knives. She felt cold, as if a cloud had passed in front of the sun. *Blanche*, she thought. *Go away, Blanche. I left you in Queens.* She pushed the whole package from her mind. She was not in a movie. She was not an imperious southern lady fallen on hard times. She was twenty-two, on a pier, in a cute bikini. She forced a smile and jumped.

AFTERWARD, THEY SAT on the sand, wrapped in towels. As the sun eased toward the treetops, Jorge proposed an expedition to the rocks. But Maddie was warm and comfortable, and had the idea that Jorge and Zar were angling for some time together. She and Liam watched them walk along the sand. Zar attempted a cartwheel. Jorge turned in a full circle in the air, landing on his feet.

"Whew," Liam said, sounding vaguely defeated.

"I bet you could do that if you wanted," Maddie said.

He smiled. "Exactly."

"Thoughtful," she said. "Modest." Then, trying to think how to ask, *Why are you here?* without it being weird: "Do you and Zar hang out much?"

He shook his head. "I'm friends with her brother. To be honest, I thought he was coming this weekend."

"Ah," she said. So Zar had duped Liam into this trip. They *were* being set up.

"It's cool, though," Liam said. "It's a beautiful spot."

She raised a hand to shield her face from the low sun. The lake was almost deserted now. No more dogs or kids or empty nesters.

"You look worried," Liam said.

She laughed. "Sorry."

"Are you thinking about the guy who's been following you?" Then, reluctantly: "Your ex?"

She shook her head. "No one's following me. My brain is just going to weird places today."

He shrugged. "It's a creepy idea. I'd be worried, too."

"No one's following me," she said again. "Hey, does this remind you of anything? This trip? Like . . . a movie? A type of movie?" He looked lost. She shook her head. "I need to stop seeing everything like it's a scene."

"That's what you and Zar do, right? I guess every now and again you need to stop and find your ground."

She quite liked that. *Find your ground.* That was indeed what she needed to do. *Where is my ground?* she wondered. "You're pretty wise for a tricycle student," she said.

"Trade cycles," he said, and smiled, and was cute, in this moment, with the orange sun softening his skin, his hair matted, his silly green swimming shorts clinging to his legs. Maddie was still fuzzy from the O-gasm, not a lot, just enough to make things more fluid, and she was stretched out in a towel on a carpet of warm sand. Maybe *this* was her ground. This right here, with the water and the seabirds and the rest of the world so far away she couldn't even hear it.

Zar screamed and pelted by, her feet digging into the earth, Jorge pursuing. Both were laughing. They passed close enough to spray Maddie and Liam with sand, then vanished into the path through the woods. Soon they were swallowed by the shadows, which had become impenetrable since the sun had dipped below the tree line.

Liam brushed away sand. "Should we go back?"

"No," she said, speaking and deciding at the same time. She shuffled closer, moving awkwardly on her elbows. Then she was against him. She tipped back her head. His lips were soft and tentative. It was a kind of kiss she hadn't experienced in so long, she'd forgotten it existed: exploratory, reverent. She had become accustomed to late-relationship Trent kisses, which were perfunctory, or else demanding. *Oh, my*, she thought. She hadn't intended for this to be anything—hadn't any plans beyond the moment—but that was rapidly changing. She might actually do more of this. His fingers brushed her shoulder, and the sensation was electric. She smiled, but that broke it, her silly stretched lips.

She took the opportunity to push herself up on her arms and look both ways to make sure they weren't scandalizing any impressionable lake-goers. To her right was empty gleaming sand. To her left, at the edge of the woods, stood a man.

She sat bolt upright. The man disappeared. It was dark; he'd been a hundred yards away. But he'd been watching, she was sure.

Liam sat up, twisting to follow her gaze. "What is it?"

Just a random person at the lake, she thought. *Not the same guy. People come and go; there's nothing unusual about a man stopping to—*

"Did you see something? Was it the guy who's been following you?"

"No," she said, although she wasn't a hundred percent sure. "I don't know."

Liam's eyes searched hers. "Let's go back to the house."

He stood and offered her his hand. She took it, feeling bad about this, as if she really were a teenager again. *You can't lead a boy on,* they had believed back then: If you got a boy excited, you were responsible for what happened next. *They get blue balls,* a girlfriend had told her during a sleepover, in complete seriousness. She still remembered the girl's somber face. *It's like a serious medical condition.* She wanted to go back in time and shake that girl, and herself, until they gained some sense.

The path was steep, slipperier than it had been earlier. Liam toggled his phone light and still she couldn't see more than twenty feet into the woods. On the way down, she had delighted in the isolation, but there was another aspect to that, she was appreciating now: There was no one around to help you.

A light bobbed toward them. "Is that you guys?" came Zar's voice. Maddie called back, full of relief, but when Zar stepped into the light, her expression was flat and scared. "What color was the car you saw? With the man inside?"

"Light blue."

Zar took her hand. "I think he was here."

What? Maddie tried to say, but the word didn't go anywhere. Zar began to lead them up the hill.

"We came up the path and he was backing out. Like he didn't realize there was a house at the end of the drive. We didn't get a good look at him, the lights were in our eyes, but it was a big dude, with a thick beard. Is that the guy?"

"Yes," Maddie said. Something had settled badly in her gut. Something she had carried with her, maybe, but maybe not: She was starting to think that this was less a case of carrying her fear and more a case of being rightfully terrified that someone was after her.

The house appeared in bright, cheery slices through the trees. Inside, Zar and Maddie went to the gray sofa. "You want me to call the police?" Zar said.

Another super situation: A cop looking at her while she explained, *I saw a man, and then I think I saw him again, and my friend saw a man and maybe he was the same one?* But that was better than huddling here as the night closed in, hoping she was wrong. She nodded.

Zar fetched her phone. "Hello," she said, her voice calm and measured. Zar was good with voice; it was an underrated part of acting. "We have a little situation here." As she began to explain, every word made Maddie feel better. *We have a little situation.* Yes. That was what it was. They were informing the police. All of that was fine and reasonable.

There were thumps on the front steps and Jorge clattered inside, his hair wild, eyes wide. Zar covered the phone. "Did you find him?"

Jorge shook his head. "Who are you talking to?"

"The cops."

"You called the cops?"

"Shh," said Zar. She spoke to the phone again, then put it down. "They're sending someone around."

"Thank you," Maddie said.

Zar nodded. "Crazy bearded stalkers following you from the city? We can't have that."

"You saw a beard?" Jorge said. "I didn't see a beard." He walked to the kitchen, retrieved a beer, and opened it. A bottle cap fell somewhere.

"You didn't see a beard?" Zar said. "I saw a beard."

Jorge set down his bottle and went into the hallway. When he returned, he had a blue baseball bat. "For if he comes back." He flipped it left and right.

"You're about to break something," Zar said.

"I'm going to go see if he's out there."

"*No*," said Zar. "The cops will show and you'll be waving a bat around in the dark. Sit down."

Jorge dropped into a chair, the bat across his thighs.

"Let's just chill. This is not the time for you to go acting the hero. Look how freaked out she is." She flapped a hand at Maddie.

"It *is* like a movie," Liam said suddenly. "It's . . ." He trailed off, embarrassed.

"What?" said Zar.

Liam shook his head. "Just something we were talking about earlier."

Zar looked from Liam to Maddie. "What's like a movie?"

"This is," Maddie said. "Four people go to the lake and there's a psycho."

"Oh, shit," said Jorge. "A slasher pic!"

"Do you mind?" said Zar. "Shame on you. And you, Liam."

"Sorry," Liam said, and he did look shamefaced.

"No more of this talk. Have some sympathy for my girl."

"It's fine," Maddie said. The movie talk was her fault, after all; she had brought it with her from Brooklyn. And better to have it out; it sounded less plausible from other people's lips. It sounded as ridiculous as it was. In real life, people weren't pursued by random psychopaths they didn't know. They weren't chased and killed for no reason.

"We'll play Boggle or something," Zar said. "Don't tell me there isn't a cupboard filled with puzzles and shit in here."

We'll play Truth or Dare, Maddie thought helplessly. *Or a drinking game or strip poker. Then we'll split up to explore and—*

"We have Parcheesi," Jorge said, rising from the chair. His eyes shifted over Maddie's head and froze.

She turned. Beyond the glass was the empty porch, the Jeep parked sideways on a patch of scrubby grass, trees moving in the night. Nothing else.

"I just saw him," Jorge said. "The fucker is out there."

He sprang to the door and wrenched it open. Zar cried out. Maddie heard Jorge's footsteps pound across the porch, then a thump as if he'd leaped the railing and landed on the grass. Zar ran outside, Liam followed, and all of a sudden Maddie was alone on the sofa. She went after the others and found Zar leaning over the porch railing. Liam was on the grass. Jorge was nowhere. In the trees, she heard crashing and breaking of twigs.

"Liam!" Jorge roared from somewhere in the dark. "Liam, I got him!"

Maddie didn't call him back, didn't say anything at all, and Liam ran into the darkness, and she should have tried to stop him, she thought. But events were moving on a track, beyond her control, like frames in a film. Liam called Jorge's name. Then someone cried out, a male voice, but belonging to whom, Jorge or Liam or a third person, Maddie couldn't tell. The noises quieted, becoming a rustling.

"Jorge?" Zar called. "Liam?" She threw a helpless look to Maddie. But Maddie was no help; she was stuck in the frames.

The rustling is the man walking toward us. He steps out of the darkness, holding something, an ax or a knife. He is no one I know, but still, he wants to kill me.

Liam emerged from the trees. Flushed with relief, Maddie started down the porch steps. But by the time she passed the Jeep, she could see that something was wrong. His head was tilted. He was holding his neck. There was a darkness splashed across his chest, stomach, and shorts. He was bleeding, she saw. He was bleeding everywhere.

Behind him, in the woods, the crack of breaking twigs.

"Run," Liam croaked.

Fear spiked her limbs. The Jeep was right beside her, unlocked, most likely, but the keys could be anywhere: on a countertop, in a drawer, on a shelf beside the conch shell, wherever Jorge had left them, even in his pockets, in the dark. The house was bright and tempting, but she had seen that movie, the one where the girl cowered in the tasteful bathroom, trying not to whimper, as the killer moved about the house, trying doors one by one, and as Zar clattered down the steps, Maddie caught her hand and pulled her in the opposite direction, away from the trees, away from the sounds, from Liam, toward the road.

A branch reached out and brushed her cheek. Zar was screaming, a raw, animalistic noise of fear, and some part of Maddie's brain tucked this away for future reference: *This is what real fear sounds like.* She stumbled over something unseen, and Zar hissed, "Go," as if Maddie were hesitating, as if she'd been about to say, *I think we should go back for Liam,* and she had not; she had definitely not; she was very, very much being a coward on that score. She ran with Zar until they broke onto paved road, where the trees parted to permit starlight. A hundred yards ahead stood a yellow streetlight. There were mailboxes and driveways, and were there people at the end? She couldn't be sure.

"Go," Zar said again, tugging her up the road.

She had the idea that Zar was thinking of the police. There was only one road: If the police were on their way, they would meet. The road curved uphill. She began to tire. Her teeth chattered.

"Come *on*," Zar said. She was fitter than Maddie, apparently. "We have to keep going."

She could see all the way back to the first streetlight. The road was clear. She should have been able to see anyone chasing them. Maybe she could go back to Liam.

"Come on," Zar said, pulling at her. "Come on, come on, come on."

They reached the main road. She saw two cars pass by, one after the other, and Zar hollered and waved her arms and gave a shriek of frustration when they didn't stop. She chased them down the road. Maddie went after her, her lungs burning. After a few minutes, Zar began to glow, and Maddie turned to see headlights blooming. They stopped and waved, but the car only moved to the opposite side of the road and flew by.

Maddie took Zar's hand. They were playing it wrong, she realized. For a car to stop, Maddie had to be *Regular Young Woman in Need of Some Assistance*, not what she and Zar had played thus far, which was something like *Crazed Female Drug Addict Wants to Attack Your Vehicle*. When the next car approached, she pulled Zar to the side of the road. She paused and raised one arm, adopting what she hoped was a plausible mix of entreaty and embarrassment.

The car slowed and stopped twenty feet ahead. Zar gave an exhalation like a sob and began to run toward it, but Maddie held her back, because *Regular Young Woman* had no motivation to run. They reached the passenger door. A horrible thought flashed across Maddie's mind: At the wheel would be the bearded man. But the car was not light blue and the driver was not bearded. He was perfectly regular-looking: young, surprised, wearing long pants and a button-up shirt. He peered at them. "Are you guys okay?"

"Not really," she said, and was relieved at the timbre of her voice, which was steady and not too full of panic. "Do you mind giving us a ride?"

"Where to?"

She didn't know the name of the next town. She pointed the way the car was going. "That way." He looked unsure, so she added, "We're really cold."

That part didn't require acting; they were both shaking. The guy nodded. There was something on the passenger seat, some kind of crate, but that was fine; she wanted to sit in the back with Zar anyway. She pulled open the door and piled inside. The guy checked his mirrors. She wanted to tell him to drive, please, go, but *Regular Young Woman* had no motivation to say that. Zar turned in her seat to stare out the rear window.

"Seat belts on, thanks," said the guy.

"Oh," Maddie said. "Yes." She nudged Zar, who started. "Seat belt." Zar's fingers were shaking so badly that Maddie had to help her. "It's okay," she murmured. "We're okay."

The car pulled out. "Guy trouble?" said the guy. His eyes met hers in the rearview mirror.

She nodded. "Thank you so much for picking us up."

"No problem." He looked at her again in the mirror. "Were you on the lake this afternoon? I think I saw you earlier."

"Yes," she said, although she didn't remember him. She had clocked a middle-aged couple, a family, a dog, and some teenagers. Not this guy.

"You and your boyfriend," he said. "On the sand."

This was the man she'd seen watching her from the tree line, she realized. At the time, she'd suspected it was the bearded man who'd followed her in the city. But no. Just a random dude. Watching her and Liam. "Is it possible I could use your—"

"Was that you? With your boyfriend?"

"He's not my boyfriend," she said, thrown.

"Oh. My mistake." He was silent. "So I guess you're just kind of a slut."

She felt poleaxed. Like he'd driven something through her. Not a completely unknown sensation. She was ten years old, dancing outside with her friends; a boy they encouraged to join in but instead chose to sit stewing on the grass: *Everyone could see your underpants.* Sixteen, a house party; a girl rolling her eyes: *Madison is flirting with evvv-ery-body.* Twenty-one, tottering in heels and a sparkly dress to a bar with two friends; a man old enough to be her father watching them pass: *Whores.* Each time, that feeling of being punctured. Was that where the expression came from, to *burst your bubble?* It felt that way: like a bright clean exterior dissolving in a heartbeat. It wasn't air that came out, though, but something sick and small and dirty.

She said, "What did you say?"

"I just don't think girls should act like that with a guy who isn't their boyfriend." His eyes flicked to hers in the mirror. "If you want my opinion."

A piece of her brain broke. *Now? Here?* She was fleeing for her life and Liam was badly hurt, stabbed, she thought, and Jorge as well, and this guy wanted to shame her? She glanced at Zar, but Zar was staring out the rear window, paying no attention to the conversation. The guy's eyes were assessing her in the mirror. She needed to keep her mouth shut; needed to nod and say, *Yes, you're right*, until they reached a town, with light, and people, and safety. But it was too much. It was too fucking much. "You don't know what the fuck you're talking about. Our friends have been stabbed. Someone's after us. A man. He called my apartment and followed us from the city."

"Hugo," the driver said. "You don't need to worry about him anymore. We lost him."

She froze. He knew the other man? She couldn't imagine how. Although . . .

You never saw who stabbed Liam.

Jorge had seen a face through the window. A bearded face, Maddie had assumed. But that wasn't necessarily true. Jorge could have seen this guy, the guy driving the car she was in right now. He could have stabbed them both, walked back to his car, and driven after her and Zar.

"Stop the car, please," she said.

The guy exhaled through his nostrils. "Really?"

Zar clutched at her. "No. Maddie. What are you doing?"

"I want you to stop the car," she said, using her assertive voice, which she more commonly deployed for queens and family matriarchs. Occasionally for an imperious southern lady.

"I mean, I will if you want," he said. "Are you sure?"

"No!" Zar's fingers tightened on Maddie's forearm. "Maddie, no!"

"Let us out."

"Okay," said the guy. The indicator began to flash. The car slid to the right and the tires began to chew stone. "It's your choice."

"Listen to me," Maddie told Zar, trying to untangle her fingers. "Zar. We have to go."

Zar's eyes searched hers. She didn't understand what was happening. She was scared as shit, Maddie saw. But she was going to trust her.

"I mean, it's your funeral," said the guy.

There was a soft noise: *clank*. Maddie turned. A silver tray jutted from the passenger seat. The crate she'd glimpsed earlier on the passenger seat was a box, with levels. On some of the levels lay mundane objects: hair, ribbon, earrings, a dull metal block. The guy turned and pushed a bright knife into Zar's chest as easily as if he were posting mail.

The blade came out red. Maddie screamed. Zar looked down at herself. Blood pulsed from a thin incision. Her mouth worked. She tried to cover it and blood flowed over her hands. She turned and tried to work the door handle. Her hand slipped. She looked back at the guy and then at Maddie and her eyes were full of confusion and fear but also, it seemed to Maddie, betrayal, as if Maddie had done this somehow. She tried to speak and blood burst on her lips in a fat red bubble.

The guy watched all this without expression, his body twisted around in the driver's seat. His hand with the knife rested on the dash, far out of her reach. And she had no idea who he was: He was literally a random stranger who wanted to kill for no reason, which Maddie had reminded herself only shortly before was not a thing that really happened, because people had motivations. Although, it occurred to her, maybe she had that slightly wrong. Even in movies, it wasn't that the psycho had no motivation; it was that the victims didn't understand it. They trespassed by accident, or unlocked a cellar they shouldn't have, or broke some mystic rule of which they were unaware. And maybe that wasn't unlike real life. Maybe everyone died like this, flabbergasted and outraged, thinking: *It doesn't make sense.*

She yanked at the door. The handle moved freely but the door did not open. She scrabbled for a lock and the guy watched her do it.

"*Guck,*" Zar said, a terrible, wet sound.

"So let me get this straight," the guy said. "You finally ditch Trent and the first thing you do is stick your tongue down the throat of some rando."

Somehow, he knew about Trent.

Maddie, we have to meet, the man on the phone had said. *You're in danger.*

He was right, she realized suddenly. The man with the beard (Hugo?) had been trying to protect her.

"You know, sometimes I wonder why I bother," the guy said. "I'm honestly like, maybe I should give up." He leaned forward, his eyes catching a gleam of light. "But then I remember the first time I saw you. What you're supposed to be like. And I won't let you ruin that. I won't let you disrespect her."

"Let me out of the car." She didn't sound so assertive this time. She was trying, but Zar was bleeding, her body slumping. And the door handles didn't work.

"You disgust me," he said. "You genuinely make me sick."

He was preparing to kill her. She could see it in the tension of the muscles around his neck. His eyes were full of anticipation, but the rest of his face had turned flat and hard and calculating. A sickly yellow glow seemed to spread across his skin.

The glow was headlights. A car was approaching.

She didn't dare turn. But she saw his eyes shift. The hand holding the knife moved lower, hovering between the front seats like the fang of a snake. He would let the car pass, she saw. If she moved, he would stab her, but his plan was to kill her after it had gone. Which meant she had to attack him. No matter how poor her odds, it was her only choice. But the blade was twelve inches from her gut and every part of her screamed to keep it that way, please, for just one more second, and one more second after that, please, don't do anything that might anger him.

The car drew closer. She was going to let it pass, she realized. She was going to do nothing until it was too late. She truly was a coward, too afraid to go back for Liam, and too afraid to save herself.

The headlights shifted. A high note yodeled in the approaching car's engine. The guy glanced away. In the side mirror, she saw the vehicle turning. As its lights swung away, no longer blinding her, she saw that it was a light blue sedan.

"Shit—" said the guy, and the car plowed into theirs.

GAVIN HAD A BEARD. HE SAT ACROSS THE DINING TABLE FROM FELICITY,
munching toast and reading his phone like it was nothing. Like there
wasn't an animal squatting on his face.

He glanced at her. "What?"

She could hardly see his lips. They were invisible. "Mmm?"

"Is something wrong?"

Well.

About that.

"No," she said.

"Okay," he said. He went back to his toast and phone.

You look fifty, Felicity thought. *You look like my father.* "How long
have you had the beard?"

He looked toward the ceiling. He had to think about it. It had
been that long. Whomever she'd been before this morning, it was
someone who would tolerate a beard on Gavin for so long that he
had to think about it.

"A year?" he guessed. "Why? You don't like it anymore?"

Anymore. She shrugged noncommittally.

He jutted out his chin. "I think it makes me look distinguished."

"Mmm," she said. Distinguished in the sense of being exceptionally terrible.

He stood, clearing his plate. "Did you go for a run this morning?" She looked at him blankly. "You were up early."

"I just couldn't sleep."

She had returned to the bedroom. It had been too dark to see Gavin—she hadn't noticed the monstrosity on his face—but she'd felt beneath the sheets until she located the egg. Sometime during the night, it had slipped down so that she was lying against it. She had picked it up with her pillow, not wanting to touch it, carried it to the kitchen, and put it in the freezer.

He dumped his plate and coffee mug into the sink. Crash, bang. It seemed careless to her. Almost ostentatious. She was being unfair. She was angry and upset because she was somewhere new and hadn't meant it. And if it was true, what Ken Creighton, the professor at Columbia, had told her, she'd come spinning out of the sky in her tornado house and squashed flat another Felicity. Somewhere behind her, in a place she could never visit, Cooking Gavin was waking and wondering where she was. "I have to run. Do you mind feeding Percival?"

The apartment contained one cat and one cat bowl. She had established this already. She had verified that she had a working staff login for the *Daily News*, as well as a phone and a driver's license, sporting a photo of her staring out from beneath awful bangs. She was reminded of a kids' book, *The Enchanted Wood*, where English schoolchildren visited fantastical realms like the Land of Topsy-Turvy, where people walked on their hands, or the Land of Birthdays, where it was parties all year round. Here was one: the Land of Unfortunate Hair Choices.

"I should be done by about two." He was wearing white pants and a light green polo. He was going golfing, she realized. It was Saturday, and he golfed.

"Okay," she said.

His head tilted. "What happened to your wrist?"

She looked. The skin was an angry pink. "I fell." His face showed no recognition. Her tumble from the subway platform hadn't happened here, she guessed. This Gavin had never taken her to New York–Presbyterian Hospital. They hadn't been burgled; she hadn't told him that she remembered having a second cat. She would have to figure out a lot of this kind of stuff. She added, "On the stairs."

"Looks nasty."

"It's fine," she said, which was kind of true; it was the least of her concerns.

He nodded. "See you tonight."

"Wait," she said, unable to help herself. "What do you want to do about dinner?"

He paused by the open door. "What do you mean?"

"Do you want to cook something?"

"Like what?"

"Whatever you want."

His expression suggested that this was the most ridiculous thing he'd heard in a while. "Can we just get takeout?"

She nodded. "Of course." She felt a twinge of something—grief?—even though he was back like he'd been before: an alien in the kitchen. She had only lost Cooking Gavin, whom she'd hardly known.

"I've got to go," Gavin said. "Love you."

"Love you," she said. The door clicked.

SHE BEGAN TO build a catalog of what had changed, but it became tedious and infuriating. One of her plants was gone. The bowls were on the top shelf, where Gavin kept putting them before she'd driven it into his head that they were awkward for her to reach. She kept catching sight of things that weren't quite right: books with the wrong covers, a frame with the wrong picture, a gym card that shouldn't exist at all. She felt as if she were wearing glasses that weren't her own.

She'd escaped the man who'd assaulted her in the street outside her apartment. He was back in the world she'd departed, along with Cooking Gavin. He could travel, she assumed. He would come after her. But she had some time. She just had to decide what to do with it.

She sat on the sofa and began to research Hugo Garrelly. For the first time, she read details of his crime—alleged crime, she guessed, since he had denied it. The judge called it *an act of unforgivable callousness and unmitigated evil.* Hugo's wife, thirty-five, raven-haired and pretty, had been seven months pregnant. The police had found Hugo with her body. He had stabbed her a dozen times. He denied guilt, which was a factor in his sentence: the lack of remorse. He was given life in prison.

Except you don't stay there, she thought. *Everywhere I go, you're out.*

She'd seen him coming out of the registered address of the Soft Horizon Juice Company. He might go there often. It was probably their clubhouse. She had more information this time, though; she knew Hugo was after Clay. And Clay was after Maddie. So she didn't need to hang around Hell's Kitchen hoping to stumble into him.

She typed: *Madison May.*

The first result was a black-and-white headshot against a studio background. Attractive, but it didn't do Maddie justice; there was no smile, none of the blinding authenticity of the real estate agent pic. Felicity tapped until she found herself looking at Tagline Artists Group, which offered actors and models at reasonable rates for a range of events. She found the phone number and dialed, but the office was closed. It was Saturday, she was reminded.

She scrolled through her contacts until she reached Levi Waskiewicz. She wasn't sure whether he would have the same number, would be employed at the *News*, or would even exist at all, but he answered on the third ring. In the background, she could hear the TV: some kind of sports. "Hi," she said. "Are you busy?"

"Nah. I'm just watching the French Open. Barty versus Degtiariva."

"Okay." She didn't know what that was.

"Tennis," Levi said.

"Can I ask you a favor?"

"Sure."

"Can we meet?"

"When? Now?"

"Yes."

He yawned mightily. "What's it about?"

She hadn't figured out how to answer that. "I can't say."

He was silent. Then the TV sounds vanished. "Well, you got my attention. Three Loaves in fifteen minutes?"

"Yes. Thank you."

"Not a problem. Degtiariva's dying anyway."

SHE SECURED A small table by the window. Levi arrived in a checked collared shirt under a black jacket that looked as if it had spent time rolled up in the trunk of his car. He looked craggy and weathered, but none of that was new. She explained that she was trying to locate a man named Hugo Garrelly, who was supposed to be locked up in Sing Sing, but, she suspected, was not, and Levi went outside to make some calls without asking her what it was about. Eventually he returned and dropped into his seat. "Your info is good. Garrelly's escaped from Sing Sing. The guy I spoke to was pissed as hell that I knew. It only just happened." He eyed her. "So how did you know?"

"I can't say."

"Mmm," Levi said. "Well, the way it went down is last night

Garrelly was arrested in Carmel Hamlet by local law enforcement. They book him, run his prints, and what comes back is that he's a registered guest of Sing Sing Correctional Facility. So they phone up Sing Sing and say, 'Pardon me, fellas, are you missing a felon?' And Sing Sing—this is the good part—says no. The cops say, 'Are you sure?' And Sing Sing is totally sure they have everyone accounted for, so would you bumbling country cops please fuck off. Twenty minutes later, they call Carmel back and now they're sweating bullets because they've actually gone and looked, and what do you know, they're missing Hugo Garrelly. Who, as I guess you're aware, is doing life for murder. Not the kind of guy Sing Sing wants to lose. So they tell Carmel to lock down and nobody move until they can get a truck there. But now Carmel is pissed at being talked down to, so as far as they're concerned, Garrelly goes nowhere until they're finished with him. That's where we are right now. With an epic law enforcement shitstorm building up around Carmel lockup."

"Why did Carmel arrest him in the first place?"

He nodded. "Good question. You should write crime. Because Mr. Garrelly, in his few hours of freedom, went back to his old tricks. By which I mean he stabbed the shit out of five people. Three are dead. People are going to get fired for this. Like, out of a cannon."

"He stabbed them? Are you sure?"

"That's what my source says."

"Who are the victims?"

Levi shook his head. "They're not releasing names. All young, though. Three male, two female."

"The survivors?"

"One male, one female."

Had Hugo stabbed five people? She didn't know him well enough to rule it out. But it was possible the police had it wrong: that the perpetrator was Clay, and Hugo had been trying to stop him. Hugo would be their first suspect, because he was an escaped felon with a violent record. Clay was nobody.

Two survivors. One male, one female. One could be Maddie. The other could be Clay.

Levi sipped at his coffee.

She said, "Do you want to come with me to Carmel?"

"Oh, boy," he said. "I was hoping you were going to say that."

LEVI'S CAR WAS a faded red Volvo P1800S, a two-door relic from the seventies that was all curves, with bug-eyed headlights and a smiling grille. "Excuse the mess," he said, sweeping fast-food wrappers to the floor. He turned the key. The engine buzzed like an angry lawnmower. "I don't know why I have this fucking thing. It sits in a garage five days a week."

"It's nice." She had been wondering whether Levi was still divorced—divorced here, that was—but after seeing the car, she didn't need to.

He guided them out of the city. As they were passing Eastchester, his phone rang. The screen said: BOO. Levi tapped. "Hey. I'm on speaker."

There was a pause. "Oh, hi, Levi," said Annalise from Ad Sales. "I was just calling about the . . . work files."

"I'm with Felicity Staples," Levi said. "From the newsroom."

"Hi," Felicity said.

"Oh, hi, Felicity."

Levi said, "Can we discuss later, or is it urgent?"

"It's not urgent. But . . . I was hoping to get it resolved sometime this afternoon. If that suits you."

Jesus Christ, Felicity thought.

"I don't think I'm going to get back to the city this afternoon. Can we take a rain check?"

"That's up to you."

"Let me see how we go in Carmel. I might be able to wrap things up early."

"I hope you can. Let me know."

"Will do," Levi said, and clicked off the call.

There was a short silence.

Levi cleared his throat. "Annalise is checking on some ad rates for me. She's—"

"I know you're sleeping together," Felicity said, to end this.

Levi looked shocked. "What?"

"I mean, if I didn't before, I do now."

"Because of the phone call?"

"Yes. That excruciating call."

Levi snickered. "Well, then, I'm sorry you had to hear that."

"Me, too."

"It's a little sensitive," Levi said. "Because she's, uh . . ."

"Married?"

He nodded. "That's it. She doesn't want to be. But it's difficult. I know how it can be." He glanced at her. "We should all get a drink sometime. She has such a great sense of humor. You'd love her."

Once Felicity had been in line behind Annalise at the deli and they got something wrong with her order and Annalise sighed like it was the most inconvenient thing in the world. Then, when the deli woman tried to apologize, Annalise cut her off and said, "Don't explain, just fix it."

"Sure," Felicity said.

"Or not," Levi said. He laughed. "It's fine. Annalise is kind of a bitch. But I'm okay with that. That's what I learned from the divorce. You begin a marriage with such high ideals, thinking everything should be perfect. When it's not, you throw your toys out of the crib. But then you're living in an empty apartment with kids who don't call. It was better with the toys, Felicity. Remember that."

"Wow," she said. This was more insight into Levi's personal life than she'd expected.

"Anyway," he said, changing lanes, "do I have to worry about my job? Are you making a move into crime writing?"

"I'm just trying to figure something out."

"It's addictive, you know. None of us who do this are in it for the money."

She'd heard him say that once before, in a different place. "Will Carmel let us see Garrelly, do you think?"

He shook his head. "Absolutely not, is what they'll tell us. But we'll see. I can be almost charming, when I want to be."

She smiled.

"So can you," Levi said.

HER PHONE RANG as they were emerging from forest on a thin road that curved across the surface of a wide reservoir. Gavin. He'd finished golfing, she presumed. She didn't pick up, and a minute later, listened to the voicemail.

"Hey. Look, I finished early because I thought . . ." There was a silence. "Are you okay? I'm not sure you're okay. I'm home and I don't know where you are. Call me."

They were approaching Carmel Hamlet. Levi was right beside her. She tapped out a reply to Gavin that she was fine, was working, and would call him when she could.

The Putnam County Sheriff's Department was part of an austere gray complex that looked like nothing so much as a jail, which, Felicity discovered from the signage, it also contained. In the lobby were rows of plastic chairs and a scuffed counter mounted with thick Perspex. On the wall was a faded poster of a grinning cop with his arm around a ten-year-old boy.

She followed Levi to the counter, where a middle-aged cop regarded him blankly. "I'm Levi Waskiewicz, with the New York *Daily News*. Who do I speak to about Hugo Garrelly?"

The woman turned and barked: "Julian!" A man in glasses approached. "Some media folks asking about Hugo Garrelly."

"What is it you want to know?"

"Sounds like you've had a real bad day here," Levi said. "Is everyone okay?"

"Three people aren't," said the woman. "Three people are definitely not okay."

The man frowned reproachfully. "The sheriff will be making a statement at noon, if you'd like to wait around. I'm afraid there isn't anything I can say until then."

"I heard five people injured. Three dead, two survivors?"

The man smiled painfully. "Like I said, there's nothing I can do to help you until the sheriff is ready."

"I hear you," Levi said. "You've been fielding a lot of press this morning, I bet."

"Oh, boy. You have no idea."

"Who's here? You must have seen at least one of the AAP guys. Aaron Jeffries?"

"Well . . ." said the man, and he and Levi began to discuss reporters Felicity didn't know.

She looked at the woman. "Are the other two going to make it?"

"Oh, gosh, I hope so. They're only kids."

"What were they doing up here? Visiting?"

"I couldn't say, but a lot of people come out for the lakes. Young people. They come up from the city to go swimming."

She nodded. "It's a beautiful town, from what I've seen."

"Thank you for saying so. It really is."

"Can I talk to the survivors? Or is the hospital here in Carmel not allowing visitors?"

"They're not just yet. Maybe in a day or two."

Felicity nodded. "Thank you for your time." As she and Levi walked toward the exit, she said: "The survivors are at the local hospital."

"Nicely done," he said. "That's good to know. The cops won't let us anywhere near Garrelly. But there's a guy around who owes me a favor, so I'm going to make a call."

"Everyone owes you a favor, is what I'm noticing."

"Look at you," he said. "You figured out journalism."

SHE BOUGHT A tasteless veggie wrap at the complex's café and ate it in the shade of a spindly birch tree out front while Levi worked his phone. Gavin had messaged her again, she saw. *Ok.* Just that. She chewed her sandwich.

"Get up," Levi said, coming toward her. "You want to see Garrelly? This is your chance."

He led her through the parking lot to the rear of the complex. Beside a set of red double doors idled a white bus, CORRECTION emblazoned on the side. Its rear door hung open. People from three different agencies were gathered, by Felicity's count: tan-uniformed deputies, cops in navy blue, and state troopers in dark gray and wide-brimmed hats.

From this crowd emerged a man in shorts and a flapping red shirt. He and Levi shook hands heartily. "Kadeem," Levi said, "this is my tagalong, Felicity Staples. Felicity, meet the best crime scene reporter in New York."

"Levi is incorrect," Kadeem said, shaking her hand. "I am the best crime scene reporter anywhere."

"He's good with words," Levi said, "but he's better with people, and that's what matters. One day he'll tell me his secrets."

"I have told you already. I make myself ready and allow the stories to come to me."

"Yeah, but really."

"I do not force myself on people like a used car salesman." One of the deputies told them to move back. "I am very sorry," Kadeem said, and the man nodded and returned to the bus.

"See?" Levi said. They hadn't actually moved.

Felicity said, "They're taking Hugo back to Sing Sing?"

Kadeem nodded. "Garrelly was supposed to be moved an hour ago, but there was a delay."

"What kind of delay?"

"Squabbling," Levi said. He gestured to the soup of uniforms. "Even I can see that."

"Yes. What do you already know?"

"Hugo Garrelly escapes from Sing Sing, stabs five people, gets arrested."

Kadeem shook his head. "Three stabbed only. The other two were injured in a collision with Garrelly's car. You should also know that shortly beforehand, one of the victims phoned the police to report being followed by a man who fits Garrelly's description, driving the same color of car."

Felicity said, "Who are the survivors? Madison May and Clayton Hors? Do you know those names?"

"No," Kadeem said, "but I am interested in how you came by them."

"Me, too," said Levi.

She didn't know how to answer that. Kadeem looked at Levi. Levi said, "Excuse my colleague. She doesn't know how this works. Felicity, what do you know?"

"I can't say."

"I thought we were helping each other," Kadeem said.

"We are," Levi said. "That's what we're doing. Felicity?"

The air was broken by the sound of a bolt being retracted from the red door. A corrections officer barked orders. The others began to reposition. The door swung open. Two deputies emerged. Behind them, a head taller than both, was Hugo, dressed in an orange jumpsuit. His hands were cuffed. He moved in a shuffle with his head down and shoulders slumped. Behind came two more officers, one steering Hugo with a hand on his shoulder. In a moment, they would bundle him into the bus.

"Hugo!" she shouted.

His head came up. He squinted into the crowd and saw her. He stopped.

"Move it," said an officer.

"Don't let him out of your sight," Hugo said. She didn't know who he meant. "He's here. Don't let him out of your sight!"

"*Move*," said the officer, and seized Hugo by the arm. Hugo threw it off and took a step toward Felicity, and she took a step back, even though she was thirty yards away, because it suddenly seemed he might be able to forge his way to her, tossing men aside. A corrections officer struck Hugo in the neck with a baton. A second hit his knee. Hugo went down. She lost sight of him among blue and gray uniforms. All she could see were arms and batons. Everyone was shouting: cops telling them to get back, cops shouting at Hugo, at one another.

"Forgive me, I must leave," Kadeem said.

"Felicity," Levi said, taking her arm. "We have to go."

There were guns, she realized. They retreated to the corner of the complex. She saw Hugo manhandled to the bus like a sack, like he wasn't even conscious.

Levi was staring at her. "What the hell was that?"

Don't let him out of your sight.

Who did he mean? Clay?

He's here.

"Garrelly *knew* you. How does he know you?"

The bus's horn blared, ragged and raw. It jumped forward, as if impatient.

"Okay," Levi said, sounding pissed. "You and me, we need to have a conversation. I can only tolerate being left out of the loop for so long."

The bus ran past them and she watched it go. She couldn't get Hugo's face out of her mind. He'd looked desperate. Like he'd thought everything was lost until he saw her.

Clay is here, she thought. *And so is Maddie.*

She'd come for answers to her own situation, not to get involved in a recurring murder. But it would happen again, she realized. Clayton Hors would murder Madison May.

"I need to get to the hospital," she said.

"Why is that?"

"One of the survivors is in danger."

"And how do you know that?"

"Levi, I can't explain. But we need to go."

"Felicity, if you're right, tell the police."

Excuse me, Officer, you need to protect Maddie May from Clayton Hors. He's killed her before.

She couldn't tell the police. Couldn't even tell Levi, unless she wanted him to think she'd lost her mind.

Don't let him out of your sight.

Not: *Don't let Clay get away.* Not: *Protect Maddie.* It was curiously specific.

"For fuck's sake," Levi said. "All right. Let's go."

She fell into step. "I'll tell you when I can."

"You better. Why do you think I'm in this job? I have to know everything."

THE HOSPITAL WAS close, a great beige brick perched on a hill, encased on three sides by forest. At reception, she was told that Clayton Hors had been discharged a few hours earlier, but Madison May was still in the ICU. In the elevator, she invented a story about being a relative, which she fed successfully to the nurse behind the ICU desk. She had to leave her cell phone behind and proceed alone, but she had, the nurse said, twenty minutes with Madison May in room 303.

She walked the hallway until she found it. There was a tall window in the door, through which she could see half a hospital bed. She knocked, waited, then went in.

The room was small and weirdly angled, as if whatever was next door was more important. To the left was a modest bathroom. Between the main door and the bed hung a curtain that could be used to create a privacy screen. In the bed, Maddie was asleep. Her face was a confusion of bruised and raw skin. The left side of her head had been shaved. From ear to temple wound an ugly laceration, jutting thick stitches. Two lines ran from her arm to a drip and a machine on a trolley.

I saw where you died, Felicity thought. *I attended the crime scene. I helped write an article about it.*

She sank into the chair beside the bed and tipped back her head. She was exhausted all of a sudden. She'd harbored the idea that seeing Maddie might grant some new insight into her situation, maybe even offer a clue as to how Felicity could get back to her old life. But it was what Hugo had described: a woman who had died before, and been attacked again. All it revealed was that he'd told her the truth. About this, and about all of it, most likely, including the part where there was no *back*. There was only *this*, or *next*.

You can make a life here, Hugo had said.

The blond man would catch up to her, eventually. He'd demand the egg. And she would have to give it to him, because the only alternative was to continue moving forward, from one world to the next, leaving behind a conga line of vanished Felicitys and bereaved Gavins. That was too monstrous to think about. She wouldn't see the trail of destruction she left, but it would be there, all the same.

Was this what Hugo did? And the blond man? And whoever else was traveling?

Maybe Ken Creighton, the professor at Columbia, had it wrong. He'd been theorizing. The eggs might actually allow travel in a way that didn't destroy people at all.

She hadn't yet figured it all out. *The egg lets you move*, she thought, *but you don't have to do anything special with it*. Because she'd moved in the middle of the night, in her sleep.

She *hadn't* moved when she'd wanted to, under the subway platform at 42nd and Eighth.

The timing mattered. That was the reason behind Hugo's watch alarms. Every so often—every thirty hours or so, Creighton had said—there was a twitch. A "bubble collision." And that was the moment you could move.

But there was one more step. Something else she was missing.

Creighton had mentioned an "observer effect." She hadn't understood at the time, and it was still a mystery.

Hugo, only an hour before, referring to Clay: *Don't let him out of your sight.*

The door clicked. She was almost dozing and jerked upright. A man stood by the bed. His face was bruised. Brown hair hung over a bandage. He smiled lopsidedly. "Sorry. I didn't mean to wake you."

It was Clay. For a moment she was frozen, caught between wake and sleep.

The smile began to slide from his face. "Are you all right?"

She blinked and sat up. "Sorry. Was I drooling?"

"No," he said, and this amused him, she saw; this put him at ease. He glanced at Maddie. "How's she doing?"

"Better, I think."

He nodded thoughtfully. "She's kind of . . . peaceful this way."

She had no phone; she'd had to leave it at the ICU desk. Was there a call button? Yes—but on the other side of the bed.

Run, she thought. *Get the fuck out.* There would be security somewhere. She could bring them. Possibly in time to stop Clay from doing what he wanted to do. Possibly not.

He rolled aside a trolley with a tray to reach the seat on the other side of Maddie's bed, unslung a gray backpack, and set it on the floor. This made it invisible to Felicity, which unnerved her. She didn't know what was in that bag. She worried that if she left Maddie, even for a minute, it would be too long.

Clay looked at her. That expression, the little half-smile she didn't believe, was back. "How do you know her?"

"Family friend," she lied. "We practically grew up together."

"Interesting," Clay said.

"How about you?"

He gazed at Maddie. "Honestly? I used to be in love with her."

"Oh?" Felicity said, and she had to be careful, because she couldn't let her feelings show.

He glanced at her, doing the loopy half-smile. "That's too much, isn't it? I've been told I talk too much."

"No, no," she said. She couldn't see his hands, she realized. He was leaning forward with the bag on the floor and who knew what his hands were doing. Her imagination vomited forth terrible ideas and she jolted to her feet.

Clay's eyebrows rose. There was nothing in his hands. Maddie's sheet was tucked into the side of the bed, unmolested.

To cover, she fooled with Maddie's pillow, as if it needed adjustment. Then she sat again. Clay studied her. "You know," he said, "if you don't mind, I'd appreciate a minute with Madison alone."

I bet you would.

"My husband will be back soon," she said. "We'll leave then."

His expression didn't alter. "You said you grew up with Madison?"

She nodded.

"Then she must have talked about me."

A trap. She shouldn't know Clay's name. "Sorry, who are you?"

"Clay."

"I don't remember Maddie mentioning you," she said. "Sorry."

"Right." He kept staring at her. Then he sat back. "Well, it didn't really work out between us."

"That's too bad."

"I haven't given up hope, though. I'm going to keep on trying."

Something beeped. She said, "Was that you?"

"Yeah. My watch."

"I thought it was a machine, and I should fetch someone."

"Nope."

"What time is it?"

"Three thirty-three."

"Funny time for an alarm," she said, unable to stop herself.

"I think it's busted," Clay said. "You don't have a watch?"

"No."

"You must have a phone."

"I had to leave it at the desk."

"Ah, of course," he said. "No recording devices."

You just told him you can't call for help.

She heard rustling. The unsnapping of a bag clip. "I lost so much shit in the accident, I can't even say."

"Oh?" she said, and rose to her feet, because that was almost like an invitation to come and look, wasn't it? He might believe she'd interpreted it that way. Clay was bent over his backpack. The flap was open, but she couldn't quite see what he had in there.

"The cops said anything missing must have been lost at the scene." He shook his hair. Flop, flop. "I've been hunting around for it this morning. It really pisses me off. A couple of things I could buy, but most of it was irreplaceable."

"What did you lose?" she asked, although she knew. *Moorings.* Things he carried to set the color and texture of the next world.

"Just stuff." He looked at her. "When is your husband coming?"

"Soon."

"I don't have a lot of time." He pointed to his bandage, giving her the lopsided smile. "I'm actually not supposed to be walking around at all."

"I'm sure he'll be here any minute."

The smile hung on his face. *He's figured it out,* she thought. *I'm resisting too much; he's suspicious—*

Clay flipped closed the top flap of his backpack and clipped it. He heaved it onto his shoulder and rose to his feet. "I might get a soda, then."

"Okay." She tried to keep the relief from her voice.

He paused at the door. "Want anything?"

"Yes, if you wouldn't mind." What was the most time-consuming item she could request? Food? Something that had to be cooked? Would he jump in a cab and pick up a cheeseburger?

"They have a machine at the end of the hall. Coke, Pepsi, and Soft Horizon Juice."

The last three words hit her with unexpected recognition. She was too slow to keep it from her face.

Clay released the door handle. He moved back into the room and drew the curtain behind him, the privacy screen that sealed them from outside view.

"What's your name?" he said, and all the false charm was gone.

She backed away around the bed. Her elbow hit the trolley with its plastic dinner tray. She snatched up the dinner tray and held it like a shield.

"First Hugo, now someone new?" Clay said. "Are you shitting me?"

"I don't know what you're talking about."

"I'm done taking orders from all of you. I'm not interfering with what you're doing. But you won't leave me alone!"

"I'm not with them."

"You must be. Then who are you?"

"I'm no one," she said, clutching the tray. "I just got caught up in this."

He was silent. "All right." He stepped to the side and gestured. "Then go."

She glanced down at Maddie. "What are you going to do to her?"

"What do you care?"

Good question. She didn't know Maddie. She was not here for

Maddie. But she couldn't let him murder her. She stayed where she was.

Clay's watch beeped. His jaw tightened. He reached into his backpack and pulled free a hunting knife: fat, serrated on one side, gleaming new. *A couple of things I could buy.* "Get out."

"No."

He took a step toward her. She raised the tray. "Are you stupid? You can leave! Just walk away!"

The thing was, she believed him. He didn't care about her. He wanted only to finish his business with Maddie May. She could stand aside and let him, and it would be just another one, another notch in the tally.

"No," Felicity said.

He lunged at her. She jerked the tray up. His eyes were already sliding to Maddie, and it was a trick, she realized; she genuinely didn't matter to him at all, except insofar as she stood between him and what he wanted. And now she was falling back, trying to save herself, so he would turn and execute Maddie with the efficiency of a man who'd done it before. Without thinking, she swung the tray, moving it from her own body to Maddie's.

The blade struck the tray and skittered across the plastic. She fell across the bed and Clay was all around her, the knife she didn't know where. His elbow struck her chin. She tried to cling to him so that he couldn't swing again.

He threw her to the floor. He'd lost the knife. She didn't know where it was. His expression was full of rage but also something that looked like grief. His watch was beeping. He whirled and thrust aside the curtain. He could have left through the main door, but instead he pulled open the bathroom door.

Don't let him out of your sight.

She dragged herself to her feet. There was a wetness around her thigh. That wasn't good. That couldn't be good. She staggered to the bathroom door and tried the handle, but he was holding it from the other side. Through the window, he stared back at her.

Unexpectedly, he released the handle. A plastic shower curtain swept past the window. Before she could decide whether she wanted to pursue him, the main door opened, and there were people.

"Felicity," Levi said. "Jesus. What happened?"

"He's in there," she said. "He's got a knife."

"Lie down. You're bleeding. Felicity."

A nurse opened the bathroom door and swept open the curtain. The room was empty.

"He tried to kill her," Felicity said. The nurse moved to the bed. "Is she . . ."

"She's fine," the nurse said.

"What happened?" Levi said. "Felicity, talk to me."

She was too light-headed to answer. She's fine. She's fine. Clay had gone. He had moved. Wherever he'd gone, there would be another Madison May. But here, she was fine. She was fine.

10

THERE WAS AN INTENSIVE MANHUNT FOR CLAYTON HORS IN PROGRESS,
Felicity was told by a serious-faced sheriff's deputy the following
morning. She'd been kept overnight by the hospital, and spent a lot
of time answering questions from people like this man, who read
from a small notebook with his broad-brimmed hat in his lap. "Just
to be clear," he said, "when you say he ran into the bathroom, is it
possible he really went out into the hall?"

"No," she said, and it didn't matter, because he assumed she was
confused.

She was eager to get moving. Her bag was by her bed, the egg
inside, and she was sure the blond man who'd attacked her outside
her apartment was coming for it. Clay had moved away, but the
blond man could have used the same moment to move in, and even
now be driving toward Carmel, chewing up the distance between
them.

She'd spent the early morning on her phone, grappling with the
academic paper she'd found online for Professor Creighton's oscillating bubble collisions—the bus schedule that said when people could
move. Because it had occurred to her that she'd accumulated three

data points: Hugo had pushed her off the subway platform late Tuesday afternoon; on Friday night, she had woken in a different apartment; and yesterday, Clay had disappeared just after 3:33 p.m. So she might be able to decode the bus schedule just by scanning every line until she found a sequence that fit.

At first, she hadn't been able to make it work: there was too much time between her first two data points. Then she remembered her argument with Hugo in the lobby of New York–Presbyterian Brooklyn. His watch had beeped, she recalled. That was another data point, between the first two. At last, she found four consecutive entries that lined up exactly right. She had done it. She knew where she was in the timetable. The next moment to move would be tonight, at 1:06 a.m.

The deputy asked her to remain in the local area for the next twenty-four hours. Felicity agreed, intending no such thing. When he was gone, she walked to the desk and got herself signed out. Levi had left the night before, but she could hire a car, or a rowboat, or something. As she reached the elevator, a nurse hurried up to her.

"I'm so glad I caught you," said the nurse. "She's awake."

She meant Maddie, of course. Felicity tried to make excuses, but the nurse was insistent, and escorted her to the ICU. A uniformed cop was stationed outside room 303, which was new. He nodded to Felicity and the nurse, who knocked and opened the door. Inside, Maddie was propped up by pillows. It was the first time Felicity had seen her eyes.

"Maddie," said the nurse, "this is Felicity Staples, the woman who saved you."

"Hi," Felicity said.

"I'll leave you alone," said the nurse.

Maddie was silent. Her left eye was half closed. Exactly how much of this Maddie was taking in, Felicity couldn't tell. "I didn't mean to bother you." She adjusted her bag. "I should let you rest." Still no response. Now it was awkward. She turned away.

Maddie said, "Who are you?"

She jumped a little, despite herself. "Just someone in the right place at the right time."

Maddie digested this. She *was* alert, Felicity realized. She was just trying to figure Felicity out. "They said he attacked me. But you stopped him."

She nodded. "That's right."

"Why were you in my room?"

She grimaced. "It doesn't matter. He's gone." This felt inadequate, and she groped for the door handle before Maddie could recognize it as such.

"I don't know who that man is," Maddie said. "I don't know why he wanted to kill me."

"You don't have to. You're safe. That's all that matters. I'm sorry. I have to go." She turned away again.

"I can't be safe until I understand."

Felicity stopped. Maddie's right eye, the open one, was clear and focused. Beneath the bruising was the face Felicity recognized from the real estate website, from the news articles.

"Please," Maddie said. "I need to know."

"They're going to look for him and he's never going to be found. Not by the police. Not by anyone. Ever."

"Is he dead?"

Felicity hesitated. But only one answer would be sufficient, and it was close enough, wasn't it? Clay could never return, so he was as good as dead, from Maddie's perspective. "Yes. I promise."

Maddie began to cry. She reached out her arms. Felicity leaned in awkwardly.

"Thank you," Maddie said. "Thank you, thank you."

WHEN THE ELEVATOR opened in the hospital lobby, a man rose from the seats and moved toward her. She had a moment, but it wasn't her attacker, not the blond man, but Gavin, the hirsute one. He wrapped his arms around her, warm and familiar-smelling. Even his beard on the side of her face: not so bad, in this moment. "I'm so glad you're all right," he said.

At first the car ride was silent, with Felicity, in the passenger seat, lost in her thoughts. As they crossed the low bridge out of town, though, she said, "I'm sorry I didn't reply to your messages yesterday." He shook his head like it didn't matter. But it did; she felt bad about that now. "You're a good person."

"So are you."

"Am I?" She wasn't feeling that. She felt like she was lying to him just by existing. Like she was wearing the skin of the woman he knew. How could she get past that? How could she ever tell him? Which was worse: to confess or to let him believe the lie?

"You just saved a life," Gavin said. "Of course you're a good person."

She couldn't stand the admiration in his eyes. "If you could change something about me, what would it be?"

He shrugged. "Nothing."

"If you had to."

"I'll be honest," said Bearded Gavin. "This sounds like a trap."

"I'll go first. I would change that beard."

He looked surprised. "You don't like the beard?"

"You look better without it."

"Huh," he said. "You want me to shave?"

"I'm not saying that. I just want to know what you'd change about me."

He glanced at her. "I'm serious. Nothing."

"Come on," she said, touched, but also aggravated. "There must be something."

"Nothing springs to mind."

"We're *going* to change. We'll get older. I might change my job. I might get into kickboxing."

"That would be awesome."

"I'm serious. You can't say everything is perfect, because it can't stay that way."

"That's different, though. That's growing old."

"How is it different?"

"We're doing it together."

She stared at him. She wanted to find the flaw in his logic but couldn't. "Why aren't we married?"

His eyebrows shot up. "What?"

"We've been dating, what, three years?"

"Yes."

She waited.

"What?" he said.

"Why haven't you asked me to marry you?"

"It's not the Dark Ages. You can ask me."

"I know. But why haven't you?"

"Honestly?"

"Yes. Please."

He watched the road. "I wasn't sure what you'd say."

"What?"

"I love you. But sometimes . . . I don't know. I can't tell if you're happy. If I propose, it forces the question. You'd have to choose one way or the other. And I worried you might choose the other."

She felt opened up. He glanced at her. He might be about to propose, she realized. She had, in fact, basically manufactured a moment in which he *must* propose. It was rushing toward her. And *that* was worse: That was a true nightmare, in which she betrayed him completely.

"Pull over," she said. "I don't feel right."

He guided the car into the emergency lane. She rolled out of the vehicle and bent and stuck two fingers down her throat. He came to her and rubbed her back. She stayed curled over on the side of the road as cars rushed by and it was terrible.

————

THEY ATE DINNER: Chinese takeout. No suggestion of cooking. She'd known that already, before she'd left for Carmel, that he was not Cooking Gavin. The mood was amiable but strange. They sat on the sofa and watched TV, a show she didn't even recognize, but which they watched together, apparently. Or, rather, Bearded Gavin had, with Previous Felicity. She couldn't follow it. She was trying to do what Hugo had said, trying to *make a life here*, but everything felt wrong. She was a wrong woman in a wrong apartment with a wrong man.

Is he dead? Maddie had asked, and Felicity had answered: *Yes.* It was a lie, but the only part of this that felt right. Saving Maddie had been the first unequivocally good thing Felicity had done since Hugo pushed her off the subway station.

I promise. She was dooming another Maddie. Clay was probably looking for her already, in a place Felicity couldn't see. He would surely find her again, like he'd found her before. Felicity's promise would be betrayed. And the egg would be used anyway, when the blond man or Hugo recovered it. If Creighton's theory was correct, and moving meant replacing, that would occur with or without her. And his theory might not be correct. It might be wrong.

She watched Gavin. She hardly even knew him.

On her thighs, Percival purred softly. As she stroked him, she gathered his loose hair. The show ended and they went to bed. Gavin looked at her. "Are we okay?"

"Yes." She touched his face.

"I feel like I'm losing you."

"No," she said, and kissed him, to close his eyes. It was unbearable, what she was doing, and she could only hope it was right. On her bedside table, her phone was set to vibrate shortly before one a.m. Beneath her pillow was the egg and a tuft of Percival's fur. She kissed him as if neither of these things were true.

AT FIVE-THIRTY, SHE couldn't stand it any longer and slid from the bed. In the living room, she drew back the blinds to reveal Percival nestled on the sofa. The table was the right way around. On the kitchen counter she found two ticket stubs to the opera, which she inspected with interest. She had actually never been to the opera. Hadn't cared to. But maybe she would like it. Her and Gavin, dressed to the nines, holding fancy drinks, chatting with people, at the opera.

The pantry suggested a takeout-leaning Gavin. In the bathroom, she found an assortment of female beauty products she'd never seen. She sniffed a perfume. She sifted through drawers and found no evidence of beard trimmers. There was a box of something named Maxi-HairGro, which gave her pause. Gavin had stupidly thick hair, like a child. They sometimes joked about it.

In the fridge were film-wrapped bowls of muesli on which someone (her?) had written days of the week. She took the Monday, added milk (skim), and the more she ate, the more she liked it.

Gavin hadn't stirred by six-thirty. Impatient, she found a set of running clothes at the bottom of the laundry hamper and headed down to the street. It was a fine morning, the air relatively clean and light. She was free from the blond man for at least a day or two, she figured, but she checked both directions anyway. The egg was in her running belt. In Prospect Park, near the baseball field, when no one else was near, she hopped the little fence and forged into the forest. There was a tan-colored rock the size of her head and she levered it up with a stick and hid the egg underneath.

On her way home, she walked by stores to see what was new. In a convenience store, she found a flavor of Oreos that she'd never seen in her life, Butterscotch Creams, and bought them. This is what she should have done last night, she realized. She might have already missed opportunities to gather things she wanted to preserve.

She explored the neighborhood, eating Butterscotch Cream Oreos. They were good but not amazing. She wasn't sure they were mooring quality, i.e., worth warping the fabric of space and time. Was there an item limit to moorings, she wondered, like a grocery checkout? Could she take as many things as she wanted?

She returned to her building. The lower step, which had been cracked for as long as she had lived there, was whole and unbroken. She took the stairs and unlocked the apartment and found Gavin at the kitchen sink. He was tall and handsome. His face was beard-free. His hair was fine; she didn't know why he had the HairGro.

"Did you eat my breakfast?" he said.

"Oh," she said. "I guess so. Sorry."

He rinsed a plate. He was already dressed. His suit was better. It had a better fit. Or maybe he was in slightly better shape. "Since when do you like muesli?"

"I felt like trying it."

"I had to eat toast."

"Sorry," she said. She watched him gather his keys, phone, and briefcase. At no point during this process did he look at her. As he approached, she stood on tiptoes to offer a kiss. It was like the brush of a bird's wings. "Have a good day," she said.

"You, too." The door clicked. He was gone.

Percival, ever the sensitive one, curled around her ankles. She sat to scratch behind his ears. She felt very taken aback by what had just happened.

She thought: *This Gavin doesn't love me very much.*

God knew they'd had mornings like this before, one or both rushing out the door, already mentally halfway to work, navigating each other like roommates. It might be nothing more than that.

Then again. The nicer suit, the hair regrowth product. He might have met someone. It felt like a stab to her heart, which was ridiculous; she'd only just arrived; he owed her nothing. Very possibly, she had done a terrible thing to a Gavin of her own only hours earlier. Still, it was shocking: an injury in an unexpected place.

She might be wrong. But she didn't think so. Maybe Previous Felicity had been unaware, like the frog in boiling water, because the changes in Gavin had come slowly. But she, actual Felicity, was seeing them all at once. He was cheating.

She had six Butterscotch Cream Oreos left and she ate them one after the other. Percival nosed her ribs. "*You* love me," she said, scritching his skull.

IT WAS MONDAY. She was expected at work, presumably. She didn't have to go—didn't have to do anything—but she had a few half-baked ideas, which would be easier to develop with the newsroom's resources. She packed her laptop into her bag.

The lobby was the same. The elevator smelled the same. As she approached the newsroom, the absence of the clock grew in her ears. When she stepped inside, she craned her neck to look at bare white ceiling with—maybe?—a slightly darker, uneven patch that suggested remedial work. For nearly a year, she had sat beneath that clock. It had invaded every moment. She had dreamed about it.

She set her bag on her desk, which did genuinely seem to be her desk, right down to a set of AA batteries she kept and never needed. She opened her laptop. Maddie's headshot was on the website she'd found before: Tagline Artists Group. She had an abandoned Instagram account that implied she worked in a coffee shop.

"Cute," Levi said, startling her. He peered over her shoulder. "Friend of yours?"

She closed the laptop. Levi was unchanged, as far as she could tell. Maybe some people were invariable: destined to be just who they were. "Can I ask you something?" she said, because she needed him for one of her half-baked ideas. "Do you shoot?"

"Do I shoot?" He glanced around. "Guns?"

"Yes."

"Why are you asking?"

"It's for a story," she said, which was a good answer to anything. "I need to learn to shoot." She detected reluctance in his silence, so added: "I'm thinking of getting a gun for protection."

"Oh," Levi said, "thank Christ." He pulled a chair from the adjoining desk and dropped into it. "Sorry. I do shoot, but I don't advertise it because I work for a bleeding-heart New York newspaper. What's prompted this? Everything okay?"

"I just thought I should learn."

"You should. I recommend it. I can even take you to a range and put you through your paces. Help you figure out what kind of weapon suits you."

There was a phrase she hadn't encountered before: *what kind of weapon suits you.* Something simple and deadly, she suspected. Something light, easy to carry, and fatal to Clayton Hors. "That'd be really helpful. Tonight?"

He shook his head. "Can't tonight. I'm dating twins."

She blinked. That was different. "Tomorrow?"

Levi burst out laughing. "Thank you for humoring me. Sure, tonight. I have nothing else going on."

"Okay," she said, catching up.

"There's a range in Woodhaven. Looks like a death trap from the outside, it's good. Open late Mondays, too. How's seven o'clock for you?"

"Seven's perfect."

"All right, then," he said. "I'll see you there."

THE RANGE WAS a low, wide brick building squatting beneath the elevated tracks with a single recessed door. Inside was a cramped space with fluorescent lighting and the lingering scent of oil and sweat. Levi was lounging in a brown chair with two cases stacked on his lap. The cases contained guns, she supposed. Handguns.

There was a sign-in process, which involved Felicity fitting herself into a grimy pair of goggles and earmuffs. A man in a tucked-in polo shirt took her through a short but emphatic safety briefing and had her sign a piece of paper to confirm that this had occurred. Then she and Levi entered a cavernous concrete space with dingy booths. At the other end of the space hung human-shaped targets, like laundry.

Levi unpacked a case and laid a gun on the counter, a solid black thing. "Now, ninety percent of this is learning how not to shoot anyone by accident. The rest is basically stand . . ." He shuffled his feet to shoulder width. "Sight . . ." He raised an imaginary gun and looked down the barrel. She had thought the sight of Levi with a weapon might be comical, but it wasn't. "And squeeze. Pow, pow." He lowered his hands.

"Okay," she said.

"That's it. Keep your gun locked up, keep it unloaded, and don't ever point it at anyone you don't mean to kill. If you do, squeeze and keep on squeezing. You have a model in mind?"

"Of gun?"

He nodded. "Gun, yes, that's what we're talking about."

"Then no."

"Some only hold five or six bullets. You don't want those. You want a Walther M2 or a CZ 75 with a magazine that gives you fifteen, eighteen shots."

"That sounds like a lot."

"It sounds like a lot because you're thinking it'll be like a TV show. In reality, you could miss him a whole bunch of times. But let's say you make two hits from your first six. What then?"

"He falls down?"

Levi shook his head. "Wrong. You didn't get any vital organs. He's spiking adrenaline. He's angry. He's hurt and scared. What did you shoot him with? A six-shooter?"

"No, I got a bigger gun, because I listened to my friend Levi."

"If you had a six-shooter, you'd be out. Not many shots, was it?"

"No," she said.

"So you have ten remaining. What do you do?"

"I keep squeezing."

"Right. You hit him in the chest a bunch of times. He goes down. Is it over?"

"No?"

"Good. Even if he has a fatal wound, he might not bleed out for two or three minutes, which is plenty of time for him to kill you. And he might not have a fatal wound. You put a lot of kinetic energy into his body; maybe he just lost his balance. Now he's trying to stand up. He looks like he wants to run away. What do you do?"

She squinted. "He's running away?"

"He *looks* like he wants to run away."

"Well . . ." she said.

"You squeeze," Levi said. "You already decided to kill him. Finish the job."

"But—"

"Too late. He wasn't running away. You're dead."

"Come on," she said.

"You think this doesn't happen in real life? You make the decision to kill him *before* you pull the trigger, not afterward."

"But if he wants to run away—"

"You don't know what he wants. Is he close enough to kill you? If the answer is yes, keep squeezing."

She took a breath.

"Make sense?"

"Yes, Levi," she said.

He nodded. "Now let's see you squeeze."

He showed her how to hold the Walther M2 and she lined up its black barrel with the paper target forty yards away. The first shot was much more jarring than she'd expected, jolting her arms down into her shoulders. And she did indeed miss the target. After thirty rounds, her wrists ached, her arms burned, and she was sweating around her goggles. At least she was hitting the target fairly consistently, which pleased Levi. They returned their gear and trooped out to the parking lot, where she watched him load his cases into his trunk.

"So where should I buy a gun?" she said.

He shut the trunk. "Do you have a permit?"

She shook her head.

"Well, you've got a six-month process ahead of you. You start with a permit."

"Six months?" she said, dismayed.

"New York gun laws are no joke. It's more paperwork than you can imagine."

"What if I want one sooner?"

He eyed her under the sodium lights. "Well, that's too bad."

"But people get guns all the time. How do they do that?"

"Like you'd expect. Person A has a gun. Person B wants it. They arrange a private transaction and no one's the wiser."

"How does that work?"

"I did a big story on it last year. Didn't you read it?"

"Sorry," she said.

He shook his head. "This is why no one likes the political reporters. You think you're writing about the only thing that matters."

"We don't think that."

"There are two channels. One, the dark web. Which isn't as dark as it used to be, or as popular, but it's still a thing. Two, listings sites. Legal because they're not selling anything. They're just connecting interested parties and telling them to obey their local laws. So what happens is one of these parties asks the other if they could see their way free to parting with their gun for a few extra hundred dollars and without the hassle of paperwork. And if they agree, they meet in a Walmart parking lot and it's done."

"Huh," she said.

"But don't do that. You'll get yourself into all kinds of trouble. Wait your six months and buy a piece through a licensed dealer."

She nodded. "Of course."

He was silent. "You sure everything's all right?"

She smiled, like: *What a silly question.* "Why do you ask?"

"I don't know. You seem different."

That was interesting. "Different how?"

"I'm not sure," he said. "Like you might want an illegal gun."

She laughed. "Levi, that's crazy."

"Right," he said.

BEFORE SHE LEFT, she sat in her car and used her phone to find a site just like Levi had described. She entered the details of the gun Levi had recommended, tapped the first result, and then a button that read: CONTACT SELLER. It opened up a message box right away, above two checkboxes that wanted to opt her in to promotional mailing lists. She didn't even need to verify her email. She wrote:

> *Hello, I'm interested in your gun for home protection. Can you please confirm it's still available? Thank you. Felicity S.*

It might take a while to find someone willing to skirt the law. And she would have to be careful: Anything that smelled off, she would have to abandon. She sent almost a dozen more inquiries before deciding to do the rest on her laptop from home, which had an actual keyboard. She put down her phone and reached for the ignition. A man was standing outside her window. She jumped. A noise popped out of her.

It was only Levi. She wound down the window. "You scared me."

He didn't smile. "What are you doing?"

He'd seen her phone, she realized. "That's none of your business."

"Are you in trouble?"

No, she was going to say, but his face was full of concern and she couldn't lie to him. "Levi," she said, "it's none of your business." She started the engine.

"Felicity—" She drove away before she could hear the rest of it.

AS SHE DREW closer to home, she felt uneasy. She'd figured she had a day or two before she had to start worrying about the blond man catching up with her. But she didn't know that. Now, driving through the night, it began to feel like a gamble. A stupid, reckless chance. Crawling along Fulton Street, she saw a motel, a shitty seventies red-brick disaster, and, on impulse, turned the wheel. She checked in, and, two hundred bucks lighter, sat on a garish bedspread with TV sounds coming through the wall. Then she wondered what she was doing. Because this, right here, could not be a long-term solution.

She dialed Cheating Gavin. When he answered, there was music in the background, a song that her Gavin had liked, which momentarily threw her. "Hey," he said. "What's up?"

She hadn't thought this through. She hadn't thought through any of it. "I'm going to be stuck at work all night. So don't wait up." Then she closed her eyes, because how could he react to that.

A short, surprised silence. "All right. No problem."

She waited. But that was it. "That's okay?"

"Sure."

This was Cheating Gavin, she reminded herself. It was probably a great opportunity for him. Once she was off the phone, he would dial his girlfriend, Vanessa, or Beth, or whatever her name was, she didn't want to know, and say, *Guess what? She's out for the night.*

"Just thought I'd let you know," she said.

"I appreciate it."

He was being unperturbed, a thing he did that always made her irrationally angry, because there was a time for being perturbed. And when she said she wasn't coming home for mysterious reasons, that was one of those times. He should be a little fucking perturbed. She had been trying to think of Cheating Gavin as a different person, not someone she knew, but this was very Original Gavin, and it broke her compartmentalization for a minute.

Would my Gavin have grown a beard, given the right circumstances? she wondered. *Would he have cheated?*

Potentially they were all her Gavins. Maybe the only reason this one seemed different was that he'd finally gotten tired of pretending he couldn't tell she was keeping one eye open for something better.

"Well, if things change . . ." he said. "You know where to find me."

She nodded, although, of course, he couldn't see her. She didn't think he was going to call a girlfriend. She wasn't even sure he was cheating, all of a sudden. How had she concluded that? From one rushed breakfast? She didn't know anything. "Good night," she said, and hung up.

SHE SLEPT TERRIBLY and woke with the conviction that she had to find them, Hugo and the blond man and whoever else there was. She had to negotiate an arrangement. She parked three blocks away from her building, resisted the urge to check on the egg she'd hidden in Prospect Park, and caught the train into the city. She had four replies from gun sellers on her phone, so tapped out the next part of a serial fiction in which she'd been abandoned by her boyfriend of three years and found herself unexpectedly alone, in a bad neighborhood, in which there had been break-ins. Of course she was prepared to go through the proper process for a permit, but was there any way the seller could help her feel safe now? Did they have any thoughts on that?

The Gothic tower on West 50th was edged in orange morning sun. A million years ago, in another place, she'd seen Hugo emerge from this building. She went right up to the revolving door and pushed through.

Inside was a cool lobby with a round chandelier, curving walls, and a wide desk. Two men in muted yellow uniforms regarded her. "Hello," she said, because she was aiming for directness. "I'm here for the Soft Horizon Juice Company."

"Yes, ma'am. Shall I call up for you?"

"Please. I'm Felicity Staples."

In less than a minute, the elevator chimed. The doors parted. Hugo rolled from between them like a truck. He crossed the lobby while she resisted the urge to turn and run, then glowered at her like she was a disobedient child. "Do you have it?"

"No."

"Then what are you doing here?"

"Nothing," she said, because she was startled. But she did actually have a plan. "I want to talk."

He exhaled derisively.

"I'll give it to you," she said. "But first I want to talk to your people."

He walked away. Not the reaction she'd anticipated. But when he reached the elevator, he turned and gestured. "Coming?"

She hesitated. But why else was she here? She crossed the lobby and stepped into the elevator. The doors closed. The car hummed.

"How was Sing Sing?" she said.

"I never made it there. They got me out first."

"Oh," she said. She wondered how that worked. But she had

more pressing concerns, like who she would see when the doors opened, and whether it would include the blond man. "I want to help you stop Clay," she said, in case she didn't get a chance to explain herself later. "I already did it once. When you couldn't." The elevator panel lit on 12. The doors opened. Beyond was a wood-paneled space with vases of flowers. Hugo led her to a sun-filled expanse of rich floorboards and white furniture where several people were lounging, all of them older than Felicity, all well dressed. They were conversing in low, musical tones, but broke off as she and Hugo entered.

Hugo gestured shortly. "She wants to negotiate."

The blond man was at the far end of the room. Sitting in a chair, staring at her.

An older man with glasses and thick eyebrows rose. "Fantastic," he said. "Well done, Felicity."

A woman approached her with rakishly thin arms outstretched, an awkward smile across her face. "Felicity? I'm Henrietta." She clutched Felicity's hands. "We're so glad you've come."

The blond man said, "Did she bring it?"

"No," said Hugo.

"That's fine," said Henrietta. "You've come to talk? That's wonderful. I know you've had some uncomfortable experiences." This might have been a reference to the blond man, or to Hugo, or perhaps to the entire fucking ordeal; Felicity didn't know. "Will you come this way?" She took a few steps toward a hallway. "If you wouldn't mind?"

THE HALLWAY WAS a checkerboard of black and white tiles, with sunlight streaming through glass at the very end. Henrietta closed the door behind them, reducing the conversation to a murmur. "Are you all right? Is there anything I can get you?"

"I'm fine, thank you."

Henrietta smiled quickly, in a way that left Felicity wondering whether it had happened. "You must have so many questions. I know you've spoken with Hugo, but he's not a talker. You end a conversation knowing less than when you began." She gazed at Felicity. She was around forty, Felicity thought, but it was difficult to pinpoint. "I must ask. Is the token safe?"

The egg, she presumed. "Yes."

"Nowhere it might be stumbled upon by a random passerby? I'm sorry to press. But the consequences of allowing it to fall into the wrong hands are . . ."

"Clay?"

"Yes," Henrietta said. "Exactly." She touched her chest, and for the first time, Felicity noticed her brooch: a silver circle crossed by five lines. Felicity had first seen that design on the wall of a bedroom, and then on Hugo's cap.

"So this is Soft Horizon," Felicity said. "I don't see where you make the juice."

Henrietta laughed lightly. "So much changes, you see. We need a way to identify one another on those occasions we don't all cross at the same time. And a place to rendezvous, without knowing in advance whether any particular location will exist. Soft Horizon is our little front. There is no juice."

"I heard it was a government research project."

"Oh, gosh. That was a long time ago. Only Dr. de Boer was involved with all that. He developed a technique for crossing over, but found himself in a place he didn't recognize—and couldn't go back, of course. Eventually he decided to form a group of like-minded individuals. But it's really nothing very formal. We're a loose organization of ordinary people who share a common interest."

"In what?"

Henrietta smiled ambiguously. "Come." She led Felicity to a room with a long table and a solid wall of glass. Below, traffic crawled through the skyscraper forest. Henrietta beckoned Felicity to stand by the window. "Here. What do you see?"

"Midtown," Felicity said.

"Yes. Midtown. Are you happy with it?"

"Am I happy with Midtown?"

"The homelessness? The injustice? Or would you change it, if you could?" Henrietta gazed at her. "I used to feel so helpless about the world's problems. The selfishness and ignorance. But Dr. de Boer showed me a way to make a difference. That's what brings our group together: the desire to make the world better. Our work is small—in a Multiverse with no end, believe me, we're very aware of our own insignificance. But we carry the best of what we find in each place to the next. Books. Art. There's a woman in India, whose name you won't know, who wrote a poem to her dying daughter, and her words were so beautiful, they softened the hearts of millions. They may have prevented a war. We took that poem with us. That is what we do, in a nutshell. Step by step, a little at a time, we preserve that which is valuable. And I'm proud of what we accomplished. We made kind, loving worlds."

Fire engine horns blared. Felicity glanced outside.

Henrietta sighed. "This isn't ours, of course." She moved to the table and arranged herself in a chair. "Before all this madness, moves were planned weeks in advance. Because the act of moving establishes a path. Once it is done, those behind are forced to follow. Which, in a practical sense, renders their moorings useless, or even lost. Only those at the head of the path can determine where it leads."

"Clay isn't waiting for you," Felicity said. "He's moving by himself."

"At a frenetic pace. Most of us still haven't caught up. So much has been lost. I truly wish you could see what we had done." She sighed again. "It's funny; do you know what I miss most? A perfume. I was in Paris years ago and passed a woman with the most incredible scent. I actually stopped her in the street so she could tell me what it was. God only knows what she thought of me. *Elucent.* I'd never heard of it. Because everywhere I'd been before, it didn't exist. But there, I was able to purchase a bottle. It became one of my moorings, so that everywhere I went, I would find women wearing it." She gave a short laugh. "I'm sorry to bore you with a silly story. Others are so much worse off. Dr. de Boer himself is very sick. All because of Clayton's obsession with that poor girl. He murders her, you know. Repeatedly."

"About twenty times, Hugo said."

"'About.' What a terrible word. It's twenty exactly. We made a spectacular mess with Clay. We were complacent and arrogant. And that girl is paying for it. Even now, some in our group consider him to be a lunatic who kills for no reason. To me, though, there's nothing particularly difficult to understand about a man who murders what he loves, and blames her for it. That's depressingly familiar." She flapped a hand at Felicity. "In any case, this disaster began when Clay managed to obtain a token. He wasn't chosen. He simply found himself in possession of it—much like you did, when Hugo gave you his. Which was terribly reckless, by the way, but a calculated risk to avoid it falling into Clay's hands." She glanced at her watch: a thin gold strap. She rose from the table. "I'd best consult with the others. Would you mind waiting? Then we can decide how we'd like to proceed."

"There's a man out there who attacked me," Felicity said.

Henrietta nodded. "You don't have to see him again. But I hope I've managed to explain a little about why we take this so seriously. You do seem like a lovely person, Felicity. I mean that. It's just that we've seen what can happen."

ALMOST AN HOUR later, the door opened. Henrietta greeted her and took her to the first room, with the white furniture. The blond man, as Henrietta had promised, was gone. The others introduced them-selves: The tall man was an academic, another was an engineer, and a woman was a business owner. Although these were ex-professions, Felicity gathered: things they'd done before they'd begun traveling the universe. She was given coffee and asked about her life. "Mark worked for a newspaper, once," Henrietta offered, and the tall man nodded gravely and said it was terrible, what had happened to the industry, which made Felicity feel like defending it. Throughout all this, Hugo lay draped across a chair like a coat.

"We have a plan to put a stop to Clay," Henrietta said finally, when Felicity was beginning to think the entire conversation would be small talk. "We want to initiate the next move before he does, us-ing moorings that will set a path to a world that will act as a trap. We'd be very glad if you would help us."

"I don't want to move. I want to deal with Clay here."

"That would be ideal, obviously," said the ex-newspaperman. "This would be a fallback."

"Either way, we must delay him," Henrietta said. "Clay's injuries will slow him down, we suspect, and the more time that you can buy us, the better. It might also give you time to reflect on what you'd like to do with the token, and whether you trust us sufficiently to return it. What do you think?"

She thought they probably intended to take it, no matter what she decided. But she nodded. "That works for me."

Henrietta smiled. "I'm so glad." She glanced at her watch, then stood. Felicity took the hint and set down her coffee. "I do hope we'll meet again."

HUGO WAS SILENT until they were inside the elevator. "They like you," he said, not looking at her. "They were impressed with what you did in Carmel."

"Okay," she said.

"I know you're lying, though."

"About what?"

"About not keeping the token. Just go ahead and ask to join. They won't hold it against you."

"I don't want to be in your club."

The elevator doors opened. "Sure," Hugo said.

"What happened to the person who was here before me? The other Felicity?" She stopped. "I need to know. Is she gone? Replaced? If I move, do I leave behind people wondering where I went?"

Hugo walked back and regarded her. "Yes."

All the breath went out of her. It was what she'd suspected, of course. She'd known it might be the case. But she'd wanted so badly to believe it might not be. "That's terrible," she said. "Don't you see how that's terrible?"

He shrugged. "Didn't you talk to Hen? The smart people can explain it."

"You explain it," she said.

He gestured vaguely. "It's not just one world. You need perspective."

"Which means what? A few people here and there don't count?"

"It's harder to get broken up about them."

"By that logic, what about Maddie? Do you even care that she's been murdered twenty times? Which would have been twenty-one, if I weren't there while you were off wherever."

He scowled. "You know where I was."

"Getting arrested. Not a whole lot of help when that happens, are you?"

He stared at her. "No, I don't particularly care."

It took her a moment to backtrack and find the question. "About Maddie?" She'd thought that was rhetorical. "You *don't* care?"

He leaned toward her like a falling tree. "There's an *ocean* of

Madison Mays. Clay could murder one a day for the next ten years and the next time we moved, there'd be another fucking Maddie May. That's the truth. And before you lecture me, let me ask you something: When did you figure out that moving means replacing? Not this very minute, right?"

"One move ago."

"One move ago," he said. "So it's a little late to decide you're not like the rest of us."

"I didn't ask for this," she said, but he was right, and she turned away.

"For fuck's sake," said Hugo.

"I don't want to join your club that goes around making people disappear."

He leaned against the wall beside her. "Look, I didn't mean to upset you. You don't have to cry."

"I'm not crying."

Hugo sighed, glancing around. "I didn't ask for this, either. I was a building contractor. My wife, Rosie, she was the smart one. She taught biology at Penn. One day I came home to find a bunch of people in my living room, and Rosie saying they could take us to other worlds. I didn't know what the hell she was talking about. I just went along for the ride. By the time I figured it out—what it meant—it was too late to debate ethics. And the way they explain it, these people, it makes sense. We keep moving because we can do good."

"What happened to your wife?"

He glanced away. "You don't want to hear that."

"I do."

"Someone gave away a token. It's a stupid story; you don't need the details. Bottom line, Clay bumbled his way into figuring out what it did. It became my job to get it back. Because these people, they're thinkers. They're not used to getting their hands dirty. That was fine by me. I had to earn my keep somehow, other than being the husband of the smart lady everybody liked. So I went after Clay. And . . . I screwed up. I thought he was just a dumb kid, who I could talk some sense into. I let him get away with it. Too many times." He shook his head. "That's my regret. I didn't see what he was."

The revolving door turned. They watched a middle-aged couple cross the lobby. If they were Hugo's people, he gave no sign.

"He set it up over two or three moves, collecting what he needed. Made sure he had everything to ensure things would happen a certain way. When I walked in my front door, he was standing in the hall, large as life. He ran. I chased. I followed him over a couple of fences. All of a sudden, I'm getting tased. And when I'm down, he uses a little spray bottle. Like he's spritzing a plant. That was where the cops found me. Like I was hiding out. Hiding from the cops in the corner of a neighbor's yard with her blood on me." He rested his head against the wall. "In the jail, all I wanted to know was whether they'd move without me. Because I was never the one they wanted. I had things—wedding rings, her birth certificate—things they said could work like an insurance policy, if the worst came to pass. I just needed them to come get me. It took them a few months to figure out how to do it. They had to be creative. And I figured that was it. But the insurance policy was worthless, because Clay had gotten out in front. He was setting a path, and what we brought with us made no difference. Everywhere we went, Rosie was dead, and I was the guy the cops thought killed her."

"I'm sorry," she said.

"Oh, but that's not the good part," Hugo said. "See, I still had hope. Anything not tied to a mooring can change, so I thought I might get lucky—the roulette ball might happen to drop on the right number and I'd have her back, just from dumb luck. But when the cops found her, some of Rosie's hair was missing. Clay killed her, cut her hair, and took it with him. So that everywhere I go, she's dead."

"Oh, God," Felicity said.

The elevator dinged. They glanced around.

"I'm going to work," Hugo said. "You want to help, maybe we can actually catch him."

He gestured. She walked toward the revolving door and he fell into step beside her.

11

ONE OF MADDIE'S CLASSES AT NYU WAS PERFORMANCE OF EVERYDAY
Life, which was about how you acted in little ways all the time, even
when there was no stage or camera. For example, at the coffee shop
where she worked, she was smilier and chattier. This was because of
implicit roles, said the teacher—*activator*, they were calling them
now—which provided small prompts and cues about expected
behavior. This was an interesting idea, although the main reason
Maddie was more outgoing at work was because if she wasn't, the
store owner, Alto, would call her into the rear office, where he sat
watching TV and security footage, and berate her.

"This is business of family," Alto would say. "This is what we
make. Not coffee. Family."

Maddie would nod seriously and say, *Yes, Alto*, which she supposed was another little everyday performance: *Woman Learning a
Lesson*. But one she was happy to play, because the coffee shop was
only ten minutes from her apartment, the tips were good, and NYU
didn't pay for itself.

"I wish I could show you," Alto said, clutching at his spine, "but I
have bad back, as you know. I cannot stand for more than one minute. Even that, very painful."

"Yes, Alto," she said.

"Smile." He pushed up the corners of his lips with his fingers. "See? Is not so difficult. Smile and treat like family."

"I hate my fucking family," said Zar, Maddie's coworker and also friend from NYU. They attended most of the same classes and had actually responded to the same ad, which had been posted in the hallways of Tisch Hall, a building shared by actors, dancers, and other young creative types brave and foolhardy enough to pin their futures on unlikely dreams.

"Shh," Maddie said. "You know he hates it when we swear."

"Alto should be fucking glad I don't treat our customers like I treat my fucking family," Zar said. There were regulars, for whom Maddie would also adopt slightly tailored personalities without entirely meaning to. For the two little old Jewish ladies who met at the same time every Tuesday over the same order of green tea and banana toast, Maddie was quiet and dutiful, like a favored granddaughter; for the lightly mustachioed guy who was writing some kind of book or script, she was curious; for the junkie who crept up when no one was looking, she was strict. Becoming aware of this was the point of Performance of Everyday Life: to realize there was no hard line between acting and not acting, and therefore stop trying to cross it. The result, in theory, was a more natural performance. But it was also something of a mindfuck, which occasionally made Maddie wonder who she was.

In June a woman began to show up every day, encamping at a table near the rear of the store and staying for hours. She wore sleeveless tops and had no-nonsense dirty-blond hair, often pulled back as she worked a laptop. She was writing an article, the woman said, although what kind of article required her to sit in a coffee shop for five hours a day, week after week, Maddie didn't know.

"It's a feature," the woman said. "About serial killers." She swiveled her laptop for Maddie to see. On-screen was a dude with shaggy hair and the hint of dimples. "Ever seen this guy?"

"No," Maddie said.

"If you do, run," the woman said. "He's a psychopath. I'm serious."

At this point, Maddie wasn't a hundred percent sure the woman wasn't a psychopath. But she nodded solemnly, another little Performance of Everyday Life.

"Clayton Hors," said the woman. "That's his name. Clayton Hors."

"I'll remember," Maddie said, and carried the woman's empty coffee cup back behind the counter, where Zar was loading the dishwasher. Maddie nudged her with her hip. "She's writing about serial killers," she muttered.

"Mmm?" Zar said, and straightened. They'd been trying to figure out the woman for a while. They'd invented wild backstories for most of their regulars, just to pass the time: The Jewish ladies were plotting a robbery, the screenwriter was a government spy, and so on. The woman, Maddie and Zar had decided, wasn't writing anything: She didn't type enough. And she didn't appear to be doing much research. Although that was true of everyone: A lot of people brought laptops into the coffee shop and said they were doing research of one kind or another, but whenever Maddie saw their screens, they were writing messages.

"Serial killers. That's what she said."

"Interesting," Zar said. "Maybe *she's* a serial killer."

"Interesting," Maddie said. "She pretends to study serial killers while looking for victims?"

"Exactly," Zar said. "*That's* what she's researching. Her next kill."

"Interesting," Maddie said.

"Interesting," Zar agreed.

In the second week, the woman was joined by a man. He was huge and broad-shouldered, with a rough beard and disheveled hair. Maddie leaned into Zar and pinched her leg. "Oh, my," Zar murmured. The man and the woman arranged themselves across the table from each other in poses that suggested familiarity yet wariness. This was an exciting development, and Maddie abandoned the smoothie she was preparing to hustle to the table. "Hi!" she said. "Can I get you anything?"

"This is Hugo," the woman said, and the man said, "Don't . . ." and then shook his head. The woman arched her eyebrows. "Don't what?" The man was silent. The answer, obviously, was *Don't use our real names*, which was amazing, and fit perfectly with Maddie's lurid theories. "Don't be polite?" the woman said. "Don't use my manners?" She looked at Maddie. "I'm Felicity. I'm sorry, I should have introduced myself before."

"Maddie," she said, even though it was pinned to her shirt. "Hi, Felicity. Hi, Hugo."

The man didn't respond. Instead, he glowered at Felicity and she glowered back. Maddie risked a glance at Zar, like *Are you fucking getting this*, and Zar, hunched over the coffee machine, was like *Oh my God, yes*. "What?" Felicity said finally.

"It's better not to get attached," Hugo said.

"Really?" Felicity said, then again with more emphasis: "*Really?*" She smiled at Maddie. "Could you give us a moment?"

"Sure." Maddie pocketed her notepad and returned to the counter.

"What was that?" Zar hissed.

"I don't know," she whispered. "Serious shit."

"Maddie," called Alto, from the back room.

"Not now," Zar called. "She's busy."

"Maddie."

"I'll be quick," she said. "Do *not* serve them until I get back."

She pushed through the grimy door with the gold-ish plaque that read STAFF ONLY. Alto was overflowing his chair, an unpacked sandwich spread across the desk in front of the monitors. "Maddie, what are you doing?"

"What?"

He gestured at the monitors. "You did not smile."

"Didn't I?"

"I saw you." He shook his head. "No smile."

She might have neglected the smile. It was possible she'd let it drop toward the end, when the woman pretending to write about serial killers had gotten into an argument with the mysterious man who *didn't want her to use his real name.* "I'm sorry."

"This is business of family."

"I know. I'll do better, Alto." She edged toward the door.

"You are prettier when you smile. That is what customer want to see. Not this." His face dropped into a pantomime scowl.

"Okay, Alto."

"Show me."

She paused at the door. "Excuse me?"

"Show me smile."

Oh my God, she thought. But there was a high-tension drama playing out at the rear table beside the patisserie cabinet and she was missing it, so she inhaled, doing a thing they called *finding your center,* and projected bright, open joy onto her face. BZZZT. Like that.

"Much better. Happy smile. Do that."

"Got it!" she said, easing out of the room. "Will do!" She ran back to Zar, who was using a rag to dry a glass without looking at it.

"He's a spy," Zar said. "The guy. Probably Russian."

"What? How do you know?"

"He looks Russian."

She peered at him. He could have been Russian. But also not. "He doesn't sound Russian."

"Oh, but they don't," Zar said. "The sleepers. The embedded secret agents."

The woman, Felicity, glanced in their direction. They busied themselves with cups. Then there was a rush of customers, and the man, Hugo, left. Afterward, Felicity seemed distracted and irritable. Just before the end of Maddie's shift, she rose and walked out.

The next day, both of them were back. Hugo turned his chair so that its back rested against the wall and jutted his legs sideways, at ninety degrees to Felicity. The two of them then conducted a guarded conversation that Maddie and Zar couldn't overhear from behind the counter. Felicity ordered coffees; Hugo drank water.

"Oh my God, he's telling her about his wife," Zar said, returning from wiping nearby tables.

"*What?*" Maddie hissed. She handed a customer correct change and smiled, for the security cameras.

"He just said his wife loved carrot cake."

"Loved?" she choked. "*Loved?*"

"Yes. Past tense."

This was amazing and changed everything. How, exactly, Maddie didn't know. But it demanded a recasting of Hugo, whom they'd pegged as the brooding villain of the piece.

"He's divorced," Maddie guessed. "No. Widowed."

"He's a narcissist," said Zar, who was less forgiving.

"He's learning to love again."

He's a con man, Zar messaged her later that night, while Maddie was lying alone in her double bed, thinking about installing Tinder. Outside her window, someone argued with a ride-share driver. *He scams women with his bullshit story about a dead wife.*

Yes, she said, because the rules of this game had come from improv class: You couldn't block an idea, only add to it. Never: *No.* Instead: *Yes, and.* So Hugo was a widowed Russian spy who was also learning to love again while he scammed vulnerable women. *But Felicity knows. When he least expects it, she's going to murder him to add to her collection.*

The argument outside died down, and, for a moment, it was quiet.

I'm thinking about getting on Tinder, she messaged Zar.

y are u not on already???

A good question. *Because I've only been single for 3 weeks??* she replied, which sounded like a good answer, even if it didn't completely feel like one. She and Trent had dated for twenty-two months. Logically, it made sense to take some time to figure out what kind of person she might be without him.

u been single for a year, Zar said.

SHE INSTALLED THE app the next day, using a publicity photo of herself from *A Streetcar Named Desire,* swigging directly from a bottle of whiskey, dressed sloppily in a sheer satin dressing gown, her hair a copper explosion, one eye closed. For her profile, she wrote:

Occasionally misrepresent things. Rarely touch liquor. Have always depended on the kindness of strangers.

A description of Blanche DuBois, which felt safer than writing about herself. And, maybe, would prompt some interesting conversations. She began to swipe. That was how it worked: She had to look at profiles and decide whether to right-swipe (yes) or left-swipe (no), and if both she and the dude right-swiped, then they could message each other. She was easing her way into it, though, and left-swiping everybody.

"What do you mean?" Zar said after class. They were changing in the Peabody room, which was full of racked costumes and smelled like mothballs and dry sweat. "Why would you left-swipe everybody?" She peered at Maddie's phone.

"I'm getting a feel for it."

"It doesn't work if you left-swipe everybody. The system breaks down. I thought you knew how to use social media. You're on Insta."

"Only to post pictures of houses," Maddie said. "I don't talk to anyone."

"That's another thing we have to talk about," Zar said. "Your weird obsession with houses. But one thing at a time. Here." She began to swipe. "Yes. No. No. Yes. Yes."

"Wait," Maddie said.

"You don't have to marry them. You don't even have to talk. You just drop the trash."

Her phone blooped. She stared at it. She had a message.

"There you go." Zar peered at her screen, then made a noise of disgust.

"What?"

The right-swipe was a blond boy in a baseball cap with his arms slung around two other boys. His message said: *Hey.*

"Never reply to those," Zar said. "The heys."

"Why not?"

"It never gets better." Zar began to wriggle into jeans. "You don't want to go downhill from *hey.*"

"I can't just ignore him."

"Oh, yes, you can. Trust me, there will be more."

Her phone blooped again. This time it was a Stephen, hugging a Labrador. His message also said: *Hey.*

"I see," Maddie said.

She did some right-swiping on the train home. It turned out to be fun and addictive and a decent pick-me-up, in the sense that she liked having people who wanted to talk to her. Although no one had mentioned her *Streetcar* reference yet. And several seemed to believe her photo was of her apartment. And this was the easy part, of course; it was always fun in the beginning, before anyone had to say no. Still, it felt like progress. Life progress. She was glad she was doing this.

SHE WAS APPROACHED during break. She didn't look right away because she was sitting on the back step of the store, near the dumpsters, reading a Tinder profile. Then she peered up and saw a

Knicks cap and a lopsided smile. It was a young guy with a map, a paper one, like a tourist from ancient history. "Pardon me." His face was ringed by bright sky, but she recognized him: the guy Felicity was writing an article about. The *fucking psychopath* guy. "I'm sorry to bother you—"

"Sorry, my break's over." She went inside and shut the door.

"Why are you locking door?" Alto called.

Everything in her body felt loose and electric. "Just a minute, Alto." He called again, but she ignored him and pushed into the coffee shop. It was a Tuesday, which meant no Zar, but Felicity and Hugo were camped out in their regular corner. Maddie walked to their table. "I think I saw him," she said, and she was trying not to overreact, but her voice came out high and thin, like an old recording.

Before she could clarify, Hugo bounced to his feet, his chair sliding backward. "Where?"

"Out back, but—"

He jumped the counter. His boot caught a glass jar of cookies, which flew into the wall and spilled. He hit the STAFF ONLY door and barged through it.

"Get behind me," Felicity said, seizing her arm. "Sit. Sit." She had one hand in her bag in a way that suggested she had something in there, mace or similar. She shuffled in front of Maddie, forcing her toward the wall.

A minute later, when this was beginning to feel slightly ridiculous, Hugo returned and shook his head. "Gone," he said.

"*Gone* gone?" said Felicity, which made no sense to Maddie. Hugo shrugged.

"It might not have been him," Maddie said, extracting herself.

"You did the right thing," Felicity said. "You can't take chances."

She nodded, but she was feeling foolish now. Other customers were staring. "Thank you," she said, although she wasn't sure what for. She returned behind the counter and began to clean up broken cookies.

——————

SHE MESSAGED ZAR, but even as she was explaining what had happened, it felt like a joke, an extension of the game they were playing, where customers were spies and murderers. On reflection, what were the odds that an actual serial killer would wander up to her and say hello—out back of a coffee shop where there was a reporter writing a story about him? It was too unlikely for words. So already the whole thing felt dreamlike. And she let this leak into her retelling and wound up focusing not on the Knicks-hat dude who was possibly a serial killer, but instead the over-the-top reactions of Hugo and Felicity.

"They're falling in love," Zar told Maddie on Saturday, buttering bread. They could see Felicity and Hugo in the reflection of the specials board above their heads.

"Are they?" Maddie said, and caught herself. *Yes, and.* "Of course they are."

"She isn't sure if she can trust him, but at this point, she doesn't even care anymore. She can't stop thinking about him. She wants to hand over the codes and flee to Russia."

"I thought *he* had the codes."

Zar flapped a hand. "They both have codes."

"Yes, and," she said, "he doesn't want her to come to Russia, because she'll be executed by his people."

"Mmm," Zar said. "A pickle."

"Can they *both* go on the run?"

"They'd always be looking over their shoulder."

"They could go to Venezuela. He has a house there."

"Oh, nice," Zar said.

"He's never been there. He inherited it."

"It's a beautiful house, isn't it?"

"Thank you so much," Maddie said to a woman dropping dollar

bills into the tip jar. "Yes, it's in the woods. There are deer. And a lake. It's a house on a lake. They could start a new life there."

Zar sighed. "We should write this shit down. Make our own parts." It had been a lean few months in terms of auditions. Maddie had gotten close a few times, particularly with a small part in a studio film titled *By the River Blue*, which would have been amazing, but instead went to an actress named Aria Astwell. That felt like Maddie's new normal: close, close, close. She was tiring of it.

"Hey," Zar said, nudging her.

She looked up in time to see Hugo reach out and put a hand on Felicity's. Just for a moment. Then he stood and left. Felicity gazed after him in a way that Maddie found complex and indecipherable, then opened her laptop.

"Mmm-hmm," Zar said. "This is all about second chances."

FUNNY SHE SHOULD say, because a few days later, while half-watching TV, who should pop up on her Tinder but her ex-boyfriend Trent. He'd used the same picture as his Facebook profile, one Maddie had taken herself, sneaking up on him as he sat waiting for her on the steps of the New York Public Library the previous winter. He was gazing into the distance, the low sun catching his jaw just right, casting him as relaxed and smart. It was a truly great picture. She wasn't sure how she felt about him using it to attract women. Fine, she guessed. She was fine with it.

For the fun of it, she right-swiped. Or maybe not *fun*, exactly. She was curious as to what her ex-boyfriend was up to. Only a minute later, he messaged her:

How's the dating pool?

Shallow, she replied. *You?*

Closed for the summer.

She smiled. She doubted he was having much trouble finding

dates. But that was nice of him to say. Uncharacteristically nice, almost. Potential evidence of a newfound maturity. She sent a crazy-face emoji, to which he didn't reply. That was fine, too. That was relaxed and smart, like his picture. She watched the rest of her show. While brushing her teeth, she checked the app, in case Trent had messaged her back, but he hadn't.

FINALLY, SOMEONE GOT her bio. His name was Mitch. He was twenty-two and looked like a swimwear model, so much so that she thought he might be a bot, or else catfishing. He wrote:

Streetcar, right?

She was delighted. It had been more than a week. *You're the first to get it.*

I'm named after one of the characters.

She found that odd, because the Mitch in *A Streetcar Named Desire* was not a great guy. The best that could be said about him was that, unlike the other guy, he didn't go right ahead and commit sexual assault. Maddie had questions for Tinder Mitch's parents.

Have you seen it performed?

No but I read the script. Your picture makes me want to see it.

She wasn't playing Blanche anymore, so that couldn't happen. She could invite him to a *Macbeth*, though, which she was doing in the fall. If he was a real human being.

"Oh, he's fake," Zar said, when she showed her the screen. They were grabbing lunch in the Village, a little corner café with foldout windows.

"What?" Maddie said.

"His picture is fake. No way he looks like that."

"But he wants to meet." Tinder Mitch had moved fast. And she was tempted, because of all her swipes, he was her favorite. Not just because of the profile pic, she hoped. "Why would he ask me out if he doesn't want me to know what he looks like?"

"Ten minutes prior, he'll message you asking if you're superficial and only care about looks."

"No," she said, gazing at her Mitch profile in dismay.

"He knows it might not work, but if he used his own pic, you'd have never swiped in the first place."

"That's not necessarily true," she said, although maybe it was true. She had become brutal with her swipes. There were a lot of boys and she had gotten into the habit of judging them in a split second. She sighed. Mitch had been a breath of fresh air, following guys who ran out of things to say after five messages, or had nothing to begin with. "That sucks."

"You just gotta . . ." Zar said, and trailed off. Her eyes fixed on something over Maddie's shoulder. "Look look look."

She turned. The sidewalk was full of people. Then she saw what Zar meant. Across the street were Felicity and Hugo. As she watched, Felicity raised an arm to hail a cab.

"Were they watching us?" Zar said.

"They think we're CIA," Maddie said, thinking: *Yes, and.*

"No," Zar said, "I mean, I think they were really watching us."

Felicity and Hugo climbed into a cab.

"The city's not that big," Maddie said. "You can run into people. They might think *we're* stalking *them.*"

Zar looked at her. "I didn't want to mention this. But a few days ago, I saw inside her bag. She has a gun. For real," Zar added, to Maddie's expression. "Not make-believe spy games."

"You're saying she might be . . ." She trailed off.

"I don't know. I'm just saying."

"Saying what, though?" she said.

"I don't know," Zar said again. They looked out at the street.

MITCH PINGED HER twice more during the day, but Maddie didn't reply. She tried conversations with some of her other swipes, to fill the Mitch-sized void, but they went nowhere, and Maddie grew dissatisfied and irritated, as if she were shopping for a thing and everywhere had the wrong color or make or was out of stock. She was making it hard for herself: Her attitude was bad. She was entering conversations like a pugilist, seeking openings for jabs. Eventually she forced herself to stop.

Later, while she was preparing noodles for one, Trent messaged her.

Can we meet?

She put down her spoon. That was a heck of a message.

Is that a good idea? she tapped.

I miss you.

It was a little too much to deal with while cooking, so she left her phone by the stove and ate spaghetti on the sofa, ignoring a show. When she came back, she discovered that he'd elucidated:

just coffee

and talk

I understand 100% if you say no

but but but

I'd love to see you

She could screenshot this and show it to Zar. It would be hilarious. And vindicating: a kind of triumph. But she didn't. It had been a disappointing day. She was, to tell the truth, sick of solo pasta. She wrote:

when?

IT WOULD BE the afternoon of the following Friday, on the steps of the New York Public Library, the very same place she'd snapped his profile picture. It would be coffee only. Not even sit-down coffee: coffee on the go. This, she decided, made it not a date. Even so, she knew very well what it was: backsliding. She and Trent might talk about nothing more than how to arrange the handover of T-shirts he'd left behind and it would still be wrong. She had already decided not to tell Zar.

The night before, in bed, she gave Mitch one last shot. She had zero expectations but felt the need to do it anyway, like a person might rattle a locked doorknob just one more time. *Hey*, she wrote, slightly ironically.

He responded right away. *Hey! Thought you'd disappeared!*

No, just busy.

Not too busy to meet, I hope ☺

Can we just talk?

Sure

But she could tell it wasn't going to work. Mitch was not a swimwear model with a curious mind who enjoyed online conversation. He was hiding his real face and wanted to trick her into a face-to-face. She wrote: *I'm just not really in a place to meet.*

I understand. This is fine.

I heard from my ex-boyfriend, she said, daringly. She waited but there was no response. *Meeting the ex: bad idea or terrible idea?*

TERRIBLE IDEA

She smiled. *What I figured.*

Seriously. Don't do it. He'll stand you up.

For all Trent's faults, she couldn't see him doing that. *Maybe.*

You watch. He's just screwing with you. If you go, he won't show up. Mark my words!

She wasn't sure why Tinder Mitch thought he knew her ex-boyfriend better than she did. *We'll see*, she said, because she didn't want to argue.

I mean why would you even want to go back to him?

She typed: *It's just coffee.*

Sure sure sure

Are you angry???

Disappointed. You won't meet me. But you'll meet him. It's not fair.

She was tiring of this. *Is that your real picture?*

A pause. *Does it matter?*

If you're lying to me? she wrote. *Yes. It does.*

Hahahahahahahahahahaha

The on-screen dots throbbed. He was writing something. She waited.

I'm lying to YOU?? What about you stringing me along for EIGHT DAYS when you WON'T MEET because you are NOT JUST REALLY IN THAT PLACE RIGHT NOW but you ARE. MEETING. HIM????? How am I the deceitful one in this situation Madison????????

She set her phone on her bedside table. Then she got up and went to the bathroom. She climbed back into bed with the conviction that she would not touch her phone until the morning. Because she didn't need to deal with this. But she couldn't stop thinking about it and finally rolled over and groped for her phone in the dark. There were a string of new Mitch messages, mostly in one furious clump:

I always give you a chance.

I give you so many chances.

You never give me a chance.

It's not fair.

Are you there?

Hello??????????

Then three minutes later:

I'm going to stab you in the heart.

She deleted him. Then she put down her phone and lay still. She should have reported him first, for what good that would have done. Too late, but it didn't matter; he was nobody. She would never meet him in real life. She stayed where she was. She didn't sleep for a long time and then it was fitful and frayed, like fabric worn thin.

———

ON FRIDAY, SHE left the subway on 42nd and headed for the library. A hundred yards away, she spied Trent near the place she'd taken his profile photo. He was even wearing a similar blue denim jacket. She felt a kick in her heart, maybe only familiarity, the fact that he was a known quantity and not a smiling veneer stretched over cruelty. But it was good to see him again.

She wasn't completely focused on where she was going and someone collided with her. She gasped. "Ow," she said. She twisted around but he kept walking, not even glancing back, his shoulders bunched. On his head was a blue cap.

She continued toward the library, but only a few steps later, stopped, out of breath. She touched her blouse and felt wetness. The pain was deep and strange. It occurred to her that the guy had stabbed her.

She turned. The guy was standing motionless in a river of human traffic, staring at her with fury from beneath a Knicks cap. She'd seen him once before, behind the coffee shop.

If you see him, run. He's a psychopath. I'm serious.

She managed a step and then another, but her knees buckled and she had to lean against the wall. Clayton Hors. That was his name, Felicity had said. But to Maddie, he was Tinder Mitch, the boy with the swimsuit model profile picture, who didn't want her to meet her ex.

"Trent," she croaked. As if he'd heard, on the library steps, the boy in the denim jacket stood. But as he turned, she saw he wasn't Trent after all. He wasn't anyone she knew. Trent had ghosted her, just like Mitch had prophesied. And she didn't understand, because as much as Trent had apparently changed, she couldn't imagine he'd become a person who would stand her up, unless—

but but but

sure sure sure

Unless it had never been Trent at all. Unless Clayton was Mitch *and* Trent. That was how he'd known she'd be here. He'd arranged the meeting himself.

Hands seized her. Abruptly Hugo was upon her, and Felicity, as if they really had been stalking her. They called to her, but there was a rushing in her ears that drowned them out. She saw Felicity mouth her name, *Maddie, Maddie,* her eyes huge and anguished. She felt bad, as if she'd let Felicity down in some way. Whatever Felicity's secret mission had been, whether it involved codes or Russians or something else altogether, it had failed somehow. *I'm sorry,* Maddie tried to say. The buzzing became a roaring and the street dwindled and fell away.

12

"LEAVE HER," HUGO SAID. HE YANKED AT FELICITY. MADDIE WAS A limp doll. Maddie was literally slipping through Felicity's fingers, because Hugo was dragging Felicity to her feet and steering her down the sidewalk, a hand gripping her upper arm, a fist in the small of her back.

"No," she said, trying to twist away from him. "We can—"

"She's dead."

But how could he know? They'd seen Maddie stop and turn and sag. Hugo had broken into a run. Only then had Felicity seen Clay: when it was too late. She'd run forward, digging into her bag for the weapon she'd carried for a week now and imagined using in a moment like this a thousand times, but it was useless; Hugo and Clay were already gone. There was nothing for her to do but hold Maddie until Hugo returned.

A man shouted after them. He thought they were fleeing the scene, Felicity realized. Because they were. She saw people with phones out, filming, but also a cluster of people around Maddie, including a man on his knees, gesturing for help. Which meant help was possible, maybe? "We have to go back."

"We stay, we get arrested. You want to help, help the next one."

She didn't care about the next one. She cared about Maddie on the sidewalk, whom Felicity had come to know so well during the previous three weeks that she was even following her Insta account with nothing but pictures of random architecture. She'd thought she was succeeding, keeping Maddie safe. "Let me go!"

His hand clamped on the back of her neck. "Walk."

"Stop it," she said, but he didn't. He steered her onto a crosswalk. She could scream, if she wanted to: There were people and she could make out like she was being kidnapped. They were enveloped by scaffolding. Then Hugo was steering her leftward, pulling open a glass door, leaving the street behind. They crossed a tired, white-marbled floor to an oak-paneled counter. A hotel, she realized.

"A room," Hugo said to the woman behind the counter, who told him, certainly, she would be happy to help. The air was cold and quiet. Felicity's nose began to run. She went to wipe it, but Hugo caught her hand and forced it down. He was being a jerk for no reason. He exchanged a small wad of cash for a green keycard and directions to the elevators, and steered Felicity toward them.

When the doors closed, she wrenched her arm free. "What is wrong with you?"

"Look at your hands."

She had blood on her sleeves. On her shirt, her skirt, her shoes.

"He timed it," Hugo said. "We're stuck here for two days."

She hated that he was already thinking about *next*, of moving on. She opened her mouth, but the doors slid apart and there was a man holding the hand of a young boy. Hugo stepped toward them, using his body to block Felicity and her stained skirt and sleeves from their view. The man said, "Excuse me," and Hugo didn't reply and didn't move and then the doors closed again.

Their room was on the ninth floor, a small, generic space with brown carpet and yellowing curtains. She sank to the floor at the foot of the bed. Hugo went to the bathroom and began to wash his hands. She watched his back. When he finished, his expression was calm and thoughtful, as if there were nothing wrong.

"You prick," she said.

He looked surprised. "What do you want from me?"

There was so much. "She *died*."

He was waiting, she realized; he thought she had more to say, and she couldn't do it, couldn't explain to him why his lack of reaction was terrible. She put her face in her hands and began to cry.

Hugo said, "You're getting blood on the bed."

She made a noise of pure frustration. "What is *wrong* with you?"

He looked disgusted. "Get yourself cleaned up."

"Fuck you."

"Lower your goddamn voice."

"Fuck you!" she shouted.

He moved toward her and grabbed her by the arm. She swung a fist that he let bounce off his shoulder. He manhandled her to the bathroom and shoved her inside. "Shower," he said.

He turned to leave and she attacked his back. She got a fistful of his hair and pulled. He grabbed her by the back of her shirt and dragged her off. As she went, she managed to take down the shower curtain, the rings popping one by one. She landed awkwardly on the shower floor. Hugo spun the taps. Water bubbled and burst from the outlet above her. She yelled in outrage and tried to find her feet, but she was caught up in the curtain. Cold water rained down on her, spattering on the floor, creating twisting pink rivulets that ran toward the drain.

"Stop it," Hugo said.

She didn't, because he should have done better; they both should have. Hugo seized one of her wrists and then the other and forced her against the shower wall. He held her as the water ran down them, his chest rising and falling, until she stopped trying to hurt him.

"I'm not moving again," she said. "Don't you get it? This was my chance to stop him. This was it."

"You can try again."

"I can't." She shivered.

His thumbs moved along her hands, washing them beneath the water. She tried to tug them away, because she didn't deserve his care and didn't deserve to be clean, but he was too strong, of course, and she couldn't stop him. He rubbed her hands until there was no trace of Maddie left.

He stepped back. Water ran down her, dripping from her red sleeves and skirt.

"You can," he said. He turned away and closed the bathroom door behind him.

SHE WRUNG OUT her clothes as best she could and put them back on. They were cold and sodden, but she had nothing else. When she emerged, Hugo was wedged into a chair by the curtains like a boulder. Like something that had fallen to Earth. She sensed this in her peripheral vision, because she couldn't look at him. She marched to the door.

"You can't leave," Hugo said. "If we're arrested, there's no one to help."

She turned. "What do you want me to do?"

"Stay. Until we can move."

"And then?"

"Finish what we started. Felicity, you'll spend the rest of your life wondering. You have to come with me. You don't belong here."

No, she thought. *I belong with the travelers, moving between worlds.* A part of her even believed it. She could almost convince herself that what Hugo had said was true, that it didn't matter what happened to each Previous Gavin and Previous Felicity, because those people were behind her. All she would be doing was moving. Bringing beauty. *Making worlds better, one at a time.*

"I'll stay in this room until it's time," she said. "But I'm not coming with you." He opened his mouth and she cut him off. "I'm not talking about it."

A grunt. An ambiguous grunt. A grunt that could have meant many things. But which she gathered mostly meant: *Fine, for now.*

"I'm tired," she said. "I need to sleep." He didn't say anything to this, either. She returned to the bathroom and hung her wet clothes over the rails. She wrapped herself in a robe and crawled under the bedsheets. Hugo didn't move. He would stay in that chair, she supposed. She would fall asleep and wake eight hours later to find him in the exact same position. She rolled over to put her back to him and curled her arm around a pillow, like a child.

IN THE MORNING, she watched TV. She browsed her phone. She ignored messages—the few she had, because during the three weeks she'd been guarding Maddie, she'd quit her job, not officially, but effectively, by ignoring calls and messages. She'd done plenty of things that were going to catch up with her in the near future, because they were the result of choices she'd made when nothing seemed as real as the woman in the coffee shop. There was a new message from Cheating Gavin (from *Possibly* Cheating Gavin), time-stamped late the previous night, that read simply "?", and didn't that say everything about the state of their relationship: that lone, tired question mark. She had effectively quit Gavin, too.

Despite this, she felt strangely optimistic. For the first time in weeks, she no longer had to fear Clay. That anxiety had filled her every waking moment, and its absence made her realize how crushing it had been. And despite the wreckage of her life, there was something exciting about the opportunity to reset—to place new words on a blank page. She had no history here, which meant she was free to make her own future.

When night fell, Hugo suggested going out. Felicity was surprised, but also eager to escape, so didn't argue. They rode the elevator to the lobby and exited onto the street, where the pavement was dark and wet, the road full of starry headlights. The air felt bright and sharp. "Where do you want to eat?" she said, thinking of a place on 36th, but Hugo took her to a Vietnamese restaurant with cramped booths and dim lighting. As they ate, she found a growing feeling of peace. It would be their last meal together. In the morning, he would leave. She wouldn't be the one to stop Clayton Hors. But no one else would have to pay for her decisions.

"I'll never know whether you get him, will I?" she said.

Hugo shook his head.

"But you will get him. We held him up here long enough. The others would have been ready for him."

"That's my guess."

"They can't, you know, let him off with a warning, because he's one of you."

"He's never been one of us."

"You know what I mean."

"Felicity," he said, "we're on the same page."

She nodded. She was just anxious. He was right about that: She would always wonder.

He was gazing at her. "Felicity . . ."

"How do you know this place?" she asked, because he was about to turn the conversation, she could see it.

He sighed. "Rosie and I used to come here."

Safer ground. "You'll be able to find her again now? If Clay is gone?"

"I can try."

"You can move to somewhere she's alive, once Clay is no longer setting the path with . . ." *Your dead wife's hair.* "His moorings."

He shook his head. "Moorings fix things in place. They can't create something you don't already have."

She blinked. "So how will you find her?"

"Without Clay, there's a chance that any place I go might be the one." He shrugged again. "So I'll move and I'll hope."

The candlelight flickered. "What kind of a chance?" He didn't answer. "One in ten? One in a thousand?" She hesitated. "One in a million?"

"A chance," Hugo said.

She didn't know what to say. He might search for years. He might search forever.

Hugo glanced at his watch. "Are you done? I want to show you something."

He led her to the back of the restaurant and pushed through a door. In the narrow hallway, he filled the entire space, blocking out light. He tested the doorknob on the left, which turned, admitting them to a gloomy . . . staircase? Hallway? She couldn't tell.

"Do you have your bag?" he asked.

"Yes," she said, and as soon as the word came out of her mouth, she realized what was happening. "Wait," she said. She heard the door close. "Wait, wait!" He had lied to her about how much time she had. She saw the faint blue glow of Hugo's wristwatch, because he had silenced the alarm, of course. The twitch wasn't tomorrow morning. It was now.

"Hold it," Hugo said, his voice rough. He pressed an object into her hands, something hard and smooth and bitterly cold. His hand enveloped hers.

"No!" she said. "No!" There was a sensation of being crushed, of her breath being scooped out of her lungs. She lost her balance in the dark and didn't know where she was.

THE DOOR OPENED. In the low light, Hugo was standing in the doorway, a silhouette; she couldn't make out his face.

"Let's go," he said.

She was still holding the egg. She was unsteady, but gathered her bag and pushed past him. She didn't wait, but walked directly through the restaurant and out onto the street. After a minute, Hugo fell into step beside her. "Leave me alone," she said.

"You couldn't stay there, Felicity. You—"

She turned and pushed him with both hands. It was like trying to shift a refrigerator. "*Leave me alone!*"

Heads turned. She began to walk and this time he didn't follow. He didn't want attention; the last thing he needed now, in a new place, was to attract police. She walked and walked and soon enough was alone. She wandered through the city like a tourist. At Battery Park, she hailed a cab. "Where to?" the driver asked, and without thinking, she said, "Home," then laughed, because of course he didn't know where that was, and neither did she.

OUTSIDE HER BUILDING, she asked the driver to wait until she'd made sure her key worked. There was a busted light in the elevator. The hallway was painted pale green instead of light blue. She eased her key into the lock, because it was almost midnight, and she knew how loud that sound could be. She slipped inside and closed the door.

A hulking shape lurked by the blinds. She sucked in her breath before recognizing it as a cat tower. A very particular model of cat tower, which she'd almost bought online a few months ago. She exhaled shakily.

Percival came bobbing across the floor. She bent and began to stroke him. Then there was a noise she hadn't heard in a long time, and at first she couldn't believe it, hadn't even been thinking about the possibility, but it was Joey, meowing, which he almost never did, and she picked him up and held him close. "Joey," she said, "Joey," and it was so stupid, but she was crying, because she'd become so used to losing things, she'd forgotten she could get them back.

SHE SLEPT ON the sofa beneath a throw rug. At five-thirty, she showered and dressed in clothes she found in the hamper. She hid her gun at the bottom of dirty laundry, wrapped in a pillowcase that never got washed. She did all this quietly, because there was a Gavin in the bedroom, she presumed. A new Gavin, whose long-term girlfriend had been silently extinguished in the night.

She couldn't think about that, so she sat at the table and began to research Maddie. She had done this so many times that she already knew where to look. First she brought up the website for Tagline Artists Group, but this time Maddie wasn't in their listings. Instead, her name and picture popped up in the client list of a Los Angeles–based talent agency, Proximate Artists. There were no records of Maddie performing in L.A., though, whereas she had definitely headlined a community theater production of *A Streetcar Named Desire*, so she still lived locally, probably in the same apartment, which Felicity had identified from previous stalking. She tried Maddie's phone number and was told by a robot the number wasn't in service. Phone numbers were a problem, Felicity had noticed. They were different a lot.

The bedroom door opened. Gavin emerged, wearing faded blue pajama pants and nothing else. No beard, Felicity was relieved to see. No fancy clothes. Nothing to suggest she was looking at a new Gavin. He rubbed his face. "Morning." He went to the fridge and pulled it open. "What time did you get up?"

"I don't know," she said. "Early."

"Did you go for a run?"

That sounded like a convenient explanation: She had risen early to go for a run. But she wasn't sure she had the physical evidence to support that. She shook her head.

He poured a glass of chilled water. "Joey's friendly this morning."

She smiled. Joey was under her chair. By his standards, this was audacious. She reached down and he nudged her wrist with his head.

Gavin came and stood behind her. "Who's that?"

"No one. It's for a story."

"She's in politics?"

Felicity shook her head. "It's a crime story."

"You're reporting crime stories?"

"Just this one."

"Huh," he said. "That makes sense, actually."

"Really?"

"You get so mad when you expose some comptroller or politician and there are no consequences. Crime, at least they sometimes go to prison." He kissed the top of her head and walked back to the kitchen. "You have to do something. You're not happy where you are. Anyway, are we doing this?"

"Doing what?"

"The shoes."

She didn't know what "the shoes" meant. "I guess," she said.

"We don't have to. I don't want to, you know, force you to make shoes."

She squinted. "Did you say 'make shoes'?"

He nodded. "Seriously, it's not mandatory. We can pull out."

She had an actor and a murderer to research. She had to figure out where they were and whether one was still a threat to the other. And then there was Hugo, whom she couldn't even think about without getting angry. Who apparently intended to drag her through worlds, whether she wanted to move or not.

She stared at him. "Okay."

"Yes?" He smiled. "I was lying. I actually really do want to make shoes with you."

"I'll make shoes." She was actually kind of interested now. "How do we . . ."

"Make shoes?"

"Yes," she said.

"I guess we'll find out," Gavin said.

IT WAS A shoe-making course—literally a class on how to make shoes—in a dusty second-floor workshop in Williamsburg. A wire-haired old man shuffled between tables, peering over his spectacles as they cut shapes from leather, cork, and rubber. There were ten other students, all of whom had a decade or more on Felicity and Gavin, causing the instructor, Herb, to refer to them as *the young man* and *the young woman*.

Her phone dinged as she was trimming her feet. At the start of the class, they had created molds by sinking their feet into shoe-boxes of pale blue alginate jelly, then fitting silicone rubber into the impression. Felicity hadn't realized she had such a haughty middle toe. She extracted the phone from her bag and the screen read: *It's done.* The sender was an unidentified number, but she could guess it was Hugo.

"Look at how the young man is holding his cutting knife," Herb said. "Very good. Pay attention, young woman. Yes, young man. Index finger along the blade. Push it straight down."

The cutting knife, Felicity thought. A strange thing to call a knife; weren't they all for cutting? But she supposed some weren't; they were for piercing, for stabbing.

"Bravo!" cried Herb, as Gavin produced a shoe-shaped cut of leather. He looked at her, delighted.

"Very good," she said. *It's done.* He could only mean one thing by that, surely.

"Want me to cut your leather?" Gavin said. "Apparently, I'm kind of a natural."

"I can cut my own shoes." That was the point of this exercise, she had gathered. To make shoes, for the simple fact of doing it yourself. Because clearly she could go out and purchase perfectly fine shoes that didn't require eighteen hours' work over three weeks and nine hundred dollars. Better shoes, even. But there was a self-sufficiency thing here. A reconnecting. Or a connecting in the first place. This must have been Gavin's idea; it was the kind of low-key excitement he enjoyed.

"I mean, you say that," Gavin said, "but you are, actually, not cutting your own shoes."

"Watch me," she said, and picked up the cutting knife.

SHE REPLIED TO Hugo with a brief but pointed message: *What does that mean?* She watched her screen bobble with the symbol that meant he was reading her message, until, maddeningly, it disappeared with no reply. She spent the next few hours getting worked up about that, finally tapping out: *What the fuck is happening?*

By nightfall he still hadn't replied. Gavin suggested a movie on the sofa and she agreed, because she needed something to help her stop thinking. An idea occurred to her. "*By the River Blue?*"

"What's that? A movie?"

"Yes."

He scrolled the TV. On her phone, Felicity found an article that suggested it hadn't been made yet: It was still in preproduction. She skimmed but saw no mention of Maddie.

"Or we could just go to bed," he said.

She felt herself flinch. "I . . . Not tonight. I have a headache," she said, like a cliché, like the dullest woman in the world. "I had fun today," she added.

"Me, too."

It was awkward and she didn't know what to do. This was a good Gavin, she felt; the closest yet to the man she remembered—although that was becoming hard to be sure about; they were blurring in her mind. Their similarities were greater than their differences. "I love you," she said, because it occurred to her that she never said it first. It was always him prompting her.

He looked at her. "I realized something about you today."

"Oh?" she said, instantly wary.

"When we were making shoes."

His expression was solemn. She said, "What did you realize?"

"You're my sole mate."

She laughed.

He put an arm around her and she curled into him. "This?" he said, nodding at a show on the TV, some kind of comedy, and she nodded and said sure, and they watched that.

THE MORNING BROUGHT a message from Hugo. She read it over and over even though it was short enough to memorize:

All good. We'll meet soon. I'll let you know.

She was glad he'd replied. But she also wanted to track him down and shake him until useful information fell out. She confined herself to a single word, *when?*, then put away the phone and forced herself not to look at it. A few hours later, it dinged with a new message:

Available now? Bring token.

"I'm going to reheat these leftovers for lunch," Gavin called from the kitchen. "You want some?"

"Um," she said. "I have to meet a friend."

"For lunch?"

"Yes." She glanced up. He was looking at her. "Actually, I'm already late." She gathered her bag and keys, feeling like a scarlet woman. "Is that all right?" she said, more aggressively than she intended.

"Sure," Gavin said.

HUGO HAD CHOSEN a coffee shop wedged between a nail salon and a laundromat on Flatbush Avenue. He was wearing a clean red shirt she hadn't seen before. He had cut his hair. She took the seat opposite, feeling slightly underdressed, since she'd run out of the apartment in chalk-pink shorts and a ratty white top. "Well?" she said.

"Want to order?" Hugo said. "I'm just having coffee."

"No," she said, but the server appeared, a dude with rolled-up sleeves. To make him go away, she ordered a sandwich. "Did you get a haircut?"

He looked surprised. "I did. Why?"

"No reason." But really, how the fuck had he found the time to do that, while she was waiting to hear what had happened to Clay.

"Do you like it?"

"It makes your ears stick out," she said. "Where's Clay?"

He smirked. Not a great look on him. Smug did not suit him. "We got him."

She refused to process this until she was certain. "What does that mean?"

"What do you think it means? He came through, they were ready. It worked just like it was supposed to. Because you and I held him up long enough in the last place."

She felt light-headed. It was what she'd wanted to hear, but now that she had, she couldn't reply, for fear of ruining it somehow.

"Every other world out there," Hugo said, "Maddie's safe, because of you."

She nodded. She ducked her head, because all of a sudden, she thought she might cry. "How did . . . what did they do to him?"

"You can hear it from them directly. They're letting you in."

She looked up.

"Thirteen minutes past eleven tomorrow morning. That's when we move. All of us. Including you. You can see it, Felicity. You can come see what the world looks like when it's not like this."

"Hugo," she said.

"I know. But if you see it for yourself, you'll change your mind. Just give it a chance, Felicity. Make an informed decision."

"I made my decision," she said. "One move ago."

He scowled. "You never met the person who was here before, and when you leave, you'll never see anyone from this place again. It doesn't *matter*."

"Is that really what you think?"

"It's the truth."

The server delivered her sandwich. She waited until he'd gone. Then she opened her bag, took out the egg, and put it on the table.

He didn't look at it. "Please," he said, and then something amazing: "I don't want to lose you."

She looked at the sandwich. This was a lot. On top of the news about Clay, it was a lot. She could feel Hugo's gaze on her like the warmth of a midday sun, and she took her time raising her eyes to meet it, because for a moment she felt untethered, as if he could pull her along in his wake simply from the sheer force of being. Drag her forward forever, never looking back.

"You don't actually make better worlds, do you?" she said, because this had been bothering her awhile, ever since the woman in the tower, Henrietta, had talked about her favorite perfume. "You don't change anything. Everything you bring with you was already there. All you do is move somewhere you like better."

Hugo was silent.

"You only make the world better for yourselves," she said.

Still no answer. He didn't try to lie, at least. There was that.

"I'm glad we stopped Clay. I'm happy you can go places where they won't always be trying to put you in prison. But I'm done." She stood and gathered her bag. "And I'm taking this sandwich."

She thought he might say something as she walked to the door. But he didn't. And she felt surprisingly okay about that. She pushed open the door and went out.

SHE TOOK HER sandwich into Prospect Park, where small children were hurling themselves around a playground. A soccer ball rolled by and she tried to kick it without standing up and missed. A boy picked it up and gave her a patronizing look. She had contemplated kids. Having her own, one day. But only in the abstract, because of what Gavin had said to her while driving back from the hospital in Carmel: *I can't tell if you're happy.* She had not been happy. But she could be, she thought. She had gained perspective. She could fix things, starting with herself.

A girl screamed with laughter and her mother told her to be quiet, she was hurting people's ears. This was real, Felicity thought. Everything around her was real, no matter how many different versions of it might be playing out in places she couldn't see.

She finished her sandwich. She was happy. She was done. She threw the napkin into the trash and began to walk home.

SHE HAD A quiet, ordinary evening with Gavin, eating in and going to bed early. In the back of her mind was a clock ticking toward eleven-thirteen a.m., the moment Hugo and the travelers would leave, but for the most part she was able to ignore it. She fell into a doze. Then she woke an indeterminate amount of time later in darkness with terror clamped around her heart. She scrabbled for the lamp. "What is it?" Gavin said.

Every other world out there, Maddie's safe, because of you.

She grabbed her phone and found Hugo's number. She pressed it to her ear and listened to it ring.

Every other world.

"What's the matter?" Gavin said. He looked around wildly, as if the room might be full of tigers.

The line clicked. "Felicity?" Hugo said.

"Is he dead?" she asked.

She heard rustling. "Felicity, it's two in the morning."

"Is Clay dead?"

"He's out of the picture. If you want me to say more, you know where to find me. Tomorrow morning, before eleven."

"I know where Maddie lives. I'm going there."

"Felicity," Hugo said, pained, "don't do that."

"Then tell me."

The silence stretched. "Look," Hugo said, his tone all wrong, and she pressed End Call. She pushed back the sheet, went to the closet, and began pulling out clothes.

"What's going on?" Gavin said. "Who's Clay?"

"I have to go."

"Where?" He looked bewildered. "What's wrong?"

She tugged on jeans, pulled herself into a sweater. She went to the bathroom and pulled dirty clothes from the hamper until she found the pillowcase with the gun inside.

"What the hell is *that?*"

"I have to go," she said again. She found her bag and keys. Percival eyed her from the sofa. Joey was a tight package beneath the chair. She saw Gavin pulling on a jacket. "No," she said. "You can't." His face was earnest and determined and she appreciated that he was doing this: that he didn't know why she was marching into the night but was on board for it. But she couldn't let him come. Gavin was just a man, who didn't know what Clay was like. "Please, please, I need you to stay." She kissed him in a way she hadn't for a while. When she reached the door, she glanced back, and he was still there, in the living room, watching her go.

13

IN MADDIE'S THIRD MONTH OF LIVING TRENT-FREE, THE KITCHEN SINK
backed up and nothing she could do would free it. She tried poking
knives down the plug hole. She made a special trip to the hardware
store and purchased a rubber plunger and worked it until her arms
ached. She made a second trip to the grocery store for industrial-
strength drain cleaner and tipped in two large capfuls of bright blue
sludge. She felt bad about that last one, because it smelled like death
and couldn't be good for the environment. Also, as it turned out, it
didn't work. She still had a sink full of scummy water.

She remembered a similar incident a summer or two ago, which
ended in Trent lying on his back, shirtless, his head stuck into the
bowels of the cupboard, doing something with pipes. What, exactly,
she couldn't say. Something involving swearing.

He had looked cute, though. On his back. With no shirt. In
the heat.

In these Trent-less times, though, Maddie was learning to be
more resourceful. She had surprised and impressed herself with
what she'd been able to accomplish with nothing more than her wits,
trips to hardware stores, and YouTube searches. When the globe had

blown in the bedroom three weeks ago, she had not phoned Trent, even though it was a deeply strange contraption that for the longest time refused to budge from its socket. She had not phoned him when the ancient SeaBreeze 2000 air-conditioning unit gave up the ghost two weeks earlier. She had phoned the super, though, as that one was beyond her powers. The super had promised to swing by in the morning and turned up at two in the afternoon, the literal moment she closed the bathroom door after hours of uncomfortable postponement, and he listened to her tale of woe (*It was making a weird noise for a while and then it just stopped*) with a skeptical air, like she couldn't be trusted to diagnose anything about an air-conditioning unit, not even whether it was working. She disliked dealing with the super for exactly this reason. But then he hadn't been able to fix it, either, and, beyond her wildest dreams, she wound up getting a replacement. She was enjoying freshly cooled air right now from a sleek white unit that had undulating fins and no damp smell.

She pulled open the kitchen cupboard and peered inside. The feature of this arrangement was a thick plastic pipe that curved dramatically before disappearing into the wall. It made a U shape, she decided. That was called a P-trap. She vaguely recollected Trent dismantling this. He'd used a bucket. That was how you cleared a blockage: You removed the P-trap part of the pipe and cleaned out whatever was crudding it up.

This was enough for a YouTube search. Her first three videos said it was a simple job that could be performed at home. They also said she might be able to remove the pipe by hand, with no tools, which turned out to be untrue. "But it's much easier this way," said a bespectacled man who reminded her a little of her father, before the stroke. The man raised a wrench and smiled, like, of course you would use a wrench, so pop down to your basement and grab one. Maddie did not have a basement. She did not have a wrench. But she had a credit card, a local hardware store, and a thirst for self-sufficiency. She watched the video all the way to the end, in case there were more tools that a person about to grapple with a P-trap might need. But aside from a bucket, which she did own, that seemed to be it.

She walked the three blocks to Ace Hardware, a cream brick building with a red awning that looked like it could do with a little home maintenance itself. Behind the counter was a little man with a huge mustache, who had been there every time she'd been in. "Back again! What do you need this time?"

"Wrench," she said, like no big deal, she was always buying wrenches.

"Against the back wall."

There was a wide variety of wrenches. It was a small store but big on wrenches. Most of the tools didn't resemble the one she'd seen the bespectacled man use in the video. Finally she stumbled upon it—it was an *adjustable* wrench; that was the key—and took it to the front of the store.

The man gazed at it unhappily. "Why you want this?"

"I'm fixing a sink," she said. "A P-trap."

He shook his head. "These are no good. Fall apart. Wait here." He raised the counter and disappeared into the aisle. When he returned, he was carrying a wrench she hadn't seen before. It was bigger, with a black grip on the handle. "Take this. For you, same price."

"Oh, thank you so much."

He nodded and rang it up: thirteen dollars and forty cents, with tax. "It is good," the man said. "A girl using tools."

"You bet," she said.

SHE WAS NOT prepared for the volume of water. She had her bucket, a dinky green thing that she occasionally used for panic clothes washing, and had carefully positioned it beneath the P-trap. But as soon as she worked the pipe loose, it vomited forth brown fluid, splashing her. The stench was overpowering. She tried to angle the bucket, but not very successfully, because the space was so cramped. She reached for her emergency towels and tried to stop the brine from slopping across the kitchen floor.

She had almost quarantined the kitchen when her phone rang. It was balanced on the kitchen counter and she wasn't going to answer it, but the screen said NEIL FOREST, and Neil was her agent, her L.A. one, with whom she'd signed six months ago, after he attended an off-off-Broadway play she was doing at the last minute because a production of *A Streetcar Named Desire* had lost funding immediately after casting her and collapsed. Neil worked at Proximate Artists and was by far Maddie's best chance at ever being cast in anything substantial. This was the third time he had ever called her.

She dried her hands on her sopping towel, tapped, and wedged the phone beneath her chin. "Hello?"

"Stop what you're doing."

Water was attempting to sneak under her fridge. She went after it with the towel.

"Have you stopped?"

"Yes," she lied, because she didn't want to have to move a fridge.

"Your life is about to change."

Now she stopped. Water oozed beneath her fridge. The way The Dream went, you busted your ass in two-bit productions for years and felt like you were making no progress, until, all of a sudden, with no warning, it happened. You received The Call.

"So there's a Calvin Anderson film," Neil said. "Family pic with Warners. *By the River Blue.* You remember we had you audition for the part of the youngest sister a few months back?"

"Of course. They cast Aria Astwell." Maddie and Aria had sat across from each other in the hallway. Aria had smiled at her briefly but otherwise remained very focused and determined in a way that had slightly gotten into Maddie's head.

"Very talented actor," Neil said. "Got a hell of a career ahead of her, once she gets out of traction."

"Pardon me?"

"Aria fell off a horse. Totally fucked up her spine. She's looking at six months of physical therapy. Maddie, they want you. You have to get to Los Angeles. As in, immediately. There's a gathering tomorrow night with Calvin and I want you there." He paused. "Are you there?"

She was on the floor, wetness soaking into her pants. "Yes." The word came out with no air.

Neil laughed. "My assistant, Yvonne, will call you back in fifteen minutes with flight details. When she does, be ready to leave."

"Okay," she said.

"Are you all right?"

She was sitting in filth. The smell alone was enough to bring her to tears. "Yes."

"Great," Neil said. "Now get moving."

SHE THREW THREE changes of clothes and toiletries into a gym bag and conducted the world's fastest shower. When she was pulling on a shirt, her phone trilled. "Hello, Maddie? It's Yvonne, Neil's assistant. How are you?"

"I'm great," she said. "I'm excited."

"So am I," said Yvonne, although Maddie had never met her. "We've all been rooting for you. It's wonderful news." Meaning Maddie getting the part, Maddie presumed. Not Aria Astwell falling off a horse. "Are you almost ready to go?"

"I'm ready right now."

"Oh, wonderful. There's a car waiting for you downstairs. Can you head on down?"

She opened her front door and glanced back at the apartment. No one had better break in and use the sink while she was gone. The P-trap was on the floor, beside her wrench.

"The driver will take you to Newark. I've sent you the confirmation number for the flight. We'll have someone meet you at LAX. I've booked you into the Waldorf Astoria Beverly Hills on Wilshire; I hope that's all right."

"That sounds great." She wondered who was paying for this.

"If you have any questions, give me a call. Anytime."

"Thank you, Yvonne."

"You're very welcome. Enjoy it."

"I will."

"Really," Yvonne said. "Soak it in. Everything you've worked for is coming true." The last word was garbled because Maddie was stepping into the elevator and she wasn't sure she'd heard it correctly. The doors closed and the call disappeared. She put her phone into her pocket. When she exited onto the street, a black Town Car was double-parked, the passenger window down, the driver leaning across to peer at her. "Madison May?" When she nodded, he sprang out and hurried around the car to open the door for her.

She slid into cool air. "Thank you so much."

"Very welcome, ma'am." He shut the door.

AT THE GATE, she had a moment. She was sitting against the wall with her bag at her feet and her earphones in. Across the aisle, a harassed couple wrangled four children under the age of six. "Jayden," said the man, "if you don't come back here right now, God help me." Another man tried to squeeze by and Maddie lifted her legs to her chest to make room and his briefcase clonked her elbow and he grunted something that might have been an apology or might not. The thought popped into her head before she could stop it: *It won't be like this when I'm famous.*

Incredible. She had been cast in a movie for five minutes.

Power corrupts, a girl with whom she'd studied at NYU had once intoned, *and being cast in a Quentin Tarantino movie corrupts absolutely*, which was a specific reference to a classmate who had indeed been cast in a Quentin Tarantino movie and immediately turned into a giant shit. But clearly the general principle applied. Maddie was already imagining it: Herself at this gate, but wearing sunglasses and a big hat that failed to hide her face, because people were nudging each other, *Isn't that Maddie May?* And she wasn't alone, of course; there was someone with her, a friend or boyfriend, and Maddie was like, *Ugh, why do they make first-class use the same gate as the rabble? It's so tiresome*, while she signed autographs and smiled flatly for selfies, and her boyfriend was like, *Actually they don't, this is your ignorant fantasy*.

"All passengers for Flight 77 to Los Angeles, general boarding is now open," someone said, possibly a recording. "All passengers, you may now board."

She snickered and the man who had pushed past turned and stared at her. *I'm sorry*, she thought helplessly. *I'm not laughing at you. I'm just in a fairy tale.*

She joined the line and showed her phone to the flight attendant, who greeted her by name, like a VIP. She walked to the plane and it was actual red carpet. She squeezed into her crappy economy seat and she could have been at the cinema, about to watch the showing of a movie, featuring her.

SOMEWHERE DURING THEIR descent into LAX, it occurred to her that Neil had not actually said: *You've got the part*. What he'd said was: *They want you*.

She had been around long enough to realize that people wanted things all the time: Producers wanted to make scripts at studios that wanted to finance them helmed by directors who wanted to work with actors who wanted to find the free time. Despite all of this wanting, more often than not, the thing did not happen. *I want* was more like *I wish*. It was actually more like: *Probably not.*

This explained something else Maddie hadn't been clear on: why it was essential for her to fly to L.A. for a party. Neil wanted her there to lock it down. To turn the *maybe* into *yes*.

By the time she reached the driver with the MADISON MAY sign, she no longer felt like a newly discovered fairy princess. En route to the hotel, he asked her what she'd been in, and she said, "Nothing, really," which was the truth. So far, she actually hadn't done squat. She was nobody. If she were to change that, she had work to do.

NEIL CALLED THAT night, as she was eating room service on her giant bed. She was wearing a white robe. The TV was the size of a table. The curtains were open and the glass was full of spotlit palm trees. It was all exactly as you would expect.

"Maddie May," Neil said, sounding like he was in his car. "I am so sorry I didn't get to you before now. How are you? Is the room all right?"

"It's amazing."

"Fantastic. I just wanted to see if you have anything to wear for tomorrow night."

Her gym bag contained a violet fit-and-flare dress, which she had stuffed inside during her four-minute exit window. It was fun and classy, and she had previously worn it with positive results. But when she'd unpacked it onto the three-hundred-thread-count sheets in the Waldorf Astoria, it looked small and cheap, like something a student would wear. "I'm going shopping tomorrow."

"No, don't do that. Yvonne will take you to a dealer."

"A what?" she said.

"He's this hundred-year-old wizard who lives out in the Hills. He'll take care of you."

"Okay," she said, wondering what that meant, exactly.

"Yvonne will be in touch. And you and I will talk tomorrow. Get a good night's sleep. You'll need it."

Minutes later, her phone buzzed: Yvonne would meet her at eleven a.m. at an address in the Hollywood Hills. She resisted the urge to ask questions and tapped out: *Ok great! Thank you!*

She'd been planning on catching up on her messages—maybe even call a few people. But Neil was probably right: Tomorrow would be exhausting on multiple levels. She turned off the TV, finished her meal, and went to brush her teeth.

THE STREETS OF the Hollywood Hills were cracked, curved, and impossibly narrow, like driveways, their houses sunken into the earth or else hidden, fortresslike, by fences or foliage. Behind a high gate and a brutalist façade, Maddie was introduced to Lionel, who was the size of a garden gnome. "Lionel collects vintage pieces," Yvonne confided to her. Yvonne herself was eight feet tall, with impossible limbs, like a baby giraffe. "When a person is finished with a special-occasion gown, he acquires it and hides it away." *A person*, in this context, meant a celebrity, Maddie guessed. Someone who would wear a thing once.

She was measured and squeezed, then spent ninety minutes being presented with a procession of gowns beyond what she could ever afford, which Lionel fetched from a room she was forbidden to enter. "This one," he said finally, and Yvonne nodded and said yes, exactly, she couldn't agree more. It was a strapless lilac tulle gown with texture across the bodice and a floating hemline, so that the fabric wafted and moved around her as if of its own volition, as if Maddie were a princess, and also magic. "Chanel," Lionel said, and Maddie opened her mouth in dismay, because that sealed it, there was no way she could afford this. But Yvonne bent and clasped Lionel's hands and thanked him and said Lionel had saved them again, how did he do it.

Yvonne saw Maddie's face. "Do you not like it?"

She chose her words. "I'm sure it's very expensive—"

"Oh, no, that's no problem," Yvonne said, apparently mortified. "We loan you the dress."

"The flight," Maddie said. "The hotel. I don't know how—"

"Maddie," Yvonne said. "It is a small investment in you, which we have great faith will be repaid. Please, don't mention it. Enjoy the dress. Keep it as long as you like."

After the dress were shoes—silver Manolo Blahniks—and hair. There was also a pair of earrings, Yvonne said, which Neil would bring for her. By the time she returned to her hotel, it was five o'clock. She did her own makeup—that, at least, she felt competent enough to perform solo—and was waiting by the curb when a black SUV slid by with Neil inside. He was wearing a light tan jacket with a white shirt. A ridiculous hunk of gold dangled from his wrist. He was more tanned than she remembered, and more fit. "You look fantastic," he said, pulling out of the hotel. Someone honked. "You're going to kill them tonight. Oh, and before I forget. Is there a box in there? Excuse the mess." He tapped the seat compartment.

She found a box. When she opened it, she was looking at a pair of earrings. They were less jewelry than chandeliers.

"You don't get to keep these, sorry," Neil said. "They're worth more than my car."

"How do I thank you for all this?"

He switched lanes. "You don't have to thank me for anything. You earned this." The traffic thickened; Neil kicked the brakes. "Okay," he said. "So the plan is to get you in front of Calvin so you can amaze and delight him and make him remember why he loved you in the audition. But I want to tease and leave him wanting more. So it's going to be kind of an abrupt end to the night for you."

"Like Cinderella."

He laughed. "That's it exactly. You go to the ball, you make the prince fall in love, and you get the fuck out before the spell wears off. You've got it."

The traffic moved off. "But he does want me?"

"He totally wants you. They almost hired you the first time. We just need to make them feel comfortable."

She nodded. He sounded convincing. But they always did. She was not convinced.

"Now, as soon as I arrive, I'm going to get caught up in a bunch of bullshit," Neil said, "so this is my apology in advance for leaving you to fend for yourself. Circulate, meet a few people, and stay clear of Calvin Anderson until I can introduce you. Because five minutes after you two meet, I'm sending you home, which will be hard to explain if you only just got there. Make sense?"

"Yes."

"Don't be overawed. All these big names, nothing scares them more than someone like you, bright and on the rise. So don't feel like you don't belong. You do. The most important thing that's going to happen at this party is that some people will get to meet Maddie May." He glanced at her. "I'm not kidding."

"Okay," she said, but he must be, of course.

"Believe it," he said.

THE HOUSE WAS a floodlit Spanish Colonial Revival featuring tall arched windows and plenty of curving black iron. She had always liked those homes, which felt very open and friendly. The driveway was a curve of white stone around a single palm tree. As they pulled in, a valet hurried toward them. Standing nearby was a man in a casually beautiful suit with an open-necked shirt and a woman in a glimmering lilac slip dress and, dear God, she recognized the man.

She had seen his films. It had felt unbecoming to ask Neil who would be at the party—who these *big names* were, exactly—and so she had not. Which was just as well, because if she'd known this man was among them, she might have thrown herself from the car.

The door popped open. "Thank you," she told the valet, concentrating on landing her newly heeled feet on the driveway.

"I've got it!" cried a second valet, jogging toward her. "This is mine!" The first valet turned. There was some kind of valet standoff. Then the first valet walked away and the new one smiled at Maddie triumphantly. There was a strange excitement about him. "Welcome to the party."

"Thank you."

"I'm a huge fan," he said. "A really huge fan."

This was so unexpected that she simply stared. Before she could say anything intelligent (*From what, exactly?*), he bounced around the car, climbed into the driver's seat, threw her one more admiring look, and drove away.

When she looked around, Neil was standing beside the incredibly famous actor and his wife. All three of them were staring at her.

"You set that up," said the actor.

"I fucking did not," said Neil.

"You *must* have set that up."

"I swear, I had nothing to do with it."

"You're Maddie," said the woman, and clasped Maddie's hand. "I'm Hannah. So lovely to meet you."

"Thank you, I'm so excited to be here," Maddie said, which would be her go-to line tonight; she had decided in the car.

"Chris," said the actor, as if she didn't know; as if anyone in the world, anywhere, would not know. He stuck out his hand.

She shook it like a child, like someone who had never shaken a hand before. "Hello," she said, because she had already used her line and forgotten the rest of the English language.

"I didn't even know anyone would be standing here," Neil said. "How could I have set it up?"

"I don't know," said the actor, "but you did it, you rat bastard."

They walked toward the house, Neil and Chris—could she call him Chris?—leading, Maddie and Hannah behind. She didn't actually know whose house it was. She had never asked. "Do you live in L.A.?" asked Hannah, and Maddie explained that, no, she had just flown in. "That's very wise," Hannah said. "Everyone who moves here wants to move away." They ascended marble steps. Hannah lifted her slip dress to keep the hem above the ground. *Like royalty*, Maddie thought. Beyond a wide double door was a high, airy lobby with a terra-cotta floor and an iron staircase curling around to a mezzanine. A dozen or so guests milled about, patrolled by servers. To Maddie's left was another, cozier room, which was also bustling.

"So Hannah and I are standing there like fools, trying to discover where her coat went," said the actor, using his performing voice, which projected throughout the lobby. Already he was drawing a crowd. "But none of the valets will look at us. Not one! We are *invisible*. Then I see Neil's car careening toward us, and I think, 'Ah, at last, a chance to corner one of these gentlemen.' Sure enough, as he pulls up, not one but *two* valets rush to his assistance. Two! 'Excuse me,' I say . . ." A joker in the audience interjected, which Chris acknowledged but did not allow to interrupt the flow of the story. "'Excuse me,' I say, 'but I wonder if I might . . .' They're paying me no attention at all. Because they are, I realize, *fighting* over which of them will have the honor of holding open the door for—no, no, not for Neil, God help us. This is a *true* story! For Neil's *companion*, an entirely charming young woman by the name of Maddie May, who is, for those unaware"—his voice dropped to a conspiratorial murmur—"rumored to be on the brink of her first role in a major theatrical production." Here he gestured to Maddie with a flourish that she'd once seen him do on-screen in reference to an object of critical plot importance. There were polite cheers, some scattered applause, which he raised a hand to silence. "Once Maddie is safely escorted from the vehicle, I seize my chance to try again with the valet. 'Excuse me,' I say. But *still* he won't look at me. His eyes are *fixed* on Ms. May. And I hear him tell her: '*I'm such a huge fan.*'"

The audience roared with laughter. She was momentarily besieged by people touching her arms.

"It is the end!" Chris cried. "My star doth wane!"

People introduced themselves. She tried to remember names: *Benji is Big, Wilma has Wild hair, Peta (Pitta?) is Pretty and Pale.* She accepted a thin champagne flute. People asked if Chris's story was true, and Maddie said the valet hadn't actually snubbed him, nor been that fawning—although that last part was modesty, since the valet had seemed genuinely starstruck, for reasons that were beyond her. "Is it Calvin's?" a man asked her. "The film you're doing?" She said she hoped so and the man nodded and said Calvin was amazing, she was getting the best possible start. This was true, Maddie thought. She was getting the best possible start. She circulated for the next thirty minutes and at no point was she left alone or required to tell people who she was. She carried her champagne flute but didn't drink from it, because if she became any more light-headed, she might float away.

The adjoining room contained a white fireplace, white sofas, and, at the very end, a collection of thronelike armchairs. Perched on one was a woman who had once played the queen of England with such ferocity that it reframed everything Maddie had thought she knew about acting. The woman glanced at Maddie and then away, before Maddie gained the wit to stop gaping.

"Look at her," said a woman she'd been chatting to. "She spotted Julie." The woman laughed and touched Maddie's arm. "It's fine."

She tried to compose herself. "She's practically why I became an actor."

"Oh," said the woman, glancing at the man beside her.

"You know what they say," said the man. "Never meet your idols." The woman gave him a look and he raised his hands. "I'm kidding. Julie is lovely. Do you want to meet her?"

She did. So badly. "I mean . . ."

"Just enjoy the night," said the woman, which Maddie found to be ambiguous. Enjoy it by meeting Julie or by not?

"Here," said the man, and took Maddie by the hand. The woman said his name, not in a good way. He and Maddie crossed the room to the throne chairs, where the woman Maddie had once watched on a loop for hours had her elbow on her knee, her chin on one hand, leaning forward to listen to another woman. She didn't look in Maddie's direction until the woman was done, and that was good, Maddie thought: respectful and also commanding. When she did turn, she executed a small tug of the lip and the barest lift of an eyebrow that was so perfect and mesmerizing that Maddie stared into her face to unlock its secrets.

"Sorry for interrupting," said the man. "I wonder if I could introduce you ladies to Maddie May, who, it turns out, is an actor because of you, Julie."

There was a small pause, during which Julie's expression changed in ways that Maddie would need to study to be able to categorize. "Is that so?"

"Yes!" she said, too earnestly. "Your Victoria was such an inspiration to me. I wore out the tape studying you."

Julie glanced at her friend, then back at Maddie. "I'd have thought you were too young for tapes."

"Disk, I guess," Maddie said. It probably hadn't been a disk, either. She hadn't meant it literally.

Julie gazed at her a moment longer. She was inserting a beat, Maddie realized. A deliberate pause to grant weight to a situation and allow the audience to digest its meaning. Maddie had the feeling that the meaning was: *This girl is something of an idiot.* "So kind of you to say," Julie said, her lips twitching into a smile that was polite yet dismissive.

Maddie and the man returned to the group. The woman was staring at him with open hostility. "Why did you do that?"

"Do what?"

"You know what."

"Hey," said the man. "Welcome to Hollywood, honey. The sooner you get used to it, the better."

"Can you not?" said the woman. "For like five fucking minutes?" She placed her champagne glass onto the tray of a hovering server and extended a hand to Maddie. "I need to powder my nose. Come?"

Maddie had felt okay, but by the time they reached the bathroom, she was shaking. The woman—whose name was Keira, if Maddie recalled correctly, Keen-eyed Keira—snapped open her bag and began to touch up her makeup. There were two ornate mirrors, each with its own sink, beneath a grand chandelier. "You good?"

"Yes." She placed her hands on the sink and breathed for a minute.

"Don't let it bother you. Her only purpose for existing is to make other people miserable."

Maddie nodded.

"Take a minute," Keira said. "Or five. We'll go out together."

"Thank you," she said, truly grateful for Kind Keira. She looked at herself in the mirror. She *was* okay. Every fairy tale had a wicked queen. "I'm fine."

"Sure?"

"Yes," she said, and she was.

NEIL WAS BY the fireplace with Calvin Anderson, the director. He beckoned. "Where have you been? I've been trying to find you all night." This panicked her momentarily before she realized this was a lie for Calvin Anderson.

"I've been making new friends."

"Well, I have one more for you. Maddie, you must remember the smartest director of our generation, Calvin Anderson."

Calvin extended his hand, which she shook. His grip was firm and warm. Behind his glasses, his eyes were a calm, deep brown. "It's good to see you again."

"Fuck, it's bad luck what happened to that girl you cast," Neil said. "Fell off her horse, I heard?"

Calvin shook his head slowly. "She didn't fall off a horse. She was attacked."

"You're shitting me."

"Someone broke into her house in the middle of the night. It's horrible. The horse story is a cover because she doesn't want pap photos of her face. Honestly, she's barely recognizable."

"Jesus, that's obscene," Neil said. "Who would do something like that?"

"I assumed it was you," Calvin said, and Neil roared with laughter.

"Well, everything happens for a reason," Neil said, glancing at his watch. "Maddie, I know you have to run in a few minutes, but would you mind holding my drink while I run to the little boys' room?"

"Sure," she said, accepting his glass. She smiled awkwardly at Calvin. "I'm sorry about Aria. She would have been really good."

Calvin nodded but didn't say anything. She began to panic a little.

"I really love the part," she said. "Clara. Since the audition, I honestly haven't stopped thinking about it."

He eyed her. "I'll be honest. I felt there was something calculated about your performance."

"Oh, interesting," she said, dying inside.

"When I watched you, I didn't feel Clara, who acts first and thinks later. I saw someone who was always a little aware of what she's doing."

She nodded. She did not have the part. There it was.

"I'm sure you'll have an incredible career," Calvin said. "There are roles for an actor like you. But I don't think this is one of them."

Ideas ran through her head. *Show him how impulsive you can be. Scream. Yell. Throw the glass into the fireplace.* Without turning, she could feel the imposing presence of Julie, probably glowering at her from her throne, or else ignoring her entirely; either way, Maddie could march over there and whack her with a cushion, like the pillow scene from the film.

No. No no no. She was being superficial. *Dig deeper,* they said at NYU. Even when you were doing well: *Good, now dig deeper.* She would impress no one with histrionics.

Start with what's real.

She said, "I think you're right. I wanted the part so much, I brought that self-awareness into the room." She raised her glass and sipped, to buy time, before realizing it was Neil's, and whiskey. "Interesting," she said again. She straightened and leaned forward. Lips parted, just a little. "So are you two gonna do it?"

This was a line from the script, which she'd performed in front of Calvin Anderson two months before. But he was right: She'd been self-conscious. She'd spent so long preparing—she'd written *diary entries* from the perspective of Clara Appleseed, the fearless and free-spirited youngest daughter of a dysfunctional family, who wanted nothing more in the world than to be with her older sisters always and forever. And all that was in her mind as she walked into the audition. She hadn't been inside Clara. She had been hovering outside, observing.

For a moment, Calvin didn't say anything. He wasn't Calvin, though. He was her older sister, Mabel. They were alone in the bedroom they'd shared as children.

"I haven't decided yet," Calvin said. "I might."

"Roy said you were lazy."

"What?"

"He said you were lazy. In bed. That's what he said."

"*Excuse* me?"

"*I'm* not lazy," Maddie said, and she wasn't bragging, not really; she was just proud of herself. "I do everything. Even . . ."

"What?" Calvin said. "No. Don't tell me."

"I want to tell you."

"Stop it."

"It's when he takes his thing," she said, "and . . ." She made a gesture, tipping back her head, raising her hand. In her head she was inspecting a prize dog at a show, checking it for lift and form, because, really, Clara had no idea about sex.

"*Mom!*" Calvin shouted.

She jumped, turned. But there was no one there, of course, except party guests, watching silently. Chris, the actor, began to applaud first, driving his hands together in great thunderclaps. Maddie turned back to Calvin, flustered, like always when she came out of someone else's head. For the first time, he didn't look like her presence was a mild inconvenience.

"That was better," he said.

"I leave you alone for five minutes," said Neil, materializing, "and you put on some kind of show. Maddie, are you not late for your event?"

"Oh," she said. "I'm sorry—"

"Calvin understands," Neil said. "We'll put you two together again soon enough, if he wants."

"A pleasure to meet you," Calvin said, and shook her hand, and people moved in, wanting to talk, but Neil put a hand in the small of her back and steered her between them like some kind of vessel, a ship carrying returning war troops. "Maddie . . ." he murmured, his breath tickling her neck. "I want you to go to your hotel and not speak to anyone. Go there and do not come out for anyone but me."

At the door, he stopped. "For the next forty-eight hours, you're the hottest property in the world, okay?"

She laughed, because that was ridiculous, but his expression didn't change.

"Go," he said. "There's a car waiting."

SPREAD AT THE foot of the marble steps were gleaming black vehicles and people in suits. She wasn't sure which car was hers, but one of the valets spied her and leaped to attention: the same one who'd made a fuss of her when she arrived. He came at her with a huge grin, and for a moment she thought he meant to hug her. "How did it go?"

She was momentarily lost. "How did . . ."

"The party," said the valet. "Did you have a good time?"

"Yes, thank you. It went very well." She was unsure how to deal with excited fans. It was a new concept for her.

"I knew you'd get the part," he said. "After what happened to Aria Astwell."

Not just a fan: a fan who knew everything. They definitely didn't get these in theater. "I don't think they've made a final decision."

"You'll get it," the valet said with finality. "Let me get your car organized. Where are you headed?"

"The Waldorf Astoria."

"Ah, the Waldorf," he said, delighted. "That's a really good choice." He led her toward a vehicle and held open the door for her.

"Thank you." He was grinning, so she added, "What's your name?"

"Clay," he said. "Clayton Hors."

"Thank you, Clay. It's been kind of a magical night."

"You deserve it. You look . . . I know I shouldn't say this, but you look perfect. Just like . . . perfect."

He seemed as if he'd been about to say something else. *I look just like what?* she thought.

"It's going to work out," said the valet. "This is the one. I can feel it."

And she did, too. It *was* working out. And she was happy she had this guy to share it with, this awkward valet, the pumpkin footman in her fairy tale, who, for reasons she didn't quite understand, cared about the moment almost as much as she did. "Me, too."

He looked like he might die of happiness. "Take care," he said, and closed the door.

14

MADDIE'S APARTMENT BUILDING WAS A TALL BROOKLYN BROWNSTONE.
The light near the door wasn't working, so Felicity used her phone to illuminate the button panel. She found the right apartment number and held the button with her thumb. After a minute with no answer, she walked down the steps and peered up at the windows. All remained dark. She went back and pressed the buzzer some more.

"Maddie's not here," Hugo said, appearing on the sidewalk. His hands were shoved into the pockets of a canvas jacket.

"Where is she?"

Hugo glanced up the street. "You want to go somewhere and talk this over?"

"No."

He sighed. "Felicity, if I tell you, you'll do something stupid."

"Tell me anyway."

"No," he said. "You want to stay in this place? All right. I won't argue with you anymore. But I won't let you ruin it for yourself." He came up the steps. "Whatever you do here, you have to live with the consequences."

"I realize how life works," she said. "Where is she?"

"She's fine. She's totally fine."

But that couldn't be true; if it were, he would tell her. "They didn't get Clay, did they?"

"Everything went to plan. I haven't lied to you, Felicity. It's over. Clay will never leave this place."

"But he's not dead."

Hugo exhaled. "No."

She was so mad, she walked down the steps, then came back up. "How *could* you?"

"Lower your voice."

"Twenty-one times. You've let him kill her twenty-one times."

"And now it's over."

"If he's *alive*, it's not over!"

"Listen to me." He went to seize her arm, but she wasn't having that. "We tried. Okay? I tried. Over and over. And it only got worse, for him and for us, and we couldn't keep going like that. So they found a compromise. Everyone gets what they want. Clay stays. We move."

She couldn't believe what she was hearing. "You made a deal? You *trust* him?"

"Of course not. But this place—this is the result of a planned move. Not by Clay, by us. And our people know what they're doing, Felicity. They've been doing it for years. Clay will stay here, in this world, because he's not an idiot. He's been searching for eleven months and he knows how hard it is to find what he wants."

"What he wants is to *kill Maddie!*"

"No," Hugo said patiently, "that's not quite right."

She stared into his face. Then she pulled away, because she couldn't look at him. Halfway down the steps, she began to run.

"Don't do this," Hugo called after her. "Felicity, don't do this!" She kept running until she could no longer hear him.

FELICITY BOUGHT A ticket over the counter for a six a.m. American Airlines flight to LAX. She was worried about her gun, having never carried a firearm on an airplane before, even though she'd detoured to the Walmart on Belt Parkway for a black-and-gray pistol case with a bright sticker that read: TSA APPROVED. It turned out to be simple: She declared the gun at check-in and the attendant asked whether it was locked and unloaded, employing the same tone with which he'd inquired whether Felicity was a member of the AAdvantage program, and Felicity said yes, and they sent it down the conveyor. "Have a nice flight," the clerk said, handing her a boarding pass.

At the gate, she phoned Gavin. She could do that, at least: tell him she was fine but had to go away.

"Where?" he said. "For how long?"

"I can't say."

"But you can. Whatever it is, you can say."

She closed her eyes. Overhead, a voice announced that flight AA171 was now open for boarding.

"Are you at the airport?"

"Please, Gavin. Trust me."

"I'm worried."

"You don't need to. I'll be fine." This was absolutely a lie, though. Whatever happened, she was not going to be fine. Best-case, she was going to kill a man for reasons no one would understand. After that, she would likely spend a good chunk of her life in prison.

Clay would not stay. Hugo had implied that this place contained a Maddie May like the one that sparked Clay's original obsession—a movie star, she assumed. And because of this, Clay would be content. But this was the purest horseshit. Sooner or later, Clay would find something in Maddie to disappoint him, because the problem was not Maddie. It had never been Maddie.

"Felicity—" Gavin said.

"I have to go," she said, and hung up.

THERE WAS NO special area to collect her gun case at LAX: It trundled down the carousel with the bags and suitcases. She carried it to the Hertz desk, and, while waiting for a girl with black nails and pierced eyebrows to locate a car on her system, phoned Proximate Artists, the L.A. talent agency listing Maddie. After two forwards, Felicity landed on an assistant who answered in a warm, lilting voice: "Hello, this is Yvonne."

"Hi, Yvonne, this is Felicity Staples from the New York *Daily News*. I'm hoping to arrange an interview with Madison May."

There was a brief pause. "I'm sorry, who is this again?"

"Felicity Staples. I work at the New York *Daily News*."

"You're looking for an interview?"

"Yes," she said, adjusting her bag. Across the counter, the Hertz girl stared blankly at a screen. "As soon as possible."

"Can I ask what kind of piece this would be?"

"A feature. Maddie is a New York resident. We're interested in running a profile."

"On her career in general? Or in reference to a particular work?"

"In general," Felicity said. "Or about *By the River Blue*."

There was a pause. Not a good pause, Felicity sensed. She had aroused some kind of suspicion. Maybe she wasn't supposed to know about Maddie's involvement in that film.

"Felicity, I'm sure Maddie would love to do that when she returns to New York. Can I get your details?"

"Actually, I'm in Los Angeles right now. I was hoping we could do something today."

"Oh, I'm afraid today is impossible," Yvonne said, sounding so sad that for a moment Felicity believed her. "How is your next week?"

"Not good," Felicity said.

"Hmm," Yvonne said, as if this was tricky, this situation, but let's see if they could find a way out of it together. "How about I get your details and I'll see what I can do?"

This was a fob-off, Felicity suspected. This was a person with no intention of following through. She gave Yvonne her phone number anyway. "I'll call you back in an hour or two."

"Of course."

"Actually," she said. "I just realized I'm going to be in your area. I could stop by your office."

"Well, I *will* be in and out today. But if you miss me, I'll get back to you as soon as I can."

"Thank you. I'd appreciate that." She hung up. Not great. She was probably not going to be able to penetrate Proximate Artists' reception. She might not even be able to get Yvonne on the phone again. For whatever reason, Yvonne wanted to keep Maddie hidden away. Maybe that was good news: If Felicity couldn't reach her, then neither could Clay. But she couldn't count on it. If it were true for now, it wouldn't be for long.

"I found it," said the Hertz girl. Felicity blinked. "Your car."

"Oh." Felicity adjusted her grip on the gun case. "Thanks." She checked her watch. A little after ten. In an hour or so, Hugo and the others would move and leave her behind forever.

She blinked. Actually, that wasn't right. Her watch had updated to the local time zone. In New York, it was already after one. They'd left two hours ago.

PROXIMATE ARTISTS LAY on Santa Monica Boulevard in Beverly Hills. Felicity missed the turnoff to the 405 on her first attempt, circled back, and spent the next half-hour inching along in a parade of cars. She was blasting air but the car was still hot. She dialed Proximate and got herself put through to Yvonne's desk, but after that was voicemail, the recorded voice of Yvonne blatantly lying to

Felicity about returning her call as soon as humanly possible. She hung up, hit redial, and nearly rear-ended a sedan. Los Angeles traffic really was insane. It was an endless series of tiny races. The receptionist apologized and said she would try Yvonne again, after which Felicity was listening to her voicemail message again. "Answer your fucking phone," she said, but Yvonne didn't.

Next she tried the *News*. The number she had memorized was wrong, of course, so she had to navigate the paper's website while fending off cars that wanted to annex her lane. The phone was answered by someone Felicity didn't recognize—not Annette, the frequent stand-in for *Daily News* photo shoots—but who recognized her, and who put her through to the newsroom. The phone clicked.

"Hello, this is Todd Schiller."

She hesitated. She'd been calling for Brandon, not Todd the intern. But now she had an idea. "It's Felicity Staples."

"Oh, hi, Felicity. Everyone's looking for you."

"Why?" she said, thinking: *What now?*

"Um, well, you didn't show for the Monday briefing."

Right. Of course. "Something urgent came up," she said. "Todd, can you help me find someone in a hurry?"

"Sure," he said, sounding interested.

"Her name is Madison May. She's an actor. I know she's somewhere in Los Angeles. But I need to know exactly."

"Do you have her phone number?"

She had tried. It was wrong. "No. Do you remember . . ." She stopped herself. She'd been about to say: *Remember when you helped me find the Soft Horizon Juice logo?* But that hadn't happened here. "I was thinking that you're good with computers. Maybe there was something you could do."

"Like what?"

She didn't want to say: *Hack in.* "Ping her?"

"Ping her what?" Todd asked. "Her phone? That you don't have the number of?"

"I just thought there might be something you can do," Felicity said.

"Do you have her email?"

"I have her Insta."

"Her what?"

"Her Instagram account." She had discovered it one move earlier, when Maddie worked at the coffee shop, and it existed here, too. It was even filled with the same random pictures of houses and office buildings, and occasionally interiors. Maddie had a thing for architecture.

"Can you message her?" Todd asked.

"No, I can only see her pictures."

"Well . . . I can think of one way, but it's a super-long shot."

"Go on," she said.

"It's pretty ridiculous. But what you'd do is look up her username on *pwned* lists."

"On what?"

"*Poan*," Todd said. "P-W-N. When a site gets hacked, sometimes all its usernames and passwords wind up dumped on the Internet."

"Did Instagram get hacked?"

"No. I mean, maybe. What happens, though, is people often re-use the same username and password on a bunch of different sites. If she did that, then one of *those* sites might have been hacked. So we'd have her credentials. You log in to her account and have access to whatever personal info she put in there."

"Like her phone number?"

"Or email. There's even a cool thing you can do where you trigger a password reset on her phone, and then when she tries to log back in, it shows you this map of where the request is coming from."

"Oh my God. That sounds perfect."

"That probably won't work, though," Todd said. "Also, it's, you know, kind of a huge privacy violation."

"Can you do it?"

He was silent.

"It's for a story," she said, unconvincingly.

"Is it?"

If Todd were older, she would say, *Yes*, because he would be asking for plausible deniability. But she didn't think that was happening. She decided to take a risk. "No. But it's important, Todd. I really need it."

There was a long silence. "I'll see what I can do, Felicity."

She closed her eyes for a moment. "Thank you."

"But seriously, don't get your hopes up. I'll call you back when I have something. Do you want me to put you through to Brandon now?"

"Yes," she said. "Again, thank you so much."

"Hold, please," said Todd, and then she was listening to a recorded message extolling the virtues of being a *Daily News* subscriber. She felt cautiously optimistic about Todd's idea, despite his warning. She now had two ways to find Maddie: via her agent and via Todd's computer magic. Ahead of her, a convertible edged forward, then, miraculously, kept moving. She goosed the accelerator, denying the advances of an SUV on her left. She could see how the traffic happened now.

"Hi, Felicity," said Brandon. "How are you?"

"I'll be honest," she said. "I've been better."

"Are you ill?"

"Not exactly. I'm in Los Angeles."

"Oh?"

She took a breath. "Brandon, if I need a huge favor and couldn't explain why, would that put too much of a strain on our relationship?"

"I don't think so," he said. "I think I'd assume you had a good reason. What do you need?"

"I have to find someone. Her film agent knows where she is, but they won't tell me."

"What did you tell the agent?"

She grimaced. "I said the *News* wants to do a profile on her."

A pause. It went on awhile. "Still they won't let you speak to her?"

"No."

"Curious," Brandon said. "All right. Give me the number and I'll put in a call."

A gap in the traffic opened to her left. She swung the wheel, stomped on the gas. There were horns. "Thank you so much."

"But before I do," Brandon said, "I need to ask you something. And I need a truthful answer."

She took a breath. "Sure."

"Are you all right?"

She couldn't answer for a moment. "Yes."

"Very well. I'll call you back."

"Thank you, Brandon."

"You're welcome," he said. "In the meantime, please take care."

SHE PASSED PROXIMATE Artists and circled the block until she found a metered park on Civic Center Drive. As soon as she turned off the engine, the car filled with heat. She cracked the windows. On the passenger seat lay her Walmart gun case. She dug out the key and opened it up and there it was: her Walther M2, snug in gray foam, alongside a red box of nine-millimeter rounds. She took it out, found the little button near the trigger that allowed the magazine to slide free from the grip, and fed it gold rounds, fifteen of them, one at a time. Then she slid the magazine into the pistol until it clicked.

She tugged at it; Levi said sometimes it only seemed to go in right. Then she put it in her lap. If she pulled back the slide at the top, it would shovel a round from the magazine into the chamber. After that, it would be ready to fire. But it wasn't time for that yet. She put the gun back in the case and locked it.

An hour passed in which Brandon did not call back. Felicity got out of the car. She didn't expect to encounter Clay in Proximate Artists and she couldn't see the gun causing anything but trouble in there, so she left it in the trunk.

The lobby was cool and minimalist in a way Felicity found annoyingly noncommittal. Behind a wood-paneled desk sat two women, one with beautiful long blond hair and one with beautiful long black hair. The blond woman smiled. "Hello."

"Hi," Felicity said. "I'm here to see Yvonne Hampson."

"Could I have your name, please?"

"Felicity Staples."

"Thank you. Take a seat, Felicity. Can I get you some water?"

She sat on a white sofa. There was a coffee table with magazines. A minute later, a short man in an open-necked shirt crossed the lobby and said, "Chloe! Where's my Chloe?" but it was nothing to do with Felicity. The receptionist beckoned. "Yvonne is on her way," she said, when Felicity approached, but looked troubled, as if this wasn't a good thing.

Felicity waited. Eventually a glass door was pushed open by a tall woman with faultless skin. This described every woman Felicity had seen in this building so far. The woman came toward her with her hand out, heels clacking, dark hair shimmering. "Felicity?"

"Yes."

"Your boss called," Yvonne said. "He said it's important to connect you with Maddie today."

Thank you, Brandon. "Yes."

"I'm going to be honest with you, Felicity. I appreciate that you're a real reporter with a real newspaper. But we're tying up a delicate negotiation, and our concern is that you might interfere with that. This morning, you mentioned *By the River Blue*. But it's not public knowledge that Maddie is replacing Aria Astwell in that role."

Whoops. "I'm just trying to set up an interview."

"We *may* be able to do tomorrow. Would that work for you?"

Felicity opened her mouth to argue, but the better option was to leverage what she was being offered. "If that's the soonest you can do."

"Can you come to her?"

"I'd be happy to."

Yvonne nodded. "We'll meet at the Waldorf Astoria, then. I'll send you the details tomorrow."

"Do you have them now?"

Yvonne didn't answer.

"I have a photographer with me," Felicity lied. She jerked her thumb over her shoulder, as if he were just out there, beyond the glass. "He likes to know what the environment will be like."

"It will be a west-facing room on the eleventh floor."

"Thank you." Her heart began to hammer. "That's very helpful, thank you so much."

THE MAN BEHIND the desk at the Waldorf Astoria was trim, balding, and sorry to inform Felicity that there were no rooms available on the eleventh floor. "Or anywhere," he said. "It's actually unusual for us to have anything free without a booking."

"Mmm," Felicity said, tapping the counter. She could feel herself developing a sweaty, panicked air. When she was physically moving, it was easier to ignore the fact that time was slipping away, but whenever she stopped, like right now, the sensation crawled up the back of her neck. "The thing is, it's important."

The man looked sympathetic. "I am so sorry."

She tried to think. If someone needed a room in a hurry, someone important, she felt like a room would appear. It was probably not especially uncommon, she sensed, for someone important to want a room at short notice, and for the hotel to make something available. "Money isn't an issue."

"Pardon me?"

"My client doesn't care about the cost of the room."

"Ah," he said. "You know what, give me a minute and let me see what I can do."

The man disappeared through a door. A lot of people had been telling Felicity they would see what they could do today. But she felt guardedly optimistic about this one. She glanced around the lobby. She'd left the gun case in the car, since it was very obviously a gun case, but she felt anxious about that, too. If this was Maddie's hotel, it was plausible that Clay would be here.

The man returned. "We can make a room available by five o'clock. Would that work for you?"

"On the eleventh floor?"

"Yes." As she dug out her credit card, he added: "However, it *is* quite expensive, as we need to expedite a cleaning crew."

"How much?"

"Six thousand and ninety-two dollars per night. With a mini-mum of two nights."

"That's fine," she said, as a part of her screamed internally. Twelve thousand dollars. Not only was she torching her future, she was bankrupting it.

"Thank you so much," said the man, accepting her card. He tapped at a screen. "Is this associated with another booking?"

She was distracted. "What?"

"Are you staying with another party? Never mind. I was thinking that if you're traveling with another guest, I could put you together."

It felt like a leading question, so she said: "Yes. Madison May." She held her breath as she watched him tap. "It might be under Proximate Artists?"

"Ah, yes. There we go."

"We're next door?"

He smiled. "Hotel policy doesn't permit me to disclose room numbers, but I have you nearby, yes."

That was fine. That would do. She would have to wait until the room was ready, but then she could ride to the eleventh floor and knock on doors. She would even have a plausible excuse if someone stopped to ask what she was doing: She would be looking for her friend, Maddie May. "Thank you."

"You're welcome. If you return at five, I'll have your key ready."

She nodded, hoisting her bag.

"I didn't think it was a coincidence," he said.

She paused. "What's that?"

"You're not the first to request a room on the eleventh floor to-day. I thought it must be related."

Her gut twisted. "Who else?"

But her expression was wrong and a frown flickered across the man's brow. "I can't disclose—"

"Clay?" she asked. "A young guy? Clayton Hors?" He wasn't going to tell her and she was leaking panic, putting the whole thing at risk. "That's fine," she said, fighting it down. Her gun was in the car and she needed it. "Thank you again."

SHE TRANSFERRED THE gun to her bag. Then she returned to the lobby and sat in a deep brown chair, the bag in her lap, watching people come and go. Every now and again, when she felt like she was pushing the limits of what the hotel would tolerate, she left and walked around the block. She called Yvonne back twice, just in case, but wasn't put through either time.

When at last the room was ready, she was given two plastic key-cards in a white envelope. She entered an oak-paneled elevator, which contained a little seat, and pressed 11. The doors closed. She slid her right hand into the bag and made sure she knew where the gun was.

The hallway was lit by chandeliers. Red carpet swallowed her shoes. She walked to her room and closed the door. She removed the gun, pulled back the slide, and let it go, listening to the soft click of a round entering the chamber.

From this point onward, she had to be careful not to shoot herself.

She placed the gun back into her bag. Then she went out into the hallway.

She moved to the door across the hall and knocked. No answer. She tried the room on the other side, but there was no answer there, either. The third door was answered by a shirtless man who thought she was with the hotel and wanted her to find his dry cleaning. When she finished with that, she tried two more doors on that side, then two on the other.

As she was approaching a fifth, a bellhop came running toward her. "Ma'am!" he called out, as she raised her hand. "Please don't do that, ma'am!" He inserted his body between her and the door. "Ma'am, you can't disturb the other guests."

"But . . ." she said, because she was in a kind of mania now, thinking she could save Maddie if only she knocked on enough doors. The reality, though, was that Maddie wasn't here. She was booked into this hotel, on this floor, but right now, she was out, taking in meetings or exploring the city or who knew. So all Felicity could accomplish by knocking on doors was getting herself kicked out of the hotel. She forced a smile. "I'm sorry. I was looking for my friend."

The bellhop watched until she returned to her room. She took the gun from her bag, set it on the desk, and pressed her fists against her face.

Maddie's with Clay. He found her first because he knows her better than I do.

She couldn't sit in a hotel room, waiting to find out whether Maddie would return. She moved to the door and peered through the peephole. The bellhop was still loitering outside. As she eyed him, her phone rang.

She jumped. "Hello?"

"Hi," said Todd. "It's me. Sorry, I meant to get back to you earlier. You know how I said not to get your hopes up?"

"Yes?" she said, her hopes rocketing.

"Well, it didn't work. I couldn't find her on a pwned list. And anyway, that idea with the password reset and the map, I think they've tightened that up. It only gives you a general area, not a precise location. So it wouldn't have helped." Into the silence, he added: "Sorry."

"Are you sure?" she said. "Is there anything you can do?"

"I'm sorry, Felicity. I looked everywhere. I even thought of checking her photos for geotags, because sometimes they have a precise location. But they're anonymized."

She blinked. All this talk of computer hacking had blinded her to something very simple. She tapped Todd onto speaker and swiped, bringing up Maddie's Insta. The feed was full of buildings and angles, as usual, but a few pictures had been added in the last few hours. The most recent was somewhere she didn't recognize: a plaza, maybe? Tables, chairs, green umbrellas. But in the background, two stores, with names she could read.

"I think I found her," she said.

15

NEIL HAD TOLD HER NOT TO SPEAK TO ANYONE FOR TWO DAYS. THOSE were his exact words. Maddie was taking this seriously, because what had happened at the party between her and Calvin Anderson, the director, had been some fairy-tale magic. Now she needed to stand back and not touch anything while her agent did agent things, until it was sure—as sure as these things could be—that Maddie had the role, and that, therefore, the rest of her life would be so different from what had come before that she couldn't imagine it.

On the other hand: She was so excited, if she didn't tell someone, she might die.

She ate breakfast alone: room service, delivered by a nice man in blue pants whose every movement was a small, brisk performance, including his exit, which he did walking backward across the carpet to the door, as if Maddie were the queen. The hotel room had a wooden table by the window, and Maddie crunched a bagel while watching palms sway in the wind and cars clump and spread themselves along Santa Monica Boulevard. Her phone sat beside her, but she was good and didn't touch it.

At nine, she visited the gym. The only other person present was a woman in her thirties working the elliptical, earbuds in, ponytail bouncing. Maddie hung her towel and stepped up to the treadmill, which had too many controls for her to make sense of. "Need help?" said the elliptical woman, and Maddie said yes, thank you, she was totally lost. The woman came over and stabbed at the buttons. "Speed," she said, tapping. "Incline."

"Thanks." Maddie climbed onto the treadmill.

The woman toweled off. "First time at the Astoria?"

"Is it that obvious?"

The woman smiled. She was older than Maddie had first thought. Quite a lot older. "I hope your visit's going better than mine."

"Oh?" Maddie said, building pace.

"I work in real estate. Short sales. You know what they are?"

"No." She did like houses, though. She had once thought of becoming a real estate agent.

"It's when the owner is selling because they're underwater. Can get messy, because there are banks and creditors involved. I flew in to finalize one that's been three months in the making and the owner's backing out. The whole thing was a delaying exercise while he renegotiated other loans. Gigantic waste of my time."

"That sucks," Maddie said, feeling strong, like she could run all day.

"Not a single man in this town says what he means," the woman said. "I shouldn't be sexist. The women are the same."

"City of dreams."

"City of fucking nightmares." The woman sighed. "Anyway, I hope you get what you came for."

"Thank you." And then, because she couldn't resist, Maddie added: "It's going well so far."

The woman's eyes traveled down her body. "I'm sure it is." She flopped her towel over her shoulder and turned away. "Enjoy it while you can." The door wheezed shut behind her.

NEIL CALLED AS Maddie was stepping out of the shower. "Have you spoken to anybody?"

"No," she said, wrapping herself in a towel. "Morning, Neil."

"Good morning, Maddie. How are you today?"

"I'm pretty good."

"Me, too," Neil said. "I'm pretty fucking good myself. Look, you don't need me to tell you this, but you knocked it out of the park last night. Congratulations."

"Thank you," she said, clutching the phone, really squeezing it.

"Now, let me warn you: This will not make you rich. We'll go back and forth and I'll get you what I can, but we're probably going to land somewhere around twelve grand for a two-week shoot. This is the one you do for peanuts because everyone will see it. Two or three pics from now, that's when I can start getting you what you're worth."

"I understand."

"Good. That makes me happy. Because, to be honest, Maddie, I'm more excited about this shit-money deal than anything I've worked on all year."

"I can't thank you enough, Neil."

"Their lawyer is calling back. Stay where you are. We'll talk again soon."

"What do I do with the earrings?" She'd locked them in her room's safe when she returned last night. "I'm nervous having them in the hotel room."

"Relax. You're the poorest person at the Astoria right now."

That made her feel better. "Can I tell my parents about last night?"

A pause. "Did you not tell your parents?"

"You told me not to talk to anyone."

He laughed. "You're fantastic. Tell your parents. But don't leave town. Talk soon."

"Bye," she said, and hung up, delighted. She dressed in one of her three outfits: a gray-check miniskirt and a long-sleeved black top. Not very West Coast. Kind of incredibly stereotypical New York, actually. Neil said to stay in *town*, not in her room: She could go shopping and spend some of her film riches. Twelve thousand dollars before taxes and Neil's commission would leave eight or so afterward: not a lot of money, but, at the same time, an unexpected fortune. And she would have done this role for nothing, would have clawed her way through mud for the privilege. So, yes, riches.

Her parents lived outside of Concord, New Hampshire. They'd moved four years earlier following a health scare: Maddie's father had complained of not being able to catch his breath and Maddie's mother had basically driven him straight to the ER, ignoring his objections, and they found a clot in his right leg preparing to make its way to his brain. Now he chewed four pink tablets a day to thin his blood, and walked to work, a small accounting practice where no one ever got too worked up about anything.

Her mother answered on the third ring. "Maddie?"

"Hey, Mom," she said. "Guess where I am?"

AROUND NOON, SHE was unable to resist the promise of sunshine and ventured out for lunch. The hotel concierge offered her a car, and maybe that was a good idea, but she couldn't really fathom exploring the neighborhood from inside a vehicle. She walked a couple of blocks east, passing concrete walls and closed blinds. A lot of Los Angeles was inside, she was discovering. You had to pass through a doorway to see it. She took a few pictures anyway, mainly of an apartment block on Brighton Way that had a roof shape she found interesting, and eventually reached something that was recognizably a deli, with outdoor seating. While she was processing an omelet, her phone rang.

"Hello, Maddie," said Yvonne. "How are you? Did you sleep well?"

"Yes, really great," she said, although, in reality, she had woken up a bunch of times, thinking about the night before.

"Do you have a minute? Something's come up. Don't worry; it's nothing. I'm just being hassled by a reporter who wants to interview you. In retrospect, something about it feels a little off, and I'm worried I might have told her too much."

"Oh?" Maddie said. She hadn't been interviewed before, not by anyone out of college.

"It's possible she's with the studio. They like to do their due diligence, and occasionally they unearth something that throws a spanner into the works as we're trying to close. I'm sure you have no skeletons in the closet, but it's best to be cautious. Where are you now?"

"I'm having lunch at a deli." She peered at a street sign. "North Roxbury Drive."

"Would you mind staying out for a few hours? Just avoid the hotel, in case she's stalking it."

"Okay, sure."

"Is that all right? I'll call you in a few hours and let you know when it's all clear."

"That's no . . ." She trailed off, because someone was staring at her from across the street: a man in a cap and sunglasses and, despite the weather, a hoodie. He was standing by the light as if waiting to cross, but, Maddie could clearly see, he already had the signal. Abruptly, he turned and walked away, disappearing around the corner.

"Is everything all right?"

"I think . . ." she said. "Sorry, I just thought someone was watching me."

"A woman?" Yvonne said sharply.

"No." She glanced around. "It was probably nothing."

"I tell you what, Maddie, why don't I take you out? We'll do a little shopping at the Century City mall. Some drinks afterward, if you can stand to meet my friends."

"Oh," she said, embarrassed. "You don't need to do that."

"I should have suggested this in the first place. Forgive me. I'm still flustered from that reporter. Let me take care of you for the rest of the day."

"This is making me feel very pampered," Maddie said.

"That you should get used to," Yvonne said.

SHE CAUGHT AN Uber to the mall, although it turned out to be so close, she could have walked. It was an enormous concrete structure with palm trees wedged onto one corner, which she stopped to photograph. Inside, it was very open and airy, not at all what she was used to, a little self-contained world where everything was the way it was because it was chosen.

Yvonne was waiting for her in the dining terrace at the top of a set of escalators. She extended her arms and they kissed each other's cheeks, like real L.A. socialites. "Thank you so much for coming," Yvonne said, although Maddie was pretty sure Yvonne was the one doing her a favor. "Neil is apoplectic at the idea that the studio is trying to talk to you before we've finished negotiating. It will be over soon."

"No problem."

Yvonne smiled. "I love your attitude." This was something Maddie could get used to: constant praise for meeting minimum behavioral standards. That had been happening a lot lately. "Would you like to see a movie?"

They took in a screening of *Calling All Martians*, which was about a teenage girl detective who was also deaf, and was much better than Maddie expected. Afterward, Yvonne told her that the actor had been replaced three times before shooting, and that one of the dogs was afraid of boom microphones, creating two hundred thousand dollars' worth of delays. It was a good way to see movies: with someone who could share their secrets.

As the evening closed in, the dining terrace became ringed with a thousand yellow bulbs like fairy lights. A man in a white open-necked shirt called to Yvonne from a glass table beneath a wide green umbrella. This was the group of Yvonne's friends, which seemed to be solely composed of producers aged under thirty. "Maddie's new," said Yvonne, introducing her. "If you want to know more, read *Variety* tomorrow."

This created a minor stir. She was given walnuts, which were a special promotion from a vegan eatery, and came with a silver tool for cracking them open. She was offered a daiquiri. This was pretty L.A., what she was doing right here. She had to grab a photo for Zar, her actor friend back home.

The next hour or so, she fielded questions about her background, favorite movies, and inspirations, while listening to other people's opinions on writers, directors, and where the industry would be once Disney owned everything. Eventually, her head buzzing from three daiquiris, she excused herself to find the restroom. On her return, she turned a corner and unexpectedly found herself face-to-face with the valet from the night before, the one with longish hair who'd been such a fan. She was startled, but he literally jumped back two steps. "Shit!" he said, then laughed. "Oh my God, I'm sorry. I did not expect to see you here. It's Clay. From last night?"

"Yes," she said, guarded, because she wasn't sure if this was a co-incidence. "Of course."

"Are you here for a movie?" He gestured behind him, where there were indeed cinemas. He was a movie buff; he had said that before. He was so into film that he'd even known she was being cast in *By the River Blue*. She supposed it made sense that he hung out here.

"I saw *Calling All Martians*."

"Hey, I want to apologize for last night. I was thinking it over and I feel like I maybe went a little crazy-stalker-fan on you."

"Oh, no."

"It's okay. You can say it. I've been cringing at myself all day."

"It's fine," she said, and it was, pretty much. "Honestly, I was happy to have someone to share the moment with."

He grinned, showing dimples. "That is super, super-kind of you. You don't know how much that means to me." He glanced around. "Can I get you something? Do you want food?"

"Thanks, but I'm with people."

He slapped his forehead. "Oh my God. Of course you are. I'm being stupid again. I'm going to let you get back to your life. I'm just killing time before my movie. I promise not to bother you again."

"Try the walnuts," Maddie said. "They're really good." She took a step and he moved to let her pass.

"I will!" he said, like this was an exciting idea. "Thanks!"

She felt good about this interaction and returned to her group. They were discussing a movie she knew nothing about, because it hadn't been made yet, but about which everyone already seemed to have firm opinions. A while later, she saw Clay make his way through the crowd and sit at a table by the glass barrier near the escalators. Over the next few minutes, whenever she glanced over, he was fooling about with the cracking tool, flipping it one way then the other, trying to insert walnuts in different ways. She found herself fascinated by how long he could take to figure it out.

Finally she leaned into Yvonne. "Is it okay if I talk to someone for a minute?" She pointed to Clay.

"Who's that?"

"Just a guy I met."

"A journalist?"

"No," Maddie said. "He's a valet."

Yvonne stared at him. Clay, noticing, blinked and sat up straighter. "I mean . . ." said Yvonne, and the man beside her bellowed laughter.

"Yvonne," said the man. "This is crazy. You have to hear this."

"I just want to help him crack a walnut," Maddie promised.

Yvonne looked unconvinced, but the man was waiting and she gave Maddie a brief nod.

Clay seemed to inflate as Maddie approached, his smile stretching, his eyes filling with delight and wonder. "Hey!" he said.

"I can't watch you do that any longer." She took the cracking tool, folded it the right way, and handed it to him.

"Oh my God." He inserted a walnut and squeezed. The shell cracked.

"Yay," she said.

"Now I feel bad. I'm not usually that stupid."

There was something about Clay, she decided. Something that felt familiar and lived-in. Impulsively, she pulled out the chair opposite and sat. His eyebrows shot up as if she'd launched them, like the ball in a ring-the-bell carnival game. "Do you mind? I know you have a movie soon."

"Fuck the movie," Clay said. "I see a hundred movies a year. I'm not even exaggerating. A hundred, minimum. That's how I saw your film. Saw the announcement, I mean. It's not really, you know, my kind of movie. But I'll watch anything."

"What's your kind of movie?"

"Anything with a good story. I hate it when they screw up the story. I don't know if it's just because I've seen a lot of movies, but I find it really clear how the story should go. When they get it wrong, that's so annoying to me. Any movie they don't screw up the story, I'm happy with."

"Maybe you should write your own."

He hesitated. "I do actually have an idea."

"Let's hear it," she said, feeling bold.

He tugged nervously at his ear. "It's stupid. You don't want to hear it."

"It's fine if it's stupid," she said, which was what she'd been taught at NYU: Before there is sharing, there must be trust. *We leave judgment outside the room, people.* "I still want to hear it."

Clay took a breath. "Well . . . I mean . . . all right. You asked for it." He wiped his hands on his pants. "So there's this guy. And one night . . ." He paused, eyeing her. She nodded encouragingly. "He leaves work, which is a shitty little electronics store. And in the parking lot, there's an old drunk dude. He grabs the guy and says, 'Hey, kid, want to know a secret? I'm from another world.' And he tries to give the guy something. He says it's a token, but it's really just a stone. Like a cold, worn-down old brick. So the guy takes it, mostly to, you know, humor the drunk dude, but the dude starts crying. He says he's glad it's over, because everything good gets left behind. Just craziness, right? So anyway, the next day, the guy wakes up and the furniture's been moved around in his house and there are photos he doesn't remember. He lives with his parents, but all of a sudden, his dad has a different job. And he's like, 'Dad, when did you get a new job?' And his dad says, 'I didn't, I've had this job for years.'"

"Ooh," Maddie said.

Clay nodded. "So the guy is really confused. And he figures out that the crazy old drunk dude wasn't crazy after all. The weird stone, the token, it moves you somewhere. To a new world. The guy tries to get home, but he can't do it. Everything he tries only moves him somewhere else, to another world he doesn't recognize. And . . . well, he starts to go a little crazy. He can't talk to anyone, no one believes him—no one even remembers the same things as he does. Finally he's literally thinking of killing himself. It gets that bad. But he goes to the movies—just walks in to whatever's playing—and ten minutes in, on-screen comes this actress. And, just like that, he falls in love."

"Oh!" Maddie said. She hadn't seen that coming.

"Suddenly he gets it. She's the reason for all of this. For everything that happened. It's a cosmic plan to bring them together."

"He just knows this?"

Clay nodded. "Did you feel something like that when you decided to go into acting? Some things, you just feel. You can't explain it."

She wasn't sure she'd ever had a moment like that. She had

doubted herself every step of the way. "This movie is more romantic than I expected."

"Wow. I'm so happy to hear you say that. Because then there's a complication. The old drunk dude at the beginning, he has friends. And the friends want the token back."

"Aha," Maddie said.

"The guy has to keep jumping to new worlds to get away. But when he does, the actress isn't an actress anymore. She's a totally different person. The guy is heartbroken, because he lost her. But he vows to keep moving until he finds her again. No matter how long it takes."

She waited. "And does he?"

Clay smiled awkwardly. "I don't know. The ending isn't done."

"It's good, Clay."

He waved her away, embarrassed. "You don't have to be nice."

"I like the people chasing him. Who are they?"

"The bad guys," Clay said. "They want to keep the guy and the girl apart. I'm so happy you like it, Madison. I'm super-open to feedback. Is there anything I could improve?"

"Nope," she said, because she had hung around artists long enough to know that didn't always go well.

"One thing. No matter how small."

She hesitated. "He first sees her on-screen, is that right?" Clay nodded. "He falls in love just based on that?"

"Yes," he said.

"I mean, as a performer, he's only seen her play a character. He doesn't actually know what she's like."

Clay shook his head. "No, he can tell."

There was an awkward silence. "Oh, okay."

He laughed. "I don't want to be defensive. It's just . . . even when you're performing, that's you, right? You're expressing a part of yourself. So it's always fundamentally real."

Fair, she supposed. "I guess so."

He grinned. "I can't even believe we're having this conversation. I feel like I can tell you anything." He glanced around. "I want to show you something."

"Okay," she said.

He dug into his pants pocket. She felt that strange sense of familiarity return, as if he reminded her of someone, but this time with a twist. He was about to produce something terrible. A knife. The thought came out of nowhere, but felt so real that she put a hand on the arms of her chair to push herself back.

Clay placed a small black bag onto the table. The material was thin and worn. A bag for cheap jewelry. Inside, something bulged.

She looked at him. "What is it?"

"Take a look."

She wasn't sure about this. It was just a jewelry bag. On a table. Outside a vegan eatery named Matty Eats. But she didn't want to touch it.

"Here." He loosened the bag's thread and lifted it by its rear corners. Out slid a gray stone. It was the size of an old flip phone, run through with dark lines. Lighter around the edges, and smooth, as if worn down over time. It made her think of chalk, like a material you might use to make something else.

She looked at him.

"You can touch it if you want," he said.

"What is it?"

"What do you think?"

She didn't know. A stone. A weird stone.

"It's the token," Clay said.

She was confused. "From your movie?"

"Madison, I've seen you as a TV weather girl. A salesgirl. A real estate agent. You're a student a lot. But not successful, not like here. I've seen you in dozens of worlds, and the first time, you were in a movie called *By the River Blue*. You were the little sister. Clara. That's how I know you'll be perfect in that role. I've already seen you in it."

She stared at him. "What are you talking about?"

"I wasn't going to tell you. But it's true, Madison. The token works."

"You're saying . . ." She had this wrong; she must. "You're the guy?"

He nodded.

She looked at the gray stone lying between them. It was a rock. A *rock*.

But she had considered going into real estate. She liked houses. Weather girl? There had been a casting call in her second year, which she'd missed because she was busy with Trent. But she might have gone. Might have gotten the job, if things had been different.

"I don't know much about you here," Clay said. "I haven't been here very long. I can't even tell you who the president is. But I can tell you about your other lives."

She heard a burst of laughter from Yvonne's table. Maddie could stand and walk over there. Tell Yvonne about the crazy guy with the idea for a movie that wasn't really a movie.

"What happens in *By the River Blue*?" she asked, because no one had that script. Even she had been allowed to see only her own scenes.

He hesitated. "It might not be the same. Whenever I move, there are changes. But in the one I saw, your first scene is at the table for a family lunch. You argue with your mom. Later you talk about boys. Fooling around with boys. Then, right at the end, after the funeral, you have a pillow fight with your sisters. An *amazing* pillow fight. You jump on the bed. Your hair is . . . everywhere."

How could he know this? He should not know this.

And his face. She couldn't see deceit anywhere. Either he was an amazing actor or he believed what he was saying.

"I've messed this up, haven't I?" Clay said. "I shouldn't have told you so soon." He sat back and ran a hand through his hair. "I forgot how crazy it sounds. Argh."

She could stand up and leave. He was half expecting it; she could see it in his face.

Some things, you just feel, he'd said. *You can't explain it.*

She could feel this. Whatever it was, it wasn't a lie.

"Tell me, then," she said, "about my other lives."

FELICITY LEFT HER RENTAL CAR IN THE BOWELS OF THE CENTURY City mall and rode the escalator. With one hand she held on to the strap of her bag, which felt like it wanted to slip from her shoulder and reveal her secret to the world: that she had a gun. The doors parted. She wound her way among shoppers to an information kiosk. There she looked for the store whose name was visible in the background of one of Maddie's pictures: MATTY EATS. According to the screen, it was part of the second-floor dining terrace, on the other side of the mall.

She moved on. With every step she felt lighter—or, *looser*, maybe, like parts of her were fraying away. Her career, her relationship with Gavin, her ability to order a frozen yogurt: Those would not be options after she walked up to a man with no history of violence and shot him dead in front of a crowd of onlookers. Those might be paths for other Felicitys, in other places. But not her.

Two lives, she thought. *I'll end two lives today.*

At the top of the escalator, wide green umbrellas crested into view, shading wicker furniture and thin tables, just like she'd seen in the picture. She scanned the crowd and it was funny, she practically walked right into them, because she was searching the terrace and they were the closest table, ten feet from the escalators, Maddie with her elbows on the table, leaning forward, as if she couldn't get enough of what Clay was saying.

Fuck, she thought. *Fuck—*

"Pardon *me!*" said a woman, the final syllable like a gunshot. Felicity had stopped like an idiot, blocking traffic. People on a wicker bench turned to see what the problem was.

She turned on her heel and walked away. Maddie had been about to look up; Clay had been about to turn; one then the other; and she wasn't ready; she wasn't. She walked around the corner and put her back to a wall. She felt like she might throw up. She closed her eyes and tried to breathe.

He's there.

Do what you came to do.

There was a crowd. She might hit someone by accident. The only way to do this would be to walk right up to their table and shoot Clay at point-blank range, without even taking the gun out of her bag.

A passing mother pulled her daughter close. Felicity peered into the store glass, and even in that pale reflection could see that she looked like someone who couldn't be trusted. She hadn't expected this part to be so hard.

On 177th Street, the stained brown carpet of an empty bedroom had been pockmarked with yellow police markers. In an alley, Maddie had bled to death, and again on a sidewalk outside the New York Public Library. She had lain in a hospital bed with her head shaved, her face black and blue.

This was how it happened: how people like Clay got away. They went unpunished because it cost too much to punish them.

She peeled herself from the wall. She stuck her hand back into her bag and curled her sweaty fingers around its secret. She breathed. She walked around the corner.

They were still seated together by the escalators, Maddie facing in Felicity's direction, Clay away. Felicity held her bag across her body. Her legs shook but didn't falter. Twenty feet away, Maddie's eyes shifted to her, but Maddie couldn't recognize her, Felicity told herself, even as Maddie's brow furrowed with something that resembled recognition but was more likely alarm, given the pale, sweating woman shambling toward her with a hand in a bag. *Please*, Felicity thought, transmitting the thought directly into Maddie's brain. *Please sit still and let me do this.*

Maddie's face filled with concern. Clay began to turn.

Felicity broke toward the table. There was a tremendous temptation to shoot before Clay could react, but she was not going to kill anybody by mistake today. She saw Clay's face, at first surprised and then angry, and he rose from his chair like a wave. He was at once too close and too far away and there was no perfect distance from which to fire, she realized; something could always be better. She lifted her bag of secrets and pulled the trigger.

She wasn't holding it the right way: not clasped in two hands with her feet shoulder width apart, but rather on a loose, idiotic angle inside her bag. As a result, it exploded like a thunderclap and wrenched violently at her wrist. Clay jumped, but not in a way that suggested she'd hit him. He lunged toward her. She fell back, trying to avoid him, and squeezed the trigger again, as Levi had told her, and then a third time.

The back of her head hit the ground. There was screaming. Not from Clay. From others, many others. Everywhere were legs. She had missed Clay, she thought. She had gone and missed him. The table had overturned. She was surrounded by bowls, cutlery, and, curiously, a walnut cracker. Maddie was on her hands and knees. "Wait," Felicity said, before she could go anywhere. "Maddie, stay." She looked around. Much of the crowd was booking it. But Clay, she saw, was not. Incredibly, he was scampering back and forth, his eyes raking the floor.

She had a bag on the end of her hand. She brought it around and pointed it at Clay.

He leaped behind a pillar. Why he hadn't taken the opportunity to flee, she had no idea, but she would take it, because the clock was ticking, running down a timer that had begun the moment she pulled the trigger, and that would end when the police arrived to arrest the crazy woman with the gun.

Clay yelled: "What are you doing?"

She was surprised by the question. It seemed self-explanatory.

"We have a deal!" he shouted. "You're ruining it!"

Right, she thought. She had forgotten about the deal. She was still unclear on why he hadn't run, though. Why he'd scurried around, hunched over, like he was searching for something.

She looked at the mess surrounding her. By an overturned chair lay a small gray block. She crawled toward it. When she picked it up, it was bitterly cold. Her own egg, she could see now, must once have been more angular. Over time, it had worn down from a shape like this. It was hard to the touch, but there was a fragility to it, a brittleness; she had always thought so. She raised it for Clay to see. "Is this what you want?"

His face contorted. "Leave that alone!"

"I thought you didn't need it anymore. Isn't that the deal, Clay? You get Maddie and you stay? So why do you need this?"

He stared at her.

"I think it's your Plan B," Felicity said. "A little something to keep in your back pocket, just in case."

"Put it down!"

But no. She didn't think she would. She had a gun and he didn't. When the police arrived, she would have a lot of explaining to do, but right now, in this moment, she had control. She spied the walnut cracker. She had to remove her hand from her bag for this next part, but it was worth the risk, so she leaned forward, picked up the cracker, and fitted Clay's egg into it.

"No!" he shouted.

He actually started toward her. She felt a little goose of fright, and squeezed the cracker as hard as she could. Clay's egg gave a noise like tearing wood. It fell to splinters, sending little bouncing gray shards everywhere. For a moment, she was so amazed, she forgot where she was. Then she looked up and saw Clay only ten feet away, his face murderous.

"I'm going to kill you," Clay said. She got the feeling there was more to this, like it was the beginning of a more detailed soliloquy, but she got her hand into her bag again and he ran, zigzagging toward an exit.

She looked back at Maddie. "Come with me." Maddie's face filled with alarm. Maddie did not want to come with her. Maddie wanted the woman with the gun to go away. "Maddie, my name is Felicity Staples. I'm here to protect you. But I have to go after Clay. Please come with me."

To her relief, Maddie nodded. Very likely she was merely playing along to appease the armed woman, but that was okay; that would do. Clay's bright T-shirt bounced toward a hallway leading to the restrooms, and there were elevators back there, too, according to the sign, which was maybe good: He might be stalled there long enough for her to catch him.

She gripped her bag. She was very worried that, despite the bag, someone might figure out she was the shooter and decide to take her down, administer a little direct justice. She held out a hand for Maddie, who was trailing, but Maddie didn't take it. The closer she got to the corner, the more she thought that Clay was hiding just around it, waiting for her. She stopped. "Maddie, I need to tell you something. The man you were talking to is Clayton Hors. He's a murderer. He's killed before. He will kill you." *He has killed you*, she wanted to say, but that would only confirm in Maddie's mind that Felicity was deranged. "The police won't stop him. Only I can."

Maddie nodded, which was pure performance, Felicity saw.

Maddie was pretending to be agreeable, because Felicity had a gun in a bag. Her wrist throbbed. She flexed her fingers inside the bag and could barely feel them.

They passed beneath the RESTROOMS sign. Felicity pressed her back against the wall and slid toward the corner. But Clay wasn't there, and he wasn't in the hallway, either, which stretched away to the elevators, where people milled at the doors, some hurrying down the stairwell, and he couldn't have moved that quickly, could he?

To her left was the female restroom. To her right, male.

He had come around the corner and realized he wouldn't be able to break through the crowd at the end of the hallway quickly enough. So he had ducked into a restroom. She looked from one door to the other. If she guessed wrong, he could escape. She glanced back at Maddie, who was drifting away; every time she wasn't looking, Maddie put a little distance between them. "Come here," she said, and Maddie did, quickly and obediently. Pretty soon Felicity was going to get distracted, and the next time she turned around, Maddie would be gone. "You have to listen to me. If I don't get him, you're going to die. He'll track you down and kill you."

"Yes," Maddie said, as if she hadn't thought about this before but it made perfect sense. "I see."

Christ, she thought. "Stay close," she said, and pushed into the men's, because she couldn't imagine Clay deciding to hide in a women's bathroom, she just couldn't. The floor was beige and gray tiles, the wall a tasteful two-tone. There was a high mirror on her right, and four more as she turned the corner. She found herself looking at a marble bench with four sinks spouting angular tapware. An orchid sat in a black vase. There were stalls. The room was empty.

He might be stealing out of the women's right now, escaping on the back of her bad psychology. Or he might be in one of these stalls.

She squatted. She saw no feet.

She didn't want to get closer because there was no room to move. He might spring out at her before she could shoot him.

She looked back. Maddie was by the door. "*Come,*" Felicity said, and Maddie did, looking not especially thrilled to be in a restroom, which Felicity understood; she was not thrilled with the situation herself. It was too small in here.

She approached the first stall and pushed the door with her foot. It didn't swing far enough, and she had to kick it again before it revealed an empty toilet. She adjusted her grip on her bag of secrets. The next stall, she gave a solid push. When the door swung back, it revealed Clay crouched there, lower than she'd expected, because he'd stolen down to the tiles, and her aim was too high, and he sprang.

Before she could react, he slammed into her. They flew backward into the marble counter. Suddenly his forearm was in her face, pushing against her mouth. Instinctively, she bit down, sinking her teeth into oddly hard flesh, like scar tissue. Then Clay's hand closed over her face and he thrust her into the mirror.

SHE FELT HEAVY. Like she was climbing from a pool, struggling to drag her weight from the water. Clay breathed in her ear. He was behind her, his arms wrapped around her, swaying slowly from side to side, as if they were dancing. His pelvis was grinding against her. His hands enveloped her own. She didn't know what he was doing. She tried to push him away.

"Shhh," Clay said. "Easy."

Maddie was gone. There were only two people she could see: Clay and herself. She was looking into a mirror. Clay was cradling her. Her head lolled on his shoulder like a lover's, like someone who had surrendered. She was holding the gun. No: Clay was making her hold it.

"You can't ruin this for me," he said. "You tried, but you failed."

He maneuvered her around, his thighs bumping against her. Now she was looking at a stall.

"I was in here," Clay said, "and you came in . . ."

She felt pressure on her finger. She tried to turn away. The sound was louder than she could have believed, exploding from the floor and walls like a slap. Clay flinched, almost dropped her, clutched at her waist.

"Ow," he said, and laughed. "Ow, shit, that's loud."

He let her fall against the countertop. She clutched at a sink to stop herself from sliding to the floor. When she managed to turn, he was standing a few feet away, holding her gun. He nodded, satisfied.

"Then I got the gun from you . . ."

He raised the gun. She hadn't seen it from this angle before. It was huge. The end of the barrel was a pit, crawling with evil things.

There was a noise.

Footsteps, Felicity thought. *Running*.

Hugo burst from the doorway. Clay cried out and brought the gun around. He fired: once, twice, three times. The tile behind Hugo burst; the other two times, Felicity didn't know where the bullets went. Hugo roared like a bear, charged into Clay, and knocked him down.

The gun bounced across the tiles. Felicity watched it go, end over end. She needed that. She had to fetch it. She tried to move her heavy body and pain lanced down her left side. But then she started to get organized, started remembering what the different parts of her body could do, and she slid down the counter and fell to her knees. Hugo and Clay were making an incredible commotion, grunting and snarling, but she didn't look at them. She had her own thing going on. She moved doggedly on her hands and her knees. Like this she crawled toward the gun.

A pair of feet appeared. Two neat shoes. She looked up and saw Maddie.

What Maddie made of this scene, Felicity could only imagine. She didn't know why Maddie had returned or what she'd come to do. "Give me the gun," Felicity croaked.

Maddie looked at her. She did not give Felicity the gun. She didn't do anything. Felicity would have to do that herself, apparently. She would have to get the gun and wrap her numb fingers around it and try to shoot Clay as he wrestled with Hugo.

She didn't know how Hugo could be here. He should have moved hours ago.

Maddie glanced behind her, as if there was someone back there, and suddenly there was: a cop in a dark blue uniform, a well-built guy with wide eyes, shouting and shoving, and then another cop appeared behind him, bigger and older, who pushed Maddie to the ground. There were boots and legs and Felicity lost track of the gun. The cops screamed to lie down and put your hands behind your head and so she did.

With her chin on the tiles, she could see Clay lying on his back. His face was bloodied. Hugo was kneeling astride him, one fist raised, his lips pulled back from his teeth, like an animal. Like a savage.

Lying on the tiles, Clay made a wet, bubbling sound. "Help," he called. "Help me."

The police were still screaming at Hugo. He wouldn't stop, Felicity saw. He had caught Clay at last, and that was all he could think about. Clay and Rosie. He wasn't hearing the cops.

"Hugo," she said. "No."

He looked at her. His head swayed. He was shot, she realized. He was barely conscious. Clay had hit him when he'd entered.

Hugo's fist sagged. The younger cop rushed forward and pulled him off Clay.

"Nice try," Clay said from the floor. His lips were swollen; the words were barely intelligible. There was blood on his teeth. "But no good."

This was her moment, Felicity realized. She had to find her gun. But there were cops everywhere, like they were multiplying, and she couldn't see where it had wound up. An officer crouched before her, peered into her eyes, and asked if she was hurt. It was gone, Felicity saw. Her moment. She'd lost it.

————

SHE WAS WRAPPED in a blanket and allowed to sit at a table on the terrace. Then the blanket was taken away and she was put into the back of a squad car and driven somewhere by two silent cops. After that, she was fingerprinted, deprived of her phone, and put into a holding cell. Each of these situations was a little worse than the one before. She suspected that they charted the increasing distrust with which she was being viewed by the Los Angeles Police Department. Someone had talked, Clay or Maddie or some bystander she didn't even know, and said, *I think she had a gun.*

She sat on a bench and gnawed at her nails. Thirty minutes passed. A young cop unlocked her cell and escorted her to a room with pleasant green walls. In a ceiling corner was a camera. "Make yourself comfortable," the cop said, and left. This was worse again, she thought. It didn't look it, but it was.

Two people entered and introduced themselves: Detective Monohan and Detective Primrose. Monohan wore little gold-rimmed glasses and was about fifty, with a beer belly pushing out his white shirt. Primrose was half his size, a Latina woman who gazed at her as if they had attended the same high school and Felicity had been an incredible bitch. She stood, but Monohan waved her back into her seat. "Sorry to keep you waiting. How long have you been here?"

"Am I under arrest?" she asked.

Monohan almost looked offended. "No, no. We're just hoping you can help us answer some questions."

"Then I want to go."

Monohan folded his hands over his belly. Now he looked disappointed. He was cycling through emotions. Beside him, Primrose's expression hadn't changed. "That's your choice. However, I should inform you, if you don't wish to cooperate, we will be forced to place you under arrest."

"What for?"

"Open carry."

So someone had seen her with the gun and told the police. But they didn't necessarily know she'd fired it. She'd had it inside the bag. It could be they were doing that thing where they charged her for something minor that would stick while gathering evidence for more serious crimes. But they might also be open to the possibility that she simply happened to be in the wrong place at the wrong time, and had drawn a gun in response to shots fired by someone else. By Hugo Garrelly, for example, the escaped felon, who they'd caught in the act of assaulting Clay.

"Any comment?" Monohan said.

She shook her head.

He shrugged. "Felicity Staples, I'm placing you under arrest. You have the right to remain silent. Anything you say can and will be used against you in a court of law. You have the right to an attorney. If you cannot—"

"I want an attorney."

"If you cannot afford an attorney, one will be provided for you. Do you understand these rights as I've read them to you?"

"Yes, and I want an attorney. And my phone."

Monohan looked at Primrose, who gave him nothing. "Well . . ." said Monohan. "I guess that's the end of the conversation." He rose from his seat.

When they reached the door, Felicity said, "What have you done with Clay?"

Monohan paused. "You've asserted your right to counsel. I can't speak with you."

"He's dangerous. He was going to kill me. You have to hold him."

Primrose said, "It's impossible for us to talk unless you waive your right to counsel."

"I don't want to waive my rights. I just need you to understand that Clay is a killer."

Monohan turned to Primrose. "Did we release him already?"

"We never had him," Primrose said. "They took him straight to Good Samaritan."

"Ah, yes," Monohan said, which was when Felicity realized that this conversation was being staged for her benefit. "Poor kid was real banged up."

"Clay is the danger," Felicity said. "Not Hugo."

Primrose said, "Are you waiving your rights?"

"No. I want an attorney from the New York *Daily News*. You can get the number from my colleague, Levi Waskiewicz, or my boss, Brandon Aberman."

Primrose stared at her with open dislike. They'd known she was a reporter, she assumed. But a reporter calling for a newspaper's attorney was worse. Worse for them. They left without speaking.

THE YOUNG COP returned her to her cell. Hours later, he came back and said she was free to go. She didn't know whether to believe this until he took her to a room where a thin-haired man in a blue suit smiled and extended his hand. "Felicity Staples? I'm Seb Leiman. Your boss called me."

"You're from the *News*?"

"I'm from Andrews and Ackerman. We do work for the Tribune papers. You're free to go, but the police would prefer that you remain in the greater Los Angeles area for the next forty-eight hours. I told them that wouldn't be a problem. Will that be a problem?"

She shook her head. "Can I get my phone?"

Seb looked at the young cop, and, a few minutes later, she had her phone. The screen was full of messages: Levi, Brandon, Gavin.

"So," Seb said, "shall we go somewhere and talk this through? My instructions were to get you released, but my sense is that the LAPD may take you back into custody in the near future, so we should take this opportunity to prepare."

"I need to go back to my hotel."

"That's up to you. Can I get you a cab?"

She had lost her gun. She didn't know what she could do without it. But she had her freedom. It might be fleeting, but she had another chance after all. "Yes, please."

"Where to?"

There were a lot of places Maddie might be. But one was most likely. "The Waldorf Astoria," she said.

THE POLICE CORDONED OFF THE TERRACE WITH YELLOW-AND-BLACK
tape. There were overturned chairs and tables and scattered plates
and cutlery, which Maddie felt a compulsion to straighten. But that
would have disturbed the scene, and that was what this was now:
a crime scene. They were all performers, locked into a script written
by someone Maddie didn't know, playing implicit roles: Witness.
Investigator. Victim.

Maddie's investigator was a woman with thin lips and heavy eye
shadow, who identified herself as Officer Weiss. Weiss wanted to
know what Maddie had seen and done, several times, from the beginning to the end. Maddie answered as best she could, feeling very
much like she was playing a part, and not even an original one: *Innocent Bystander #2* from some midweek TV show. Even her lines
felt recycled. *It happened so fast. I didn't really see. I don't know.*

She did not tell Officer Weiss that Clay claimed to be from another world. If he was telling the truth, exposing his secret would
put him in danger.

Her phone rang. Officer Weiss motioned for her to take it. "Are
you all right?" Yvonne said, as soon as Maddie swiped. "My God. Are
you okay?"

"I'm fine," Maddie said, as if reciting a line.

"I can see you. I'm right here." Maddie looked about until she spied Yvonne across the terrace, behind a strip of police tape. Yvonne wasn't being interviewed; she was just a bystander. An extra. "When you're done, I'll take you back to your hotel, okay?"

"You don't have to do that," Maddie said, although maybe it was a good idea.

"I feel so bad. I see you're with the police. I'll wait right here until you're done."

"Thanks," Maddie said.

"That was her," Yvonne said suddenly. "The woman they arrested. That's the journalist who's been stalking you. Felicity Staples."

She felt startled. "Are you sure?"

"Yes! I already told the police. She was trying to track you down all day."

She didn't know what to make of that. "I'll call you when I'm done," she said, because Officer Weiss was waiting. She put down the phone. But almost immediately, it rang again: Neil, her agent, this time, presumably phoned by Yvonne. Or he might have seen the shooting on the news. Maybe Maddie's parents had, too, and would be phoning her next. She hoped not, because she didn't want to frighten them.

"Do you need to get that?" said Officer Weiss.

Maddie shook her head. "It's okay."

"The initial shots," said Officer Weiss. "You didn't see where they came from?"

She shook her head.

"But you did see the woman with a gun. A woman who identified herself to you as Felicity Staples."

"Yes." They had been through this. "I saw her walking toward our table. Then there were shots. Then people were running, and Felicity Staples was on the floor, and I saw her take a gun from her bag."

"Could she have taken out the gun earlier, but you didn't notice?"

She shook her head. "I was looking right at her."

"The man in the restroom," Officer Weiss said. "Did you see him at any point prior?"

"No. I'd never seen him before."

Officer Weiss nodded, writing in her notepad.

"Who are they?" Maddie asked. "The man and Felicity Staples? Why were they here?"

"We'll know more tomorrow," Officer Weiss said, delivering her own line. Then, more genuinely: "He's an escaped felon. Best guess is he's the shooter."

"What about Clay?"

"He's suffered some injuries, but I think he'll be all right."

"Why did the man attack him?"

Weiss hesitated. "Your friend tried to wrestle the gun from him. That's his statement." She eyed Maddie. "Is that what you saw?"

"I didn't go into the restroom until the end."

Weiss nodded.

"Is Clay . . ." She trailed off.

Officer Weiss raised her eyebrows. "Is Clay what?"

You have to listen to me.

He's a murderer. He's killed before.

"Wanted," Maddie said. "With a police record or something."

Officer Weiss studied her. "Do you want me to check?"

"Yes, please," she said.

Weiss nodded. Officer Weiss was understanding. Weiss was looking out for her because she was Innocent Bystander #2. "Wait here."

She waited. Ten feet away, a man in a blue suit scraped debris into a plastic bag. The night had grown cold.

"No record," Weiss said, returning. "He's a model citizen. Does that answer your question?"

She nodded. "Thank you."

"All right," said Officer Weiss. "Let's get you home."

———

SO SHE DIDN'T need a ride from Yvonne: Officer Weiss drove her back to the Waldorf Astoria. In the lobby, she handed Maddie a card and said to call if she had any questions, or if anything else came to mind that she thought the police should know. Otherwise, Maddie was to expect a follow-up in the morning.

She rode the elevator to the eleventh floor. She entered her room and set her heavy bag on the bathroom counter. In the mirror, her reflection appeared calm. A little strained around the eyes. Her hair needed brushing. On balance, though, there wasn't much to suggest she'd just been involved in a shooting, after sharing a table with a man who claimed to be able to walk between worlds. Who had been *searching* for her because, in a place she'd never even been, he'd fallen in love.

Such a strange idea: that there were more of her, somewhere she couldn't see. A dozen Maddies, playing different parts, as if in a play with many stages.

Her first thought had been that Clay was mentally ill. He had built a fantasy world in his head and dropped her into it.

You have to listen to me. If I don't get him, you're going to die. He'll track you down and kill you.

He's a murderer. He's killed before.

But if Clay was delusional, so was the blond woman. And the other man, who'd charged into the restroom. All three must share the same delusion, because the woman had taken a walnut cracker and broken that gray stone, the thing Clay called his *token*, like it meant something. They behaved like characters in the same scene, operating from the same premise.

What if it were true?

They want to keep the guy and the girl apart, Clay had said. *The bad guys.*

The man was an escaped felon. The woman, Felicity Staples, had been stalking Maddie around town. Clay had no police record. All this fit with the idea that he was being pursued by bad guys.

He will kill you, the woman had said. *The police won't stop him.*

"Things a bad guy would say," Maddie told the mirror. "To keep the guy and the girl apart."

Her reflection looked anxious. She undressed and stepped into the shower. Water coursed down her face. Steam rose.

SHE DID HER hair and her makeup, then sat on the bed in her hotel robe and zapped through TV channels. Five people injured, according to the news. No deaths. And surprisingly brief coverage; just a few minutes and then on to a baseball story. As if it happened every day.

She considered room service. She was hungry and the hotel food was amazing. But she resisted, because she didn't think this night was over, and if anything else was going to happen, it would happen soon.

An hour passed. Then came a knock at the door. Not a phone call, a buzz from reception. A knock. She moved to the door and set her eye to the peephole.

In the hallway, distorted by the lens, stood Clay. A hoodie was pulled tight around his face, but she could still see that his left eye was swollen and half shut. His right cheek was bruised purple. His lips were patchy with dried black blood.

"Madison, I know you're there. I can see your shadow."

She said nothing.

"Please open the door. We need to talk. Please." His voice broke. "I don't care what else happens. But I have to see you. I can't bear to think you might hate me."

She glanced back at her hotel phone. She could call security and have them up here lickety-split. This was something she would do if she believed what the woman had said, that Clay was dangerous. She put her eye to the peephole.

Through the lens, his head was huge. "Stand back so I can see you." He obeyed. "Turn around. I need to know you're not carrying anything."

He pushed back the hoodie and lifted the shirt at his waist, revealing pale flesh. He turned in a circle. No weapon that she could see.

"Madison, I hate that you're afraid of me." When she didn't respond, he shuffled closer, as if trying to see her through the peephole. "Those people . . . They want to kill me, because I took their token. They lie. They always get between us." He glanced over his shoulder, as if they might be coming for him down the hallway. "Please let me in."

She unlocked and swung open the door. His face lit up. He took a step like he might grab her hands or hug her or something, which she wasn't quite ready for, so she stepped back. "We can talk. But you have to keep your distance."

He grimaced. "I understand. That's totally reasonable."

She led him into the room. The door eased closed behind them.

"This is nice," he said, looking around. "Did Neil arrange it? He was your agent in another place, too. You were in a TV show there, but it wasn't very good."

She pointed at the bed. "Sit."

Clay lowered himself onto the end of the mattress. A smile kept surfacing and disappearing on his lips, like he couldn't suppress it.

"Clay, I'm scared and confused," she said. "I need you to be totally honest with me."

He sobered instantly. "Of course."

"If you lie to me, you'll never see me again."

His eyes widened fractionally. His face was very expressive, despite the injuries. He nodded. "That's fair. I always want to tell you the truth, Madison. The only reason I hold back sometimes is I'm scared I'll lose you."

There was a chair at the desk, which she turned around so she could sit and face him across six feet of carpet. "Is it true?"

"Is what true?"

"All of it. Everything you told me. Your movie."

He nodded emphatically. "Yes. That's how it really happened."

"The stone you showed me. It lets you . . ."

"Move to other worlds. Yes. I've done it dozens of times."

"But she broke it. The woman at the mall."

"That doesn't matter. That's the point, Madison. I don't need it anymore, because I found you. If you can just not be mad at me, everything is fine. I don't want to move. I want to stay here with you. You're the reason for everything."

His body was taut angles of anxiety. He hadn't shifted his eyes from her for a moment, and it was like a spotlight, she thought suddenly. She'd been loved before, but not like this.

"Madison, I just need to know. Do I have a chance?" He dropped his head, breaking eye contact at last. "I know I don't deserve to ask."

She felt cruel, keeping him at bay. But she needed more information. "Who were they?"

A spasm of anger crossed his face. "Hugo. Felicity."

"They're the ones who have been chasing you?"

"Yes."

"For the token?"

"Yes."

"Is that all they wanted?"

He glanced up. His eyes danced to the right. A lie was coming. "Yes."

She waited, giving him a chance to rectify this, but he let it pass. She stood. "I want you to leave."

He gaped, his poor ruined lips hanging. "What? Why?"

"If they want the token, why did she destroy it?"

Panic spread across his face. "No! Wait! I'm sorry! I'm sorry, Madison! I'll tell you. There's more. Please, give me a chance to tell you."

"You had a chance."

"I know," he said, and moaned. "I want to, Madison. I'm just so scared of losing you." He swallowed. "I did some bad things. In other places. I was all alone and I didn't know what I was doing. And that's no excuse. I know. But I was so messed up. I'd lost everything." He wrapped his arms around himself. "They didn't just want the token back. They wanted me to stop moving. But I had to, Madison. So I could find you." He put his head in his hands. "I can't look at you."

She decided to be direct. "She told me something about you."

Clay's head jerked up. His mouth hung open in an almost comical depiction of shock.

"In the dining terrace," Maddie said. "The woman."

He gave a cry of anguish, startling her. He rose from the bed, bunched his hands into fists, and pressed them against his forehead.

"Sit," Maddie said, alarmed.

"They always ruin it!" Abruptly, he moved and punched the drywall. When he withdrew, a hole gaped. Maddie rose half out of her chair, but his shoulders slumped and he sank back to the bed. "It's over."

The spotlight was gone. It had been overwhelming and uncomfortable, but its absence felt like the moment of leaving a stage, or when the director called "Cut," reducing her to ordinariness in a moment. She almost wanted to move to him, raise his chin, and make him look at her again, to get it back. "Clay, I don't know that woman. I've never seen her before. I want to hear it from you."

He shook his head, still not looking at her.

"Do you trust me? Then trust me with the truth."

"I can't." His voice was thick with grief.

"Why not?"

He balled his hands into fists and beat them against his forehead. It was so fierce that she cried out for him to stop. He writhed and slid from the bed to the floor. "I'd rather die. I mean it. I'll kill myself. I'd rather be dead than have to see your face when you hate me."

She stared at him, frozen. Something flickered in his eyes, a kind of calculation, as if another person was inside him, behind all the histrionics, watching this scene play out from a distance. But then he blinked, and that person was gone.

"Good-bye, Madison," he said. "I won't bother you again."

Before he could stand, she dropped from her chair. She crawled toward him across the carpet on her hands and knees. His eyes widened. When he was close enough to touch, she said, "Don't go."

A soup of emotion washed across his face. The spotlight was obscured, and she reached out and gently pushed back a lock of his hair from his face, until all she could see in his eyes was her own reflection.

"I understand," she said, "what it's like to do things, when it's not really you."

He began to cry. He looked away. "You don't. You can't."

She turned his face back. "You were in pain. You were lost and confused."

He nodded.

"Did they hurt you?" she asked. "The people you . . ."

Clay grimaced. "Yes. But it wasn't their fault."

"You were in pain and you lashed out."

His shoulders shook. His chest heaved. "I shouldn't have. I'm so sorry for what I did, Madison. I'm truly so sorry."

She thought she could see it now. The woman at the dining terrace hadn't told her the full story because Maddie wouldn't have believed her. Clay hadn't told her because he feared her reaction. But she was, in a way, perfectly equipped to understand. How many times had Maddie watched herself on a screen and been disgusted with what she saw? How long had she practiced a line or an expression in the mirror, doing it over and over, infuriated at her failure to get it right—to *be* right? She'd spent her whole life shedding versions of herself that weren't good enough. That were wrong.

Clay wanted the best version of her. Of course he did. That was what she wanted, too.

"They were me," Maddie said. "The people you killed."

He froze. For several moments, she couldn't tell what he was thinking. Whether he was thinking at all. His mouth closed and opened.

"It's all right," she said. "Clay, I understand." She wanted to see the spotlight again, which had disappeared behind a cloud of doubt. She put both her hands on his face, feeling his rough, bloodied skin. "You love me. Not someone *like* me. Not me but different. Me."

He nodded. And there it was. The truth.

"You'll never do it again."

He shook his head, tears spilling down his cheeks, running down her fingers. "Because I found you, Madison. I'll be good to you always. It will be different now. It will be so different."

She was starting to cry, too. "I believe you."

She leaned forward. Into the spotlight. She made it slow, so that he could see what was happening, had time to anticipate it.

Their lips touched. She kissed him once, softly. He gave a small gasp for air. It was the strangest thing. She pulled away a half-inch, leaving the air between them laden with possibility. Then she sat back on her haunches. His face was incredible.

"I need to go to the bathroom," she said. "Wait here."

When she reached the bathroom door, she looked back. He was gazing after her with pure adulation. "I love you, Madison."

She smiled, opened the door, and stepped inside.

As she closed the door, she was hit with a wave of revulsion. Everything she'd suppressed for the last ten minutes tried to come out of her at once. She bent over the sink. For the sound, she turned the faucet. She didn't have long, she suspected. But she needed a moment.

In the mirror, her eyes were wide with terror. That was new, she thought; Clay hadn't seen that. She'd kept it tucked deep down while she was playing the role of a woman in love with a murderer.

I'll kill myself, he'd said, and that had almost broken her. Because he'd meant it, at least in the moment. But that moment would have been followed by another. And another, and another, and in one of those, he would change his mind. He would decide that he wasn't the problem; she was. That she wasn't even the woman he'd fallen in love with. She was someone else, someone wrong.

Her bag rested on the counter. She opened it and drew out the thing she'd taken. The thing that, in the restroom, when Clay and the large man had fought, had come spinning toward her, and which she'd picked up. She'd only meant to keep it safe. Give it to the police, when they arrived. But the words of the woman had kicked around her head: *The police won't stop him.* She'd seen how angry Clay had been when the woman destroyed his stone. Which meant there was truth in her words—and Clay's. So until she'd figured it out, Maddie had decided to do what she did best: perform.

She inspected the gun. It was heavy. She hadn't used a firearm before. She wasn't entirely sure how it worked. The woman had discharged it, though, which should surely mean it was ready to go.

Her eyes rose to the mirror. Her reflection was a wreck. Her reflection couldn't kill anyone. That was the problem. She just wasn't that kind of person. She could be facing a man who surely meant to kill her and still not act to save her own life, because she was, in her heart, kind of a coward.

In the mirror, she exhaled. The lines of strain around her eyes softened. The fear fell from her face. She found her center, and became someone else.

SHE ENTERED THE bedroom. Clay was on his feet. His face was different. He had been changing, too. In his eyes was the person she'd glimpsed earlier, the calculating one. She'd kept him at bay with sympathy and kindness, and, playing fully into his fantasy, a kiss. But she'd taken too long in the bathroom, and now he was back.

She wasn't hiding the gun. His eyes landed on it. He yelped and scrambled backward across the bed.

She aimed and squeezed the trigger. The sound was gigantic, like a mountain breaking open. It was so startling that she temporarily forgot who she was. Clay tumbled off the bed. She couldn't see him anymore.

"Madison," he croaked. "Wait. Please."

She didn't say anything. She didn't have any lines in this scene. It was a very mechanical part. But a part of her wondered, for a moment, if that had been what any of them said, the other women, in other places: *Wait. Please.*

His arm appeared. His sleeve was bloodied. She must have hit him somewhere. He rose from behind the bed with his hands out. "You have to underst—"

She squeezed the trigger again. This time he jerked back. His head hit a framed picture and dislodged it. Her next shot was wide, popping the drywall beside his shoulder. The one after that seemed to strike him in the chest. He doubled over and fell to the carpet.

She moved to the corner of the bed. She felt calm. She knew what she was doing. Clay was curled over, his fingers clenched in pain. His leg slid along the carpet, up, down. His teeth were bared. His eyes moved to her. He might have been trying to curse, or beg, or say he loved her. She couldn't tell. All these things were possibilities. They might be happening, in other worlds. She sighted him down the barrel and squeezed the trigger again.

THERE WAS A banging on the door. She felt a disorienting, coming-out-of-her-head moment: the jarring instant when there was no more character, only her, unclothed and unsure.

She was in a hotel room, wearing a robe, and holding a gun.

On the carpet, Clay's body lay still.

She moved to the door. It occurred to her to put down the gun, so she did that, on the side table. When she peered through the peep-hole, she saw not police or even hotel security, but the woman from the dining terrace, Felicity Staples.

She opened the door. Felicity came inside in a rush, shouldering Maddie aside. Her head whipped from side to side. "Where is he?"

"Behind the bed."

Felicity pressed Maddie to the wall, stepping in front of her. Then she spied the gun on the side table, snatched it up, and ran in quick, balanced steps, the gun in two hands, pointing down, like a professional. She reached the end of the bed and looked at what was behind it.

"I shot him," Maddie said into the silence. The words were shocking. Now that there was no part to play, she felt dismayed. What had she done? She was in a hotel room with a dead man. "He didn't have a weapon. I just shot him. I murdered him." She covered her mouth.

"Thank God." Felicity crossed to the kitchenette and began pulling drawers open. "The twenty-second one, that can be yours." She raised a knife, inspected it under the lights, then, satisfied, returned to the bed and knelt beside Clay. "He came here to see you?" She glanced back.

Maddie nodded.

"All right. Then you got into an argument. He threatened to kill you. You had to shoot him to defend yourself. I was here. I saw the whole thing. That's what we tell the police."

Maddie nodded without understanding. All she could think about was what she'd done.

Felicity seized her by the arms. "Look at me. It's going to be okay now. It's going to be okay for you everywhere. You're going to live because of what you did. You did exactly what you had to."

There was determination on Felicity's face, but something else, too: relief on a scale that Maddie couldn't quite fathom. Felicity had seen it before, she realized. She had seen what happened when Clay was not stopped.

"Thank you," she said.

Felicity pulled her in for a hug, fierce and tight, like she might never let Maddie go. "Thank you," she said.

SHE HAD EXPECTED TO SLINK AWAY WITHOUT FANFARE. BUT AT FOUR-thirty, Brandon Aberman called everyone into the *Daily News*'s meeting room, where there was a cake, plastic cups, and an oversized card that said CONGRATULATIONS. "Felicity Staples came to work for this paper seven years ago as a bright young cadet with a promising future," Brandon declared, once the small audience had settled. "And I can say today that we didn't entirely beat it out of her."

There were cheers.

"Not for lack of trying," Levi added, twisting the cap of a wine bottle.

"We got a few good years out of her as a political reporter," Brandon said, "before Levi dragged her into crime reporting and ruined her." Levi protested that he'd had nothing to do with it. Brandon raised a finger. "I say 'ruined' in the sense that we are ruined without her, as she's leaving us for a far better newspaper."

People laughed. Todd, who had been an intern but was now taking over her job, applauded enthusiastically.

"Nevertheless," said Brandon, "despite my sadness, I'm buoyed by the thought that some small part of her future success will be because of what she did here. And because it is *so* nice to be able to do one of these where the person isn't quitting the entire fucking industry." More cheers. "To Felicity!" Brandon called, and they echoed her name, raising their plastic cups, which Levi had been filling. "To the future of journalism!" he added, to mixed feedback.

She drank. She ate three slices of cake. By five-fifteen, most people had excused themselves, but she was hanging around, reluctant to leave. The newsroom clock was *thwack-thwack*ing its way through the hour, and she was even going to miss that.

"*Mmf*," said Levi, approaching with a drink in one hand and a slice of cake in the other. "It won't be the same without you, Felicity."

"You're not getting rid of me that easily," she said. "I'm going to call you all the time, because I need your contacts."

"Yes," he said, pointing at her. "Do that. Great point."

"You *are* drunk."

"Actually, I'm grieving. A colleague just told me some terrible news." He leaned toward her conspiratorially. "Annalise from Ad Sales. Her marriage is over."

"Oh," Felicity said. "Wow."

"She finally walked out on her no-good husband." He made little walking motions with his fingers. "Poor girl. Woman. Poor woman. I've been through a divorce. I know what it's like."

She nudged him with her hip. "I'm happy for you."

"Are you implying that . . . Annalise and I . . ."

She nodded. "I am implying that, yes."

He snickered. "This is the problem with working around a bunch of reporters."

"The problem is you're not very subtle."

"Well," he said, topping up his cup from the wine bottle, "that may be true. You might have me there."

"I should go," she said. "It's getting harder the longer I stay here, and I don't want to carry a cardboard box on the subway in rush hour."

He nodded. "I'm glad we got to work together. Even though you never told me the truth about what got you started."

She blinked. "What do you mean?"

He waved her away. "Forget it. Me and my big mouth. Go be happy."

"Tell me."

He glanced around. The room was empty. "Hugo Garrelly breaks out of prison, flies across the country, and shoots up an L.A. mall with a Walther M2. The same night, an obsessive fan breaks into the hotel room of an up-and-coming actress, and she shoots him dead."

"Uh-huh."

"Lot of bad mojo in one night, in two places only a few blocks apart."

"It's the economy," she said.

"Ha," he said. "Except you're in both places. The restroom where Garrelly gets cornered. And the hotel room where Maddie May is attacked."

She tilted her head. "What are you trying to say, Levi?"

He shook his head. "Nothing. It's just the kind of thing that sticks out to someone like me. You know how it is. A piece doesn't fit right, so you keep tugging on it until something falls out."

"Maddie didn't want to be alone. We met before Garrelly started shooting, and afterward, we decided to hang out. Neither of us knew anyone else in the city." This was what she'd told the police.

"Yes," Levi said. "I'm sure that's it." He eyeballed her, then laughed. "Forget about me. I'm genetically incapable of minding my manners. You're going to make a great crime reporter, Felicity. You have a knack for it."

He extended his arms. She stepped into them and they hugged.

"Sing Sing will allow visitors eventually," Levi said into her hair.

She stepped back. "Pardon me?"

"They've had him locked down for six months, but that can't last. Sooner or later, people will be let in to visit. To ask questions."

She eyed him, unsure what this was: A piece of harmless gossip? A warning? "I don't have anything to hide, Levi. I was in the wrong place at the wrong time."

"Of course you were." Then, like he couldn't help it: "Twice."

"I have to go," she said. "Thanks, Levi. I learned a lot from you."

"I wish I could say the same," he said.

FOUR DAYS LATER, there was a thick yellow envelope in her mailbox marked NEW YORK DEPARTMENT OF CORRECTIONS. She stared at it for so long that a man who owned a dog that had once peed in the elevator said, "Excuse me," and she had to move to let him by. She carried the envelope to her apartment and sat on the sofa beside Percival.

Inside was a smaller envelope, white, stapled to a form letter that informed her that she was receiving a missive from a convicted felon. The communication was subject to monitoring, and if she had any questions or complaints about that, there was a number she could call. On the form were two dates, one for ORIGINAL APPLICATION and one for APPROVAL GRANTED, and they were three months apart.

Joey leaped onto the sofa. She gave him a scratch, to reward his bravery. Then she tore open the envelope. Inside was a single page, handwritten:

Dear Felicity,

I've been allowed to write this letter, but I don't know if it will get to you. If it does, I hope you'll visit. I know we had our differences

*and I don't blame you if you don't want to see me, but I hope the
fact that I came back means something.*

My people moved without me.

*It's hard to get news here, but a CO told me Madison May is
in a big movie. I'm glad to hear that.*

*If you visit, I would like to ask a favor. I know this might make
you stay away, but this might be my only chance, so I have to ask.*

*Before we last met, I put something in a pool outside a bank.
By now it might be gone, but if you can find it and return it to me,
I would be forever grateful.*

*Yours sincerely,
Sing Sing Correctional Facility
Hugo Garrelly, #411002*

SHE FLEW OUT to Los Angeles the next day. It was the first time she'd
returned to California, and during the flight, she debated whether to
message Maddie. On the one hand, Maddie had impressed upon Felicity that she should let her know if she was ever in town. On the
other, Maddie was in the process of becoming a major star, and Felicity didn't want to turn up like some unwanted relic from the past.
In the end, she sent: *In L.A. for the day, hope you're well F xxx*, and
put away her phone.

She parked beneath the Century City mall, one level down from
the last time. Riding the escalator upward, she felt like she might be
able to glance around and see the ghosts of six months prior: Maddie
and Clay, Hugo, maybe even herself, clutching a bag. At the top, she
turned right, away from the stores, and departed the mall for bright
sunshine. She'd studied a bunch of online maps and come to the con-
clusion that the "pool" Hugo had described in his letter must be a
rectangle of aging concrete on Avenue of the Stars, which did indeed

front Wells Fargo, and was close enough to the mall that she could imagine Hugo selecting it as a temporary hiding place.

It was smaller, smellier, and dirtier than she'd imagined. She walked a circuit, noting the gardens on each side that were filled with gray rocks, all of which looked quite a lot like what she was hunting for. Hugo had said he'd put it *in* the pool, but this was less disgusting, so she began to sift through the rocks on her hands and knees.

Forty-five minutes later, she'd collected nothing but dirty looks from a security guard in a gray uniform, who occasionally came out of the Wells Fargo and put his hands on his hips and went back inside. She straightened, studying the pool. The water was too murky to make out the bottom, but it was not deep, presumably. She sighed.

She kicked off her shoes and set them with her keys and phone. Then she climbed over the short railing and slid in.

Water closed around her up to her waist. Her feet touched slime. "Gahh," she said, because why did an ornamental pool need to be that deep? It was ridiculous. She waded a short distance, but she wasn't going to find anything with her toes, so she put her face beneath the surface.

When she forced open her eyes, there was a whole underwater world in front of her, with shafts of light and floating detritus. She searched for a few minutes, coming up every so often for air, and then the security guard was running toward her and hollering. "I dropped something," she said. "I'll just be a minute." She ducked back under.

"Get out of my pond," said the security guard, when she surfaced.

"One minute."

"No, not one minute. Get your ass out of there now."

"I'm not hurting anyone."

He produced a phone. Calling the police, Felicity assumed. She did not want to be arrested for trespassing in a pool. But she didn't want this to be for nothing, either. She waded toward the far corner, where she hadn't searched yet.

"You have to get out now," the guard said.

"You think I'm doing this for fun?" she said. "You think I want to be in here?"

"I don't know what you want. But you can't be in the pool."

"Is this *your* pool?" she said, because he was being very protective. But she couldn't fault him for that. He was doing his job. "I'll be one minute."

"No. No minutes."

"One minute," she said, and went under again. In the far corner was a plastic bag. She forged toward it, gripped it, and hauled it out of the water. Inside was a gray stone.

"You found it?" the guard said aggressively. "What you were looking for?"

She began to wade toward him. "Yes, thank you."

He watched her silently. When she reached the edge, he stepped forward and offered his hand. She took it and he hauled her out of the water.

"Thanks," she said, dripping.

"That's what you lost?" he said, eyeing the stone.

"It has sentimental value," she said.

SHE SQUELCHED BACK along the sidewalk with the plastic-wrapped egg in her pocket. While waiting at the crossing, her phone rang. "You're here?" Maddie said. "Where are you?"

She was in the shadow of the mall where it had happened. "Beverly Hills."

"Where in Beverly Hills? Can I come to you?"

"I don't want to bother you," Felicity said, because who knew; Maddie could be doing Hollywood things.

"It's no bother," Maddie said firmly. "I can't tell you how long I've been looking forward to this. Are you free now?"

"I am. But I'm wet."

"You're wet, did you say?"

"I had to get into a pool in my clothes."

"You're so fascinating," Maddie said. "I'm sure you'll dry. It's L.A."

They met at a café on Wilshire Boulevard, which Felicity walked to, like a New Yorker. Maddie was right: She dried. By the time she pushed open the door, even her shoes were quiet.

Maddie rose from a table, wearing an emerald knitted dress, her hair a few shades lighter than it was the last time Felicity had seen her. She came forward and they hugged. "Hi, oh my God," Maddie said. "I'm so glad you came."

"Your hair is amazing," Felicity said.

"Amazingly time-consuming. I spend half my life in front of a mirror now. It's not healthy." She gestured to her table, where sat a young woman with remarkable cheekbones. "Felicity, this is my friend Zar." Zar rose and shook Felicity's hand. "We were together when you called. She'll stop bothering us in a minute."

"I just need a sandwich," Zar said.

"She wanted to meet you," Maddie said.

"The person who saved your life, yes, that's true," Zar said, gazing at Felicity as if Felicity were the movie star, not Maddie.

"I don't know if that's what happened," Felicity said.

"It is," Maddie said. "Zar, stop looking at her like that. You're embarrassing her."

"I'm not," Zar said, and laughed. "Maybe I am. I'll get out of your hair. Thank you for saving my friend, Felicity Staples."

Maddie ushered Felicity to the table, which was tucked away in a corner of the café. "We went to NYU together. I brought her out a couple months ago, when things started to get wild with my career."

Felicity nodded. "It's so good to see you."

Maddie smiled: a wide, beautiful expression that put Felicity in mind of the first time she'd seen her, as a real estate agent, on a website. "You, too." She glanced around. "You know, I saw him here once. He was watching me from across the street. I didn't realize it was him at the time, but it must have been. He was following me."

It took her a moment to realize who she meant by "him." "Do you want to go somewhere else?"

"No, no. I'm in this area a lot. All the ghosts are gone by now, I think." Maddie smiled. "I wasn't sure I'd ever see you again."

"Why not?"

"I thought you might leave."

"Oh," Felicity said. "No, I'm not going anywhere."

"I don't really know how to think about it," Maddie said. "Sometimes I can't remember exactly what happened. I'm not sure how much was real."

"I remember. Ask, if you want."

"Maybe it's best not to. I could let it be a kind of dream."

"If you want," Felicity said, although, if it were her, she would want to know.

A moment passed. Maddie laughed. "I'm a little nervous. He's gone, isn't he? That's my first question. Is he really gone?"

"Yes. God, yes."

"I know he died. But I keep thinking about how he came from somewhere else. He went to places where I was . . . a real estate agent. Or a bartender. Or this, but with different hair. That's right, isn't it?"

"Yes."

Maddie nodded and sipped at her water. She was building up to something, Felicity sensed. There was another question she was almost ready to ask. "He's not the only one who moved from place to place. You did, too. And your friend. Hugo Garrelly."

"Yes."

"He hasn't gone anywhere, though," Maddie said. "He's in Sing Sing."

She nodded again. "He lost his chance to move when he came back to help me."

"Is that what you do? Move places to help people?" And before Felicity could think how to answer: "I've thought about visiting Hugo. But I don't know why he was there. At the mall, I mean. I feel like I owe him."

"You know what? Don't visit Hugo. They don't move to help people, Maddie. And you don't owe anyone anything. Just go enjoy your life."

Maddie was silent for a moment. "Is that what you're doing?"

"Exactly," Felicity said. "That's what I'm doing."

"It's a choice, then? You're not stuck, like Hugo?" There was a short silence. Maddie laughed. "I'm sorry. These questions are so personal."

"I'm here because I choose to be," Felicity said, which was kind of true, starting from roughly the moment she'd collected Hugo's egg from the Wells Fargo pool. "What is it you really want to know?"

Maddie glanced away, embarrassed. *She wants the egg,* Felicity thought. It should have occurred to her earlier. It was a magical transdimensional portal key—who wouldn't? "I was thinking . . . and I know it's silly . . ." Maddie leaned forward and planted her elbows on the table. "If there are more of him, could he . . . start again?"

Felicity blinked. "Oh, shit, Maddie. In none of the other places does Clay get a token. You never meet him. None of us do. He's just a sick kid. End of story."

"Are you sure?"

"I promise. Forget him. Seriously. Him, Hugo, all of those people:

Forget them. There are enough assholes in this world for you to worry about."

Maddie gave another small laugh, this time of relief. "Thank you." She wasn't going to ask about the egg, Felicity saw. She never had been. "I won't forget about you, though. Not ever."

"Well, that's fine," Felicity said. She was glad she'd come. "That's fine."

FOUR WEEKS LATER, she received a phone call from a woman who told her in a brisk monotone that a fifteen-minute visit with inmate Hugo Garrelly had been approved. Felicity parked in a small lot off a narrow road that ran alongside the prison's apparently endless concrete wall. In reception, she stood in line with a dozen or so other people, including a depressing number of children, and showed her papers to a man with small glasses and pink cheeks. She was an hour early, because apparently that was the rule. Eventually, she was taken to a room with four chairs facing glass panels. Behind one of the panels was Hugo.

He had a wired phone to his ear, but for a few moments, she stayed where she was and just looked at him. He had lost a lot of weight. He was clean-shaven. She sat and picked up the phone. "No beard," she said.

"They don't force us to shave," Hugo said. "But if we choose not to, we get solitary. I held out awhile."

She nodded. He was nervous, she thought. Not in a way that most people would see. But she could tell.

He said, "Did you get it?"

"Straight to the point," she said. "As usual."

"Well?"

"Yes, I got it."

He blinked rapidly.

"I got pretty wet," she said. "It was a whole thing."

He shifted his weight. "Felicity—"

"I realize you saved my life. Clay would have killed me if you hadn't come back. Would have killed Maddie, too, by now. I want you to know I appreciate that."

"But you're keeping it," Hugo said.

She sighed. "I almost threw it away. I almost destroyed it. Because I think it's shitty, what you people are doing. But it's not my token. So I'm giving it back."

He bowed his head for a moment. His face was full of relief. "You can't mail it to me. You have to find a guard who—"

"Please," she said. "I'm not an idiot. I'll get it to you."

He nodded.

"Do something good with it, if you can. Because what you're planning—spending your days looking for someone you might never find—that's not actually a life." She raised her hand and wiggled her ring finger. "Did you notice? You didn't congratulate me."

"You're engaged?"

"June wedding. I'll send you an invitation." This was a joke, but he didn't smile. "Gavin, in case you're wondering."

"Which one?" He gestured at his face. "The beard?"

She shook her head. "He makes shoes. But doesn't cook."

"Huh," Hugo said.

"They're all the same, though," Felicity said. "That's what I figured, eventually."

He nodded.

"Except me," she said. "I think I changed. I have you to thank for that, I guess. My wedding day, I'll have a drink for you." A silence fell between them. "Maddie says hello. She's an actor now. A real one."

"I heard."

"Oh, of course." He had mentioned that in his letter. The silence stretched. He was already thinking about the egg. Planning how to use it. "Well," Felicity said, "that's it, I guess." She rose. "I hope you find what you're looking for. If I don't see you again, have a nice life."

"You, too."

"Thanks," she said. "I'll try."

THE CURTAIN CAME DOWN, AND THEN WENT UP AGAIN, AND REPEATED this two more times, and finally Maddie hurried offstage to the echoes of applause. She wiped the greatest excesses of makeup from her face and wriggled out of her 1950s A-line skirt. She hung it and her blouse where the costumer would find it, dressed for the current century, and headed for the lobby.

The audience was milling there, still talking excitedly. A woman of about seventy spied her, her eyes lighting up, and Maddie stopped and smiled as the woman tottered toward her. In theory, Maddie had plenty of time to walk the three minutes to South Street and catch the 39 bus downtown. But it was Boston, where timetables could not be trusted.

"You were wonderful," the woman said, clutching her hands.

"Thank you," Maddie said. "You're so kind."

"You should do this professionally."

"Oh, no," she said. "I don't think so."

"You *should*. I've seen every production at this theater for the last thirteen years. You're the best."

Maddie laughed politely, because she actually *had* considered doing this professionally—not seriously, but as a kind of daydream, which came and went. Especially in moments like this, when she saw that she had done something: had moved people somehow, to somewhere else, for a short while. She'd once even applied to NYU's drama program. But then her father had suffered a stroke, and after that, looking at her booklets and forms, drama had felt silly and impractical. She wound up getting a BFA at the New York School of Design instead, then an entry-level position at an architectural firm in Boston, where she mostly sat in client meetings and carried a laptop. One day, though, not too long from now, she hoped to create spaces: interiors of daring and dash, where shapes aligned in ways that comforted and contained. On weekends, for fun, she did community theater. This season: *Who's Afraid of Virginia Woolf?*

Across a sea of heads she saw Jamahl, who played her Nick, still in costume and makeup. He met her eyes and raised a champagne flute. Jamahl was very arrogant after performances, for about fifteen minutes. He was a good guy, but also kind of the reason she was glad she didn't go into acting professionally. "Thank you so much. But I really have to go."

"Oh, of course you do," said the woman. "Parties, I'm sure."

She had an hour and a half on a crummy coach to Concord, New Hampshire, en route to her parents' house. If she were lucky, she wouldn't be seated next to anyone too drunk or too chatty. "It was great to meet you. Thanks for coming to the play."

"You're so wonderful!" the woman called as she walked away.

DURING THE TWENTY-MINUTE bus ride to South Station Bus Terminal, she flipped open her screen and began to sketch. There was a client pitch on Monday, a corporation looking to refresh their work spaces. Maddie was a million miles beneath the notice of the people who would actually contribute competent design ideas, but she had thoughts. She inserted her earbuds and began to draw.

She was lost in shelving ideas when a man seated across the aisle leaned toward her. She removed her earbuds. "I'm sorry?"

He was looking at her screen. "What is that?"

This was why she didn't usually catch the bus. "My work."

"Looks cozy," he said. "You make warm throughlines."

Maddie eyed him, puzzled. "Do I know you?"

He shook his head. "I don't think so."

"Do you work in design?"

"No, I've just picked up a few things in my travels."

She wondered where you traveled to pick up terms like *throughlines*. She didn't want to know. She would be off this bus in twenty minutes. "It's just a sketch."

"You're talented. You'll do well."

"Thank you," Maddie said. She reinstalled her earbuds and returned to her work. But over the next few minutes, she found herself glancing at the man across the aisle again. She couldn't shake the feeling that she'd met him somewhere. He was familiar in a way she couldn't place. She took out her buds. "Are you sure we don't know each other?"

He looked mildly surprised. "I don't think so."

"What do you do?"

"Me?"

"Yes," Maddie said.

He glanced around. "I check on people."

"What, like a parole officer?"

"No. Not exactly." The bus wheezed to a halt. A woman in an ancient blue hat tottered down the front steps and off into the night.

"Are you a cop?"

"No."

"Then what are you checking?"

He shifted in the seat, which could barely contain him, because he was huge, tall, and round-shouldered. Slightly grizzled face, but handsome, with a beard and a cap. "I'm making sure they're happy and safe."

"Let me get this straight," Maddie said, because it was the weirdest thing she'd ever heard. "Your job is to travel around making sure people are happy and safe? Who pays for that? Is this a service for overprotective parents?"

"Not the parents," he said. "It's no one they know."

She began to feel that this whole conversation might be a fiction. "You're talking about guardian angels, then. People looking out for you and you don't even know it."

He smiled ambiguously.

She laughed, because this fantasy was a nice one, worth indulging for a minute. "What if they're not? The people you check on. Not happy and safe. What do you do?"

He shrugged slightly. "Hasn't happened yet."

"Oh, okay," Maddie said.

"You don't like the idea?"

"It's a nice concept. I'm just not sure it's, you know, a real thing."

The man's watch beeped, and he glanced down. "Ah," he said, standing. He had to hunch over to avoid hitting his head on the ceiling. "My stop."

She peered outside and saw the flat red brick of Northeastern University. "Who are you checking on tonight? A college student?"

"No," he said. "I already met her."

The doors hissed open. He clomped down the steps. She wanted to say something, but her brain was jammed up all of a sudden.

"Nice to meet you, Maddie May," he said, even though she had absolutely, definitely not mentioned her name. The doors thumped closed. The bus pulled away from the curb. She turned to stare out the window. The man stayed on the curb for a moment, watching her, then tugged down his cap and began to walk away.

ACKNOWLEDGMENTS

In other worlds, this book is much worse, because I didn't have the support and critical insight of my dedicated early readers. Although I guess there might also be worlds in which I had even better early readers. Huh. So thanks a lot, Kassy Humphreys, Jo Keron, Todd Keithley, and Charles Thiesen.

Luke Janklow and Claire Dippel are brilliant readers, strategists, and life coaches in every world.

My editor, Mark Tavani, was instrumental in steering this book's early development as it tried to figure out which version of itself it wanted to be.

Jen, as always, makes me want to be my best version. What my world looks like without her, I don't want to know.